THE FOUNTAIN

The Fountain is a love-story, set in Holland during the First World War. Lewis Alison, prisoner of war, is given leave to stay at Enkendael castle, which belongs to the van Leydens. Baroness van Leyden is an old family friend, and at Enkendael he meets again her daughter Julie, whom he remembers as an intelligent and beautiful child to whom he had been a kind of unofficial tutor. She is now married to a Prussian officer, Rupert von Narwitz. Half against his will, Lewis finds himself attracted to Julie. When von Narwitz is sent to the castle to convalesce, he and Lewis become friends, despite the attachment between Lewis and his wife.

Charles Morgan uses the setting of his own imprisonment in Holland as the background to this story, but it is the acutely observed and tenderly portrayed love-affair between Lewis and Julie which is the essence of the novel: he insists on its spiritual aspects as much as the physical attraction, while never losing touch with reality.

Charles Morgan, who died in 1967, was one of the most important English novelists of the years between the wars. His work earned the highest praise from contemporary critics, and this reissue will help to remedy the unjustified neglect of his work in recent years.

'His novels are novels in which the song of life is always perceptible. A poet is latent in each of their principal characters . . . his prose gives to love, even in the suggested presentment of its physical powers, a universal tenderness.' Paul Valery.

'As one reads one forgets everything, enchanted by the beauty of the setting, fascinated by the subtlety of the spiritual reasoning, the provisional speculations, the ethereal love-story.' J. C. Squire on *The Fountain*.

THE FOUNTAIN

Charles Morgan

Introduction by Leonée Ormond

THE BOYDELL PRESS

© The Estate of Charles Morgan 1984

Introduction © 1984 Leonée Ormond

First published in BOOKMASTERS 1984
by The Boydell Press
an imprint of Boydell and Brewer Ltd
PO Box 9, Woodbridge, Suffolk, IP12 3DF

ISBN 0 85115 237 6

Printed in Great Britain by
St Edmundsbury Press, Bury St Edmunds, Suffolk

INTRODUCTION

Charles Morgan was born in 1894, the sensitive son of a successful civil engineer, who placed him in the navy at the early age of thirteen. After six years of service, Morgan persuaded his reluctant father to let him resign and take a degree. The first world war intervened, and it was not until 1919 that Morgan began his university career. This was also the year of his first novel, *The Gunroom*, an exposé of conditions in the navy.

Morgan did not hit his stride as a novelist until 1929 when he published his third novel, *Portrait in a Mirror*. From then until his death in 1958, he was one of the most esteemed and successful writers of his generation. He was gifted with a finely chiselled prose style, well attuned to those themes which attracted him: the nature of the imagination; the profound relationship of love, religious aspiration and death; and, above all, the analysis of the forces which drive a man to pursue a particular woman, whatever the cost in social and emotional terms. Morgan's most important novels were written in the first part of his career, in his last years the faultless prose remained, but without the passion which renders the earlier novels so remarkable.

The Fountain, Morgan's fourth novel, was based upon his experiences during the First World War. Its setting is Holland, where Morgan was interned on parole between 1914 and 1917, a part of his life which he later described as 'Time Out' comparing it to the grand tours of the eighteenth century. Not quite twenty at the outbreak of war, Morgan had been expecting to go up to Oxford in the autumn of 1914. Instead, he volunteered to serve in the Royal Navy, 'not, alas, in a ship. The ships were full, the Fleet was at sea'. He went with the Naval Brigades to the defence of Antwerp, and was there when the city fell in October 1914. Finding retreat to the coast cut off, 'some 500 men' surrendered in neutral Holland: 'as a result I find myself in Groningen, a prisoner of war on parole'. In January 1915, Morgan was moved to the fort of Wiericker-schans, between Leiden and Utrecht, and then, a year later, he joined two other officers in an estate cottage belonging to the van Pallandt family at Rosendaal in Guelderland.

After nearly three years in comfortable confinement, Morgan returned to England on *The Lapwing* in November 1917. When the boat struck a mine, he survived, but lost the manuscript of *The Gunroom*. This violent aftermath to the peaceful Dutch years finds no place in *The Fountain*, where the stress falls, not on the imminence of death, but on timelessness, on patterns of contemplation and meditation. Early drafts of the novel show that Morgan reached this decision slowly. In one deleted passage his hero, Lewis Alison, recalls the retreat from Antwerp, and the embarkation from the railway station:

> On the platforms were great crowds of men waiting to be entrained and the air was full of the grind of their nailed boots on asphalt, the clatter of rifle-butts, the squeak of leather. The platforms stretched beyond the crowds into a moonlit night, and, beyond the platforms, the rails continued, engraved in white by the needle of the moon.

The novel combines Morgan's memories of this unique period with a romantic love-story, drawn from imagination. There was no beautiful Julie von Narwitz at Rosendaal, only Madame Loudon, a woman of eighty-six, of whose youthful beauty Julie's is an imaginative projection. After the war, Morgan was briefly engaged to an heiress whose parents rejected him as unsuitable, and he may have drawn upon this episode for his account of the social gulf dividing the middle-class Lewis from the aristocratic Julie. Morgan intended to suggest that his lovers are drawn by exceptional circumstances into a relationship which seems to have no future. 'They would not match each other in tastes or position in the ordinary work-a-day world. So to the girl this is a *temporary* adventure; to the man it is all of a piece with his dominant idea that life in Holland is detached—is "bracketed in the narrative of life".'

The love story is one aspect of a continuous dialogue between flesh and spirit, carried on throughout the novel.

From the opening pages we are reminded that 'Women never leave you alone. They come in like water into an old ship'. At Enkendaal, Julie threatens Alison's 'singleness of spirit which . . . he desired above all else to cultivate'. He wants to believe that body and soul can co-exist, but finds it hard to unite them: 'Not to kill the senses or to hate them, he thought, but to discover an inviolable ghost in the sensible body is the highest and most difficult art of the saints.' The conflict remains unresolved at the close. Sailing to England with Julie, Alison sees that he will go on fighting for his spiritual independence: 'it was in his nature; vainly or not, he must fight it to the end'.

Like most novelists of war, Morgan was attempting to formulate and understand his experiences. In May 1929, when he was planning *The Fountain*, he told another former internee, Roger Barrett: 'the point is that life in Holland then was, in the strangest way, a life within life—a sort of spiritual island, and so a delusion'. The novelist was thirty-five when he wrote this. More than twenty years later, he had come to see the Dutch experience as a 'gift of God', 'imprisonment was a blessing. It gave me a chance, it even compelled me, to sort out my values—to discover what I deeply cared for in life, and why.'

The protagonist of *The Fountain*, Lewis Alison, is thirty when he arrives in Holland, closer in age to the man who wrote the novel than to the man whose experiences it recalls. Like Morgan, Alison has been prevented from taking a degree at Oxford, in his case by the death of his father. Alison's pre-war life as a publisher is superficially unlike Morgan's, but it is easy to see here the pressure and frustration of the artist with a family: 'I've been at it ten years. I took my father's place when he died. Up-hill work.'

Alison joyfully decides to spend his 'Time Out' in satisfying a long-held ambition to write a study of the contemplative and meditative life: 'following the development of spiritual concepts in England since the Renaissance and relating them with the philosophies of a remoter past'. He is not a Christian, nor a religious historian: 'His care was to ask whether there was not a perceptible unity of all the higher endeavours of the human mind.'

This sounds a little like Mr. Casaubon's 'Key to all Mythologies', and not the least of Morgan's triumphs in this novel is his ability to convince us that Alison's task represents a tangible goal. In the end, like many before him, Alison falls back on an edition of papers, translations of the work of a nineteenth-century Dutch writer and historian, Dirk van Leyden. This more limited undertaking, ready for the publisher by the end of the novel, is very different from Morgan's own Dutch achievement, *The Gunroom*.

The opening books of *The Fountain*, 'The Fort' and 'The Castle', are dominated by Lewis Alison. Only in a handful of paragraphs does the reader move outside this perceptive consciousness, which often reveals its depths in a profound sense of place. Some of the finest prose evokes Alison's responses to the fort at Wierickerschans, a part of actual experience which Morgan originally planned to omit: 'It was a period of great fascination. But to begin so far back would leave the book's theme unstated for too long.'

Having written several chapters of a novel which began with Alison's arrival at Enkendaal, Morgan changed his mind, and began work on the five chapters which make up 'The Fort'. This opening book was re-written four times, and in the course of revision Morgan omitted a number of striking passages. Among them were the scene at Antwerp station quoted above, an account of Alison's sense of release at the death of his brother, and a fuller analysis of Alison's relationship with his rough alter-ego, the pilot, Herriot. All these revisions, like the removal of much detail about Alison's fellow-prisoners, clarified the main theme. 'The Fort' became less autobiographical with each re-writing.

At the end of the first book, on the evening before his departure for Enkendaal, Alison recognises that in the year since his arrival at the fort, he has been exempt from the processes of nature. 'I am frosted in knowledge and cannot renew myself. I listen but hear no voice. I am like a tree in which the sap does not rise.'

Alison takes up the notion of stillness, which has been his ideal, and relates it to death, the death of absence, of being forgotten. Against this he sets the children glimpsed over the canal, suggestive of a renewal of life from which he is cut off:

> Next summer the water would lie still perpetually; none would swim in it; and the children on the opposite bank, seeing no movement on the ramparts, would forget those who had moved there sooner than they forgot the beings of a tale. They would forget them as they forgot the dead.

The idea of fairy-tale, of temporary enchantment and unreality, is associated later in the novel with the relationship of Alison and Julie. At a moment of acute tension in that relationship, Alison's mind goes back to the fort:

> The fort is empty now, he thought; the barbed wire is dangling from the poles; but every evening the children on the opposite bank turn to watch the train as it passes and wave their caps. Soon this room, also, will be empty. I shall be on my way to the Castle. When I return to sleep here to-night, I shall be entering a strange house. It is already strange to me, he added, raising his head, as strange as the fort would be if I went back to it.

In earlier drafts of the novel, Alison's active self is attracted by plans for escape, while his spiritual self draws back. In the final text, there is little inner tension. Thankfully rejecting ideas of returning to the active life, Alison sends home for his books. To his mother 'it seemed so strange that you should care to think of them in these dreadful days'. She would prefer him back at war, revenging his dead brother. Much of this first year is spent in reading: Plato, Thomas Aquinas, Isaac Newton, Jeremy Taylor. Morgan touches on the names and ideas, without attempting to explain the precise nature of Alison's researches. He deliberately leaves most of the quotations unattributed.

When he agrees to move to Enkendaal, Alison is drawn there largely by the thought of the castle library. His interest is the seventeenth century, the golden age of Dutch culture. Morgan, whose own interest originated in an early reading of J. Henry Shorthouse's historical romance, *John Inglesant*, chose the age of Charles I for his special subject at Oxford. He planned to write a civil war novel, drawing on the Verney papers. In *The Fountain*. Lewis and Julie have Shorthouse in common: 'Fénelon led them to Bossuet, Bossuet to Molinos, and from Molinos the way was easy to Inglesant and the seventeenth century in England, a subject of which they never grew weary.'

John Inglesant presents a sympathetic view of the Spanish priest, Michael de Molinos, the founder of Quietism, a form of worship which forbade strenuous religious activity, and instead commended a passive acceptance of the will of God. In its perfection, Quietism, to which Morgan confessed himself 'attracted', led to a total annihilation of the human will, and a state of mystic death. Taken to its logical conclusion, it denied the need for a church, and Pope Innocent XI condemned Quietism in 1687, imprisoning Molinos for the rest of his life.

Other writers of Morgan's generation felt the pull of the seventeenth century, Rupert Brooke, Virginia Woolf and T. S. Eliot among them. Morgan's delight in the work of the mystic and religious writers (particularly Henry Vaughan, from whom his wife was descended) placed him closest to Eliot. The Anglican community at Little Gidding, founded by Nicholas Ferrar, was a source of inspiration to both men, providing the title for one of Eliot's *Four Quartets*. Morgan, and possibly Eliot, found Ferrar by way of *John Inglesant*.

Alison's search is not for religious truth, but there is a clear debt to Quietism in his philosophy. Julie tells her husband that Alison wants 'to be still, listening . . . He calls it the stillness of an axis at the centre of a wheel'. Alison is not the only character in the novel who seeks invulnerability and private stillness, but his approach, through reading and scholarship, is peculiar to himself. There are other paths to 'the untouchable, the timeless thing—were not all these struggling by different paths towards one end, an ecstasy invulnerable because it is "out of the senses"?' Old van Leyden, who scorns reading, has self-protective silences, he retreats into his own consciousness. Some characters can escape in the extremes of sexual passion, while others, like Herriot, find it in speed: 'I want to fly for the sake of the flash of seeing that comes now and then—almost as if one died bodily, and escaped from oneself and saw out on the other side.'

Julie absorbs herself in looking at a much-loved painting.

Morgan originally intended this to be Bellini's *Agony in the Garden*, but remembered that it was in London, and not in The Hague, and substituted the more apt *Adam and Eve in Paradise* by Rubens and Velvet Brueghel. When Julie sees it, the narrator comments: 'works of art that men love are a cloister where they may have absolute retirement and a cooling of their fevers in this world'. Such islands are easily accessible to saints, or to the simple, but others can find them only in art or nature: 'Every man, who is not a devil, has his own retreat, his intact island, ringed about with the waters of the spirit, where he may live his own life and not be pursued; and from which he may set out on his own voyages.'

Water and islands are important images in *The Fountain*. The title is glossed with a quotation from Coleridge's 'Dejection: An Ode', a poem where Coleridge laments his failure of imagination. The calm evening presages a storm, but even that will not lift feelings of deadness and depression, will not allow the fountains of his spirit to flow:

> [I may not hope] from outward forms to win
> The passion and the life, whose fountains are within.

By omitting the first four words, bracketed here, from the heading to his novel, Morgan softened the negative, implying, as Coleridge does not, that inner release may perhaps come from outward influences.

Associations of rebirth make water an appropriate central element for Morgan's novel. The fort is surrounded by a wide canal, which as Lewis Alison thankfully notes, cuts it off from the world, divides one part of his life from the other. There are lakes around the castle of Enkendaal, and water falls in a cascade between two of them, suggesting other connotations for water, those of timelessness and continuity: 'Whoever occupies that room, Lewis thought, must hear the splashing of the water day and night until at last it becomes a part of silence, as the active routine of a monastery, because it is regular and persistent, must become the rhythm of meditation, and as breathing is an unwilled rhythm of life.' The room is Julie's, but the emotions which Alison describes are his rather than hers.

In the centre of the upper lake is an island or eyot, which becomes a symbol both of Lewis Alison's existence in Holland and of Rupert Narwitz' wish to release himself from earthly ties. At the end of the novel, Narwitz spends more and more time alone on the island, almost dying there on one occasion. Morgan planned that Narwitz should die by suicide, but changed his mind, to remove this burden of guilt from Julie. She comes to dread her husband's death, which she has foreseen in a visionary moment during a party at The Hague:

> she knew, as if the scene were reflected for her in the Ruysdael, that Rupert's body was lying now partly buried by earth; she saw the back of his head protruding and the heel of a riding boot. She imagined herself running to his side and kneeling on the loose earth; his head turned; his eyes stared at her. 'Rupert!' she said, but he didn't hear her, didn't know of her existence.

One imaginary scene blends in her mind into another, the face of the porter at her hotel, telling her that Alison has left no message. Then both merge into the present, with the voice of her hostess asking her to play bridge. 'Long afterwards, lying in bed, Julie was awakened, whenever she was about to fall asleep, by the same voice asking if she would play bridge, and in her mind she began to tap the glossy cards with her fingernail.'

These experiences in The Hague culminate in the experience at the Mauritshuis when Julie finds her own place of refuge. Morgan attempts to move the focus of the novel from the man to the woman. In the first half of *The Fountain*, we experience Julie through her effect on Alison, his mixture of admiration and irritation, his sense that she represents a threat, his memories of her as a child. From these fragmented reactions we must build our picture of the novel's heroine.

In the second half of *The Fountain*, the reader's viewpoint alternates between those of Julie and Alison, possibly to the detriment of the novel as a whole; Julie is never as convincing a character as her lover. In *The Fountain*, Morgan was not simply concerned with the ironic truths of *Love's Labour's Lost* or *The Princess*: that those who shut themselves up with books will discover that they cannot escape their own sexuality. We must believe that there is more to Julie than beauty and social grace. The novelist perhaps implies that she can supply a lack in Lewis Alison, but he never quite says so. She responds to the romance of history, is associated with the harmonies of music as she is with the delights of painting. Even in The Hague scenes, however, there is a danger that she will emerge as no more than a wayward rich girl, burying her sapphires in the snow to see the effect of light, and giving away her new evening dress to the maid. In earlier drafts, Morgan filled in more of Julie's background, but later removed this social solidity, leaving his heroine more mysterious, but even less believable.

The climax of the relationship between Julie and Alison is at the end of the second book, 'The Castle', where two outward struggles provide parallels to inner tension. One is a keenly fought tennis competition, which is itself juxtaposed to an historical event, the indecisive naval battle of Jutland of May 1916. Julie, the English wife of a German officer, is herself an embodiment of conflict, and her too obvious despair at what appears to be a British defeat exposes her to censure. It also produces her unexpected victory in the tennis tournament, followed by her declaration of love to Lewis Alison. The prominence of Jutland in this episode suddenly brings the war into the foreground. Earlier, reports of Neuve Chapelle, the advance on La Bassée and the sinking of the Lusitania have scarcely disturbed Alison. He has been able to keep the war at bay, outside the charmed circle. Morgan removed all other references to the course of the war in his revisions of the novel. When Julie breaks down the walls between the lovers, it is appropriate that war news should provide the catalyst. The inaccurately reported results of Jutland are neither qualified nor corrected. Instead, the war retreats once more into the distance, until the final chapters again set up a juxtaposition, this time of the fate of Germany with the rapidly approaching death of Rupert von Narwitz. He finally dies at 11 o'clock on 10 November 1918.

Julie apart, Morgan triumphantly avoids the danger of literary cliché throughout *The Fountain*. His central theme of invulnerability and stillness finds its apotheosis in the most unexpected place, in Rupert, Julie's Prussian husband, who only enters the novel towards the end. Terribly wounded, Narwitz' control of physical suffering has already taken him far towards Lewis Alison's ideal. His whole will to live is in the hands of his beautiful young wife. When he recognises that she has loved another man, he deliberately puts this last link with the world away from him, symbolically, and ironically, handing her over to Lewis Alison, when Julie's concern is now only with Narwitz himself.

During the last months of Narwitz' life, he asks his wife to read aloud Turgenev's *On The Eve*. This 'absolute' novel, which Morgan greatly admired, suggests a series of parallels and contrasts with *The Fountain*, like the story of Nausicaa, which is associated with the lovers, Alison and Julie. Julie chooses to read out the passage where Bersyenev tells Elena Shakov about his friend, Insarov, a Bulgarian revolutionary, with whom she will fall in love. In *The Fountain*, this reading follows closely on Julie's description of Alison, given at her husband's request. Narwitz returns to the subject of Turgenev in his first conversation with Alison, telling him that 'the character of Insarov, when he comes . . . prevents it [*On The Eve*] from being a masterpiece'. He prefers the opening scene where Bersyenev and the sculptor, Shubin, talk of life in general and of love in particular. For Shubin love is a means of personal happiness, but for Bersyenev 'to put oneself in the second place is the whole significance of life'. Rupert Narwitz interprets this as Turgenev's apologia for his long platonic relationship with Pauline Viardot. The whole discussion of *On The Eve* opens up a series of ironic connections. In the Turgenev novel, all three men are in love with one woman, but once Elena has discovered Insarov, she flowers into womanhood. Narwitz' preference for the opening scene prefigures his pleasure in long conversations with Lewis Alison. The end of *On The Eve* is tragic, Insarov dies, Elena disappears, and the words which end the chapter from which Julie reads could apply to either book: 'something dark and secret had entered his heart; he was sad with an unpleasant sort of sadness'.

Lewis Alison's response to the notion of taking 'second place' is almost involuntary: 'It seems to me that to discover what to put before oneself, in the first place, is the whole problem of life.' For Narwitz, 'Death is the answer': in the understanding and knowledge of death man can be born again. Narwitz' words have the force of a revelation to Alison: 'Here is a great man, here is my master! and, looking again at Narwitz, he added almost with terror: To betray him is to betray myself.'

There is much Christian imagery in this part of the novel. As Narwitz touches the hem of Julie's garment, he feels life returning. Julie tells Alison: 'The joy we had then is turning into thirty pieces of silver.' Morgan was even accused of plagiarising the Bible for Narwitz' death scene, '"Into thy hands, I commend my spirit", and when he had spoken thus, he gave up the ghost.'

From the start, Morgan envisaged problems in writing the conclusion to *The Fountain*. His early scheme took a sternly moral line: 'The isolation of "life within life" is broken down; the lovers' false illusion is shattered; like Adam and Eve, they see their own nakedness.' Adam and Eve, appropriately envisaged through seventeenth century intermediaries, the painting in the *Mauritshuis* and Milton's *Paradise Lost*, provide an effective parallel. If Narwitz is God appearing in the Garden, however, he is unwilling to take on Divine attributes, denying that he has the power to forgive and free his wife. In his plan for the novel, Morgan went on to summarise the final chapters: 'the lovers are left, free to marry, free to satisfy themselves, outwardly with a "happy ending" and yet with the life and death of this tormented man lying between them—their only enduring riches being their knowledge of him'.

In April 1930, Morgan sought the advice of his wife, the novelist Hilda Vaughan: 'I've been worrying and worrying about the end of my book and uncertainty about it has been holding me up. I can't really account to myself for their deciding to marry. It seems to me rather revolting in a way, with the ghost of the dead man between them.' After turning the question over in his mind for several weeks, Morgan found an explanation. Julie was a 'spiritual courtesan', a woman 'who changes the depths of her individuality in accordance with the changing demands of men'. In her marriage to Lewis Alison, Morgan believed, Julie would be able to respond to both his spiritual and his sensual nature: 'he feels her to be, not merely the mistress of his body, but an inspiration of his work, a condition of it'.

The final books of *The Fountain*, 'The End' and 'The Beginning', written after this flash of inspiration, represent the novelist's determination to avoid the sentimental cliché, to end on a strong note. Morgan's style becomes deliberately unromantic, as the lovers contemplate what Julie's mother calls 'the doom of an English middle-class marriage'. The vivid Julie of the earlier books passively allows events to propel her towards The Hague and England. In his revisions, Morgan excised several passages where Julie's stream of consciousness becomes too explicit, too concerned with the practicalities of the future. After cutting one such reverie, he noted in the margin: 'Tighten up Julie's thoughts.' Through Morgan's omissions, Julie's decision to rejoin Alison is delayed until after the moving scene when she is driven to confess her adultery to her step-father. Only as she drives away from Enkendaal does excitement take over, followed by what Ramsdell describes as a 'stiff, and reasonable, and determined' manner. As Morgan's Adam and Eve leave the Garden of Eden, it is with a will to succeed in the real world. The novelist's own fundamental truthfulness had, after many months of hard work, led him to an appropriate and credible outcome, where Alison and Julie do not merely fall back upon each other, but determinedly set out to challenge the future.

The Fountain is one of the best English novels of the inter-war period. The issues which it raises are not simply those of war and peace, but of man's need to maintain an inner life in the face of human and social pressures. Morgan's compelling prose celebrates the contemplative virtues, but the outcome of the novel is far from escapist. In the final paragraphs, Lewis Alison is still willing himself to find inner stillness, even while business and marriage close in around him. The title of the last book, 'The Beginning', suggests challenge and maturity, expressed through the lines of Milton, which stand at its head:

> The world was all before them, where to choose
> Their place of rest, and Providence their guide.
> They, hand in hand, with wand'ring steps and slow,
> Through Eden took their solitary way.

LEONÉE ORMOND

> " from outward forms to win
> The passion and the life, whose fountains are within."
>
> COLERIDGE : *Dejection.*

> When a man proceeding onwards from terrestrial things by the right way of loving, once comes to sight of that Beauty, he is not far from his goal. And this is the right way . . . he should begin by loving earthly things for the sake of the absolute loveliness, ascending to that as it were by degrees or steps, from the first to the second, and thence to all fair forms; and from fair forms to fair conduct, and from fair conduct to fair principles, until from fair principles he finally arrive at the ultimate principle of all and learn what absolute beauty is. This life, my dear Socrates, said Diotima, if any life at all is worth living, is the life that a man should live, in the contemplation of absolute Beauty . . .
>
> PLATO : *Symposium.*
> Trans. ROBERT BRIDGES.

CONTENTS

I

THE FORT

Be still, my soul, be still; the arms you bear are brittle.

A. E. HOUSMAN

CHAPTER ONE

ON an afternoon of January 1915, a small train dragged itself across the flat Dutch countryside in the neighbourhood of Bodegraven, carrying a group of English officers under guard. Their heads appeared continually at the windows, for, though their destination had been kept from them, they judged by a restless movement of the guard that they were near the end of their journey.

Lewis Alison, a dark, craggy man of more than common height, gave no sign of sharing in the general curiosity. He stayed in his place, seeming to have wrapped himself in a composure not easily to be disturbed. Thirty years had left upon him more than their accustomed mark—not upon his physical appearance only, but upon his manner, delaying his smile and giving an air of deliberateness to his speech and movement. Vigour and eagerness lay in his eyes, and his hair, full and black, had the glisten of youth upon it; his body was pliant and his cheeks could darken with colour when whipped by excitement, but his good looks were of maturity, and owed so much to something austere and self-disciplined in his expression that it was hard for one who had not known him in the past to imagine him as a very young man, sanguine and impetuous. But while he sat in this train, which the early twilight of winter was already filling with shadow, even his boyhood might have been guessed at by one who watched him closely. When he spoke, there was in his voice a mingling of quietness and animation which made him master of his company. Throughout the morning and the afternoon he had spoken little. A book on his knee had occupied him, and the

3

turn of his fingers as he lifted a page suggested a loving reader.

Among the Englishmen in the train were a few airmen, brought down by engine-failures into neutral territory, but the greater number were of the Naval Division that had retreated from Antwerp three months earlier. Separated from their men, with whom they had been living in an internment camp at Groningen, they were now being taken to closer imprisonment in a fortress. In Lewis's compartment were two former sergeants of marine, Lapham and Shordey, upright in opposite corners like dogs on trust; Ballater, long and fair and handsome, stretched out at ease; and Sezley, still so much of a boy that, when he withdrew his head and shoulders from the window and turned round to communicate in high excitement what he had seen or guessed or thought of, his words came tumbling over one another, and he had often to stop and draw breath in an audible gasp before he could continue. Other officers had from time to time wandered in from the corridor, stayed a little while and gone.

"This fort we're going to," Lapham was saying. "Wonder what kind of a place it is? Ever served in a fort, Shordey?"

Shordey's eyes twinkled above his puffy cheeks. Now, as always, he seemed about to make a joke, but he shook his head and said nothing.

"I did once," Lapham continued. "At Sheerness. Windy sort of place. But I didn't mind it. The young officers did, though."

"You had the wife with you," Shordey said.

Ballater smiled and, seeing that Lewis had at last closed his book, asked: "Do you imagine we're going to be shut up in this place for ever, Alison? I can't get the idea of it."

Lewis took up a pipe from the seat beside him and tapped it on his boot.

"I've been trying all day to get the idea of it," he replied. "It's odd in these days and oddest of all in the middle of a war. But it wouldn't have seemed odd in the past—to be shut up. Whole communities shut themselves up. I've often thought I'd like to go round the world in a sailing-ship. Day after day, nothing but your own job."

"What did these fellows shut themselves up for, Alison?" Shordey asked, wrenching himself out of his speechlessness. "What was the idea? Religion and so on?"

Lewis hesitated. The answer to that question would be an answer to all the questions that had for many hours, for many years, perplexed and enchanted him. Then, suddenly, fascinated by so profound a riddle, he began to speak of the monastic ideal of earlier ages, saying that there were two aspects of it, the devotional and the contemplative. "The struggle for some kind of stillness within oneself seems to run right through history," he said. "In cities and market-places as well as in monasteries. In forts, too, and camps and prisons. It's a question of how to attain it. To worship a particular god is only one means; so is seclusion; neither, perhaps, is a necessary means." Even Sezley turned from the window to listen to him. His audience was held by his argument and by the evidence of his eyes and voice that he had deep personal concern in it. He said much that surprised them, but nothing for effect—nothing that did not spring from within himself.

"I believe you'd have been a monk if you'd lived then," Ballater said. "You'd like to be a monk now if you had the chance."

Lewis at first made no reply. Then: "I've no sort of religious vocation," he answered. "Anyhow I have a business to run and people dependent on me. . . . But in the fort," he went on with hungry eagerness, "there'll be none of that. As long as we live, it's the only chance that any of us is likely to have to be completely independent." He checked himself abruptly and leaned back in his corner.

"It's all very well for you," Ballater said. "You won't be without a job. You have your history to write."

"Without the history," Lewis replied, "I'd still be glad of the fort."

"But who's to look after the business?" Lapham asked. "What's your line, Alison?"

"Publishing. Alison and Ford. Educational books mostly,

and books of reference." Lewis's words came from him in jerks, forced by a reluctant memory of the past. "I've been at it ten years. I took my father's place when he died. Up-hill work. Still," he added, "that's over. Everything be-gins afresh to-day."

But Lapham's mind had run on.

"You may have your history," he said. "But what's the rest of us to do? We're not all monks by a long chalk. No women an' no job. It's worse for the married men than the single, though you may think different, Ballater."

Ballater replied cautiously: "As for girls, the old mon-asteries didn't always keep them out."

"They'll get in somehow—never you mind," Lapham said after a moment's reflection. "Visitors' days. Poodle-faking in the dog-watches. Women never leave you alone. They come in like water into an old ship. First your mother. Then your wife. Then, when you think you're through with it, your daughter worryin' at you. You never get clear. This fort mayn't be as peaceful as you looks for, Alison. Things have a way of coming in, you know."

"They have indeed," Lewis answered. "I've spent my life finding that out."

The train groaned, rattled and was silent. It had stopped without show of reason among the meadows.

"It can't be here," Sezley cried, leaning out yet farther. "There's no station, no platform, nothing."

But a Dutch captain with a precise voice and a blond, silky moustache went from compartment to compartment, smiling and repeating monotonously: "Will the gentlemen please to go down here?"

"Like a butler announcing dinner," Ballater said.

"Yes," the captain was heard to explain, "this is the place. There is Wierickerschans, the fortress where you go —you see the ramparts with the trees over? That is your new country mansion."

Alison rose and slipped his book into his pocket. Six months ago he had been travelling every day from home to office, from office to home, having no thought that his way of life could ever be changed. Even the desire for a

different life had fallen asleep within him. This evening,
when he took up that volume again, the gates of the fort
would have closed. For months, perhaps for years, they
would not be opened.

"Come on," he said. "Let's get out."

Coat collars were turned up, pipes lighted and khaki caps
pressed down against a blustering wind. The Englishmen
climbed on to the line. With a guard of some fifty Dutch
privates shambling before and after them and the blond
officer in their midst, they set out across country.

Ballater and Lewis Alison walked together. At Antwerp
they had served in the same battalion but in different com-
panies, and not until they had passed several weeks in
Groningen were they drawn into a loose friendship. What
bound them was not a shared interest but a humorous liking
or tolerance that each had for the other's foibles.

"Personally," Ballater said, "monasteries aren't in my
line. No opening for talent." His face, clear red and white
in complexion, moved in an easy smile.

Lewis wondered what Ballater would do in the fort. What
would they all do?—and he looked at the men surrounding
him. Some were naval officers or former naval officers re-
joined for the war; some schoolboys, still in the adventure
of a commission, no older than his own brother who had
been killed at his side during the crossing of the Scheldt.
Some, like himself, were mature civilians, brought by a
medley of chances into the Naval Brigades. Lapham and
Shordey, being old soldiers, would make themselves snug
in Purgatory itself, anxious only that marching-orders
should not disturb them. They would settle down to a
routine of pipes and beer and five-cent Nap, outwardly
resigned. But imprisonment, even the easy imprisonment
that lay before them all, was a distinguisher of men. None
knew what would befall him here nor what he might become.

Lewis was possessed by the fantasy of this mild walk
into prison. Near him, Herriot, a Flying Corps pilot,
and Dacres, his observer, were plodding on, shoulder to

shoulder. Even Dacres's chubby face wore an expression of
melancholy—a grotesque, ridiculous crumpling. He was
taking stock of the Dutch guards, the broad fields, the
chances of a dash for liberty. When he spoke of this,
Herriot growled and shook his head. "Not a hope. We'd
be in the dykes."

They went on in silence, and Lewis knew what bitterness was in Herriot's mind. Dacres was an amateur of adventure; if he did not escape he would soon console himself; but Herriot was a dry, frosted little man, cool, wary,
without illusions, and to fly was his life. He cared for
nothing else except unending games of patience. Flight was
to him a necessary drug; without it his imagination became
erratic and his fingers twitched above the cards. "I must
get out," he had said at Groningen. "This war's my one
chance. There'll never be another until I'm too old." He
lifted his grooved, sallow face out of the collar of his coat
and gazed at the fort, a tree-lined eminence seemingly
afloat on the ground-mist.

"Well, Alison. Like the look of it? This ought to be the
place for you. Though why, I doubt if I understand. What
is it you want?"

"That's a hard question."

"I know—but answer it."

"If I say that what I want is peace of mind——"

"That's too vague," Herriot interrupted. "May mean
anything. Lapham has peace of mind when he's had a good
dinner and his pipe is drawing."

Lewis hesitated. "There's no answer to your question,"
he said, "that doesn't sound like a boast. . . . What I want
is stillness of spirit."

"It doesn't sound like a boast except to fools," Herriot
answered. "It's what we all want—though damned few of
us know it. But it's to be found in an office or an aeroplane,
not only in a hermit's cell. . . . Some people have to shut
themselves up. Maybe that way's right for them. Depends
on the man. If the wrong man dives into solitude he goes
mad—or, what's worse, he goes stale. Why you should shut
yourself up, I don't know. You're not one of the incapables

of this world. I know your story; Ballater told it me; and a man who's left in charge of his family when he's still an undergraduate and pulls a business out of the fire isn't an incompetent. It's not the sort of efficiency that I'm capable of. A mother, two sisters, a young brother to educate—I'd have deserted them in a week. I did desert my own wife and children. Still, if you can stick that, you can stick most things."

"It wasn't altogether a question of sticking it," Lewis said. "It was at first. In a way it was right up to the end. But I don't take a hero's credit. I began to be proud of it— almost to like it. That's the devil of it all—that half of me began to like it. But running a business and a family wasn't what I wanted to do. This"—he lifted a hand towards the fort—"is what I've wanted inside me all my life."

"Well," Herriot said, "to every man his own fanaticism —as long as he's got one. It's a queer choice for you to make. You can do your job outside and do it damned well. Men like your company. And women too," he added, shooting a glance upward. "You could play hell with them if it amused you. You look as if you'd burn them up with your austerity—and that's a candle they'll always die in. Not all women, perhaps—the silly ones like a smoother passage— but the women worth having. . . . Look, man, there's what Ballater calls your monastery. Shout! Why don't you shout and sing and dance? I should if I saw an Avro make a landing in that field, ready to take me away."

"No, you wouldn't," Lewis said. "You'd be too excited to speak and too doubtful whether you'd get clear. This is my chance, but God knows what I shall do with it."

"Nothing would keep me from my job," Herriot exclaimed. "Not a hundred mothers and sisters and brothers —nothing but that prison. Nothing ever has. But this place is the end for me, if I can't get out of it quick. . . . Observe the corpse walking to its grave."

In the fierce extravagance of that jest there was so deep a sadness that Lewis could find no answer to it. There were peace and joy in his own heart. In the fort, he imagined, day would follow day in slow, empty routine. He would look out over this calm, mist-bound country that separated him from all external claims and watch the spring appear. In summer, greenness would enrich it; in autumn, the few belts of trees would flame and darken; this winter or next there would be a snowfall and the canals would become a network of black cords laid upon the snow. Hour after hour, season after season, in no conflict of duties, he would do what all his life he had wished to do.

"I'd like to be a saint," said Herriot suddenly.

"A saint—why?"

"It would be exciting, that's why. Anything is that you can go mad about. The hopelessly sane men are the bores. Dacres, for instance." He jerked his thumb. "A good fellow, but sane as a stationmaster. You have the merit of being mad, Alison. Half-mad anyway. Lord in heaven, think of going mad about a history book! And a history of the contemplative life at that! That's what you want to write, isn't it? It's a good world when you see the joke of it." And he added slowly: "I suppose there's a technique of contemplation—same as in flying. You've got to learn it from ABC. And no good then if you haven't the right nerve."

They were approaching the fort—a high flat mound that was evidently a hollow square, for above the grassy ramparts were visible the tops of trees growing within on a lower level. On each of the great earthen bastions at the corners of the square was a wood of tall elms. A canal, wider than any common moat, lay about the base of the ramparts. It had been made, they soon discovered, to encircle the fortress, to which a guarded bridge was the only entrance. As Lewis crossed the bridge, he paused, with a feeling of delight and finality, to look down into the waters of the canal.

Inside was a paved courtyard, flanked by buildings chiefly of one storey—long narrow bungalows stretching out on either side to the full breadth of the old fortress. High above their roofs stood the gatehouse rampart, a steep bank already equipped with arc-lamps, sentry-boxes and barbed wire. It overshadowed the room that Lewis found was to be his dormitory. Through the windows on one side, nothing was to be seen but this great rampart and a narrow path that divided it from the buildings. On the other side, the prospect was more open. Here, beyond the path, were a few yards of turf, fringed with barbed wire and bordered by a stagnant inlet from the moat. The main ramparts of the fortress rose out of the farther bank of this strip of water. Their earthy bulk stood across the world, but above them and their soaring elms the twilit sky was visible. From this quarter in the daytime the sun would for a little while make its way into the room.

Ballater and Lewis chose beds within a few feet of each other and sat down upon them. Baggage was being brought in, but their own was not yet come and they had nothing to do. Other officers, whose place was in this dormitory, were standing about in knots, hesitant and restless. "What are we going to *do* here?" Ballater said. "We shall be lucky if we aren't at each other's throats in a fortnight."

Sezley was handing round lumps of marching chocolate. "Rations for the troops!" He was as excited as a girl at a party.

Among the baggage that had come was Sezley's gramophone. He turned it on, and soon Lauder's voice was grinding into the dusk. Someone began to sing, was shouted down, and persisted in his singing. A chorus sprang up and in the midst of it the gramophone choked and died. A grey hush fell on the room.

"This place will be damp, so near the water," and Ballater stared up at the whitewashed walls. It was now too dark to see whether they were patched with wetness.

Sezley was examining his gramophone. "Can't see a thing. Anyone got some matches?" He looked over his shoulder at the brass oil-lamps hung from the ceiling. A chair was dragged across the boarded floor; a match fizzed and illumined the faces looking upward. "No oil." But Sezley prevailed among the shadows; soon a jarring of the needle was changed to a stifled rag-time, and Ballater said:

"That's one of the snags to your monastery. You won't have a room to yourself night or day."

But nothing could now disturb Lewis's tranquillity. While he sat on his bed and the noise of the room drummed upon him, his mind returned to a time when, still a child, he had felt that he was at the gate of a mystery which, if he could but open his eyes anew, would be revealed to him. To learn how to open his eyes it had seemed necessary that he should be alone, that he should be still with an absolute stillness, until his self that was blind had fallen from him like the skin of a snake. Within the apparent form of all things was another form, waiting to appear; within stones another stone; within the vitality of trees a secret and ghostly sap; beyond God who, he had been taught, was his Father in Heaven, another god whose being sprang, not from instruction and rule, but from his own apprehension. As he grew older, he had perceived in certain books that their authors had been seeking what he sought, and scholarship had become a passion in him, a means, not of learning only, but of association with minds coloured as his own. To their diverse voyages he would now return, seeking always in them that discipline of stillness beneath which, if any man perfectly attained it, his blind self might be shed like the skin of a snake, and he be changed.

He went out into the dusk, wishing to visit the ramparts before others came and to walk among the great elms on the bastions. But there was a gate, heightened with barbed wire and padlocked, across the path leading from the courtyard on to the main ramparts, and a Dutch lieutenant appeared out of the arc-lamp shadow of an elder bush to say that he might not go by that way until morning.

"It would be too simple," he explained in an English that came from him uneasily, as though, while he spoke, he were nervously collecting it from a book of idioms. "The outer ramparts cannot in the night be closely guarded. You would escape, *niet waar?*"

Escape. All day that word had been repeated—in the train, in the meadows, by groups of men unpacking their gear and setting up photographs in the dormitories. They had chattered of tunnels and barges and disguise. They would learn Dutch, they said, and had asked Lewis, who had already made progress in the language, whether he would help them. As he walked under the darkening and austere sky, watching an electrician in overalls inspect an arc-lamp circuit, the word escape seemed to come to him from another age. It was a thing you could pick up between your fingers and toss in your hand like an old coin, thinking of the remote world in which it was currency. But he heard his own mind say: "It's our job to get out of this place if we can," and his eyes were on the barbed wire, testing it.

In the messroom, he found Herriot with his patience cards, sitting at the end of a long empty table covered in red chenille.

"Cut to me, Alison, and bring me luck. I've made a bet with myself. Every card I don't get out keeps me in this place a week."

Lewis stretched across the table and cut the pack.

CHAPTER TWO

THOUGH a letter from his mother came in each English mail, and Janet, the elder of his sisters, sent out copies of *The Times* in which local casualties were marked in red ink, more than a month passed before any sign was given that Lewis's request for his books had been received. At last his mother wrote:

". . . The books and notes you asked for have been sent. I fear you will think we have been slow in sending them, but everything in England is so difficult nowadays —so many forms and regulations, and things one needs to do for the men, and the poor brave fellows who are fighting must come first, as you, dear, much though you love your books, would be the first to admit. And besides, now that Nancy is married, Janet and I have to do everything, and it was always Nancy you told about your things. She knew where to lay her hand on them.

"Before I forget—I met Mr. Ford in London the other day and he said I was to be sure to tell you the business keeps steady, but all publishing is very slack. He has to do everything himself now you are away, and he is getting old, but he will carry on, he said, without you. I think he has always been a little touchy because the business improved so much after you joined it when your poor father passed away. I have never liked him. So different from his daughter. Oh, Lewis, I do wish your engagement to Elizabeth had not been broken off. It always seemed so suitable to me.

"But about your books. I was surprised when your

letter came. For a time I could not make my
about books—it seemed so strange that you should care
to think of them in these dreadful days when we have all
one object only, to avenge our dead. Vengeance is mine,
saith the Lord, I will repay. But we must help. Even in
the little work Janet and I do here at home we feel that.
It is a consolation. But afterwards I said to myself you
must have your books since you asked for them and God
has decided you may take no more part in this struggle
unless Holland is shamed into doing as Belgium did. So
I went up to your room, past poor Peter's door (his little
place is just as he left it and some of his writing still on
the blotter), and I looked for the books and papers as you
told me. How many you had in that locked cupboard!
I used to think it was account-files you kept there. Some
on your list I could not find. I grew tired looking, and I
thought you would not mind; but there will be enough to
occupy you in your sad idleness. In the end it was Elizabeth
who packed them and arranged to have them sent. She
wanted to look for others, too, but I had burned your list
by then. She has never really told me how your engagement was broken off when she visited you in the camp at
Walmer. She says you both wished it, but I have never
heard of such a case. I used to think she was such a well-
balanced girl—always so quiet and so modest about the
share in the business and the money she will have from
her father some day. But perhaps the war has upset her
in more ways than one. You cannot imagine what trouble
I have had with the maids since the camp began in Harbury
Park! Young people of every class seem to be very much
on edge. When I told Elizabeth that you were to be moved
to a moated fortress from which it would be impossible to
escape, she said: 'Thank God! That's his chance, then.'
Of course I am thankful you are safe, and if she had been
still engaged to you I might have expected her to say what
she did, but she told me, when I asked her, that she was
glad because for once you would be compelled to stop
fighting other people's battles and to lead your own life.
What she meant I really don't know. I said, how could

she say such a thing?—as though she thought you would rather be reading in idleness. She could not answer me, of course, but went on cording the crate without looking at me. So strange. And when I thought it was done with, she found a volume slipped under a chair—one of Plato's it was and in Greek—and she *would* open up the crate again and put it in. I am sure that I was right and that, though she is now a little overwrought, she is still genuinely fond of you, as you will find on your return, whatever may have happened at Walmer. I should go on writing to her if I were you.

"I envy you, dear, being able to settle down so easily to your old hobby. I wish I could read. It would distract my mind. But since Peter was taken I keep thinking that if he had been on your left instead of on your right when the piece of shell came, he would have been spared, and I am always picturing the dreadful scene. It comes between me and my book and I can read nothing but a newspaper. But you are more composed. That is wiser and better, I suppose, if one is capable of it. The books left here three days ago. . . ."

Lewis took the letter with him on to the ramparts, intending to read it again as he walked, but a green woodpecker came over, summoning him, and, with a delicious flight of the mind, he watched it on to a tree on the farther side of the moat. Here, in meadows sparsely bordered with willow and poplar, lambs with great ears and spindly legs were hastening after ponderous, greyish ewes. Now and then he could hear their bleating, borne to him on a thin, wintry breeze that scudded the surface of the water, and rooks were pairing in the elms overhead. Winter is breaking up, he said, and into the calm thought that among the many birds in this place he had seen neither blackbird nor thrush and but one robin, another thought was thrust like a dagger—that the break-up of this winter was herald of a campaign.

Fifty years hence the little girl among the ewes in the nearest meadow would remember that on the disused mound at Wierickerschans she had seen figures, said to be those of Englishmen, moving to and fro, but she would have no care for them or for the remote wars. The lambs, with their absurd, stumbling grace, might enter into the pattern of her mind, or the heron, solitary inhabitant of the marsh; and Lewis knew that he also would see the heron and the lambs, and hear again the movement of the rooks above him, when all else of this day had fallen to greyness and the trivial gleams of the past; would see them, it might be, when he was unable to imagine his mother's face, so long would she then have been in her grave. Now, with the crumple of her letter in his fist, he imagined her at her little table in the morning-room, saw how the sunshine revealed the white in her iron hair, listened to the dashing strokes of her nib. She was noisy and violent in nothing else, but she wrote, in a jingle of bangles, as if each correspondent were a mobilized army hungry for dispatches and each post the last. Only the letters she sent to Peter at school had been written on her knee by the fire, silently and in pencil.

Looking back on his past and on his mother's letter which seemed to have sprung from it, he smiled over them as he would have smiled over the narrative of another's life, the life of a friend whose secrets he was but now beginning to understand. He had always supposed that it was the need to maintain his home that had bound him to it —that, and his mother's reliance upon him. But what bound me, he said now, was what always keeps men from going their own way . . . and he could not complete the thought. Some flaw in himself, perhaps. Or was the world, in the exercise of its power over one who wished to become independent of it, subtler than the moralists commonly supposed, binding him, not by his vice or weakness, but by his strength and a flattery of his virtues? The grip of a wife, he thought, not the inducements of a mistress.

The packing-case at last followed his mother's letter. Sezley ran into the smoking-room with news of its arrival. It was necessary, he knew, to the writing of "the history,"

which, because he liked Lewis, he had romanticized in his
impetuous mind. He entered from the courtyard with the
headlong floundering of a puppy, for he expected to find
Lewis alone. The emergence of a senior baldhead and a
pair of blood-rimmed eyes from behind a lowered copy
of the *Statesman* of Calcutta abashed him, but he was not
abashed for long. The crown and star on Jedwell's shoulder-
strap had not in the fort their Indian validity; and anyhow
he hadn't been by any means a colonel when he retired.
Sezley drew in his breath to speak. Then, seeing that
Lewis, at the table by the window, was writing, he hesitated again and advanced a few paces—over Jedwell's feet
—without speaking.

"Oh, you're only writing a letter!" he exclaimed at last.
"That's all right. . . . I say, your books have come, Alison.
There's a whacking great packing-case dumped in B Three.
Going to open it now? Shall I help?"

Lewis was glad to put away his letter. It was to Elizabeth
and hard to write. Words that had been the currency of
their betrothal might pass no more between them, and
there was as much artificiality now in the deliberate omission of these words as had formerly crept into their use.
She also would feel the constraint. "A bleak letter," she
would say, and her little smile would shroud the death
within her. He remembered the first touch of that death—
how once, while he kissed her and her body clung to him,
she had known suddenly that his mind was not in her
passion, that he was waiting for her to cease. Her knowledge had been the cause of knowledge in him. She had
not understood; nor he; they had been silent and had
fought long against the truth. At last, bidding him farewell
at Walmer, she had accepted—with how much courage!—
what he could not deny. To write to her now in the chilled
idiom of friendship, to wound her with each careful gentleness—but there was no other way in which he might write,
none less cruel. Except when he made himself write to
her, she was never in his thoughts. He was writing to a
stranger.

"I wish, Sezley, that you wouldn't come into a room

like the squirt of a siphon," the statesman of Calcutta remarked, removing the gold rims of his glasses from the
red rims of his eyes.

"Sorry, sir."

"And will you please notice that there is an abundance
of floor-space not occupied by my feet?"

Sezley was baffled by so much elaboration. "Sorry, sir,"
he repeated. "My fault."

"Your fault? Not at all. The fault of the god who made
you."

Sezley had not the gift of silence. "Anyhow," he said,
the colour rising in his cheeks, "I don't see what there is
to make all that fuss about. I didn't tread on your feet. I
cleared them. I——"

"What are these books of yours, Alison?" Jedwell amiably
intervened. "Something to read?" And the question, as he
considered it, not seeming to be as intelligent as he had
hoped, he added: "Nothing much to do in this hole except
read."

"Alison's writing a history, sir," Sezley answered, his
temper past.

"But history," Jedwell said, "is being made. . . . A history, may I ask, of what?"

Lewis might have let the question slide; it had been
asked for the sake of asking. But he could not resist watching Jedwell's face and saying:

"A history of the contemplative life."

"The what?"

"The contemplative life—particularly in England since
the Renaissance."

"But who lives it?"

"You know India and I don't, sir, but isn't it true that
in India——"

"In India, yes. I know. But you said England. Who lives
it there? Who and how and why and with what effect?"

"That's a goodish summary of my book," Lewis said.

The *Statesman* of Calcutta fell to the floor. A lively
interest had made Jedwell a changed man.

"Are you really writing that book—seriously? Then let

me tell you this. You can't write about the contemplative life unless you're the sort of man capable of living it."

"I know," Lewis said. "It's much more important to me to become a man of that sort than to write the history. But you must have a concrete task to live by while you're learning—worshipping God, or shepherding, or illuminating manuscripts, or writing a history. It's all one."

Jedwell twisted a button on his tunic. "I see. That sounds like sense. Look here," he added, his hand shaking a little and his eyes coming up in compelled shyness, "if you want the Indian stuff—and I don't see how you can do without it—I know about that, or did once. Might have been better for me if I'd known a bit less. Lot of good it's done me. . . . Still, we might talk, if you care to."

Sezley had been swinging Lewis's attaché case on his finger.

"Aren't you coming, Alison?" he said, and, as they crossed the courtyard: "What's the matter with Jedwell? I've never seen him like that. He doesn't know anything about it, does he?"

"Yes, he does," Lewis answered.

They went to the dormitory together. In it, hunched over a drawing-board, was Ferrard, a naval officer who, like Ballater, had left the Service as a midshipman; a Scot with high cheek-bones and tight lips and dark, curving eyebrows that gave to his face an expression of amusement and surprise. The white sun of early March shone on his paper. Looking over his shoulder, Lewis saw a map of the fort.

"Alison's books have come," Sezley cried.

"What the hell does he want books for?" Ferrard answered, carefully wiping the pen that he was using for red ink. Then he became aware that Lewis was at his side. His eyebrows went up into his forehead and his lips flickered into a smile. He grasped Lewis's arm. "Look here, Alison," he said, "you can help me," and while he explained his difficulties they leaned over the map together. The greater part of its outline was complete—the two islands connected by a narrow arm of land; on the smaller, the courtyard,

the dormitories, the gatehouse and the bridge leading to
the outer world; on the larger, the square of the main ramparts with a vast quadrangle, containing the garrison's
quarters, enclosed in it, and, at its corners, the wooded
bastions. "It's the external dimensions that worry me."
He pointed with his pencil. "What's the breadth of the
outer canal—there?"

"Does it matter?" Lewis said.

"I don't want to leave anything to chance." Ferrard
lowered his voice that he might not be overheard. "I've a
Belgian in Rotterdam making outside arrangements. I want
him to have his car—there. . . . And either there . . . or
there . . . I shall do my get-away. It will be dark. We might
not make contact unless the staff-work's perfect—so this
map. . . ."

As they discussed the scheme, Lewis perceived a flaw
in it and suggested an amendment.

Ferrard looked at him. "You're a queer bloke, Alison.
Thanks for the idea. But why did you tell it to me?"

"Isn't it useful?"

"I know. But if I'd had it, I should have kept it to
myself."

"It's not so precious as all that."

"It's damned good."

"You're an enthusiast, Ferrard, you know."

"Well, we all are on this job. . . ." Ferrard was about
to speak again, checked himself, sucked a paint-brush and
considered his words. "Look here, I'll tell you what I'll
do," he said at last, with the seriousness of a diplomat
conceding a continent. "I'm tied up in this scheme with—
with two other people. And it won't work for more than
three. But one of them thinks he may have a better line
elsewhere. Anyhow he may not be able to raise the cash.
If he falls out, I'll take you in. . . . Or perhaps you've
something of your own?" He added swiftly: "No, that's
not a fair question. . . . Let's leave it at that. If there's
a vacancy, I'll give you first refusal. No need to decide
now."

But why this elaboration of map-drawing? Lewis wondered as he turned away towards the packing-case, summoned by Sezley's shout for attention. Why the coloured inks, the paint-box, the measured printing, the dolphin and compass in the north-west corner? The Belgian in Rotterdam would not profit by so much decoration. It was unlike Ferrard to waste his time. He was a good officer, a quick, unspectacular worker. Only in the fort, where all men were changed, would he have drawn dolphins earnestly as though persuaded that he might escape on their backs.

Sezley was prizing open the packing-case, and Lewis saw at once how small a part of his library could be contained in it. His task appeared before him like an impenetrable forest; it seemed that he had been pretentious and childish. He sat back on his heels before the packing-case, thinking: My history is little nearer than it was, but his discouragement vanished as soon as he had a volume in his hands. In the packing-case it had been separated from the others. It's the Plato, he thought, that Elizabeth put in at the last moment. But she passed from his mind; he could think only of his books, their names suggesting to him many connected posts in the historical system that he had imagined. Since the Renaissance, contemplation, by which he meant the stilling of the soul within the activities of the mind and body so that it might be still as the axis of a revolving wheel is still, had taken new forms and had cultivated in old forms a new significance. Mathematics, perceiving and measuring the order of external nature, had discovered in new men those very qualities that the perception of God had discovered in their predecessors. Might not this unity be the unity of his history? He saw the books before him as the quarries from which stone for his building was to be hewn. Sezley turned them over and built them into patterns. When pillars of books stood upon the floor, Heber's edition of Jeremy Taylor was found spread over the bottom of the box. Sezley looked into it.

"Sermons," he said. "Prayers. A Life of Jesus."

"Read it," Lewis said.

"Read it?"

"Where your left thumb is."

Sezley read, kneeling on the floor:

" '. . . and whatsoever is good, if it be a grace, it is an act of faith; if it be a reward, it is the fruit of faith. So that as all the actions of man are but the productions of the soul, so are all the actions of the new man the effects of faith' . . . I say, shall I go on?" Then suddenly: "What about shelves? There aren't any."

CHAPTER THREE

SOMETIMES a group of officers made voluntary and escorted marches into the countryside that lay about the fort. Ballater went always, because confinement tormented him; Ferrard went "to get to know the country," carrying a notebook furtively in his pocket and a miniature compass in the palm of his hand; Jedwell went, none knew why, for he did not enjoy going. But Sezley, who enjoyed everything, enjoyed this. If he was walking ahead, he would remember that he must speak instantly to Ferrard in the rear; if he himself had fallen behind, it became at once necessary to communicate with Dacres in front. He ran continually up and down.

"That boy," said Jedwell, "makes one feel like an old ram bothered by a sheep-dog puppy."

Lewis, urged by Ballater to join in these marches, soon discovered that Jedwell was unable to communicate what he knew, or had known, of Hindu philosophy. He began hopefully but his mind wandered; he would lose himself in anecdotes; nothing for him was clear. Or being launched in exposition, he would be seized by a paralysis of language, by some obscure embarrassment at hearing his own lips speak these things and his own voice yield again to the emotion of them; and he would become once more the half-humorous, half-crusty little man, ridden by whisky and quinine, that he appeared to be. Soon he abandoned his vain attempts, but he and Lewis had formed a habit of walking side by side and did not break it, their silences serving them perhaps as well as words could have done.

Lewis saw that snowdrops were blooming in the gardens;

24

they were planted in grass and seemed to be larger, more starlike, less timid flowers than at home; and an hour later, under a sky threatening one of the showers of snow that were common in those early days of March, the grass seemed to be lighted from within and the white flowers to be ghostly shadows upon it.

When the march was over and the group was breaking up in the courtyard, Jedwell cleared his throat and said: "Where do you work, Alison?"

"Where I can, sir. There's generally some room fairly empty, according to what people are doing—the smoking-room or the messroom or B Three. And the ramparts when I'm not making too elaborate notes. In a few weeks it won't be so cold out of doors."

"Ever seen my room?"

"No, sir."

"Care to look? It's not much of a place. But it has a lock."

They inspected it together. Its breadth was scarcely greater than that of its window; its length, containing the door and the bed, could be covered in four paces. A chair, a table, a trunk, an iron washstand, and a row of pegs made up its furniture. On the table, in a silver frame embossed with the heads of Reynolds's angels, was an enlarged snapshot of two figures; an Indian girl looked back over her shoulder at Jedwell, who disregarded her. On the wall was pinned a great map of the Western Front.

"I keep it up to date," Jedwell said. "I like to move the pins and wools according to the bulletins. But it isn't up to date," he added fretfully. "Not nearly. The names are so difficult. Once I get wrong, I never seem to get right again." He straddled the chair and set an empty pipe between his teeth. "Well, there's the room if it's of any use to you. It's not quiet. Nothing is. Ballater's making a garden patch outside the window; he talks about it; you might think it was Kew. And you'll hear Sezley's voice through the partition. Makes me feel like the infant Samuel. But there it is. I use it only to sleep in."

"But you'll want it in the evenings?"

"No. I play picquet with Grove in the evenings. You can pay me rent if you like. Pay it in kind. Keep the map up to date for me. Make that your job." He rose, stared at the map, uprooted a pin and allowed a bight of green wool to drop over the bedrail. Suddenly, in an outburst of irritation, he dragged all the wool into his hands; it hung from him, the pins glistening. "You start afresh. I can't do anything right these days." Then, in his old voice, prim and regulated, he said: "You can turn the lady face downwards if she disturbs the contemplative life. . . . Though she knew a bit about it. . . ." And he added, as though answering a question: "She died at Benares. When you've done, you might stand her up again. And do you mind not smoking in here? I never smoke where I sleep."

In the weeks that followed, Lewis was happy as he had not been since childhood. It seemed that the world had indeed ceased its concern with him.

Day after day, reading at Jedwell's table or watching from the ramparts winter's stubborn decline, he allowed the idea of his own book to grow unforced within him. He was not impatient, for the history was not to him an end in itself but the symbol of a way of life, a means of disciplining and co-ordinating it. The completed work did not appear as a prize that should urge him to present anxiety but as the labour of the man he must study to become, and the end, being so far off, seemed scarcely to be of this world.

The form of the book must be historical, following the development of spiritual concepts in England since the Renaissance and relating them with the philosophies of a remoter past; but the task before him was not to give an account of certain mystical thinkers and even less to compose a religious history. To identify the contemplative with the mystical purpose would be to identify a mountain with one of the many streams that sprang from it. His care was to ask whether there was not a perceptible unity of all the higher endeavours of the human mind, whether Plato's purpose was not linked more closely than was commonly understood with that of Aquinas, and Vaughan's with Newton's. If this unity existed, what was its nature? Was it limited to men of genius? What was its significance in the lives of men and women not knowingly of the contemplative sort?

Pressing upon him, as though it were an external force and not the product of his own argument, was the thought that, though the contemplative life was rare, the contemplative desire was universal, being, in the spirit, what the sexual desire is in the flesh, the prime mover of mankind. Contemplative stillness, he said, is but the name for a state of invulnerability, and to be invulnerable is what all men desire. Even the desire for immortality, springing from fear of death and having its fruit in the doctrine of the resurrection, is less than the desire to be invulnerable, being part of it. The desire for immortality can never be flawless; it is streaked with a longing for rest, for annihilation, or with Hamlet's terror of immortal dreams. But the desire to be invulnerable is flawless; it is consistent with man's longing for rest and with his eagerness for life—it is, indeed, the only reconciler of them; and it implies a supremacy even over dreams.

Newton seeking a final order in external Nature; the saints of the early Church, striving to identify themselves with God and to lose themselves in Him; the philosophers who, having no thought of resurrection, devoted their lives to the quest of absolute truth, the untouchable, the timeless thing—were not all these struggling by different paths towards one end, an ecstasy invulnerable because it is "out of the senses"? Men of a different temper, he added, pursue the same quest in the senses—in the apprehension of speed which, while it lasts, excludes the apprehension of time; in the arts, themselves sensual, from which they that have the gifts of the spirit proceed to the core of the spirit; in love that builds its citadel in the midst of the city; in lust even—that bliss of nakedness which, like a torch in the night, drives darkness back and, in the same instant, blinds the beholder to all but itself. To enter by some means into a condition that excludes all but itself is every man's purpose. He will snatch at the promise of even a ghost of that condition; his pleasures, his loves on earth, his art, his philosophy are valuable to him in proportion to the strength of that promise contained in them. He will lose the world for love because in his heart he wishes to lose the world, to shake it off, to armour himself in an ecstasy against it. He sees all things moving about him; he sees all consciousness in flux; he desires, if it be but for an instant, to be as the gods are, to be invulnerable, to be still.

And Lewis, feeling as a traveller feels who comes suddenly upon a limitless prospect when he has believed himself to be enclosed in a narrow pass, began to think of contemplation, not as the exceptional province of genius, but as the crown of all men's hopes—a condition of vital peace, he said, that carries the everlasting within it, and he returned to the Plato before him, hearing in it now, not the speech of one man only, but the argument of mankind.

When short leave on parole began to be granted to those who applied for it, he did not apply, and an invitation that he received from a Dutch lady whom he had known long ago in England was refused. He would not be turned from his work. Having experience sometimes of that brilliant lightness of spirit which is the reward of prolonged meditation, he found pleasure even in the weariness that followed a day's labour, and would lie awake in his dormitory, hearing the slow, rasping breath of those who slept there and feeling that his own presence among them was unsubstantial, that his life in his mother's home at Chepping and all the world's claims upon him had been wiped away, that he was indeed shedding his old individuality— "like the skin of a snake"—and being made anew. These passages of delight were swiftly followed by knowledge that they were delusions. Between sleeping and waking the fort would appear to him to be a dream, and he would lie still, ridden by that hot anguish of disappointment which is the trickery of happy dreams.

But it is no dream, his heart cried suddenly. To-morrow, during the morning, he would work again in

Jedwell's room or, if the wind dropped, under the elms, sheltered by a scoop of the ground, pausing to gaze up through their branches at the sky, aswirl with ribbons of cloud. Two ravens were building, he remembered; the sun armoured them in gold when they moved. Over the rookery, kestrel were active, and, though the grey-backed crows chased them continually, they returned again and again. Everywhere, in defiance of gusts of snow, life was being renewed. Primrose and daffodil were out, and the air at noon would be fresh and warm with a taste of flowers in it.

On the opposite bank, he thought, staring into the darkness over his bed, larks will be singing; and it may be that by to-morrow morning the cattle will be in the fields. As he lay with a rough sheet dragged under his chin, imagining the long, gentle course of the succeeding day, the red and green wools and the shifting battle-fronts became entangled with the discourse of Timaeus, and, spent in thought, he sighed with the tranquillity of passion appeased, and, turning on his pillow, slept until morning.

As April passed, and French's dispatches on Neuve Chapelle appeared in the papers from home, and kingcups came out on the island in the moat, Lewis began to go on to the ramparts later in the day. There was delight, not only in his study of Plato, but in emerging from it—a blessed knowledge that he might return when he would, and that, though books were left behind, their wisdom would accompany him and maintain a ghostly world about him, glowing in his spirit as the memory of a summer's day continues though darkness fall. Even material things were affected in his sight by this afterglow of meditation. They appeared now in a special calm, always at a little remove from himself; and when, in the evenings before dinner, he went out eager for company after many hours of silence, the earth seemed to be newly revealed to him, as it had been long ago when for the first time the Odyssey changed in his mind from words into music.

The brown sail of a barge, whose hull was concealed by the deep canal-banks, would rise out of the meadows and dwell long in the great landscape, seeming to have fallen asleep in anticipation of dusk; and always, out of the glazing of the sun, a train appeared. Its wreaths of smoke drooped into the canals and vanished, as if the earth had sucked them down. From the windows, heads were thrust out and handkerchiefs waved—always, it seemed, the same heads, the same handkerchiefs. The regularity of that little train linked day with day. Time had forgotten this everlasting scene. All that Lewis saw was endowed with wonder and grace, as if whatever was evil in the world had been emptied from it.

His delight was sharpened by the peril of all delight, a voice within him saying: "If this should be taken from me!" And he held these enraptured evenings jealously in his heart, scarcely knowing whether it was in bliss he trembled or in his prescience that the world would rob him of it. A thick hedgerow pressed against the fence that separated the path on which he walked from the inward slope of the rampart, and at last the spring so abundantly increased in it that the great internal square of the fort, where the Dutch garrison had their quarters and tennis courts were being laid down, could hardly be seen through the palings and the foliage, and he looked outward as he made his circuits, seeing how the canal thirty feet below began to draw new and deeper colour from its reeded shores and how with the lengthening days the horizon extended. The narrow path, curling to embrace the bastions, was overlaid by shadows of the trees that it encircled. Each evening they cast a bluer accent on the earth, and the slash of gold stood higher among their branches.

A few officers were generally out at this hour and, personal routine being now firmly established, Lewis knew whom he might encounter. Willett, who said that in civilian life he was a professional strong man, would hold the path, a coat of yellowish tweed dragged over his bulging chest; and at his side, with head thrown back and bony nose uplifted, would be Gestable, padding along in rubber-soled shoes with the loping gait of a tall, shivering dog.

"Finished the history of the world?" Gestable would say, and Willett show his teeth in an amiable grin. Or a young Harrovian, named Carroll-Blair, with sharp creases in his grey flannel trousers and wrists like brittle twigs, would draw Lewis into argument. They would walk up and down together in the circle of a bastion, and, others joining them, the argument would deepen and increase, Lewis with delight leading it and drawing the truth out of his companions by challenge and prompting. Nothing stimulated him more than this testing of himself in them, and men who were ordinarily timid of argument, falling carelessly into the group, stayed under the compulsion of interest, held as by a story, and, without knowing it, revealing themselves.

One evening early in May, Ballater, coming up as he often did after watering his patch of garden, found Lewis alone. He began to speak of the agriculture of Holland, using it as an excuse to draw in a subject of which he was guilelessly fond—his uncle's Wiltshire acres that he would inherit and certainly reorganise. From the Ballater acres his way was easy to his Angevin pedigree and his un-varying success with women, who, it was implied, found an Angevin courtship irresistible. Lewis gravely led him on until, at the peak of his gallant solemnities, perceiving a light in Lewis's eye, he stopped, and rubbed his cheek, and pretended with disarming laughter that he had not expected to be believed. No one so easily as Lewis could persuade Ballater to laugh at himself and enjoy it, and to no one, in consequence, did Ballater reveal so much of what lay beneath his boasting—a passion for Nature, for land, for the legend and spirit of the countryside, which induced in him a specialized love of Hardy and Words-worth and tempted him to water-colour painting desper-ately sincere. He could be more proud of his water-colours than of his pedigree; but the woolliness of his trees smote him, and often he abandoned his brush and sought an outlet in the secret composition of descriptive essays, choked with the names of little-known grasses and flowers.

One of these essays he now brought out of his pocket

He invited Lewis, as a scholar, to criticize it. "Of course,"
he said, "I'm not a writer and all that, but I do know about
curlews." They sat down on the edge of the rampart, side
by side. Lewis was careful to criticize nothing but the
prose of the essay, leaving its sentiment unquestioned, for
natural history was Ballater's religion; his knowledge of it
was hedged about with prides and faith, and this writing
was an oblation to his god. Life in the fort marvellously
exposed the lovable and childlike secrets of men. That is
why Ballater bears so patiently with my freak of scholarship, Lewis thought. It must seem a mad waste of life to
him. But he treats me always with the smiling respect
appropriate in country squires towards the men of letters
they have tamed.

"Last time it rained," Ballater said, when the essay had
been folded and put away, "there were no leaves on the
trees." He looked up at a cloudless sky, thinking, perhaps,
of his garden. "It will be good to hear the raindrops
pattering on leaves when it does come. Sounds like summer. But, as the evenings become lighter," he added,
turning away from Lewis and kicking his heels into the
turf, "it will be harder to escape."

"Are you planning an escape?"

"No, as a matter of fact I'm not—not yet. But it worries
me. I ought to, I suppose. Everyone is. They sit about in
corners making plots; but it's a game more or less; it would
be the devil of a shock to most of them if they found themselves on the other side of the barbed wire. That's where
the Dutch are so wily—giving us short leave on parole
now and then. It keeps people from being bored, and
boredom's at the bottom of most escaping stunts. Aren't
you ever sick of this place? If it weren't for short leave now
and then, and my patch of garden and the birds, I'd go
mad. . . . Why don't you ever take leave?"

"I have my job here," Lewis said. "Even you can't take
your garden to the Hague."

"But if we were given permanent parole—there have
been vague rumours of it—we could live where we liked
in Holland. You could do your history even better then."

But life in any other part of Holland, with liberty to come and go and choose one's own conditions, would not have the intactness of this life. Here nothing moved but thought. "In this place," Lewis said, "we eat what we are given; we sleep where we are told to sleep. There's no question: 'Shall I go to the Hebrides to-morrow? Won't it be damnably selfish if I do this or that?' We can't go to the Hebrides or anywhere else—that's final. There are no obligations, no ties. Money has ceased to exist—and time. We are living on earth but we're as independent as ghosts."

"First rate," said Ballater, "if the life of a ghost satisfies you. But I want to ride. I want more people—different people. I want women, too—oh, not simply for the obvious reason. It amuses me to see them and talk to them. Don't you want that?"

They sat for a little while without speaking, at ease in their own thought. The evening train appeared; the clatter of it came to them across the moat and died away in the distance.

"Can you still hear it?" Ballater said, long after it was gone. He rose and stretched himself. "We'd better go down. They'll be clearing the ramparts soon. I hate being herded off by some damned corporal."

They had begun to walk on together when they saw advancing towards them the figure of the Commandant—a strange figure, tightly encased in a dark cavalry uniform, high and square at the shoulders, clipped at the waist. The head was carried at an upward tilt, like the head of a dog walking on its hind-legs; the breeches had the bulge of leg o' mutton sleeves in the 'eighties; the shanks were covered by patent-leather hessians that ran to sharp points at the toes and picked their way through an imaginary mud. The hands were gloved, and a tasselled switch hung by a loop from an extended wrist.

"At any moment," said Ballater, "the figure may dance."

As he approached, the Commandant threw up both his hands in an exaggerated gesture of recognition and delight.

"Ah!" he said, bestriding the path and showing his teeth in a wide, pink smile. "I have good news!"

Their thought was instantly of the war, though they could not understand why the Commandant should have come out on the ramparts to give them news of it.

"News? What is it, sir?" Lewis asked.

"Shall I tell you?" the Commandant exclaimed, warmed by their curiosity. "Or shall I keep it a secret? Friday morning will, perhaps, be soon enough. Will you do me the honour to take luncheon with me on Friday? And you also, Mr. Ballater? You also have an eye for ladies, I am told. . . . Ah yes, little rumours creep up from the Hague of how when Mr. Ballater goes on leave—but it is not you who are the conqueror on this occasion, Mr. Ballater."

Lewis said: "Have you yourself made a conquest, sir?"

The Commandant smiled his youngest smile and touched his grey hair. "Alas, I am old as you see—but perhaps not so old that—well, we shall see, we shall see." Then, leaning forward, he laid a forefinger along the side of his nose, in the manner of certain Dutchmen when they are coy. "No, it is you who have conquered, Mr. Alison. You, who refuse always to take leave. You will not go to the ladies. So the ladies they come to you. Can you guess? I will give you a hint. It is a very great lady."

"Oh," said Ballater, "do you mean that the Queen of Holland is to visit the fort? There was a rumour of it some time ago. I thought it was nonsense."

The Commandant laughed aloud. It was evident that his news, whatever it might be, had given him extreme pleasure. "No. Not the Queen, Mr. Ballater. Guess again. One more hint. A lady whose husband belongs to a very ancient, noble family. . . . But there, you will never guess. How could you? I never dreamed of such a thing myself. I will tell you." His voice changed to solemnity. Taking Lewis and Ballater by the arm, he drew them on towards the gate that led down from the ramparts. "I have had orders from the Ministry of War to prepare to receive the Baron and the Baroness van Leyden on Friday

—Leyden van Enkendael, you understand. They happen
to be sleeping on Thursday at Utrecht. They will arrive
Friday at 12.50. And why are they coming you ask? To
visit our fortifications?—no. To visit me?—och!" He
threw out his hands. "It is to visit Mr. Alison they come."

Ballater, who never blushed to say those things that
earned for him more leave than was given to any other
officer in the fort, said: "But they would scarcely be
coming, would they, sir, if anyone but yourself were commanding the fort?"

"You think so?" the Commandant replied thoughtfully.
"Well, I did know Leyden a little when I was a young
man. It is true that in our army all the officers are not of
the nobility. However. . . ." He clapped his hands together.
"So that is arranged? Our little luncheon party? There will
be one lady only—Mevrouw van Leyden herself. Your friend
is a sly dog, Mr. Ballater. Even now he does not tell us
how he came to know the van Leydens. And I hear—un-
officially, of course—that he refused an invitation to Enkendaal.[1] The Minister inquired whether I had refused him
leave and if so——"

"The explanation's simple enough, sir. I don't really
know the van Leydens at all. But the Baroness's first husband was an Englishman."

"I remember. A relative of the Marquess of Harbury?"

"He was a writer," Lewis continued. "My father published his books. Our home happens to be on the outskirts
of Harbury Park. That's all. I knew the Baroness as Mrs.
Quillan."

"And her beautiful English daughter no doubt?"

"She was a child."

"But even now, Mr. Ballater, you notice your friend
does not tell us why he refused an invitation to Enkendaal."

"I was settled here, sir."

The Commandant smiled knowingly. "Shy? But they
are very simple people," he said, adding with a glint of
malice: "Indeed, Mevrouw van Leyden has no reason to

---

[1] *Enkendaal*. The modern, official spelling is used in the place-
name, but the old Dutch, *Enkendael*, is retained in the family's title.

be otherwise. She was born a Hoek. You know the story, Mr. Ballater? She was governess at Enkendaal twenty-five years ago; beautiful but of no family. Then she married the Englishman, Quillan. Leyden never lost touch with her. He used to visit at Lord Harbury's whenever he went to England—calling at the house of Mr. Quillan, you may be sure." He chuckled and stroked his cheek. "And when Leyden became a widower, it wasn't long before the lady was back in Enkendaal. . . . But they are charming. Charming. We should not have refused, Mr. Ballater, I think? To stay in the country with beautiful ladies? Better than than the fort, *niet waar?*"

"Who are these people?" Ballater asked, when the Commandant had returned to his own quarters, waving his hand like a schoolgirl in high spirits. "Why are they coming here?"

"Just in kindness," Lewis answered. "To visit prisoners and captives."

Ballater smiled. "And the girl—the daughter—what's her name?"

"Julie Quillan. Gräfin von Narwitz, now."

"Did you know her well?"

"Yes, once. I was ten years older than she. An unofficial tutor, more or less, until her mother ran away to Holland."

"Really beautiful?"

Lewis hesitated. "I think of her as a child. She did come to England three years ago when her father was dying. She must have been eighteen. I saw her for a moment at the funeral, but scarcely to speak to. In some odd way she didn't seem the same person. . . . But yes; really beautiful."

"Is she coming, do you think?"

"Probably not. The Commandant said van Leyden and his wife. Julie may not be in Utrecht. Anyhow, it was probably thought that a girl who married a Prussian officer three months before the war couldn't be a visitor here."

"But she's English."

"She was."

"Anyhow," Ballater said, "it ought to be an amusing

party. The Commandant flourishing his nobility. . . . You'll have to give your Plato a rest on Friday afternoon."

The first dinner-bell was ringing and officers were moving across the courtyard on their way to the messroom.

"Look," Ballater exclaimed, "Ferrard and Gestable prospecting again."

"Prospecting? For what?"

"Escape. . . . D'you think they'll ever do it?" he added to Herriot, who had come up at Lewis's side. Herriot threw a glance over his shoulder at Ferrard.

"No," he said. "They're non-starters. They talk too much. This escaping business is becoming a disease with some people," he went on, taking Lewis's arm as they moved off towards the messroom.

"All the same," Ballater put in, "I suppose it is our job to get out if we can."

Herriot turned on him with a sneer. "I dare say it is for those that haven't a mind of their own. But I scheme to get out because I personally want to get out—not because my country needs me. Flying happens to be my job and I can't do it here. But if my job were to study Plato, I'd study Plato and be thankful. These boys intent on being heroes with wire-cutters sent out to them in cakes— it's all cant, though they don't know it. There are only two ways out of this place, anyhow, and they'll never use either of them."

"What are the two ways?" Ballater asked.

"One is to bribe the whole guard on the bridge. You need money for that—more than I've got. There's one other way."

"Do you know it?"

"I do; but I'm not ready." Suddenly, with a pressure of his arm, Herriot drew Lewis out of the little stream of men wandering in to dine. "Look here, Alison," he said. "After the war, let's meet. I may be through with flying then." He put his foot on a wooden bench that stood outside the messroom, and smoothed out a piece of paper on his knee. "I shall get out, and I'll tell you how. Read that."

In the fading light, Lewis saw that the paper put into his hands was the printed form, issued in the Commandant's office, that each Englishman was required to sign before taking short-leave on parole.

WIERICKERSCHANS
Bij BODEGRAVEN

In consideration of my being permitted to go from Wierickerschans on leave to............from 8.0 A.M. on ....until midnight on.............I.......... promise on my word as an officer that during that time I will not escape, and I will not prepare a future escape or assist others to escape.

Signed....................
Date......................

"Well," Lewis said, "how does that help you?"

"Read it again," Herriot answered quietly, "omitting the first 'not.' I have a facsimile, all but the one word, coming from England—same paper, same print. When it comes, I put in for a week-end in the Hague. When the day comes, up I go to the Commandant's office; he gives me one of his own forms to sign; I pick up a pen and ask him about the weather. While he looks out of the window, I pocket his form and sign my own. 'I hope you have a good time in the Hague, Mr. Herriot.' 'Thank you, sir.' And off I go, report in the Hague, shift to Rotterdam. I shall be home before they miss me."

"They'll ask the War Office to send you back."

"And d'you suppose the War Office will send back a pilot for the sake of a quibble? They want me; the Dutch don't. Once in England, I'm safe enough. And when I'm gone, no one will ever get out of this place again. I'm glad for your sake. Why should you escape? It's not a question of being killed. It's much better to be dead than to lead someone else's life. Here you *can* lead what you know to be your life. When I go," he repeated, "that settles it. You can do your own job in peace."

The bell was ringing again and they went into the mess-room together. After dinner, the poker players settled to their game. The chink of beans in their saucer was answered by the swirl, the rattle, the drop of a roulette ball. Outside the messroom, Lewis found men walking up and down in pairs, between the buildings and the barbed wire. The name of the *Lusitania* recurred again and again, but sometimes they were silent as they passed, guarding, he thought, a secret of escape. Sometimes it was of swimming they spoke, or of the hard tennis courts that the Government had laid down; often of women, of theatres in London, of good wine, good food. Jerram, who might be seen each morning, seated at a desk, preparing himself to become an actuary, walked under the arc-lights, discoursing in a raven's voice of the philosophy of mathematics. And the arc-lights, shedding their glare on the barbed wire and the silver gravel and the burdock at the water's edge, drawing an intense blackness out of the little branch-canal that separated the living-quarters from the great mass of the ramparts, awakening in the ramparts themselves a harsh green sliced by metallic shadows, blotted out the sky and enclosed all life within the compass of a stage whereon these figures went to and fro continually in a wheeling pattern of flash and gloom.

Lewis, having taken his fill of the night air, went on to his dormitory. Here, so early in the evening, he could generally be alone. To-night Lapham and Shordey and Willett, seated on trunks round an upturned sugar-box, were playing a game of their own that they called poor man's poker. When he was undressed, their game broke up. They gathered round his bed, on which he had propped himself—a book across his knees.

"Look here, Alison," Willett said, "I don't want to interrupt you, but there's something we should like to have your opinion about. The point is this. Ferrard and Gestable and I planned an escape together. Bribery was part of it; it meant money; I've tried to raise my share. Well, I'm a kind of showman in private life—strong man and so forth —and I'm poor; I have to send money home; I can't raise my share of the bribe and the outside expenses of a car to Rotterdam and all that."

"And we're poor, too, Shordey and me," Lapham put in. "We and Willett rows in the same boat. That's how it is. And we thought that if you, Alison——"

"Let me," said Willett. "The point is that if a dozen and more run a scheme it won't cost more than for one or two. Divided up, it'll come cheap. There are lots of poor men in the fort. Alone they can't do much, but bring them together and it might be a damned fine show."

"I see," Lewis answered.

"My idea is a tunnel," Willett continued. "It would take the hell of a time and there are all sorts of difficulties, but the chief one that I can see is keeping the people together. You know how everyone goes his own way in this place; we're a howling democracy. Lapham and Shordey and I will do the dog-work. What we want you to do is to be the brains behind the thing. You give the orders. We'll see they're carried out."

"The long an' the short of it is," said Lapham, "that the scheme wants officering. Me an' Shordey and Willett's been bickerin' about it already. If you came in——"

"But why me?" Lewis asked.

"To start with, you're not mixed up in any of the private stunts," Willett replied. "And it was you who hit on the one idea that gives Ferrard's scheme the least chance of coming off. Anyhow, people will listen to you who won't listen to any of us."

"Why should they?"

"Because you've a mind and they know it. And you don't shout and get worked up. You wouldn't come in on a thing of this kind unless you meant to go through with it. That's why."

"In this place, you know," Lewis said, "I haven't laid myself out to be a man of action."

Willett was not to be shaken. "That's why, too. The place simply rattles with men of action. There's a Dead-Eye Dick in every corner. I'm sick to death of 'em. And they're sick of themselves."

Lewis glanced at the book lying open on his bed; the point of his finger was still marking the line at which he had ceased to read. Then he looked up into Willett's eager face—a blunt-featured, honest, attractive face with eyes slow but bright, hair thinning at the temples, and a mouth good-humoured and firm. I shall be in the thick of it, Lewis thought.

Willett sat down on a chair beside the bed. "I don't pretend to be anything of a scholar," he began, "but I respect other people's jobs—if they're genuine. I don't understand what you're driving at, Alison—I mean the way you live here—but I'll lay what you're doing's worth doing. I don't want to hedge you into running this poor man's scheme. Some of the people in this place are just shirkers—too damned lazy to stir hand or foot. If we want them to dig, we'll rope 'em in. They won't stand up against public opinion. They'll come and be heroes because that way's easier—you see if they won't. But if you feel that your job's to stand clear—well, that's that. But I'll say this: until we actually get out, the thing oughtn't to trouble you much. We shan't be able to dig for more than a few hours a day—perhaps only for a few hours a week. You'll have time for your own work, too."

"It's not a question of time," Lewis said.

"What then?"

"It's a question of how your mind runs—clear, or silted up with other things. There are some jobs that can't be done with half your mind—starting and stopping, like a bus-horse."

"I see. . . . Then you'd rather we hadn't asked you?"

"Yes," Lewis answered. "I wish to God you hadn't. But since you have, I'll do it—if in the end it's necessary. But it's up to you to sound other people. You've got to get the team together. They may not want it—or may not want me."

"Give us a fortnight or three weeks," Willett said. "There are some useful people on leave. We'll have to wait until they come back. Then we'll ask you again. It may come to nothing."

"Very well," Lewis replied, picking up his book.

In his thought of the van Leydens, in Herriot's plan of escape, in this scheme of Willett's, the world had approached Lewis through the swerving of his own mind; but it receded again. To-morrow he would be undisturbed. To-morrow and for many to-morrows he might be at peace. "It may come to nothing," Willett had said, and he forgot Willett and the Commandant's luncheon party; he shut them away from him. Outside, the wind was rising. When at last the groups in the messroom broke up and flooded the dormitory with talk of Atlantic transport and Jerram's straight flush to a knave, he thought of the canals ruffled in the darkness and of the sentries on the ramparts bending their heads to the wind. If the breeze increased, the barbed wire would sing with it.

During the night he heard often the twang of wire on the stakes, heard it until its shrill vibration and the slow lash of the risen wind became an unperceived accompaniment to silence. On a little table at his bedside he had built, as was his custom, a shelter of books for his candle, so that the light disturbed none of the sleepers but fell on his book and hands.

The storm ran its course and died away. Now and then the regular breathing of the dormitory was broken by the creak of springs and the gasp or muffled cry of a dream. The Dutch sergeant, on his rounds, standing in the doorway with a shaded lamp, stared at the lighted head and shoulders of the reader, not in surprise, for Lewis's nightwatch was familiar to him, but as children stare at a picture that disturbs them, they know not why. Sometimes the Englishman was not reading, though his book was open, and the sergeant, encountering the wide eyes that included him in their gaze but seemed not to recognize his presence, was fascinated by the origins of a vision that he could not share. He shaded his lamp the more carefully and, going at last, quietened his tread, not wishing to be long a solitary witness of this struggle or to infringe this isolated power. But he returned again, drawn by a curiosity stronger than his reluctance, and at his third visit, when the morning light was clinging like a mist to the edges of the blinds, he found the candle out, the shelter of books laid down and Lewis asleep with one hand fallen from the coverlet and the other curled above his head.

CHAPTER FOUR

"Sweet vernal is over, and nearly all the ewes have lambed," Ballater was saying, as he and Lewis went together into the Commandant's quarters, whither the van Leydens had already been taken. "I think it's the best moment of the year. Hot days and cold evenings. Better than April. Much better than June." He had a pastoral independence of mind. Though he would earnestly discuss politics and the war, they were not in the core of his thought. Like a peasant, like a child, he preserved his own values with a stubborn and lovable innocence. And it was he who smoothed away the awkwardness of the van Leyden's visit, for after luncheon he permitted neither Lewis nor the Commandant to be their host, but showed them the fort, as if it were his country-house, with an irresistible pride of ownership, telling them of his fishing, his jay, his golden oriole in the orchard opposite, explaining the work he had done in his garden patch, and, when he heard a reed warbler merrily singing across the water, waving their attention to it, as if it were a member of an orchestra that he had summoned for the pleasure of his guests. The Baroness, after a cold beginning, was full of praise for Ballater when she heard of the Wiltshire acres. "What a charming friend you have, Lewis! You must bring him to stay with us. Or, if you will not come, then he must come alone." And van Leyden, delighted to find in Lewis an Englishman who could speak Dutch, talked proudly of his library in the Castle at Enkendaal. "You must come to see it. It would interest you, Mr. Alison. He can have permission, Commandant, *niet waar?*"

44

"But certainly he can have permission to visit the Castle at Enkendaal," the Commandant replied. The words Enkendaal and Kasteel fascinated him; he could no more keep them out of his conversation than he could prevent his corseted body from inclining a little whenever the Baron van Leyden addressed him. "But Mr. Alison," he added, "has always refused to take leave."

"Och!" said the Baron. "How is that? Julie says you taught her when she was a child. I wish you'd teach her again. She needs discipline, heaven knows! . . . But, though I'm not a scholar, I know their ways. My uncle Dirk would never leave his books unless it suited him. Invite yourself when you please."

The idea of having a pupil, a mind that he might impregnate, filled Lewis with excitement. Into his conversation with the Baroness this excitement entered. He laughed with her, and pleased her more than he had done hitherto; but he was thinking that, in the days when he had gone to Natton Lodge to teach Julie, Mrs. Quillan had appeared to be heavy and dull, with the beauty of a stiff flower always drooping towards him on its long stem, and that the child, full of fire and grace, had never seemed to be her daughter.

"You did not bring the beautiful Madame de Narwitz to-day?" the Commandant ventured, hoping that this compliment would recommend him to Julie's mother. "No, no, of course," he added hastily, seeing a shadow pass across the Baroness's face. "It would be difficult. . . . I understand."

"No," said the Baroness, with sharpness in her tone. Then, turning to Lewis: "She wished to come. She wanted, she said, to see her schoolmaster in his cage."

At this the Commandant laughed heartily, wrinkling his lips under his clipped, white moustache, pressing his gloved hands to his waist and throwing back his head. The Baroness stared at him coolly for a moment; then turned away.

It was understood before the van Leydens went that Ballater was to visit them early in June. Meanwhile, the tranquil routine of the fort continued unbroken. Willett said no more of his project and Lewis imagined that it was postponed; then ceased to think of it. Herriot made no move.

One evening at dinner Herriot leaned across the table and poured wine into Lewis's glass. They had so often shared their wine that Lewis gave no more acknowledgement than a movement of his hand; the talk was not interrupted. Ballater announced that he had been sowing radishes; Jedwell didn't believe that the advance of the Allies near La Bassée could be maintained. Lewis continued a conversation with the Dutch captain.

"Anything you want from the Hague?" Herriot broke in. "I'm going on leave to-morrow." Lewis understood then that the wine in their glasses had that night a special significance; it was the last they would drink together, for Herriot would not return from the Hague; and he was sad, as though this were an old friend he was losing. The day became suddenly memorable and he cast his mind back over it, remembering how Ballater had given him a pair of field-glasses with which to observe the movements of a reed warbler on the farther side of the moat, and how, while he stood with the glasses to his eyes, a little group had assembled behind him, eagerly discussing the resignations of Fisher and Churchill. The edge of the moat was deeply fringed with yellow iris, ablaze in the sun, and apple blossom was coming out.

These fragmentary details, by which alone day was divided from day, persisted in his imagination while he walked with Herriot in the courtyard after dinner. He could not free himself from the thought that they would never see each other again, or would meet as strangers, their intimacy lost. After the war, if both survived, they would speak of to-night—this walking up and down together, their unconfessed reluctance to separate, the little incident of the wine, and would struggle to recapture the vanished mood. But they would fail, and, after a few hours of friendly pretence, part, leaving over their next meeting an intentional vagueness.

Never before had he been so strongly aware that in each instant of their lives men die to that instant. It is not time that passes away from them but they who recede from the constancy, the immutability of time, so that when afterwards they look back upon themselves it is not themselves they see, not even—as it is customary to say—themselves as they formerly were, but strange ghosts made in their image, with whom they have no communication.

He heard Herriot saying: "D'you know, Alison, this ache of mine to fly—I lose trust in it sometimes, just as you lose trust in your own job. Often one flies just for the excitement of speed and power, but that's nothing. Any fool of a passenger gets it—it's little more than a physical thrill. I want to fly for the sake of the flash of seeing that comes now and then—almost as if one died bodily, and escaped from oneself, and saw out on the other side. But I can't tell you what it is I see. I can't even remember it myself. It will be the same with you. Some day the kind of exaltation you told me of, that comes to you after days and days of thought, will suddenly become more than it has ever been before—and you will *see*. Then you'll come back, just as I come back to earth, and you won't be able to tell what you've seen—or remember it. But the thing you can't describe and can't remember will be the whole of life to you. Sometimes you'll call it God, and sometimes you'll feel that it's nothingness and that you've given up your life to nothingness. . . . And in what way you'll reach it, I don't know. Maybe through solitude. I doubt it. I believe you'll find what you're looking for *in* the world, not in withdrawing from it. Work, women, responsibility —you'll have to accept them and go through with them."

"If you're right," Lewis said, "after all this—and after I've learned from this—I shall have to start again."

They walked in silence beyond the courtyard, down the length of the buildings. The windows of the messroom threw patches of yellow light on to the small brick of the path, drawing a plum-like bloom out of its redness. "We'd better put in an appearance," Lewis said. "The Dutch will think you're conspiring." They entered the room and stood, propped by the wall, at a little distance from the roulette players.

"It's odd," Herriot said, shaking dead pipe-ash into his hand, "how our heavens seem to differ and yet are alike. I reach mine, as much of it as I shall ever reach, by going in a machine up into the air. But I'm a little man. You may become what I can never be—the invulnerable man, passed beyond harm. I can never be that. But our ideas come out of the same basket—or seem to to-night. Perhaps they won't again."

Half an hour later the roulette cloth was rolled up and they went to their dormitories amid a little group talking of systems.

In the morning Herriot went on leave and did not re-appear. The arguments provoked by his escape soon died, but the community was affected. Already, by grants of short leave, the character of internment had been changed; now restlessness increased; perhaps, it was said, perma-nent parole would be given. Preparations for tunnel-digging were continued by those who had no desire for parole or, desiring it, were without faith in diplomats; and Ballater, having flattered the Commandant into taking a benevolent interest in gardens, proudly imported a spade. Rampart and messroom and dormitory were eager with rumour from the Hague. The fort had ceased to include the lives of its inhabitants.

After his visit to Enkendaal, Ballater returned to the fort at midnight. To his disappointment, Lewis was already asleep, and he was forced to turn in with his triumphs untold. In the morning he fared no better. He loitered in the messroom after breakfast, discussing with Ferrard, who was annoyingly stubborn and would not give way, whether a carp should properly be cooked in milk; and when he had despaired of Ferrard, he found that Lewis was already inaccessible in Jedwell's room. He had therefore to content himself with the silent planting out of candytuft. He pulled a few radishes, intending to pull only a few; but, he thought, if I pull them all at once there'll be enough to go round the mess. This would win fame for his garden, and the prospect of it was his consolation in an unprofitable hunt for a mole.

"Pretty good crop of radishes, sir," he cried as Jedwell passed.

"Ah, Ballater, still at your garden," was the reply, given without a turning of the head.

Perhaps Jedwell had not heard. Ballater stared at the back of the little man's skull and at his ribbed neck. But he'll be glad enough to eat them, he thought, returning to his quest of the mole.

His afternoon was more fortunate. For once, he had no need to persuade Lewis to be idle. Lewis himself suggested that they should play tennis, and, when tennis was done, they fetched towels from the dormitory and went down to the landing-stage on the edge of the western ramparts. They swam and lay in the sun and swam again. "Hot!" Ballater said.

He was waiting, had long been waiting, to be asked his news of Enkendaal, but Lewis appeared to have forgotten that he had been there.

"You seem to be taking a day off," Ballater said. "Are you working to-night instead?"

"Not to-night."

"What's wrong? Are you stuck in the book?"

Lewis stretched his bare arms across the grass. "No. I read pretty steadily this morning. But this place has changed. And I've got the tunnel on my mind. Where to begin. How to begin. How to get through the floor—there's concrete, you know, under the wood."

"Oh, to hell with the tunnel," Ballater answered. "Too much like work on a day like this. I'm warm and dry already. . . . And, anyhow, I believe we shall be given parole before the tunnel's through. If we're not, and the tunnel's discovered or fails in some way, it will give the German Legation an excuse to have parole washed out and leave stopped. This place isn't so bad if you can get leave now and then. But I don't want to spend another winter here. The tunnel's more risk than it's worth."

"But you're in on it?"

"Of course I am. You can't say No to a thing like that. You came in on it yourself. I did because you did. Run by Willett and Shordey and Lapham, it would have been hopeless. Now at least there's a sporting chance, though it is a devilish poor chance, if you ask me. Don't you agree?"

"About one to a hundred."

"Then we're wasting our time?"

"As long as we don't realize it too acutely, I suppose it doesn't matter. But I should like Willett's 'poor men' to have a run for their money."

Ballater turned over on his face and threw his towel aside.

"When we do get permanent parole," he said, "if we ever do, the place I should like to live in is Enkendaal. They were talking about it at dinner. The Baron said, Should we like to live in Enkendaal? I thought at first he meant in the Castle. But he meant on the estate. They own the village and all the land for miles round. Such country! Heath and pine. We went up to a place where you can look out between two woods right across to the German frontier. The Baron said if I wanted country and you wanted books we couldn't do better in Holland. He'd give you the run of his library."

"Did you see the library?"

"Yes. We went up there, into the tower."

"What kind of library is it?"

"Enormous. Great thick walls and——"

"I mean, what kind of books?"

"Oh!" . . . Ballater was wriggling across the grass towards his cigarette case. When the first wreath of smoke had twined into the air, he had forgotten about books. "You'd like the place," he said. "There are two great lakes at the foot of the tower—and the lilacs. . . . I admired them, and Julie gave——"

"Julie?" said Lewis.

Ballater smiled. "Well, I don't call her that to her face yet. In fact, I don't call her anything. I can't call a perfectly good English girl Narwitz. She doesn't look in the least Narwitz. . . . Anyhow, she made me wear a sprig of lilac in my button-hole at dinner—took away my carnation and put the lilac in. There was a man there called Alex van Arkel; they call him Aguecheek behind his back; he was furious about the lilac, because she hadn't any for him. I don't like that man. He wears a bracelet. Pro-German probably. And when he wants to annoy Julie he pretends that she must be pro-German too. You should see the colour come into her cheeks."

"I liked the Baron," Lewis said. "It's odd; I can vaguely remember now having met him at the Quillans' years ago, but until he came to the fort I'd forgotten that I had ever seen him. Did you talk much to him?"

"Shooting chiefly. And agriculture of course. He was frightfully interested when he found I really knew something about it. . . . But you can talk to Julie about anything. Except, I think, it's better to keep off the war. She's on edge about that. Not that she lets most people see it, but I saw it. I can often see what's going on in a girl's mind. And I think I was rather a relief to her because I'm English. I wish I could do something to help her. I believe I could if I were living there."

"Help her?"

"Well . . . in the Castle . . . everyone round her Dutch. And every Dutchman who comes there——" Ballater pressed the stub of his cigarette into the earth. "I don't blame them, poor fools. She's beautiful enough to make you want to cry. Do you know, once when she and I——"

Lewis had risen to his feet. "I'm going to swim again," he said. They walked down to the brink of the water together, and Ballater put a watch into Lewis's hand, saying that he was going to sprint across the moat.

"I used to be fast at Dartmouth. You might time me. I don't think I've lost much of my speed."

In sixty-two seconds he touched the farther bank and began to return leisurely, pausing to lift a long white arm out of the water and to shout: "How long?" Being told, he disappeared with a splutter of satisfaction and came up again with a great threshing of arms and legs. As he swam, the water ran out in a twisting spiral of gold and steel and foam. Beyond him the countryside was red with sorrel and yellow with buttercups.

He stopped swimming and for a moment lay extended on his face, his hands dividing the calm surface before him, his body rippling through a little cloak of bubbles. And Lewis remembered how he had said: "She's beautiful enough to make you want to cry,"—an unexpected saying in Ballater, who now threw his shoulders out of the water and began to turn somersaults with a ridiculous grace, emerging at last breathless and in grinning expectation of applause. Lewis was trying to imagine her, but he saw at first only the shadowy figure of a child known in the past; then, suddenly, he saw her cheek as he had seen it when Ballater spoke of the colour rising in it. He could not imagine her face, but her cheek he saw and the swift flow of colour and the flash of the eyes, though the eyes themselves were unimagined. He laughed at Ballater and dived into the water after him.

They swam down the canal and across to the farther bank, visiting the reed warbler's nest. "One egg," said Ballater. "Now I'll race you to the boom;" and at the end of the race they lay on the water, exhausted, silent, while birds hung and arrowed in the air above them. Inaudible waves lapped at their temples and slid over their ankles and wrists. Without speaking they swam back and stretched themselves out again on the hot boards of the landing stage.

It was resolved that the mouth of the tunnel should be under Lewis's bed. A large boring should be carried across the room, and the earth from it packed handful by handful in the nine-inch space between wooden floor and concrete foundation. Under the path, under the rampart and its barbed wire, a narrow tunnel should then be pushed forward to the inner edge of the moat. The broader shaft would become a receptacle for earth from the narrower; the need for close, laborious packing would cease, and the narrow shaft, once begun, make swift progress. One night, perhaps in early autumn, twenty-six men would assemble at the moat's brim beneath an unsuspecting sentry. They would launch off into the water together. The sentry, in an embarrassment of targets, would miss his aim. At worst, twenty-four would clamber up the farther bank. Three might get to Rotterdam; two, it was hoped, to England.

To turn back a flap of linoleum and hinge a trap-door in the floor-boarding was easy enough. But how was the concrete to be broken? Lewis remembered that Willett was by profession a strong man and that the Commandant was of genial disposition.

"I can't get exercise, sir, not the right kind of exercise," Willett said. Exposing his muscles, he made it clear that they were deteriorating; his livelihood was slipping from him; when the war was done, his wife and children must starve. "Ja, ja," said the Commandant, "I will see what I can think of," but Lewis had already decided that what Willett needed was a heavy crowbar from the garrison store. This was obtained. Willett exercised himself with it conspicuously; the garrison, passing through the court-yard, were confirmed in their opinion that the English were mad; the Commandant, when he had guests, brought them to the window of his quarters to observe Willett's behaviour. They were well entertained by it.

Meanwhile two clubs were organized. The Photography Club, under Ballater's control, obtained permission to import oxygen, in which the Commandant saw no evil. The Boxing Club, advertised on the messroom notice-board, invited the Commandant to be its Honorary President, and he knew at once how wrong he had been in supposing that the Englishmen disliked or laughed at him. "There is no greater honour," he said in a little speech after dinner, "than to be invited by your countrymen to share in their sport"; and for the first meeting of the Boxing Club, held in B Three dormitory when dinner was over, he put on his smartest uniform. Never since his coming to the fort had he enjoyed himself so much. The boxing itself was tedious, but he applauded with all his heart. To accept a few drinks, to refuse many more with a wag of his finger and a shake of his head, to unbend in a manner befitting a gentleman who knew how to preserve his dignity and yet be a "sport"—what could be more delightful? "To-night we are all sports together, isn't?"

"Yes, sir," said Ferrard, lifting his glass and his eye-brows, "all sports together! *Vive les Pays-Bas!*"

"*Vive les Pays-Bas!*" cried twenty-six Englishmen in chorus.

The Commandant rose to the toast. How the English-men cheered! How they sang! But their taste in music was execrable. Men of no other nation would play three gramo-phones together and shout them all down. But let them shout. Let them sing. The legend of this great party would spread to the Hague. No one could say hereafter that a Commandant was a failure who was thus welcomed into his captives' grotesque entertainments. At eleven o'clock he bade them good-night and withdrew. A few revellers escorted him to his lodgings and serenaded him. He thanked God that he had the gift of popularity. It was odd that he had ever doubted it.

A week later the Boxing Club met again. The Com-mandant was invited but, feeling that habitual unbending might be bad for discipline, he made gracious excuses. The blinds of the dormitory were drawn. Drink was brought; three gramophones played; Sezley and Gestable put on boxing gloves and were prepared to box if any in-trusion by the garrison staff should make boxing necessary. But they did not box. They stood in the ring and applauded themselves. The room was full of men shouting and sing-ing and stamping their feet. To the sentries a few yards away, the uproar did not differ from that in which, a week earlier, the Commandant had shared. They continued on their beat; the child-English were drunk again; German officers would certainly have behaved with more dignity. Meanwhile Lewis's bed had been pulled out of its corner. The flap of linoleum was turned back, the trap-door opened. In each *crescendo* of cheering, Willett attacked the concrete with his crowbar.

The material was stubborn and the attack prolonged. What had been a joke became a business. Spontaneity died. The cheering of boxers who did not box, the singing of bawdy songs by sober men, the intervening silences, the artificial cries of laughter and partisanship with which each hush was raked—all these it was necessary to orchestrate and control. Lewis stood on a trunk with an ivory hair-brush in his hand. He began to take pleasure in calling forth new combinations of sound; they excited him and made him laugh. A group in a distant corner broke into song whenever his brush was pointed at it; another group sprang into obedient competition; when he stamped his feet, all feet were stamped; when he beckoned sound to-wards him, sound came; when both his hands were stretched out in repression, the uproar weakened. He sig-nalled to Sezley and Gestable; instantly the room was full of the thud and patter of boxing gloves beaten against a wall. A glance towards the crowbar having told him that Willett, with lips set and sweat running from him, was rested and prepared to attack again, he threw his clenched fists high above his head, the ivory brush flashed in the shine of the oil lamp, and the impact of steel upon concrete was drowned in yells of victory and groans of disappoint-ment.

"That's enough," Willett exclaimed at last, standing clear. "You can dig to-morrow. Keep the party going till we've closed down the trap and squared off."

For a little while the noise was continued. Lumps of concrete were packed away into a locked trunk; by day they would be taken out to the ramparts one by one and dropped secretly into the moat. The meeting of the Boxing Club dispersed; members who slept in other dormitories reeled into the night, singing drunken catches, their gait carefully unsteady, their arms linked.

Gestable, inspired by the part he was playing, invented a liquorish quarrel. "Never been m'sober i'me life!" he protested with truth. And even Carroll-Blair's thin voice was to be heard uplifted in Harrovian song, which was all the song he knew.

Lewis, in bed at last, picked up a book but could not read. Night rounds are made at fixed hours, he thought. If we have to dig late, we can avoid them. But better dig in the early evening. There are no dormitory rounds before midnight. The shriek of a distant train reminded him of his coming to the fort, of plodding across the fields at Herriot's side. The noise of the shouting and the throbbing wail of the gramophones were still in his ears. He saw again the faces of the singers uplifted towards him, their open mouths, their fixed eyes—they had been like a ring of dogs howling at the moon; and he felt again the ivory hairbrush under his fingers. While the scene lasted he had been excited by it, had even been proud.

Ballater, in blue silk pyjamas, looked up from the magazine he was reading.

"Well?" he said. "All right? . . . pretty good staff work."

Sezley was lowering the oil lamps by their chains and puffing down their chimneys. The room fell into darkness and silence.

Lewis and Ballater shared a watch as diggers and carriers. One evening, when they were in the tunnel together, working by candlelight amid the thick smell of earth and crumbled masonry and stale air, Ballater dropped the tool he was using and said quietly: "It's a marvellous night outside. Did you notice? The Plough bright as if there were a frost, but everything sniffing of summer." He scraped sweat from his forehead with the edge of an earthy hand. "This hole stinks like the double-bottoms of a cruiser. . . . Come on, let's get the loose stuff shovelled back. We haven't room to work," and, kneeling across the tunnel in single file, they began like two dogs to scrape earth backward between their legs. This done, it was Ballater's turn to hold the candle while Lewis attacked the earth-face.

"My God, Alison," Ballater said, "why are we burrowing here like moles? When you came into the fort, did you imagine yourself doing this?"

Lewis was struck, not only by the shaft of irony that had touched Ballater, but by a feeling of guilt and desolation.

"No," he said. "I didn't see myself as a man of action."

"Never again? Not even after the war?"

Lewis was struggling with a ledge of earth in which stones were deeply embedded. When he had broken it down, he replied:

"Perhaps never again. I didn't swear to that. But I did swear to myself that while I was here and had this god-sent chance——"

He could not continue. In the confinement of the tunnel every conversation but a demand that the candle should be held higher or lower became ridiculous, and he returned to his work in silence. But his thought ran on. Solitude and a discipline of peaceful scholarship might prove, as Herriot had often suggested, not to be his ultimate way of life; he didn't know; that lay in the future; some day he might have strength enough to preserve an absolute still-ness of the spirit, even amid the activities of the world. But if ever this was to become possible, it could be made possible in him, he believed, only by the discipline of quietness. The opportunity had been given him. He remembered with what delight and with what assurance he had welcomed it. Now, by every evening in the tunnel and by every thought of escape, he was betraying it.

"I'll take over," Ballater said, exchanging his candle for the tool with which Lewis had been digging. "You've been hacking at it like a madman. I shall take life more easily. . . . It must be nearly time for our reliefs."

Work had begun again, when a sound behind them, at the entrance of the tunnel, told that the trap-door had been hastily closed.

"Someone coming," Ballater whispered, and ceased to dig, that the sound of his tool might not be heard above ground. "Better put out the candle."

"No light can show through if they've got the lino-leum-flap down. If they haven't, we're done."

"Still we may want the light later on. The Lord knows how long we may not have to sit here if Willett can't get rid of the man, whoever he is. It may be the Commandant come to be affable. He might stay for hours."

"If he does," Lewis added, "he'll notice that we don't come to bed."

"Oh, Willett will invent some lie."

"Can't go on lying for ever."

"Anyhow," Ballater said, "we shall quietly suffocate."

The candle was put out. They lay in darkness on their stomachs and waited. Lewis forgot that he was in the tunnel, and the bitterness of his self-reproach passed from him. We make ourselves, he thought, by struggle and rule, but a force deeper than our will, deeper than our consciousness, corrects our making. To cultivate the man of intellect is not enough, for stillness is a quality of the whole man. We are like the strings of a stringed instrument which, slackened in any part, are dead; they can yield no music but the music proper to themselves and then only if their tension be just. Each man must discover the perfect tension of his being—in action or solitude, in love or asceticism, in philosophy or faith—by continual adjustments of thought and experience; and he asked himself whether the particular seclusion of the fort might not be a phase from which he was emerging. What development of his scholarship would attend the fresh impulses stirring within him? But if the tunnel succeeds, he added, there may be no more scholarship. His longing for seclusion returned, but for a seclusion that seemed to him, as he strove now to imagine it, less wintry, more beautiful and flowering, than that by which he had been bound.

He opened his eyes in the darkness and saw the pale glimmer of the fist on which his cheek had been resting.

"The trap-door is being opened," Ballater said.

The gleam in the tunnel increased.

"All clear now," said Willett, in the hoarse whisper of one who had a habit of conspiracy. "You fellows still alive?"

Weeks passed in digging and alarms. That he might not cease to read, Lewis imposed daily tasks on himself and performed them, but he was restless and troubled. When

news was brought to him in Jedwell's room that the tunnel
had been discovered, he started from his chair, thinking
at first only of the failure of his enterprise, but, as he went
towards the dormitory, joy mounted within him and he
thought: Now I shall have peace. Now there'll be quiet
again.

A servant in the dormitory had noticed the crease made
by the continual turning back of the linoleum and, his
curiosity aroused, had come upon the trap-door. Whether
the man made this discovery by chance or had been sent
to investigate by Dutch officers aroused by some suspicion
was not known; certainly he remained firm against threat
and bribery and could not be prevented from making
his report. The Commandant was at first indignant. The
English officers had betrayed his trust in them. They had
rewarded his kindnesses by doing their utmost to ruin his
career. Their ingratitude was shameful. Had he not come
himself as a friend to share their entertainments in this
very room? An attempt was made to suggest to him that it
was a duty of interned officers to escape if they could, but
he was beyond reason. If he was allowed to remain serious,
they were lost; the wildest penalties would be imposed upon
them; no weapon could now be effective against him but
ridicule; only his vanity could be touched. While others
argued and the Commandant raged, Ferrard brought salvation.

"In this very room we drank and we laughed," the
Commandant cried. "We trusted one another and were
friends. And you——"

"Yes, sir," said Ferrard quietly. "We were all sports
together. *Vive les Pays-Bas!*"

The ring of serious, disappointed faces began to smile.
The Commandant saw mouths opening to laugh. The
intolerable levity of the English, who would laugh at anything! Then, suddenly, as he perceived that they were
laughing at him, his expression changed from anger to a
pitiable embarrassment. An instinct of self-preservation
enabled him to see their joke. He was delighted because he
had seen it.

"*Les Pays-Bas?* The Low Countries? That was it—the tunnel under the ground? Even then—so early?"

He threw back his head and outlaughed them all. Before his mood could change, they began to show him their tunnelling equipment: old pyjamas stained with earth, their entrenching tool, the electric torches that had displaced candles which in the foul atmosphere of the inner tunnel would burn no longer, their stores of earth, Willett's crowbar, the rules and agenda of the Boxing Club.

"And I was your President!" he exclaimed, when the purpose of the Club had been made clear to him. But his face fell when he was invited to inspect the tunnel. "Won't you go down and look at it, sir?" Ferrard suggested. "We can lend you some kit." Should he preserve his dignity or in pyjamas regain the esteem of these barbarians? He smirked and hesitated. Pyjamas were brought and he suffered them to be put on over his uniform; gloves were provided; a scarf was tied over his head. His grotesque figure, having climbed through the trap-door, sank on its hands and knees and began to crawl into the hole.

"That's the end of that," Willett said gloomily, and turning to the servant who had discovered the tunnel, a timid little man in brown overalls, he exclaimed with bitter good-humour: "Are you the one man on earth who won't take a bribe?"

"Ja, mijnheer," the Dutchman answered, understanding nothing.

Lewis turned away with a smile. He could have shouted his gratitude for this saving farce. A weight had been lifted from him. This evening, the tunnel under his bed would be empty; he would light his candle and re-build his screen of books. He was free again; and when he returned to Jedwell's room, it seemed to have recovered much of its former composure.

had caused in him, quickened his sense of exhaled individuality. He seemed to hold in his hand not a letter,
a thing completed and therefore sparkless, dead, but the
animation, the moving essence, from which it had sprung,
and the name Julie, not Julie Narwitz, seemed to him a
kind of wordless confession; for, he thought, her signature,
when her eye falls upon it, does not appear to her as a
label which, like a number, is useful to distinguish her
from others, but as an expression of herself of which the
ever-changing secret eludes her. While she was writing,
the word Julie was for her a coded summary of her
mysteries. Between the J and the e she was lying, her
inmost self as much expressed and as much concealed as
when, in that other visible but clouded formula—her body,
she lay extended long ago on sunlit grass, or stood looking
up at him, being then a child.

The child also, he remembered suddenly, had used the
same word: Julie. Imprisoned in memory, but gazing at
the run of ink in the word before him, he saw for an instant
the child, with elbow cocked and pen in hand, writing
this letter; then, as memory released him, saw her change
under his eyes into woman. The change brought with it a
stinging, pervasive delight—the whip of a gust on a still
day. She, too, must have been aware of the gust, the sweet
invigoration, the heady sharpness of it; for that reason she
long delayed her letter, and, when she did write, wrote as
though the calm were unbroken. Reading again her easy
phrases, he felt the stress in them. Why hadn't he come
to Enkendaal? It was lovely at this time of year. He might
find books in the library that he needed; besides, it would
be good to see him again, the Dutch were so dull. "I think
I'm changed a great deal, but you won't have changed at
all. When I was twelve you always seemed so old that you
can't have become older—perhaps younger again. There's
consolation for you!" Then news, stiff and brief. How
sorry they all had been to hear of the discovery of the
tunnel! It must have been sickening after so much work!
Then, with a twinge of nervousness perceptible in the
raising of the key: "You won't mind your pupil's being

married to a German husband? He's different from most
Prussians in some rather important ways. I believe you'd
like him. . . . You'd talk philosophy together." After the
words "like him," a word had been begun and crossed
out. "I believe you'd like him better than——?" "Better
than I do," Lewis guessed, but it was no more than a
guess. If that was what she had intended to write, in how
forced a mood of mock seriousness she must have written!
He saw her plan the graceless joke, begin to write it, then
fall back before its shrillness, her taste prevailing over the
embarrassment that had stood at her elbow, dragging her
pen into protective commonplace, jerking it into staccato
concealments.

Two days later came another letter in the same hand.

My dear Lewis,

　　　I think the letter I wrote must have been a very
silly one. I was feeling all the time that I didn't know you,
and that you would turn my letter over thinking that the
little girl you knew was pretending to be what she wasn't.
I couldn't get it clear. And it's not much clearer now, is
it? But if you ever come out of your monastery, I'll try
to make intelligent amends. And now, how do I finish a
letter to you? The way I used to end when you were at
Oxford was—

With love from
JULIE

His reply to her first letter crossed the second. They
did not write again.

The diplomats did their work at leisure and the autumn
passed without assurance of general parole. That it would
in the end be granted there was little doubt, for the Dutch
themselves were eager to be free of the responsibilities and
expense of a garrison, and Ballater, who was always well
informed, brought back with him, after each of his adventurous visits to the outer world, authoritative statements
that on such and such a date parole would be signed. The

dates passed and on each occasion there were reasons,
which could never recur, for fortune's having tricked him
into a mistake.

"The only thing that worries me about leaving the fort,"
Ballater said, "is that I shall have to leave my garden behind, but up at Enkendaal there's a cottage belonging to
a man called Kerstholt that has a garden, and if we took
rooms there——"

The canals were clipped in winter and the barbed wire
was furry with snow before it became certain that, in the
third week of February, they would leave the fort, not to
return. Three officers rejected parole, preferring banish-
ment to an island in the Zuyder Zee. A few months earlier
Lewis would have chosen to join them rather than go out
into the world. Now, listening to Ballater's description of
the great solitudes about Enkendaal, the heaths and elms,
the lakes upon which the Castle looked down, the library
in its tower, he consented to do what Ballater wished. The
fort had grown old for him, perhaps because he had allowed
it to grow old. At Enkendaal also there would be seclusion,
and a seclusion continuously refreshed by the changing
moods of the countryside. In heath and lake and forest,
becoming day by day parts of his own life, there would be
a serene quickness that could never exist for him in a landscape of which he remained a withheld spectator. Though
for several weeks he had been working without disquiet
and was happy within the enclosure of these snowy ramparts, he knew that he was but in the infancy of the life
he desired and must proceed beyond it.

"I was half afraid you wouldn't come," Ballater said,
and at once allowed his plans to overflow. "As a matter of
fact, I more or less booked Kerstholt's cottage when I was
at Enkendaal, though I didn't tell you then. There's room
enough for two of us and for a couple of our own men we
can get up from the camp as servants. And there's a garden.
And a shed I can have for a car. There's only one trouble.
Kerstholt has his wife's relations coming to stay, and we
can't get in until early April. I'll go to stay at the Castle
late in March and have everything fixed in the cottage

before you come. Can you put in your time until then?"

"I'll go and dig in libraries at Leiden and Amsterdam and the Hague, and collect more books."

"Good," said Ballater. "I'm going to buy a car. Do you know anything about cars?"

On the last day he would spend in the fort, a day of February so boon and mild that it seemed already to have spring in it, Lewis went out on to the ramparts carrying with him one of the few books that he had saved from the crating of his library. It remained long in the grip of his arm while he observed in a mood of peaceful acceptance how the new year, whose movement he would no longer witness from this place, was repeating the miracles with which the old had received him. The cottage gardens beyond the moat were flecked with snowdrops; in the elms, rooks were pairing again; and I, with my crate of books that must go with me everywhere, he said, I am frosted in knowledge and cannot renew myself. I listen but hear no voice. I am like a tree in which the sap does not rise. And he began to ask himself, as he had asked many times, by what discipline he might attain to that stillness which should enable him to hear and to that brilliance of perception which should enable him to see. But the disciplines and compulsions of life are not all; they are what a man may do for himself, but he cannot do all. As he cannot be a poet by will, or a lover by will, neither by will alone can he become a creature of the spirit, but by a yielding, an abandonment—he put the thought away from him for he could not complete it, and sat down among the elm trees that overlooked the water, wondering whether the elms at Enkendaal of which Ballater had spoken stood near the brim of the Castle lakes. Here their images and the image of the grassy bank on which he was sitting were so held in the metallic surface of the moat that they seemed to be engraved upon it. He would remember the fort by their quietness even more than by the grey shadows and flecked, infrequent sunshine of Jedwell's room, more than by the delight of the summer days when he and Ballater had swum together. Next summer the water would lie still perpetually; none would swim in it; and the children on the opposite bank, seeing no movement on the ramparts, would forget those who had moved there sooner than they forgot the beings of a tale. They would forget them as they forgot the dead.

"And what is the book, Alison?" Jedwell said. "It looks like an old one." He sat down beside Lewis and let the pages run beneath his thumb. "German, too? What is it— prayers?"

"And other things. I've pencilled a translation here and there." Recalled by the book to the earlier movement of his thought that morning, Lewis took it from Jedwell and, opening it at a passage which had long troubled him and which for his own help he had translated, he forgot his companion and began to read silently:

"When I was a boy, God held my hand, but I escaped from Him, and in my youth, having need of peace, I said: I will find Him. I scoured the city with my lamp, well-trimmed, and so bright that my companions envied me it. I searched the countryside diligently; I inquired of the stars with a candle; I was humble and crawled the earth, looking into the holes of foxes and beneath the petals of flowers. But I found neither truth nor rest, for, like a witless child and many a learned man before me, I had forgot what it was I sought. So I set down my lamp and my candle, I threw away my keys and wept, and straightway His light was within me. When I returned to the city, I was not empty of it. Now I am in the liberty of His prison though all the world hammer at the gate. Give me Thy hand, O God, when Thou summonest me forth."

The German Protestants, he thought when he had read and read again, were in the earliest days men who feared their own learning, even while they laboured to acquire it. Though their maturity was in rebellion, their childhood had been in submission, and no one outlives all his childhood. What was meant by "I threw away my keys and wept"? Keys of dogma, perhaps, which had been renounced. The lamp was of learning, the candle of a faith too weak, but the keys— It was vain to press for the detail of allegory. The upshot was plain.

At the end of the same volume, he remembered, among Prayers for Several Occasions was one that might well have been written at the same time, though no commentator had marked the similarity of thought:

"Grant, Eternal Spirit, to us who kneel before Thy darkness that it may become light by Thy Grace, for we have but a sickly spark within us. Blow upon us with Thy breath, though we feel it not; lead us, though we follow not; receive us, though our pride reject Thy consolation; for save by Thee we cannot come to Thee and, unless Thou showest it, there is no end."

At first he was interested only to probe the mind of the writer and to ask whether, when he wrote, praying for compulsion to faith, he had already passed, though he did not know it, beyond a condition of inquiry into an ardour of faith. How else could he pray thus? How far was this man, who had stood so long between self-vindication and self-abandonment, advanced on his way towards mystical ecstasy? How far on the road to Damascus? And because the way to Damascus seemed to Lewis but one of the many ways of contemplation, he considered this writer's progress upon it with the detachment of a student; but soon his attempt to project his mind into the thought of another, that he might the better understand it, transmuted analysis into imagination, and, struggling to re-create the circumstances that had here drawn learning to its knees, asking himself what had been the nature of the apprehension spoken of in the words "and straightway His light was within me," he found an answer not of reason only. There seemed to be, not indeed a light within him, not a voice or a touch, but an encirclement of himself, and within the encirclement a visitation, so that, though he saw as he had seen, and heard as he had heard, the outward sense being still present and unchanged, he was yet aware of other eyes seeing through his eyes, of another individuality moving behind the reasoned movement of his brain. Into this individuality he wished to fall back but could not; it stayed behind him and at a remove, attendant but not possessing; and presently it ceased to be, and he was on the ramparts alone.

When he had risen, he saw a little figure walking slowly along the western rampart. Before disappearing round the corner, Jedwell turned and waved to him.

II

THE CASTLE

For contemplation he and valour formed,
For softness she and sweet attractive grace.
MILTON: *Paradise Lost*, IV. 297-8

CHAPTER ONE

FROM unpacking books which he had brought with him that day from the Hague, Lewis had fallen into reading them, and, the afternoon being now advanced, had drawn near to the window that opened upon Kersholt's garden and was holding a volume towards the light. He was lost in it and happily lost, for its subject was so much in harmony with his own mood that the writer, leaving the seventeenth century, had thrown a spell of intimacy over the solitary hour that Lewis had spent in his company— the intimacy of speech, even of tranquil argument.

"Meditations in order to a good life," this writer was saying, "let them be as exalted as the capacity of the person and subject will endure, up to the height of contemplation; but if contemplation comes to be a distinct thing, and something beside or beyond a distinct degree of virtuous meditation, it is lost to all sense, and religion and prudence. Let no man be hasty to eat of the fruits of paradise before his time." Here Lewis paused, and looked up sharply, allowing the volume to close upon his finger. Beyond the garden, footsteps were approaching, and an accompaniment of voices, Ballater's and a girl's. He withdrew from the window, feeling certain that Ballater, who had not expected him to arrive until nightfall, would not suspect his presence.

He would have liked to put the intruders out of his mind but could not; and, kneeling beside a packing-case, he listened to them as their voices became distinct and their steps sounded in the gravel of the little ascent between the lane and the cottage. Their conversation was

73

animated and gay; evidently they were delighted in each other's company and Ballater was already at ease. He is always soon at ease, Lewis thought. That is the charm of him to me as well as to women. He treats every woman, neither as a stranger nor as quarry, but as if he and she had long ago come to a smiling agreement that she should not be his mistress—an agreement capable of being rescinded.

They were standing beneath the window, and Ballater, with a delightful, childlike boasting, was telling her solemnly—for he was always solemn about the little attainments of which he was proud—what he would do with the garden and how by next spring it would be transformed. "Next spring!" she said. "The war will be over before then. You will be in England again."

Lewis ceased to listen. Though he had known Julie when she was a child in England, he felt now detached from those memories and was eager to fortify himself in detachment from them. He began again to order his books in their shelves and to wonder whether so much care was wasted—whether this precious time of isolation in Holland would end before the coming of another spring. Then, in the garden, he heard his own name spoken. Kerstholt, coming from his own quarters at the back of the house, was explaining in Dutch that the other English officer had arrived more than two hours ago. "Alison?" Ballater cried. "Where is he, then?" He raised his voice and shouted: "Alison! Alison! are you there? Here's an old friend of yours come to see you." Lewis did not answer. There were matches in his hand, for he had intended to light a candle, but he let them return with a little clack into the bowl of the candlestick.

"I expect he's gone for a walk," Ballater said. "Unless he's hiding."

Julie dropped her voice. "If he's hiding—do bring him out."

"He can't be. Look, there are no lights in the windows. It must be getting dark inside. Besides, why on earth should he hide?"

"He might," she answered. "Do see." And in a dancing tone, mischievous and wilful, she repeated: "Do bring him out."

Ballater laughed at her. "You sound very fierce," he said. "As if the poor devil were a badger in his earth. Are you a huntress?"

She laughed back—a laugh of challenge and mockery and enticement. Until then, Lewis had been indifferent to her, content to wait among the shadows until she and Ballater were gone. Now her laughter invaded him; he grew hot, as if she had struck him in the face with some stinging flower; and even when she went away, Ballater having offered to walk across to the Castle with her, the sting—the turbulence it had provoked and the unacknowledged delight of it—increased in his memory. The room was not quiet now as it had been before her coming.

And as he moved from sitting-room to bedroom, carrying great armfuls of books, he began to understand that, though the laughter he had heard was that of Julie Narwitz, the laughter that was still sounding in his mind came from a remote past in which he had been a very young man and Julie Quillan a child; and he remembered how one day, when he was an Oxford freshman and he and she were wandering together through the Harbury meadows, she had patted his pocket for the shape of the volume that was bulging in it and had asked him to read it to her. "But it's Greek," he had said, "and you have enough to do in Latin." A clumsy, stupid saying, which she had disregarded. Opening the book at random, "Please read it, Lewis," she had insisted, and, with her child's hand in his, had walked beside him while he read, checking him now and then at a line while she tried to imitate the sound of it, and, when he solemnly corrected her, teasing him with her laughter. When they had walked a little while, she had dropped on her knees in the grass, still holding his hand so that he was drawn down beside her. Turned upon her face, she had lain with no movement but of her breathing, the white nape of her neck, where the long hair fell away on either side, exposed to a dapple of sunlight amid the flickering shadow of beech leaves. She persuaded him to translate the story, which had been of Nausicaa.

Not long afterwards, she had been taken away. A pupil had gone, an airy companion, a pleasant child—no more it had seemed to him then. The sudden curtailment of his Oxford days, his entry into his father's business, the responsibility that fell upon him at his father's death, the straitening and self-discipline of life from that time forward—these had curbed his spirit; the Odyssey had been put away—all his odysseys; the dreaming and, it seemed, the memory of them. But the memory of his association with Richard Quillan's child had persisted as an undertone to all emotion, a secret that he had not been able fully to discover to himself. From it even now he sheered suddenly away, picking up the Odyssey from a pile of books, carrying it to the window-light, and telling himself it was not for a personal reason, but for the merit of the tale, that there seemed to him to be no story equal in magic with the story of Nausicaa.

When he looked up from the Odyssey, he saw Kerstholt in the garden—a veritable Dutch peasant, short, high-shouldered and sinewy, who carried his years with stubborn and ungraceful vigour. Observing the Englishman at the open window, the old man asked what war news there had been in the Hague that morning. There was nothing, Lewis replied, that had not been told before. "You don't hear the guns in Enkendaal?" he added. "No," said Kerstholt. "It's quiet, Enkendaal," and so quietly did he say it, as if a deeply rooted tree were speaking in the interior of a forest, that Lewis's mind was emptied of disturbance and he also began to think of the seclusion of Enkendaal where, ringed about by guns and delivered from the pressure of existence, he was free to create a new life within himself. He went down into the garden and talked to Kerstholt, who grinned and exclaimed because an Englishman spoke Dutch so well. "Do you know the flowers and the trees, Jonk'er? Did you know Dutch before you came to Holland? Of course, the Freule Julie is English

and she speaks Dutch, but she won't speak it if she can
help it. Always English or French with her—and now
German, may be, since she married a German." The old
man's tongue ran on; he was curious to know how an
Englishman, who was neither Baron nor Count, was a
friend of the Baron van Leyden van Enkendael. "There
are not many Dutch he would allow to take rooms in my
cottage, so near to his own Castle."

Lewis explained that Julie and her mother had lived
near his own home in England.

"Ah, that is how it was," said Kerstholt. "I remember
they told me. Then you are just a friend of the Freule. . . ."
And he added after a long pause: "Of course, she is not van
Leyden."

Lewis went out of the garden and found himself in a
narrow lane, hedged on one side but lying open on the
other; he could see how the ground fell away towards
the few houses lining the avenue that led to the Castle
gates. The Castle itself he could not see, but he had been
told where it lay, and he went on through the dusk, looking for a wood that Kerstholt had said he would presently
find before him. "If you walk straight on through the
wood, you will come out by the pavilion—a little place
like a pepper-box where the Castle ladies sometimes take
their tea in summer—and below the pepper-box you'll
see the lakes, Jonk'er, and the Castle stands on the other
side of the lakes." Lewis did not greatly care whether or
not he came upon the Castle that evening. To be alone
was all his desire, and, coming to the edge of the wood,
he paused and held his breath. There was no sound but
the rustle of leaves and far away a faint movement of
water. The lakes must have a fall between them, he
reflected, and, climbing the low bank at the roadside,
entered the wood.

The undergrowth was very dark, but, this extreme spur
of the wood being not more than a couple of hundred
yards in breadth, the thickening day was visible beyond
it. The smoother trunks were streaked with light. A grey,
luminous stream appeared to be flowing down them, and,

from the tops of bushes, glazed leaves of evergreen threw up the sky again. On the farther side of the wood there was a vague shimmering, as though the outskirts, and the outskirts only, were wrapped in a gigantic cobweb of light, but this dissolved as Lewis approached it, and he saw before him, just beyond the wood, and on raised ground that concealed any farther prospect, a little pillared building with a flattened dome and ornate capitals. I might work there if the van Leydens will let me, he thought. Beyond it are the lakes, and no one is likely to come by the wood; it would be an island in effect.

But when he reached the pavilion, he saw that he had misjudged its position. It was farther from the water's edge than he had suspected. At his feet was an expanse of shelving ground along which a path, that appeared and disappeared among close shrubs, followed the water-line; and, crossing this path, was another that connected the pavilion with the shore. The sharp point of land to which it led was almost met by the nose of a miniature peninsula thrust out from the farther bank. Between them, water flowed from lake to lake in a soft cascade. The fall was not more than the height of a child; and the cascade was spanned by a bridge. On the peninsula, over a gleam of steps, was a low block of darkness that seemed to be a boathouse but was hardly to be distinguished from its background, for behind it the Castle's chief tower rose out of the waters of the upper lake. This tower, a great-girthed cylinder of ancient brick, was little superior in height to the other buildings of the Castle, which lay clustered beyond it; but it had the character of Dutch grandeur, a superb austerity, an aloof composure, and the eye was held by its rooted plainness. Two slits of light shone in its upper part, repeated in unrippled elongation by the surface of the water below. Whoever occupies that room, Lewis thought, must hear the plashing of the water day and night until at last it becomes a part of silence, as the active routine of a monastery, because it is regular and persistent, must become the rhythm of meditation, and as breathing is an unwilled rhythm of life. Even in

the contemporary world and for such a man as he, it must
be possible to reduce all worldly action to the plashing of
water day and night until it became at last, though unceasing, a part of silence wherein the spirit was free. Then
might not all the life of the flesh, its delights and torments,
even the plain earning of bread—the going every day to
office or factory, the performance of labour that seemed
to have no heart in it, be recognized as that of which
spiritual sanctuary was the essence, as the necessary condition of it? Not to kill the senses or to hate them, he
thought, but to discover an inviolable ghost in the sensible
body is the highest and most difficult art of the saints.
Solitude would have no meaning if it were not encircled,
nor peace if it were not threatened. In the fort, life stood still,
but it was crowded and stagnant—an enforced monasticism
without rule. Here, day after day, I shall live in an enclosed freedom without need or possibility of escape from
it. He felt the excitement and awe of a child who for the
first time recognizes his own individuality and sees himself, a solitary and adventurous figure, travelling through
a virgin landscape from birth to death. An indefinite sweep
of seasons rolled ahead of him like a great moorland, un-
mapped, unconfined, a continent of experience; and he
became impatient even of the dusk and eager for the
morning to which the sun would awake him in his bedroom at the cottage. In the act of waking, he would remember that a day of early spring lay before him, the
first of many days not to be counted or distinguished—
an empty day, indivisibly his own, whose very air, quick
but still, would have the quality of meditation; and he
would welcome it, and each of its successors, with a silent
cry of the heart as a new gift miraculously given.

In the middle of the upper lake, beyond the shadow of
the tower, he saw again now what his eyes had previously
seen but his mind had not recorded—an eyot thickly
wooded and shaped like a pair of blunt boats lashed gunwale to gunwale. Whoever occupied the room in the tower
would learn to know the seasons and the weather by the
changing appearances of the eyot and of the water round

it; and would, perhaps, if observation reached back into childhood, invest it with a thousand legends—seeing in it the ship that Poseidon changed into an island as she returned from Ithaca, or another ship launched in a private dream. It would be easy in this place to dream a dream into reality. In so great a quietness, while the evening sky lay in the water of the lake and the scud of a bird was the silent drawing of a diamond across a mirror of steel, it was hard to understand that the scene was not perpetual, but must be resolved into night and morning and be consumed in the succession of days.

But though one who had attained to that spiritual detachment within the world which was the destination of philosophy might see an earthly image of it in this scene, Lewis perceived, with a sensation of humility that was akin to fear, that for him nothing existed but the image, the reality being infinitely distant. And not the supreme reality only, the inviolable sanctuary of the saints. After the war, he would live as he had always lived, plainly and without affectation, performing what tasks were required of him; but he wanted to be able to endure disappointment without bitterness, to learn to accept the burdens of his life in England without the necessity of guarded and enforced patience, to receive immediate beauty without being prompted by it to hunger for beauty unattainable. He wanted to create within him a retiring place which the fret of common existence and the hot breezes of desire and fear and ambition should be powerless to disturb. How far he was even from this lesser end, he knew well enough, and how unschooled in travel. He stumbled from thought to thought, from book to book, from dream to dream; he had scarcely learned to ask his way or to understand the answers he received. He could not hold steadfastly to his course; there was a weak discipline upon his meditation; a girl's laughter could make him swerve from it, leaving him angry and afraid. Even now, he added, while I have been standing here and have seen the water darken at the foot of the tower, perhaps I have been waiting to have that anger renewed in me, for several minutes have gone by since I seemed to hear the brush of shoulders against the bushes of that narrow path and the approach of voices.

So he went forward, and, rounding a wall of bushes, came upon a little open space that looked out over the lakes. At the edge of it she and Ballater stood, their backs towards him, the pallor above the water describing their figures with a lucent edge. Her arm was raised to point towards the Castle.

"I have that room in the tower," she said, "where you see the lights. I can get away from them there."

"But do you dislike them?" Ballater asked.

"Dislike them? Well . . . no. But I don't belong. I'm not Dutch."

"Nor are we for that matter."

"There's no need for you to be. You are strangers. Your pedigree doesn't affect the kennel. Your mother wasn't a Hoek and didn't marry into a litter of Leydens." She turned abruptly. "Walk with me to the bridge. Then you must go back."

As they advanced side by side, she lifted her head, checked herself, and suddenly ran forward.

"Lewis!" She took both his hands in hers. "Look," she cried over her shoulder to Ballater, "didn't I tell you he was my schoolmaster?" for Lewis had stiffened at her touch and could not answer her. "He used to kiss me when I was a defenceless child."

Still holding his hands, she leaned away from him, searching his face; he felt the weight of her body on his arms, the curl and pressure of her fingers in his.

"Lewis, where have you been—walking? alone? We went to the cottage and shouted for you. Kerstholt said you had come up from the Hague hours ago. I wanted to see you. You don't know what it is to have English people here. Mr. Ballater and I. . . ."

Her chatter ended; she released Lewis's hands and stood before him.

"Am I what you expected?" she asked, and, giving him no time to answer, she went on in a changed voice: "Your

being here doesn't seem real even now. I think of you
wandering about Daddy's library in Natton Lodge—your
arms too long for your sleeves. O Lewis, I've so much to
tell you."

"I too," he said, "think of you as you were then."

"And now?"

He laughed and hesitated. He saw that Ballater had
charmed her. He himself must seem awkward and old; it
was a mocking sentimentality in her, less than half serious,
which had made her speak of their early days together.
And, observing her beauty, seeing how she challenged his
opinion of it, he said with forced and stifled breath:

"You are almost in the dark. I can see nothing."

She seized his hand, ran with him across the clearing
to the place where she and Ballater had stood side by
side.

"Now there's light," she said. "What do you see?"

The curve of her shoulders, the uplifted pallor of her
face, her throat's gleam, her body's suppleness, her eyes
like the challenge of a bayonet in a quiet path—he could
not tell her what he saw or how he was in arms against the
invasion of his being. He said quietly: "You are mad still,"
and, even as he spoke, blamed himself for having said an
unusual thing that betrayed emotion in him.

"Am I?" she answered. "An older kind of madness,
then."

"Older?"

"I'm not a child."

"Of course not."

Seeing her look at him doubtfully, he remembered that
she had never been sure how seriously to take him. "You
know I'm married," she began, and added deliberately:
"—to a German."

"I know."

"Then I'm not a child," she repeated with a child's persistence, and continued swiftly: "Lewis, what's the matter?
You are hating me. Why? Because I ran you out here? Has
that offended you?"

Hating her? He felt again the touch of her hand, and

grasped it. He said "No," glad that his face was almost concealed from her.

"But you *were* hating me? Why?"

"Perhaps because you're not a child still—or because you are."

Ballater came up, bareheaded. He stood grinning at them, his weight on one leg, like an affable stork.

"Well," he said, "isn't she beautiful? And you have known her all these years, Alison, and let her escape to Holland!"

"I was carried off," she replied, and added with elaborate carelessness—"I'm imprisoned, too, if you knew it."

"Can one imprison ghosts?" Ballater said.

"Ghosts?"

"You look like a ghost in this light." He laughed at her. "As if you had risen from the lake."

She held out her hand. "Then you must say good-bye to flesh and blood."

Ballater stooped over her fingers and kissed them with an elaborate flourish. "To see if you are flesh and blood," said he.

"And you, Lewis? . . . No, you must kiss my hand too. This isn't England, and I'm a ghost."

He had taken her hand in his and she would not release him until he had done obeisance. She would not release him. Her first tone of nervous mockery was in her voice. "If you will not," she said, "I shall hold you here all night—or I shall kiss you."

He bent quickly over her hand and put his lips to it.

"That's a penance for hating me, Lewis, dear. Don't always hate me or you will have to do penance again." She went down towards the bridge and suddenly looked back: "In the morning, I'll absolve you, perhaps."

CHAPTER TWO

Lewis spent the morning in the seventeenth century, a noble period in Holland, and in England, he was inclined to think, of all periods the greatest. Yet how can one compare, as "greater" or "less great," phases of history? The adjective is a dangerous one which may become the empty rhetoric of a criticism too lazy to define its pleasures and distinguish their sources. A student of history, he thought, must beware of supposing that the men of the past are arraigned before him for his approval or condemnation; he is not their judge. Nor is he what many historians are content, and even eager, to remain—a visitor with a cloak of darkness, a notebook and a curious eye, loving facts, as avarice loves diamonds, for the value given them by their rarity. An historian has much in common with an artist; he must yield himself to his subject and become a creature of the time he investigates, standing apart from it only now and then, as a traveller, wishing to examine a map which he alone possesses, may for a little while leave his companions, soon to rejoin them. He must be able to accept the limitations of contemporary vision that he may experience its intensity, endeavouring to feel, and not merely to understand, the Elizabethans' terror of youth's departure, and to participate in that exquisite insanity of passion which gave to their actions a desperate fire, to their lyrics a charming melancholy, not now to be recaptured. Not to be recaptured? Lewis asked himself. Who knows? For youth has become precious again; life is threatened and short, its end terrible and violent; once more death's hand is on every boy's shoulder. But not on every girl's, he added, as it was in the ages of pestilence, and though there are women whose love for men will enable them to see, with men's eyes, how time has shrunk suddenly to this day, this hour, this sweet and vanishing instant, and how, by that shrinking, the spirit of man is driven in upon its ultimate defences, such women are few, as poets are few, and many will suppose that but one conclusion may be drawn from the saying "to-morrow we die." And by women, poets are ruled. Women give an age its colour; not because they themselves are omnipotent but because men, being children first and last, see their god through women, and have no peace but at the breast and no imagination of rebirth but in the similitude of a womb. Solitary men are like cut flowers in a pot; they are beautiful but they wither, being without nourishment; yet, if man consent to be nourished of woman, he, like a flower, is rooted and held; there is no escape until his earth receive him again.

Coming upon this knot in thought, making again his perpetual discovery that asceticism, which is a stage in the spirit's journey, is also a refusal of the nourishment by which that journey may be sustained, he turned away from it and back to the book on his knee, saying to himself: All thought leads me to this thought. How was I led to it from thinking of the way in which history should be studied? And resolute not to wander again from his page, he continued to read until at about one o'clock he heard Ballater's footfall on the gravel and went down to join him.

They must call on the Baroness in the afternoon, Ballater decided when luncheon was over, and might well walk over the moors until the time came. As they walked, he spoke eagerly of his management of the household affairs of the cottage, inviting Lewis's approval of his arrangements, telling how he had chosen as servants two seamen, Reeve and Garkie, from his Antwerp company, and demonstrating in what ways his insight into character

had been justified. There was something charming and
ingenuous in his pride; he was delighted by praise of his
skill in choosing a dinner or a new wall-paper and told
more than once how Julie had smiled upon his handiwork.
"The men and I haven't been here a week, and yesterday
she said we'd done wonders. She was sure no woman would
have made so many changes in the time. . . . But then
women make the devil of a fuss about running a house,"
he added. "If you know your own mind and stick to a
clear routine, it's easy enough."

Without this streak of pompousness, this blind spot in
his humour, Ballater would have been a less amusing,
because a more superficial, companion. That anyone so
gay could also be so solemn gave to his character a saving
touch of mystery; you never knew on what subject he
would be solemn next. When, seeing the moors and woods
stretch out to the horizon, they spoke of the van Leyden
estate, his thought flew to the Ballater acres and soared to
his ideal landlordism. His uncle's land was the best in six
counties, he declared proudly, but it needed scientific
cultivation. "That's what I mean to study here. Not that
even in Holland some of 'em aren't pretty stubborn against
new ideas. The other day I was talking to old van Leyden
about sugar-beet, and I threw out an idea of my own—
just threw it out, you know, to see what he'd say—and he
tugged at his beard, and hummed and hawed, and said
that had never struck him! Seemed impressed, but he
won't *do* anything, you know. He's too old, like my own
uncle. But Goof[1] van Leyden. . . ."

Lewis had already heard of Govert van Leyden, called
Goof, a younger son who had a place of his own at the
Huis ten Borgh, half *château*, half farm.

Outwardly a correct young man and an ardent agri-
culturist, he was believed to have lighter interests in the
Hague and, indeed, at the Huis ten Borgh itself.

"I can get over in twenty-three minutes in the car,"
Ballater said. "I'm going to work there."

"All arranged? You've been quick."

[1] Pronounced *Gofe*.

"Well, you see, Goof is keen on experiments in sugar-beet."

"Has he made any?"

"Not yet. But he will."

Ballater believed it. He believed, too, for the time being, that it was the earnest farmer in Goof that was attracting him to the Huis ten Borgh. His pink face was grave as he spoke of "modern ideas" and of the agricultural blindness of England which, when he went home, he proposed to remedy.

"Perhaps I ought to go into Parliament," he said. "And I shall have to marry, too. You can't run an estate—anyhow not as I should like the Ballater estate to be run—without a wife."

"Is that the only motive?"

"Well, one must have a son to inherit the property." It was said without a flicker, and not until they had gone forward half-a-dozen paces did Ballater's face move in a smile. "I dare say there are other reasons too. The devil of it is to choose the right girl."

"Is there a candidate?"

"In a way—yes. . . . As a matter of fact there are three."

"Equal chances?"

"Roughly—at a distance."

"And all willing?"

A silence implied that, until this moment, Ballater had not doubted their willingness. "I'll show you their photographs," he said. "But, of course," he went on, "your idea in life is to make a kind of island for yourself. Probably you'll never marry. But owning land's a responsible job—and a damned fine job. Land is in my blood—the land itself, not just what can be got out of it. Farming, good farming, is more important than anything on earth, but it won't be farming only that takes me to the Huis ten Borgh. Although it's scarcely ten miles away, it's fresh landscape—a lower level, almost in the dyke country. From the upper windows you can see the Rhine and the flat meadows beyond. I don't know why—the view's utterly different—but it reminds me of looking across the valley at home.

Nothing you see is the same—colour, skyline, cultivation, all different—and yet, for me anyway, the two countries have the same character. D'you ever feel that? You think I'm mad about country. You don't feel it as I do. My God," he said, staring at the moors, "I'm glad I came to Enkendaal. The Hague's good enough for a few days, but I couldn't live in a town."

It was true; it had the ring of truth; and Lewis perceived that Ballater's passion for Nature, underlying the vanities with which he entertained the world, tormented while it delighted him, because he could find no way of expressing it. "I can't describe what I see. I try to paint it sometimes—just water-colour, you know. It sounds damned silly, but I love it, though I dare say I'm no good. I've never been taught," he added, as if that were explanation enough. "But I've been out sketching with Julie, and she says that with practice——"

Vanity, having reasserted itself, was overcome by a recollection that Julie had been quoted before. "Look here, Alison. We've got to live together. When I begin to sing my own praises, you tell me . . . What was the news in the *Telegraaf* this morning? I was in Enkendaal and didn't see a paper."

"Nor did I," Lewis admitted.

"Would you ever? If I weren't here, I believe you'd forget there was a war. You'd drop out even the bulletins."

"No, I shouldn't forget," Lewis said, "but it's true that the newspapers. . . . If I were in England," he continued, "I should read them every morning and evening. When we were first shut up in the fort, I read them. And you remember the map Jedwell had on his wall—with pins, and red and green wool—I used to help him set it whenever there was a movement on the western front. But even Jedwell gave up his map. It isn't indifference. It isn't just selfishness either. . . ."

And while Lewis was hesitating, Ballater said unexpectedly: "I know what you mean. At least, I think I do. You mean there's something almost indecent in civilian keenness: pins, and red and green wools like some damned parlour game; or rushing in with a good bulletin as if it were the result of a steeplechase. . . . But one wants to know all the same."

"Here we are—shut up," Lewis answered. "We've given parole; we can't escape; we can't help in any way, even as civilians in England can help. We are as much out of the world as if we were dead. What we do or don't do makes no difference to a living soul. As long as we live, we shall never again be responsible to ourselves alone. And we don't know how long it will last—years perhaps; or Holland may come into the war next week and we find ourselves in the trenches the week after. It gives me a feeling, as far as the war is concerned, of absolute fatalism. This bit of our lives is in brackets—ours, our own as the rest of our lives can't be; and the bulletins and cartoons seem to belong to something outside the brackets."

They walked on in silence until Ballater exclaimed: "But it makes things look pretty queer inside the brackets, Alison. The more natural and ordinary a thing is, the harder it is to believe. When I'm out sketching, it suddenly comes over me—'You oughtn't to be dabbing here with a brush,' and I look at Julie—English, German officer's wife—telling me I have too much colour in my middle distance. It's mad. And these moors. Listen to them. So quiet you can hear the wind in the gorse—and there's scarcely a breeze. . . ." But suddenly Ballater became aware that he was floundering. "Everything's back to front," he abruptly concluded. "It's no use thinking about it."

They said no more on this subject until, having made a wide circle over the moors, they were approaching the Castle by the avenue that skirted one bank of the lake.

"What your idea comes to," Ballater remarked with relish, as if, while they walked, he had been turning a question over in his mind and had come unexpectedly on a pleasant answer to it, "is that, while we're here, we can do as we like and damn the consequences."

"That sounds as though you had a plot?" Lewis answered.

"Plot?"

"It's in your face."

"No—I—at least, I was only imagining——" He broke off, shot a laughing glance at Lewis to discover how much he had guessed, and added, with the mockery of a sigh: "Anyhow, I don't believe the theory holds water. I dare say we are irresponsible in a way. Still, even here, one has to conform—up to a point. Your sins find you out."

"Sins?" Lewis said. "Oh, you mean women—is that it? . . . I didn't say we were irresponsible, but that we were responsible only to ourselves."

"I don't see the difference. . . . And if I was thinking of women—which I wasn't," Ballater said, acknowledging his own lie in an unconcealed smile—"suppose one did have a go with some girl up here, well, wouldn't that be inside the brackets, too? The thing wouldn't drag on, as it would at home—women are liable to take everything seriously if they have the chance. For ever and ever, amen. But here there'd be no for ever and ever. When we went back to England, that'd bring the curtain down short and sharp . . . not that there are any women in Enkendaal; none to speak of any way."

The last denial, spoken with a forced easiness, showed to Lewis the direction of Ballater's thoughts; but Julie's name, which a swift impulse prompted him to speak, was checked on his lips by a momentary tension of his whole being, a shock of self-discovery, that made it impossible to speak of her. And it would have been ridiculous to be angry, he told himself after a little while, for over Ballater's mind thoughts of women passed like sunlight over water on a variable day, and, even if it had been Julie of whom he had been thinking, already he had ceased to think of her and was saying in the anxious tone of a master of the cere- monies that, if the Baroness was out, they must turn down the corners of their cards. But how many cards should they leave? The Baroness; her stepdaughter, Sophie; the old man himself—Ballater began to count them. "Oh, and Julie, too, I suppose. You know," he added, "they have their own etiquette in this place. We ought to have found out the details before we came."

Their ignorance was not exposed. At the point where the avenue ceased and the approach to the Castle widened into a great oval garden, walled for fruit trees on the curve farthest from the lakes, they were encountered by van Leyden himself, wearing gaiters and a faded black coat cut away short over his hips—a straight, wiry old man whose grey beard, trimmed to a long point, gave to his face an air of elaborate courtliness strangely contrasted with the plain, good-humoured, almost boyish intelligence of his eyes.

"So you have come, Mr. Alison?" he began, speaking English smoothly and slowly as if he were translating his thought. "And how do you find the cottage? I hope Kerstholt looks after you. . . . Everyone is out, I believe," he continued as they approached the house. "But come in, come in, both of you. Mr. Ballater can tell me more about sugar-beet until the ladies return."

Ballater fell easily into the trap.

"About that idea of mine, sir——" he began.

Van Leyden chuckled. "It doesn't work, my good friend. I told Goof it wouldn't—but Goof, he knows everything better than I do."

"But you said you'd never heard—were you pulling my leg, sir?"

Ballater could laugh against himself and laughed now, but van Leyden, who had let slip his little joke unintentionally, ceased to chuckle, blaming himself, Lewis thought, for having allowed a foreigner to see that he had been making fun of him. His apple cheeks tightened and his eyes twinkled above them, but he would not laugh. He led the way into his own room—part sitting-room, part office—and gave his guests chairs and cigars. Determined to put Ballater at his ease, he began to talk gravely of agriculture, pulling down records from his shelves, politely changing gulden to sterling when he mentioned prices, and never forgetting to ask questions about the Wiltshire acres. Ballater leaned back in his chair and, having said with becoming modesty that, of course, everything at home was on a relatively small scale, talked, as landowner to landowner, of the subject that warmed his heart and weighted his voice with importance. The old man, his duty done, twisted a paper-weight and, with stolen glances towards the window, listened for the return of the women who would set him free.

"They ought to be home," he said when a silence had fallen. "Can't think what keeps them."

Lewis asked whether Julie also was out driving.

"Julie? I doubt it. I wasn't thinking of her. One never knows where she is. She may be in the house somewhere." It was spoken not unkindly but in such a tone as made it clear that, in van Leyden's mind, she was separate from his own family—little more than a lodger among them, and Lewis, while he drew the Baron on to talking of his library, asked himself how she lived in this castle—how the English child had grown up here. She must have been lonely then, he thought, if she's a lodger among them still.

"Julie promised to be a reader when she was a child," he said out of his private thought.

"Ah, indeed. Of course you knew her well in those days. I suppose she went her own way then as now."

There was no interrogation in the Baron's voice. He was speaking only to cover his unwillingness to be reminded of the time when his wife was not his wife. What Julie had been he seemed not to care; perhaps his imagination had never compassed her then or since. She was not a van Leyden, and you did not become a van Leyden by nine years or by a lifetime spent among them. And yet, Lewis thought, he speaks of her with a twinkling affection, as though she were a pretty toy that it amused him to have on his shelf.

The Baron's first wife had been his cousin. Allard, married now and heir to Enkendaal, Sophie who lived on unwedded and of whom Ballater had given a sour report, Jan who was in the Legation at Washington, Goof at the Huis ten Borgh—all these were her children, doubly van Leyden; but Mrs. Quillan had once been Mejuffrouw Hoek, the governess of Allard and Sophie—and Julie was that governess's alien daughter. Alien not by birth only,

but in will and mood, Lewis thought, looking into the
heavy intelligence of van Leyden's face, which, though
evidently that of a man skilled in his own business, had
in repose, when there was no glint of laughter to quicken
it, the dullness of a close and stubborn mind. Above it,
on a wall of red and gold embossed leather that was
being turned by the years into a general black, hung three
portraits in gilt frames—the portraits, beyond doubt, of
three earlier van Leydens. In this room, they also had
dropped pipe ash or snuff on to estate ledgers and done
the patriarchal business of a burgomaster of Enkendaal.
They differed in feature; no common physical mark, unless perhaps the outward turning of their ears, pronounced
that they were of one family, but relationship was as plain
in their expressions as in the lip of the Hapsburgs. There
was a woodenness common to them all, a strange mingling
of toughness and benign irritability. Jealous of their rights,
but without the spirit for tyranny; rulers but not leaders;
solid, competent, enduring, dull, they had been masters
of Enkendaal because, recognizing their limitations, they
had not looked beyond it. And yet, had there not been a
van Leyden who resisted the Spaniards and died in resistance? "Willem van Leyden," Lewis asked, "did he
live at Enkendaal?"

"Which Willem—Long Ears?"

"The one the Spanish burned."

"Ah! the Leyden martyr! No, he didn't live here, except
for a few months when he was a boy. The Huis ten Borgh
was his—a fine place in those days; but the Spanish—how
do you say *verwoesten*?—plunder? sack?—the Spanish
sacked it. Willem lost everything—his money, his house,
his life. Did you know his mother was Scottish?" the old
man added, as if that were needed to explain his ancestor's
rashness. "And in the Scottish mother there was a streak
of French—not a safe mixture, eh?"

"Not safe?"

"Well, your Stuarts couldn't keep their thrones or their
heads for ten minutes. What is the use of having a thing
if you don't keep it, and do good with it, and make it

grow?" He picked up another cigar and bit it. "The Festons," he added suddenly after a gap of thought, "have France and Scotland in their blood."

Lewis did not answer this, for it seemed to invite no answer. Julie's grandmother had been a Feston, daughter of the fourth Marquess of Harbury. Where France and Scotland entered into the pedigree, Lewis did not know, but van Leyden knew and had remembered; in speaking of Julie's descent, he had given his explanation of her—a convenient explanation, this dangerous mixing of blood, which, when once he had seized upon it, perhaps nine years ago, had answered with a magic formula many of the questions that she might otherwise have provoked. He had had no need to ask himself more about her than he might have asked about a pet animal of alien breed. Naturally incurious, hating the labour of imagination, he had allowed France and Scotland to absolve him from it.

In this rigidity of mind, which was implicit in his tone when he spoke of Julie, there was an element so masterful that Lewis could at once smile at and admire it. It was the defect of a quality without which neither van Leyden himself nor his ancestors on the walls could have been the men they were—men capable of cutting distractions out of their lives as a gardener cuts out weeds, thus enabling the narrow plots of their activity to be sturdy, ordered and fruitful. But to live with such a man and in a world commanded by him?

I could live with him, Lewis thought. I should admire him as I always admire men, even the dullest, who know their job and keep their noses to the grindstone. And he found himself envying the rebels in life, not only the great rebels whose rebellion was justified by genius but even the rash, mistaken, foolish ones, who cut such a sorry figure in the world. A queer envy in him! In the past he had always been inclined to draw satisfaction from the rash failures of little men who had overshot their mark and become ridiculous; to smile at them had been to console himself at his own grindstone, to approve his own caution, to read modesty and virtue into it. And lately, though he had learned not to sneer at failure, he had condemned rebellion for another reason—that it was the contrary of acceptance, which had become for him the rule of life that he most desired to receive. Why, then, when he thought of Julie living with the van Leydens, did he envy her those qualities of sparkling, wayward vitality which she must have paid for with unhappiness? Little could she have gained by them. Unable to answer his question, and wondering at himself that he should envy what reason told him was not enviable, he passed suddenly through one of those blank spaces of thought wherein a blinding flash of the mind banishes an old subject and admits a new, seemingly inconsequent. If she were here now, he thought, she'd be huddled in this chair and despise me as she despises van Leyden, or respect me as she may respect him—or, no, not despise, not respect, but pity, with a mocking, contemptuous, affectionate pity. She is young. If she were in this chair, her suppleness would conform to it; when she rose, she would move with a weightless rhythm, as if drawn into the air. But I shall drag my feet in, throw my weight forward, pitch myself up with a thrust of my hands. If I played Rugger still, I should be a veteran. He remembered the hands which beside the lake she had thrust into his—the spring of the fingers, the interior softness, the run of the blood. He saw his own, lying on the leather before him. He had always been a little proud of them—long, chiselled, revealing the bone. But the skin at the knuckles was losing its elasticity; the nails were drying; soon these would be the hands of middle age. With what aloofness she would consider them and him! He was set. He was grave and set. Like a puppy, she would amuse herself by teasing his gravity. And yet: Ten years, he said, ten years isn't so much. To be thirty is to be young—van Leyden would say so! But he could not persuade himself. In her view, he was not her ally—rather, in solid gravity, van Leyden's. "My schoolmaster!" she had said, "My schoolmaster!"

He lifted his hands out of his sight and grasped the back of his chair.

Van Leyden was hoisting himself. With compelled vigour he crossed the room and dragged at a silken bell-rope beside the hearth. In answer to the bell, a butler entered, dressed like an English gardener in Sunday black, but wearing white cotton gloves.

"Tea."

It was brought on a large silver tray. Among the tea things was a dish of fruit, and van Leyden, when his guests were served, began to eat an apple with slow, munching satisfaction, and to talk to Ballater, who was instantly away in the Wiltshire orchards, of the cultivation of fruit, almost whining in his impatience while Ballater's discourse continued but becoming benign again as soon as he had established an interruption. He gave his own views loudly and slowly, as if he were uncertain whether he could be understood, shaking his head now and then over some perversity of Ballater's like a hairy dog that is irritated by water dripping over its eyes. From apples to the library, of whose ancient contents he was exceedingly proud; from the library to crops; from crops to horses; from horses to pedigrees; from pedigrees—but from that subject he never strayed very far, men, horses and apples being rooted in it. Conversation dragged on. A map was spread over Ballater's knees; van Leyden's voice and his scraping forefinger were explaining it. Clouds gathered over the sun, which would not appear again that day. Outside the long window a cluster of rhododendron bushes was growing stiff in the quietened light; on the lowest pane a sparrow, perched on the framework, was scratching and tapping with its beak.

Staring at the sky above the bushes, a calm, vaporous sky, glazed yet, where the clouds were unfolded, with winter's transparent steel, Lewis fell back from the self-examination that had lately disturbed him into an untroubled repose, upon which the clock, the slow pendulum, the little activity of the sparrow, the crackling canvas of the map were, now and then, delicious accents. In the midst of this quietness he became aware that, standing behind him, Julie had laid her hands upon his. He lifted his face. She was stooping over him, her expression a

laughing demand for silence. None had heard her enter;
Ballater and van Leyden were close upon their map; like
a child she would surprise them. For an instant, while she
hung above him, he was admitted to conspiracy with her,
and her hands, warm from their gloves, communicated
with a firm pressure her urgent secrecy—communicated to
him, yielded to him, a light, exquisite, eager confidence.
It was as if she had poured her own youth into him, as if,
by her failure to perceive that rigidity of his mind which,
he had supposed, separated him from her, she had given
him her own suppleness, admitting him by a recognition
of kinship with herself to a life that he had believed to be
dead.

For a moment, having no thought but of wonder and
pleasure, he did not attempt to rise, and, when he would
have risen, she held him in his place, moving her head and
smiling. "Don't let them know yet that I am here," she
seemed to say. Indeed, her lips moved as though she were
whispering, but no sound came from them, and Lewis,
seeing her face above him and from so unusual an angle,
felt the wings of unreality touch the instant as if, in the
fulness of a dream, he were on the edge of a discovery that
he was dreaming. It was an experience less than thought,
more fragile and elusive than accepted feeling—a gleam
of magic instantly lost; but to him, who had for long believed himself to be shut out from the lustre of such enchantments, it brought an inexpressible delight—the rapt
but momentary ecstasy of one who has imagined in himself again the breath of an expectation long since abandoned, of an emotion forgotten and put away.

Van Leyden now looked over his shoulder and said
briefly in Dutch: "Just come in?" before turning to the
map again. But the map was gone; Ballater had risen, all
smiles. Soon the three of them were on their feet before
her.

"I've been here ages," she said, "watching! You didn't
know, did you?"

"No," said van Leyden. "But what if we had?"

"What if you had? Nothing, I suppose. Except that I

might have stabbed you in the back, Uncle Pieter, before you had a chance to growl at me."

"Growl?" said van Leyden. "What do you expect me to do? Dance, because you have come into the room?"

She was talking to Ballater, while van Leyden, with stiff knees and lower lip thrust out, rocked from foot to foot before the fireplace, looking at Lewis now and then and making a little grimace as if to say, "Yes, I know I was sharp with her, but she gets on my nerves. She's like quicksilver." Lewis, watching her enjoyment of Ballater's easy company, felt, not jealousy, but a slow humiliation. It was not that he was now excluded from her intimacy but that he had ever supposed himself to have been admitted to it. The excitement of a moment ago was gone. There had been after all no significance in the chance of her having shared a childish joke with him. Whoever had happened to be sitting in that chair by the door, she would have leaned over him and made him her partner in secrecy. When she might have a free choice of the man with whom she would talk, it was to Ballater she went. So be it. Ballater was closer to her in years.

She was sitting on the corner of a leather fenderstool, looking up, her head thrown back, her lips parted. Ballater having pretended to scold her for some imagined wrongdoing, the colour moved in her cheeks while she answered him and her eyes shone; but suddenly her eyes came round to Lewis, lingered in some provocative curiosity that he could not interpret, and were turned away. She raised her voice; Ballater broke into laughter; she joined in it; the room, seemingly, was theirs. Why this little arrogance of behaviour—this defiance of the quiet of van Leyden's own place? It was contrary to her breeding, and Lewis had begun in his mind to blame her for it when he perceived that it was not deliberate. Embarrassment had touched her; this was her unchosen way of release from it.

"I'm sorry, Uncle Pieter," she said. "I've invaded your territory."

He looked at her with puzzled good-humour. "I don't know what's the matter with you to-day. You're usually quiet as silk in here. D'you know," he went on, turning to Lewis, "she used to come to this room when she was a child and curl up in that chair and sit like a mouse for hours. God knows why. I must have been dull company."

"I thought you might talk to me," she replied. "You never did."

"Well," said van Leyden, "what was there to talk to you about?"

Ballater, seeing that her face was changed, had knotted his brow; her seriousness perplexed him. He tried to draw her from it, but his light-hearted question missed its mark. She was staring at the armchair towards which van Leyden had pointed and from it raised her eyes to the window in a long abstracted look. Then, with a little wrench of her whole body, she roused herself and was Ballater's again. The cloud had passed; van Leyden had not perceived it; his hand was on Lewis's arm.

"Come," he said. "I promised to show you the library since you're interested in such things. We can leave these children to amuse themselves."

The tower, van Leyden explained as they crossed the hall, had been greatly changed since it was built; or, rather, not the tower itself, but the approaches to it, for it had survived a fire at the end of the eighteenth century by which a great part of the old castle had been gutted. Only the topmost storey could be reached by the main staircase. The lowest—"we dine there when there's a big party"— was approached through the drawing-rooms and a long series of passages and antechambers. Thence a stair built into the thickness of the wall led up into the library.

"The stair stops here?" said Lewis when they stood in the great circular room.

Van Leyden pointed to an oak door opposite that by which they had entered.

"There used to be another wall-stair going upward. But it's black and slippery—none too safe. Not used now. . . . Nor is the library, if it comes to that."

Cleaners and housemaids came here, but none came to read. The books and shelves bore no accumulation of dust; the thick carpet gave out its faded colours; a broad central table, a reading-stand and a couple of shelf ladders had been lately polished; a group of padlocked boxes, of the kind seen in lawyers' rooms, gleamed still, though their black enamel had been dulled by the years; but there was no sign of common usage. On the table stood a dried inkpot, an empty pen-tray, a pink blotting-pad whitened by age, a wooden bowl of rusted pins. Two of the three window embrasures, each the size of a small room hewn out of the stone, had been used for miscellaneous storage: dead toys were there, dead skates, a canoe, dead games in battered cardboard boxes, a woman's bicycle with the broken strings of its skirt-guard dangling in a melancholy fringe over its spokes.

Van Leyden put his hand on the bicycle with clumsy timidity. A sentiment, not a happy one, seemed to compel his movement; the machine had over him some power of association to which he would not confess. While he touched it, he pretended not to know that he was touching it and with his other hand waved Lewis's attention elsewhere. But, his thumb catching the lip of the bell, he could not forbear to press it. There was a grinding sound, weak and toneless, as if a mile away some little, rusty gate had moved on its hinges.

"*Kapot*," he said.

A thick word that had become ludicrous, for when a thing was broken that urgently needed repair, Dutch servants would always stare hopelessly at it and say that it was *kapot* in a slack, indifferent tone which implied that no one would ever be fool enough to mend it. *Kapot* and *morgen*, the formulae of blank resignation and perpetual postponement, had seemed to the English officers to be national phrases of the Dutch; and, hearing one of them spoken by van Leyden as an epitaph on his first wife's bicycle, Lewis had to turn swiftly towards the shelves to conceal the twitching of his lips.

Van Leyden did his utmost to be a good host in this

treasure-house of his. He pointed to a few volumes of
conspicuous value; rehearsed dutifully what others had
told him of them; admitted at last, with a contraction of
his shoulders and an apologetic movement of his hands,
that he was not competent to be a guide. "I had an uncle,
my father's younger brother—Dirk van Leyden—he'd
have told you. Used to sit here all day, writing, writing,
writing. Those tin boxes are full of his stuff. . . . You look
at it some day—all sorts. Verse even. He sat at that table.
There's his inkpot. You see where the carpet's worn thin?
He used to shuffle his feet."

"What did he write?" Lewis asked.

"Oh—ah—all sorts," van Leyden repeated. "There
was a professor from Leiden came here once in my father's
time. He wanted to publish some of it but my father
wouldn't let him."

"Why?"

"Family history."

"You feel as he did?"

"The less one says, the less chance one gives to some
scribbler who isn't one of us."

"Then it was good of you to say I might see it."

"You? But you are not Dutch. It would give you no
satisfaction to discover some little thing about us and
build it up and build it up"—van Leyden spread out his
hands—"until every school teacher in the country could
purse her lips whenever our name was spoken, and shake
her finger and put her eyebrows into her forehead—och,
you don't know how much interest they take in us! You
English are different. You have no curiosity about people's
grandmothers. You might be better if you had more of it—
but not too much, not too much. You forget too quick; we
remember too long."

He touched the tin cases with the toe of his boot. "It's
not all uncle Dirk's," he said. "There are other manuscripts as well. Some of Mary Stuart's letters—the wife
of William of Orange. You are welcome, if you wish to see
them. . . . Then I'll get the key."

Lewis would have stayed him; another journey by the

tower-stair was an undertaking for so old a man. But van Leyden brushed him aside. "No trouble, no trouble," he said, and evidently he wished to go—for courtesy's sake, perhaps, no service to a guest being troublesome to a van Leyden, but also, Lewis suspected, because the library bored him and he was glad of an excuse to leave a book-worm to a solitary examination of it.

The library changed when he was gone out, as human beings change and reveal new qualities in themselves when they are freed of company that is a restraint upon them, and Lewis found that the room itself had a value for him independent of the books contained in it. He was not a connoisseur of rare volumes. It was the patience of books that he loved, their absolute passivity, which endured all things in man. It was a miracle that a book, neglected for years, being taken down at last, should sing instantly with Shelley's voice and that the voice should be unchanged by all the operations of fortune. And if, while he read the argument of a master, his attention should wander from it and drift away into his own follies or prides, to this master he might return unreproved as to no other, books having no need to forgive. The argument would be con-tinued; if he misunderstood, he could turn back and it would be repeated—endlessly repeated without irritation, without scorn; if he rejected it, he might lay it aside and it would not intrude itself, would not complain or threaten or protest. It was the godlike aloofness of books that he loved. But, as the word godlike struck upon his mind, he thought: But we have made gods in our own image; they are angry or merciful; they pardon or condemn, and he remembered how, when he was a small boy, being in some way disgraced before his family and having no one to whom he might turn, he had found an Irish terrier curled up on the stairs in a patch of sunlight and had flung his arms round its neck and wept. "Alison, Chepping"—he saw again the engraving on the collar and felt the wiry hair on his cheek. His comfort then had been, not in any godlike quality, but in the blessed inhumanity of dogs, in the terrier's absolute detachment, more healing than tolerance or pity, from the worldly confusion into which the small boy had fallen. The blessed inhumanity of books! he said to himself now. That must be their secret for me. Yet their inhumanity must not be coldness; it must be a transcending of the heat of life which still dwells in them as the heat of the sun may be said to dwell in an oak tree. And though, just now, I thought that I loved this room better than the books contained in it, without the books it would be cold; it would be a tomb. I couldn't walk up and down, up and down, feeling this silence enclose me like wings. When I stood still, listening, it would be loneliness, not solitude, that enfolded me.

He began to ask himself whether long ago, in some forgotten dream, he had visited this room, for he seemed now, not to have come, but to have returned, to it. If he had dreamed of it, how had the dream continued? Well, he thought, struggling against an overpowering mood, dream or no dream, I know how reality will continue; the Baron will come back with the key—and there is his step! But van Leyden did not appear, and the force of indefinable expectation resumed its sway over Lewis until he knew that the moment through which he was living was a gate between a life and a life. Yet he was not unquiet; rather did he seem to have entered the innermost court of quietness itself, where, like a stream from the ground, a fountain of the spirit was rising. He understood that he would come again and again to this place, and watch the hours and seasons circle about its walls, and find, if he had constancy enough, such peace as he might carry always within him through the world.

Perceiving how much of fate the room held for him, how suddenly all the dreams of his life had been gathered together in it to be betrayed or fulfilled, he looked at it anew as a man will look into the face of the bride to whom his irretrievable pledge is given. The lofty ceiling, the prodigious thickness of wall, the long vertical shafts of light diffusing themselves at the mouths of the embrasures and throwing upon the inner shelves a pallid, web-like gleam that might have been the earliest evidence of a new day—these had lately been strange to him; he trembled now before their intimacy. But why am I trembling? So a monk might tremble, seeing his cell after his final vows had been taken. But this is no cell; I am no monk. This is a room in which, with van Leyden's permission, I shall work. No more than that. The old battle between his aspiration and the humility to which he had trained himself was refought in his mind; he shied away from his own vision, telling himself that the intimations which had swept his being were the intimations of a saint and, therefore, presumptuous, unnatural, deceptive in him. Let no man be hasty to eat of the fruits of paradise before his time, Jeremy Taylor had said. It was a warning to ordinary men not to mistake emotion for vision, a warning that he would do well to accept. He accepted it now without falseness, recognizing his own limitations, but the thought that the solitude of this room was pregnant with discoveries for him persisted, and he did not seek to repel or deny it. I shall be alone here. I shall pursue my task and thread all my hours on it. It will not be, perhaps, a contemplative life that I shall lead; contemplation is too high a word. But I shall have a single mind, and no single mind is barren.

At peace with himself and seeing his way before him, he went to one of the windows and looked out upon the lakes. At the end of the farther lake, where the curving drive passed out into the road, a bare-headed woman was standing on the bank—a motionless figure crowned with a fleck of white. Beyond the gate a loaded cart came down from the woods, went on its way towards Enkendaal, and was presently lost among the trees at the roadside. The white-haired woman vanished into her lodge. In all the scene there was no human sound or movement, no movement but a shudder of the water now and then and a ruffling of the trees, no sound but of the little waterfall which, being near the foot of the tower, sent up its soft plash and purr to the windows.

Above the fall, the upper lake stretched away to the right. A great expanse of water, it curved round the tower and was cut off from view at last by the masonry of the Castle. Over it afternoon had begun to fade in a starless sky. Though twilight had not yet come, the distinguishing forms of the clouds were dimmed, and the low, wooded hill on the opposite bank, from which Lewis had looked out on the previous evening, was losing its foreground. Among the darkening shrubs green shone here and there with a sad brilliance, and on the eyot, when a breeze lifted the foliage, little tongues of yellow and green flame appeared to move over the branches. The eyot would be doubly beautiful when autumn came. Flames would burn in it, and beneath a late sun of October the water be fired by them.

Remembering that the earth was at war and that when October's sun was on the lake he might not be there to see it, Lewis discovered an intense bliss in the quietness of the scene before him. A veil was drawn between him and all things external to this scene. He thought of the war as if it had been fought long ago and of his mother and sisters as people who had once played their part in the village history of Chepping. Imagination of them brought into his mind another face, the face of a girl standing before him with tears in her eyes and her lip twisted by a grief she could not control. Elizabeth: he said the name aloud. He tried to imagine what she might be doing now and to reprove himself for having written to her so seldom while he was in the fort, and then only to thank her for having packed his books and to answer her letters after long intervals. But he could not reconcile her with the present; her letters seemed to have been written by a ghost to a ghost. Nothing of her remained but the tears she had at last been unable to check and had been too miserable to conceal. They had rolled down her face, which she had not turned away. The recollection of her frozen agony cut him—but like the recollection of a scene in a tragic play witnessed long ago. Her love and their parting belonged to a dead life, and the time in which she had lived for him was faded—was faded as his old self was fading while he looked down upon the lakes. Here all confusions will be taken from me. I am

alone . . . I am alone, he repeated as if by repetition of
the word he could ensure the privacy of his soul.

When, beneath the tower window, two small figures appeared on the peninsula and moved out towards the boat-
house, his mind was slow to accept their presence, and it
was with the reluctance of a sleeper awakening from a
dream that he identified them. Ballater and Julie. They
were climbing into a boat. Ballater was going home by the
short way across the upper lake; he would disembark on
the opposite bank, wave to her, disappear among the trees;
she would bring the boat back. Lewis watched them without disturbance—the little figures, the toy boat, the ringed
puddles where Ballater lazily dipped his blades.

But they went up the lake, not across it, and, as soon
as they were lost to sight, Lewis's mind began to hunger
after them. He thought of the air moving on their faces,
the stiff throb of the rowlocks, the cut of water under the
boat. Soon Ballater would cease to row, and, resting on his
oars, would look up at the Castle and speak to her. She
would dabble her hand and shake the drops from it on
to the opaque surface of the lake. "Cold!" Lewis imagined
her tone and how there would be a rim of coldness on the
warm flesh of her wrist. Last night I kissed her hand, he
said, and flinched. He saw her again leaning over the back
of his chair; her breasts had touched his hands; there had
been a moving pulse in the cup of her throat.

The library, when he turned back into it, was dark and
unquiet. He was glad when van Leyden entered, carrying
before him a reading lamp of fluted silver and over his wrist
a pair of keys joined by a fragile chain.

CHAPTER THREE

LEWIS and his host came down from the library and through the antechambers side by side. In the drawing-room a maid was closing the shutters and a youth in an alpaca jacket and felt shoes held a taper in his hand.

Van Leyden snapped at him in Dutch. "Not the candles, Willem. Two lamps, no more. Oil may be short before long."

"Mevrouw . . ." Willem began.

"Nonsense. Take your orders from me. . . . And listen. The English officer is to use the library when he pleases. Sometimes morning, sometimes afternoon. See there are pens, ink, paper—everything. What else do you need, Alison?"

"A waste-paper basket," said Lewis in English, his Dutch failing him.

"*Prullenmand. . . . De jonkheer is schrijver. Twee prullenmanden.*"

"*Goed, Mijnheer.*"

Van Leyden, who still held in his hand the silver lamp he had carried into the library, was moving towards the door when he jibbed and turned aside, pretending a sudden interest in a Troyon that hung on the wall.

"Give them time to get upstairs," he said, and Lewis, glancing in the direction of his alarm, saw a group of three standing by a long table in the hall, greyly illuminated by the dusk of high windows. The Baroness and Sophie were returned; the butler was attending them. Where was Anna? Why was she not there to take their wraps? the elder woman was asking, while the younger stood aside, grim and silent, with a bleak, curling smile on her lips.

Sophie despises this usurper who was her governess, Lewis said at once to himself, and he imagined that behind the slanting eyes and prompting the curled smile was the thought: Old Jacob, too, remembers when she was Juffrouw Hoek. But Sophie was too proud to give Jacob the confidence of her glance and he was engrossed by his vain wish to conciliate the Baroness, holding out his arms like white-gloved clothes rails while she piled her belongings upon him.

"Who?" she was heard to say while the Troyon was being examined and the group in the hall was lost to sight. "Who? Why can't you speak up, Jacob?"

"I heard clearly," said Sophie's voice. "Jacob was reporting, Ella, that the two English officers had called."

"Have they gone, Jacob?"

"They weren't seen to go, Mevrouw."

"Where are they, then?"

"One went to the library with mijnheer, Mevrouw."

"And the other?"

There was a pause. Jacob seemed to be recovering himself. Was he hesitating to say that Julie had gone with Ballater on to the lake? Though Julie was not van Leyden, Lewis did not doubt that the sympathy of the men-servants would be with her.

"Perhaps the other went back to Kerstholt's cottage, Mevrouw."

"Och!" cried the Baroness. It was the noise made by a small puma before it is sick. "You are so stupid, Jacob. You say one thing and the other. Questioning you about the simplest thing is like—but why are we in the dark? Didn't I tell you that the silver lamp was to stand always in the hall, on this table?"

"Ja, Mevrouw."

"Where, then, where? How do you expect other servants to obey when you—I'm beginning to think you are getting past your work. If you cannot remember——"

"Here's the lamp. Here's the lamp, Ella," van Leyden

called. He turned away from the Troyon, whinneying annoyance into the roll of his moustache so that the grey hairs reared themselves under his nose. "Baiting the servants like that. Baiting. . . ." Lewis heard him murmur as he went out into the hall. "Here's the lamp, my dear; I took it into the library to show Dirk's papers to Mr. Alison."

Lewis was introduced to Sophie. A gently venomous woman, he thought at first; then—but a pitiable one, and venomous only because she knows that she is pitiable. She gave him a hard, limp hand, too old a hand for one whose years could not be more than thirty-five; could not be more, for the Baroness was forty-five and had been Sophie's governess. Sophie gave him a forced smile which said: "It's useless to smile at you. You won't like me either. I've too much experience to hope that you will." So grey was she (though her hair was black and without gloss—like a negress's hair, but straight and smooth), so grey and tall and shabby, that she made him think of a long moleskin coat on a hanger, worn and moulted. "Your friend has gone home?" was all she said. "That's a pity. . . ." And long afterwards, with a flash of the whites of her eyes, she asked her father: "And where's Julie, I wonder?"

The Baroness held Lewis's hands between hers. In the van Leyden tradition of hospitality she was welcoming a guest to the castle of which she was mistress, and again Sophie's lips began to curl. Lewis was glad when his hand was released. How cleverly, in an attempt to preserve her youth, the Baroness had preserved everything except youth itself—the yellow hair, the glistening teeth, the tight flesh, even the tone of girlish eagerness that her voice could still summon. "You must come to tea. When? To-morrow? Thursday, perhaps? And on Sophie's birthday you must both dine here."

As Lewis walked down to the lodge, he saw Julie rowing across the lake alone. Ballater must have landed on the opposite bank and would be home before him.

That night, in his bedroom, he turned and returned the pages of the Phaedo until his candle overflowed its bowl, for he wished to observe again, and observe closely, how Socrates pursued the theme of the spirit's detachment from the flesh, which had dominated his own mind in the library of the Castle. It seemed at first that Socrates was at fault. Thought was best, he argued, when she took leave of the body and had no bodily sense or desire, and he added that a true philosopher must have a firm conviction that only after death might he find wisdom in her purity. This was good reason that a philosopher should welcome death, but was it equally good reason, as Socrates appeared to believe, that a man, while living, should struggle continually to separate soul from body—"to live as nearly as he can in a state of death?" For if separation of soul from body was impossible in this world, as Socrates himself allowed, would not the body, crying out against the stress of attempted separation, become a more conspicuous part of consciousness than when the impossible detachment was not attempted?

Folding the book against him and leaning back on his pillow, Lewis wondered what the answer of Socrates would be. "Each man must strike his balance between soul and body according to his nature," Socrates might say, but this reply would be in conflict with his own argument that men should study "to live as nearly as they can in a state of death." For, to live in a state of death, Lewis thought, is to seek not a middle way, but an extreme; it is to separate and unbalance, not to balance, the soul and the body. In this Socrates is an extremist, he said, picking up the book, and runs on the same path with mediaeval asceticism.

Was that true? He looked out across the dark room questioningly, as though the philosopher were before him and he might read his face. He felt that he had been arrogant, and must certainly have been blind, in thus disputing with one whom it was necessary only to understand. How often before had he, in common with Socrates's own disciples, imagined that he had his master in a corner! He turned back the pages that he might follow the argument again, and, as he read, he saw that there were indeed logical discrepancies in it, but that its wisdom survived its faults, as a great character survives its errors. If I compare phrase with phrase, he said, I am led astray by the opposition of words, the words soul and body having such a cloud of meaning attached to them as darkens their use. Words are elastic symbols; they yield differently to differing tensions of thought; and though I may imagine that I can trip Socrates with a quibble, it is I who fall, not he, for his intention is plain—that each man ought to cultivate "the habit of the soul gathering and collecting herself into herself from all sides out of the body; the dwelling in her own place alone, as in another life, so also in this as far as she can." That last phrase, "as far as she can," marks the difference between Socrates and the mediaeval ascetics: To them the body was evil; they schooled themselves to hate and destroy it; and, finding that it was indestructible except by death, they allowed their hatred of the supposed evil to grow until it became a corruption of the cherished good. To Socrates the body, though often evil in its effects, was not of itself evil; it was evil only in dominance; it was to be mastered, not destroyed; and the problem of a good life was that of learning how to subdue the body while it lived.

That, Lewis thought, is the doctrine of Socrates as nearly as I can understand it, and he put out his candle and lay down, believing that he was ready to sleep. But his mind remained active, slowly approximating philosophic debate to his personal life and relating it to emotions of which he was scarcely aware. The argument of Socrates seemed to depend upon two things—first, upon belief in the immortality of the soul, and, if that were assumed, then upon a belief that body and soul were opposed to each other. The first belief is implanted in me, Lewis thought; I could not if I would, rid myself of it; but I am not persuaded that soul and body are in opposition.

Is it not possible, he asked himself as he lay in darkness, that the body is an instrument of the soul, not merely a limitation upon it that we must study to outgrow? Is human love a limitation upon the soul? Socrates seemed to think so, for he said the body "fills us full of love and lusts, and fears, and fancies of all kinds, and endless foolery." Endless foolery! Lewis wanted to ask Socrates: Is it not possible that the Body is too inclusive a word and that we ought rather to think of bodily things as being of two kinds—those bodily things that serve the flesh only, and those that serve the soul as well as the flesh? The first kind ought indeed to be subordinated; the mind ought not to be given to them; like the acts of breathing and walking, they should produce neither pleasure nor pain nor any awareness of themselves. But the second kind are the contributions of this life to the growth of the soul and, though they ought to be regarded not as of themselves valuable but as being of a contributory value only, we ought not to despise them or confuse them with the first kind. And it is part of the duty of a philosopher to decide what bodily things are of the first kind, spiritually valueless, and what of the second kind, spiritually contributory. And I would say that human love is sometimes of one kind, sometimes of the other. Nor is the distinction by any means made clear by the presence or absence of carnal desire. A mother's love for her child is not, within her consciousness, carnal, but it may nevertheless be a love that occupies her mind with earthly aspirations and prevents the growth of her soul; if so, however selfless, it may be without spiritual value. And a man's love for a woman, though one of the expressions of it be carnal, may be the very air in which his soul grows. The distinction is hard, so hard that, in making it, reason combats experience; instances appear that contend with every rule, and we fall back at last upon intuition, choosing to make our way by the sun of poetry rather than by the map of argument.

He passed the next day and the next in desultory reading and speculation at ease, content that, while he wandered alone through the countryside, his mind should take what course it would. It was as if he were a very young man full of opportunities and unfettered in his choice of a way of life. Leisure and freedom, coming to him now after he had supposed that they had passed him by or that he, in years and responsibility, had stiffened beyond the enjoyment of them, brought with them the wonder of a miracle, and again and again he would be delighted, not by the fruit of thought, but by the discovery that thought had become his natural companion. Ballater, returning from the Huis ten Borgh or from a sketching expedition with Julie, would ask: "What have you been doing all day?" and, being answered with the truth, say that if Lewis had been writing a book or reading for an examination he could have understood this determined solitude, but that as it was——

"What on earth do you do with yourself?" he asked.

But Ballater could be tolerant of a friend who differed from himself and was amused and made curious by Lewis's drifting way.

"Julie wanted to come in here with me," he said one evening. "She has an idea that you're hiding from everyone. I told her she'd better leave you alone."

"What did she say to that?"

"She laughed and asked why—were you asleep?"

"And you said?"

"That as far as I could make out you were in some kind of a dream of your own. Anyhow I kept her out. I was right, wasn't I? You don't want her in here?"

Lewis said yes, he had been right; but, hearing in imagination how Ballater and Julie had laughed together over him, he understood that his drifting was perilous, and determined that henceforth he would pursue regularly the task that had engaged him in the fort. But he was still without an established routine of scholarship as he walked with Ballater to the Castle on the evening of Sophie's birthday.

"Why are you so determined to keep Julie out of the cottage?" Ballater asked. "You don't dislike her?"

"No. I don't dislike her."

"Well?"

Against his reason, beyond his knowledge of himself, a

defensive anger stirred in Lewis. "Why did she want to come in?" he cried. "She's shallow and vain and cruel. Why on earth should she want to disturb me?"

Ballater stared and laughed. "Good God, what's the matter with you? You don't mean that! Shallow and vain and cruel!"

Lewis perceived at once the extravagance of his words. They had been drawn from him by some thought that he could not now recognize as his own.

"No," he said, "I didn't mean it."

"Anyhow it's not true."

"No. It's not even true."

In the drawing-room of the Castle he felt that his words, and the secret, indefinable impulse that had prompted them, made it hard for him to look at Julie. There was a double guilt upon him—of having betrayed his solitude with thoughts of the woman, of having struck and abused the child, for the childlike aspect of her was one from which he could not escape. Certainly he could not escape from it now. The van Leydens and their friends disregarded her as they would have disregarded a child tolerantly admitted to their adult company. A knot of them was gathered on the hearthrug, another by the stiff brocaded window-curtains on the farther side of the room; sometimes the edges of these groups broke away and a guest with a deliberate air of strolling at his ease would pass from hearth to window or window to hearth, jerking up his chin and tugging at his waistcoat before launching himself into the intervening continent of gilt and beeswax. Allard van Leyden, while making one of these social journeys, checked himself at the great circular table beneath the unlighted candelabra. He looked into the mirror standing there, frowned, hoisted his chins out of his collar and resettled his tie.

"Well," he said amiably, "been out riding much?"

"Not much," Julie answered, and he passed on towards the bearskin rug to explain to his sister, who was receiving congratulations on her birthday, why his gift to her had been delayed. His tail-coat set in a horizontal ruck over his thighs; there were tufts of black hair and a signet ring on the fingers interlaced behind him; there was finality in the back he turned on Julie—the finality of a cart-horse with its head in a bag and its rump turned outward from its stall. Those who stood with him were as firmly set—his wife, Madame Allard; Goof, solidly handsome, with long dark lashes, a moustache trained upward from a straight mouth and his father's high, apple cheeks; Sophie, whose sallow forehead and suspicious eyes were almost on a level with Allard's; and three friends whom Lewis had not seen before, a youth named van Arkel with curled canary hair and a white face that his feminine hands were forever touching—an Aguecheek twitching his pedigree; Count Sordel, a gruff barrel of a man whose voice and laughter seemed to be echoed in the bowels of the earth; and Corrie Sordel, pretty as a squirrel, highly coloured as a doll, but considered unfortunate, Ballater murmured, because, though she took no exercise and drank chocolate, only her ankles were fat enough to satisfy Dutch requirements of ample beauty. They were discussing the blockade, for Allard's gift to Sophie had been delayed by it.

"Oh, I do think it a shame!" said Corrie. "Poor Sophie, how disappointing!"

"It will come in time," Sophie answered.

"Unless," Sordel observed, "the fishes have it."

"But why Dutch ships should be hindered I don't understand."

Goof remarked that it was the fortune of war. Allard said that he agreed—unquestionably it must be considered in that light, but he wished that he could get some English playing-cards. The groups gathered a little closer to hear how, while playing bridge on Tuesday evening, Allard, being strong in spades but weak in diamonds, had tried to indicate to his partner that——

"But, of course," said the canary-haired youth, "one does need to be accustomed to one's partner, doesn't one? Like marriage, isn't?"

"You can't say 'isn't' in English to end an interrogative sentence," Goof remarked.

"Of course, you can. *N'est-ce pas? Niet waar?* Every language has it."

"Not English," said Goof.

"Let's ask Julie," Corrie suggested.

"No, no. Leave Julie. She has her English boots on to-night," Allard said without moving his back. "Goof is right. Anyhow, Julie knows no more than the rest of us about English. It's only a bit better than her Dutch. She hasn't really a language at all, though she speaks four of them."

"Mustn't it be funny," said Corrie, "not to belong anywhere?"

There was a pause. All the horses shifted in the stable, considering the humour of the filly excluded from it.

"Napoleon did not belong anywhere," Goof observed. "Whenever I think of Napoleon, I always think how surprised he must have been to find himself married to Marie Louise. It must have been for him the climax of his career, though he'd have been the last man on earth to admit it."

The significance of this saying made its way slowly into Lewis's mind. The Baroness had drawn him aside to show him a case of ancestral miniatures, being particularly anxious that he should notice a frame of diamonds in which one of them was set, for on the top of the frame was a little basket of diamonds and rubies—"not a flower-basket as you might suppose," said she in the explanatory tone of an official guide—"not a flower-basket, but a guillotine basket. She was French, though she looks Spanish, and Pieter's—how do you say it?—Pieter's great-grandfather saved her, and brought her out of France, here to Enkendaal. And when they were married. . . . The rubies represent blood, I always think—blood from the basket. . . . And more than a hundred thousand florins the frame is worth. . . ."

"Napoleon did not belong anywhere," said Goof's voice, a pronouncement as unexpected as a pistol shot. While the Baroness had chattered of blood and rubies, Lewis had been fascinated by the heavy dreariness of the conversation behind him, for he seemed to be overhearing not the particular dialogue of a particular evening, but the words of the years, of the accumulated past, of a thousand assemblies in this drawing-room before dinner. They knew each other so well that they had nothing to say. They were so carefully trained in politeness that they could not be silent, so nurtured in a tradition of affability that they could not cease to be affable. All night they would continue; all night?—all their lives they would continue, had continued to tell how, being strong in spades and weak in diamonds, they had tried to indicate to a partner, who had not been "one of us" that . . . But you need to know your partner—like marriage, isn't? Marriage? Out of the depths of Sordel the rumbling recognition of wit inherent in the very word. Out of Mademoiselle Corrie a tinkling tribute. A growl from Allard, and from Goof a brief essay in English grammar. Van Arkel was a wit; he had but to say "marriage", and every hoof in the stable thudded its muffled applause; every hoof but Goof's and Goof perhaps was a rival wit—no, not a wit, the van Leydens were not frisky, but a dictator on the hearthrug, the explicit intelligence of the family, with a shrewd contempt for a youth whose feminine fingers were for ever stroking a pale cheek. The essay in grammar had not a pedantic purpose; it was a way of taking the wind out of the sails of wit felt to be intrusive and disturbing. Into this conversation no disturbance might enter. It was the conversation not of men but of the hearthrug, of the quarter of an hour before dinner, of all the quarters of an hour before all the dinners that had ever been eaten in the Castle of Enkendaal. It was not of to-day; it was ancestral, and Goof, having his back to the clock, was presiding over it.

"Mustn't it be funny not to belong anywhere?"

Lewis said the enamel frame on the extreme right was, he thought, a pretty one, and looked over his shoulder to see Julie standing where Allard had left her, turning and turning the edges of an old copy of the *Berliner Tageblatt*; and he saw her run ahead of him through the Harbury meadows and throw herself down in the dapple of a beech tree. So deeply now was she withdrawn into herself that she seemed to have no eyes for Goof's group or for the little knot that surrounded van Leyden by the window; to have neither sight nor knowledge of them and to be invisible to them. Ballater was leaving van Leyden's side and approaching her. She looked up, spoke to him, but her movement and speech did not lead her out of the remote world in which her spirit was wandering.

"Mustn't it be funny to belong nowhere?"

"Napoleon didn't belong anywhere," Goof remarked, and while Lewis bent again over the miniatures, he began to understand that this saying, which for him had been endowed by irrelevance with the insane originality of Wonderland, was for the van Leydens a commonplace, it seeming to them very natural that the marriage of a Buonaparte with a Hapsburg should be the climax——

"Yes," said Allard, "it must have been a great embarrassment to him."

"Not a bit," Sophie put in, "upstarts don't notice. They are so obsessed——"

"Oh, do you think so?" cried Madame Allard. "I think they notice all the more."

"Well," said Goof, "I knew a man once—you know the kind I mean—I wouldn't swear he had coloured blood, but his mother spent most of her life in Java, and—well——"

"You mean," Corrie put in helpfully, "that if you clapped your hands, he'd run up a tree?"

"Precisely," Goof replied, nodding his head. "Well, this man——"

"Dinner is served, Mevrouw."

"But the frame with the basket," said the Baroness, "is the gem, the peak of the collection. Will you take in Julie, Mr. Alison? As Allard would say, she is in her English boots to-night! He means only that—but there, you understand. What a tragedy, the war! What a tragedy! Good men on both sides. It is the privilege of a neutral to say so. Almost our only privilege I sometimes think."

They passed through the antechambers. In each a double candlestick threw its light on to panels of Utrecht velvet and the gleaming edge of picture frames. Julie's hand was on his arm.

"So we are dining in the tower? I thought——"

"Always on birthdays," she said, and afterwards: "Lewis——"

"Yes."

"Who is going to win this war?"

"God knows."

"But you must feel—you must feel, in your own mind, one way or the other. Sometimes—listen—sometimes I think I want England to win more than anyone in the world wants it. But for me to want that—oh, if only one could go to sleep and wake up when it's all over. Or not wake up."

He thought that the man in front had heard her. The bristles of the neck revolved a little above the collar; the head seemed about to turn. It did not turn, and Julie's voice, the voice of a frightened child, began with a sharp drawing of breath—

"Lewis. If by any chance——"

He laid his hand on hers. Like a pony that, having seen ghosts, is steadied by a familiar touch, she trembled and was still. She was silent while they entered the tower and silent while the van Leydens began to drink their soup.

"I wonder," she said slowly, "what blessed chance brought you into Holland of all men on earth?"

CHAPTER FOUR

WHEN Lewis opened his eyes next morning and saw the leaves of the birch tree outside his bedroom window fluttering in full sunshine, his mind was filled with a delicious strangeness as if, for a reason that he could not remember, the world had been transformed since last he awoke to it. "Reeve, how late is it? Why are we being called so late?"

"Mr. Ballater, sir, he left orders you was both to have a lie-in this morning, seeing you was at the Castle last night."

The sun had long been up; it was the light in the room, then, that had made the world seem unfamiliar. But it is not the light in the room, Lewis thought, that fills me with gladness, but a light within me; and as memory ordered itself in his awakened mind he remembered his putting his hand on Julie's, her quivering response, her obedient quietness. The pleasure he had in this recollection was one of relief and discovery—of discovery that Julie was not isolated from him by her gaiety and youth; of relief and wonder that in a human contact he had not failed. For since his father's death, he had given to the world few indications that the man of business he seemed to be, the discreet elder brother, the careful, regular, accountable citizen, was indeed a creature of his will, not the expression of his nature; and this schooled reticence of which, as it became habitual, he had ceased except on rare occasions to be aware, had frozen him so that he could not give of himself. Now, suddenly, he had given, and to a woman; his power to give had been recognized by her; and throughout the evening by a thousand magical communications of her reliance she had welcomed him into an intimacy with herself. There had been no luxury of secrets, no spilling of confidence, no current of sentiment but that which drifted, with a half-mocking glitter upon it, out of their association in the past. They had spoken, Lewis remembered, of the Odyssey and she had exclaimed that she had forgotten what little Greek she had known. "You must teach me again," and he had wondered how the Greek characters would look, written in her hand. "But my own Greek is stale," he had said. "I can read Greek, but I can't read it as a scholar." She had asked him what work he intended to do while he was in Enkendaal. "Are you going to write a book?"

"I'm preparing to write one—but the preparation means more to me than the book."

"Why?"

"You are like Ballater," he had answered with a laugh. "He can't understand why anyone, who isn't actually writing a book or reading for an exam., should want to be alone as I do."

"But why do you want to be alone?" Julie had asked. "I go for solitary walks by myself and ride by myself, but sometimes, I think, I'm almost afraid of being alone."

"Perhaps I like it for the same reason that you're afraid of it. We want to escape from ourselves—you into company and I . . ."

"Well?"

". . . And I into a solitude where self is lost. Where I confront it and see through it."

"That's like you, Lewis, my dear," she had said with a smile. "And may no one follow you?"

"No one can. That particular phantom one hunts alone."

How she had answered this, he did not know, but he remembered that a look of fear had come into her eyes which faded as she spoke of indifferent things and returned when she said abruptly, as if she supposed him to be familiar with the sequence of her thought: "Lewis, I had a letter from Rupert to-day. From the front. He's hunting your phantom, too."

A sudden embarrassment had seized their conversation, and to put an end to silence he had asked:

"Is your husband a philosopher?"

"All Germans are to some extent. It's a part of their sentiment—or their sentiment's a part of their philosophy."

"Does he write to you from the trenches of philosophic ideas—in this letter, I mean?"

For a moment she had lowered her head; then had faced him with shining eyes.

"This letter? I haven't opened it." And she had added deliberately, as if she wished him to question her: "I've left it in my room in the tower, since this afternoon when it came."

"But why?"

"Because. . . . Some day I'll tell you, Lewis. Not now. I'm happy to-night just talking to you."

Again, as the scene drifted through his mind, there was a gap in Lewis's recollection, and soon he and Ballater were breakfasting together, Ballater saying: "You didn't seem to enjoy the party last night?"

"What on earth makes you say that?"

"I thought you were feeling rather out of it. You clung to Julie as if you were afraid to speak to anyone else. And the amusing thing was that she let you. She's a minx that girl." Ballater rose from the table and began to fill his pipe. A good-humoured grin spread over his face and his eyes shone. "I suppose she thought she'd annoy me and that I'd come running to her this morning. As a matter of fact I had intended to take her out in my car to Goof's and to do some sketching with her. But I'll give her a lesson. I'll go to the Huis ten Borgh alone. And when she asks where I am, don't you tell her."

"D'you know," he said later as he climbed into his car, "I don't wonder the Baroness married her off young. She must have been the devil in this place."

Lewis smiled. "I'm sorry for the Baroness," he said. "The ex-governess living in the Castle—she must have had a fight to keep her end up."

"Sorry for her!" Ballater exclaimed, his hands on the

steering wheel. "Since she heard about the Wiltshire place, she's behaved like a well-preserved tigress who expected me to make love to her but would scratch me if I did. She's a snob if ever there was one. She's more van Leyden than the van Leydens themselves. Look at this marriage to Narwitz. You can bet your life she engineered it. The Narwitz family are out of the top drawer even by the Leydens' own reckoning. Now she's mother-in-law to a Narwitz—a fine slap in the eye for Sophie—that's what matters to her. And the wretched Julie's married to some Boche she never thinks about."

"Does she never think of him?"

"Well," said Ballater, "I know her pretty well by now. She'd talk to me about him if she talked to anyone."

Half the morning had passed when Ballater was gone; in less than two hours Reeve would be ringing his little handbell to announce another meal; and to avoid the interruption Lewis thrust his head through the open window of the kitchen and said that he wanted no luncheon to-day—he was going to the library at the Castle and would not be back until evening.

There was blue sky above the Castle, and, between the great tree trunks of the avenue, the wheeling sections of the lake held streaks of blue in their grey ripple. This is how spring comes in England, Lewis thought, when spring has been delayed; at night you go to bed remembering the winter and in the morning summer is come. The grass at the foot of the trees was bright and fresh; yellow and white flowers had sprung up among it; and where the sun fell on the barrel of the tower, the dark masonry and the creeper mounting it threw out a radiance of gold and green by which the water was enriched—the water and, it seemed, the air above the water, for the atmosphere of that morning, particularly in its contact with the surface of the pools, was charged with a golden opalescence; the windows of the Castle shone with it and the plumage of birds was washed in its brilliance as they passed through the air. Soon it will be May! Lewis began

to count the April days, and, thinking that the war must
certainly be decided before the third winter, he imagined
the tranquillity of his own summer spread out before him.
Even the summer would end. He looked at the trees, the
Castle, the flickering water, seeing them all as parts of a
vanishing interlude in the reality of his own life; and that
they might not escape him he halted in the avenue, listening to the rustle of an unseen bird in the foliage but hearing
time drumming in his ears.

Out of this dream he lifted himself and went forward.
In the tower, the sound which was now a part of the restlessness of the spring day would become the faint whisper
of a perpetual waterfall, independent of the rhythm of
time. He longed for this sound, and when he had been
admitted to the Castle and was mounting the staircase of
the tower, he listened for it, his hand cold on the stair-
wall, and not hearing it yet, ran forward until he stood
among the books, and the waterfall came to him like a
murmur from within the shelves.

Here indeed the hours went by in untroubled calm, there
being in old books, as in a country churchyard, so deep and
natural an acceptance of mortality, that to handle them
and observe their brief passions, their urgent persuasions,
now dissipated, now silent, is to perceive that the pressure
of time is itself a vanity, a delusion in the great leisure of
the spirit. As one who lingers among tombs, though at first
weighed down by the evidences of death, is at last soothed by
so great a witness to its insignificance and finds wings in his
heart that shall transcend it, so does he whose rest is among
ancient writings pass from a despair, in which all endeavour
seems fatally destined, to a high, winning exaltation. In
these volumes controversy is perished and the politic heats
are cold, but there come from them certain imperishable
voices freed of their temporal occasions, even the great love
songs having transcended the flesh that begot them; and
the solitary reader, seeing that many arrows aimed against
time are blunted on its shield while others are made birds
of the air and fly out of the archer's sight above the battle,
is compelled by the necessity of faith. On earth time is

invincible, he says. Therefore I will not be at war with it but draw my bow at a venture. Whither the arrow goes I know not, but into an air it goes where there are powers to raise and sustain it.

In these thoughts Lewis was quietened. He took down volume after volume from the shelves. They were written in many languages, but more of them in English and French than in Dutch. Here, he perceived, was a library of great range, but, above all, an assembly of the seventeenth century; and, seeing that many of the books were not old but came from the press forty or fifty years ago, he concluded that Dirk van Leyden had contemplated some vast work—a history of seventeenth-century Europe, perhaps—and had industriously added to the library that his ancestors had bequeathed to him. Yet scarcely of Europe; the range, though wide, was not wide enough; too many of the books looked upon England. He must have had an English track of his own, Lewis thought, but there's no telling what it was—the constitution, the Church, the Puritan divisions, foreign affairs, domestic manners, there's material here for the study of them all. He felt a friendly sympathy with Dirk, for this was a period of English life that had long fascinated him. His imagination continued to hover over the seventeenth century, and with a volume of Evelyn in his hands he thought: When Evelyn was a boy of ten there were people who could tell him of the Armada in their own childhood—Elizabethans through and through; when he was old, Blenheim had been fought. And he imagined the many others far from Whitehall, respectable townsmen, small gentlemen in the country, who had been engaged in the changing fortunes of the period. What a story might be written of one of them, the pivot, perhaps, of a numerous family, divided and redivided against itself by conflicting loyalties. At one end of the tale would be the conservatism—the very odd conservatism—of the surviving Elizabethans, grandparents in the opening scenes; at the other, the children of the eighteenth century would be looking back with cultivated indifference on the moral heats of the past; and, in the midst, would be that complex struggle of conscience which gave its character to seventeenth-century England. There were men living to-day who had seen greater and swifter changes, but it was not the extent of the change in the seventeenth century which attracted Lewis but the nature of it—a change from within, he reflected, the root of the contest having been in men's minds, not in their material conditions. Trivial, greedy, vain, ignorant—men of the seventeenth century could be all these things; he did not shut his eyes to the follies of the period; it was not for any supposed romantic perfection that he loved it, but for the close contact that it allowed between philosophy and affairs, and for its recognition, which began to wane with the Restoration, of a certain aristocracy of the spirit.

What a story, if one had sympathy and imagination enough to tell it! Though he did not think of himself as a story-teller and the tale would never be written by him, the idea of concentrating while in Enkendaal on the seventeenth century and using some group of characters as a vehicle of research leapt up in his mind and burned steadily there. He seemed to have come upon the immediate task he had been seeking as part of his greater undertaking. In imagining the life of the past and striving to penetrate the minds of particular individuals, he would move towards apprehension of the whole period, and, while he linked generation with generation and entered into their dreams, he would lose himself in the antique thought. With a pile of books beside him, he sat in one of the embrasures so that the window light was easy on his page and began to read the *Silex Scintillans*:

> Quite spent with thoughts I left my Cell, and lay
> Where a shrill spring tun'd to the early day.
>> I beg'd here long, and gron'd to know
>> Who gave the Clouds so brave a bow,
>> Who bent the spheres, and circled in
>> Corruption with this glorious Ring,
>> What is his name, and how I might
>> Descry some part of his great light.

I summon'd nature: peirc'd through all her store,
Broke up some seales, which none had touch'd before,
    Her wombe, her bosome, and her head
    Where all her secrets lay a bed
    I rifled quite, and having past
    Through all the Creatures, came at last
    To search my selfe, where I did find
    Traces, and sounds of a strange kind.

Sometimes, when he raised his head that a thought might resolve or a cadence declare itself in his mind, he heard the waterfall, but soon the external world fell away and the genius of Vaughan spread wings between him and the passing hours.

His eyes were not upon his book when the larger of the two doors to the library—the door by which he himself had entered—swung open, and Julie, without knowledge of his presence, crossed the room, carrying in her hand a volume that she returned to its place. Before the shelf she stood, her arm raised, her body stretched. He spoke her name, and, as she heard it, a tremor passed visibly through her limbs, and, dropping her arm, she turned, not with the wrench of surprise but with the supple alertness of a fawn that, hearing an unexpected sound, swings to it and listens. The world came with her, but not instantly, not fully. Lewis was looking at her out of a profound detachment and, though he recognized her and spoke her name, he was still seeing her in isolation from the circumstances of her world—seeing not Julie Narwitz, not the Englishwoman who lived at the Castle and whom he had known as a child, not even the girl whose intimacy had been so unexpectedly won last night, but a being that seemed to be in part the creature of his thought, to have emerged from his own imagination—a lovely body caught in the air, eyes filled with a wondering inquiry that reflected his own wonder, hands clasped on the breast—not *this* woman, not woman even, but speed suspended, movement perpetuated in stillness, a grace borrowed from light itself.

The mist of illusion passed from her. The world appeared and she with it. But she was not for him as she had been; and would not be again.

He asked: "Did I frighten you?"

"No, but I was thinking of you when you spoke, and your voice seemed to come out of what I was thinking."

"Weren't you choosing a book? Your finger was crooked to pull one down."

"Still," she said, "I was thinking of you. I knew you had been in the library this morning. I supposed you'd gone home since then. And, when you spoke, I was imagining you alone in your cottage, and wondering what book you had chosen to read, and thinking that I'd almost lost the habit of reading and must teach myself. . . ."

Her speech, that some powerful emotion was driving towards the edge of confession, became breathless and ceased.

"You must have been here five hours," she said. "Have you had no food? What have you been working at?"

He answered that he had been passing from book to book, and told how an attempt to recreate in his mind the life of the seventeenth century had seemed to him a useful, concrete prelude to——"

"A story?" she cried before he had finished speaking. What was to be the plot of his story? Who was the heroine to be—a Royalist or a Parliamentarian?"

"My heroine? I hadn't thought of her."

"Oh, but there must be a woman!" Julie exclaimed. "There'd be no story without her. . . . The men would be spinning their theories and she'd be pretending to, pretending, I mean, even to herself; but all the time she'd be living her own life and seeing the men as men, apart from their theories; seeing into the men themselves—right through the principles that divided them."

"A romantic heroine!" Lewis said.

"Romantic! Not in the least. They are the romantics. She's a realist."

She was sitting on the floor, her feet curled under her, her supporting hand in a patch of sunlight that lay on the carpet, and, as they talked, the sun moved to her shoulder, her throat, her breast and side, enveloping her save where Lewis's shadow was spread. Half serious, half mocking, she discussed his supposed story with him, which by now had become her story, and though she was so close to him and seemed to enjoy his company, he could not but observe how remote was her habit of mind from his own. He saw the seventeenth century from the point of view of the English middle-class; his purpose was to see it whole, and, correcting his prejudices when he was aware of them, to form a balanced judgement of it. She, too, would balance judgement in her mind, but could not in her heart. She would admit the King's unreason; Cromwell, of course, had right on his side; but still, when intellectually she had given Cromwell his due, he remained for her an intruder into a drawing-room, a foreign element that had thrust itself into the continuing reality of life. She spoke of the Great Rebellion as if it were a storm that had blown open the drawing-room window and wrought havoc before it could be shut out again—a natural and inevitable storm, perhaps, and one that had had the merit of clearing the air, but a storm that in the course of Nature was bound to exhaust itself, a rough, exceptional phenomenon. Reality to her was the social life of privilege. Her view was not narrow or arrogant; she was trained in sympathy with those whose lives lay outside her own; she admired artists, poets, philosophers, and said that she often wished that she had been brought up to a profession, but when with genuine feeling she had discussed Vaughan's poetry, she asked at once whether he was related to the Vaughan who was at Agincourt, and after they had been speaking of Comus she wondered on what terms of intimacy Milton had been with the Egertons. And why not? Lewis asked himself. It was delightful to try to imagine the performance of the Masque at Ludlow; it was reasonable to inquire into the conditions of Vaughan's life and into his heredity.

"But why are you laughing?" Julie said.

"You live in a *salon*," he answered, "and on the lawns outside a great country house. Sometimes you drive in your carriage to visit people and gather knowledge of the world; but you never get out and walk. Sometimes artists and poets and philosophers are among your guests. Milton has his turn, and you have the same smile—and rather a different respect—for the Russian ambassador."

She laughed merrily. "You mean I'm an incurable amateur."

"I mean that your world's different from mine."

"I wasn't so very different when I was a child. My father was poor and a writer."

He shook his head. "It's no good, Julie. Your father may have been poor, but you lived inside the grounds of Harbury House and I lived outside them. Shall I confess— my mother's often told me that she wanted your father to be my godfather, but she didn't dare to ask it—or, rather, my father wouldn't let her."

"Why on earth not?"

"Because your father was the grandson of the old Marquess and my father knew him as a publisher knows an author. At least it began so."

"But, Lewis, they were friends—old friends."

"Afterwards. At first they were professional acquaintances. 'It's always a mistake,' my father used to say, 'to presume on a professional connexion. We shouldn't like it if the grocer asked me to stand godfather to his son.' My father's view was the old English one—that a man's class is his own and that he should be proud of it."

Julie turned over the leaves of a book that was lying on the floor beside her.

"What is more," she said at last, "I suppose my father was only an amateur writer. A volume of scholarly essays about once in six years." She sighed and smiled. "Oh well, I suppose it's true. Perhaps I am an amateur. But need we remember it so desperately? I could help you," she added, raising her face to Lewis's, "if you wrote that book. There are advantages even in being an amateur. I know about furniture, I know the dress of the period—and china and silver. I know—or I know roughly and can find out more accurately—what flowers there were in England then. I won't let you stock your garden with the wrong flowers. Even Mr. Ballater admits I know about flowers."

She made a smiling grimace and Lewis asked her opinion of Ballater.

"He's funny," she said, "isn't he?—like a big graceful dog, always bounding up to you with some achievement in its mouth and wagging its tail in triumph and expecting to be patted. Very different from you, Lewis." Then, with abrupt return to the seventeenth century, she added: "And music—I could tell you about that. Above us, at the top of the tower, I've a little den of my own, next my bedroom. I have a clavichord there as well as my piano. It is very old—seventeenth century—a *gebunden* clavichord. My husband gave it to me, and I brought it from Germany. He was a scholar of old music and used to make me play it to him; I loved that more than anything. . . . Couldn't your heroine be a musician? Why not she and others in the family? It's more probable that, in England about the time of the Civil Wars, she'd have been playing the virginals; but clavichords weren't by any means unknown. And I can play you the music she would have played— mostly Tudor music, I expect. And later you can hear the Restoration changing the whole style, mode having developed into key. Byrd to start with; Lawes for the transition; then Purcell. If she was young at the time of Naseby she might easily live on beyond Purcell. You must make her a musician," Julie insisted. "The old instruments have lovely names," and springing up she set a ladder against a bookcase and brought down from a shelf of rarities Verschuere Reynvaan's Musijkaal Kunst-Woordenboek in the Amsterdam edition of 1795.

As she spoke of music, her manner grew more tranquil, and, instead of breaking from one subject into another with swift transitions, she continued in a narrative of her delights. Lewis, turning Reynvaan's pages, was well content to listen and to think that, while her mind was given to what she loved, she became a child again. Her expression never ceased to be animated; even in sleep, he thought, there would be something eager and adventurous in it—

but now her animation was grave and deep, as it had been while she listened to the legend of Nausicaa.

"Why do you look at me as if you were seeing a ghost?" she startled him by saying, but so absorbed was she in her subject that she forgot her question when it had been asked and soon she was wondering whether the heroine of his book should be better pleased by music when she was gay or when she was sad. "And yet that isn't quite what I mean," she added. "It's when I'm excited that I need music—even solemn or mournful music. My husband used to say that if only there were a wine that didn't cloud the mind as well as stimulate it, one should get drunk on it and then listen to music. I know what he meant. I feel as he did about it. But you are different, Lewis—the other kind of human being. It divides the world into two groups: those who take their music drunk and those who take it sober."

"Those in whom thought is an attribute of feeling," he said, "and those in whom feeling is an attribute of thought. I feel because I have imagined, you imagine because you have felt. Is that your distinction, Julie?"

"Like a book," she said, smiling. "And which is your heroine to be, Lewis? I believe you think that because, as you say, I'm an amateur, I'm incapable of feeling or imagining anything very deeply, but I can imagine her. Think of her, beginning life tucked away in the country, supposing everything to be secure and settled. Imagine a girl, brought up to Church and King, who married without knowing it into the other side—married, I mean, some Puritan whose conscience was as genuine as her own and who loved her, and loved her more and more until she was frightened, for she had married very young; she scarcely knew him. She respected him but didn't love him, but she thought she'd become accustomed and held on. And she was beginning to be calmer, less frightened when suddenly. . . ." Julie was pale; her hand closed over her knee; her knuckles tightened. "Then, suddenly, the war came, and the triumph of his side. Think of how, after being separated a long time, they'd meet and look into the faces of the strangers they had married long ago and half forgotten, and how, feeling that their marriage was a dream that by some cruel freak had become real, she'd start living with him again." She broke off, and presently said in a toneless voice: "Then the Restoration. And afterwards—oh, all their lives to the very last, bitter memories and conventional tolerance and stiff concealments for each other's sake. And right at the end their children wondering why on earth their old-fashioned father and mother still couldn't bear to speak of . . . I could imagine the seventeenth century, Lewis. It's not so far off."

There had been so much of her own life in this imagined history that her eyes were full of tears. "Now you know," she said, when she could not conceal them, "why it's good to have you here."

"Because I'm English?"

Passing him, she stood at the window and looked out over the lakes. When he had risen and was standing beside her, he saw that her hand moved towards him, closed upon the air, and was withdrawn.

"I'd have gone to England long ago and found work to do there," she said. "Even though he is on the other side, I'd have gone. But I'm German now. They would never let me in."

"And in Germany?"

"I'm allowed there, of course. But my husband sent me out. I could only have lived with his family. It's better here, I suppose. And not only that—he didn't want me to be in Germany. It was part of his sentiment that he and I weren't to meet again until, as he said, we had ceased to be enemies. He asked me which side I wanted to win. I said I would support his side—I would do what was required of me. But he repeated his question—he's the honestest man alive—whom did I want to win? I told him the truth. We had been speaking in German, but after he had thought for a little while he said in English: 'Then it would be an agony for you to remain in Germany. You might grow to hate me. God knows, I might grow to hate you.'" She continued with difficulty. "We spent one more day and one more night together. Then, next morning, we said good-bye and I came away. It was time. I was beginning to hate him. Until then I hadn't. I don't now. But that morning . . ."

"But however the war goes," Lewis said, "the wounds will heal."

She looked him in the face. "It's not the war only," she answered.

In the long silence that fell between them, Lewis began to see the husband whom she feared, whom she scarcely knew, whom she respected but could not love. She had spoken of him as of one who belonged already to the past, but in both their minds he was present now—"a dream," Lewis repeated to himself, "that by some cruel freak will become a reality." But if he should be killed? And meeting Julie's eyes he knew that the thought of death had been shared by her, for she was stricken now as she had not been by all her memories.

"Lewis," she said, "will you do something for me? Will you let me play to you?"

"Now?"

"Yes, now. I can't go down and wander about the Castle alone. Come up and let me play. The walls and the doors are so thick that no one will hear or disturb us."

With a key that stood in the lock she opened the second door of the library—the door of which van Leyden had said that it was no longer used—and, passing through with Lewis, closed it behind her. The staircase on which they found themselves was almost dark, but through a slit in the wall, itself hidden from them by the interior masonry, a weak light entered—enough, when their eyes had become accustomed to the gloom, to reveal, in narrow triangles, the form of steps spirally ascending. The air was dank and chill, and the walls sweated. Each step, blunted at the edge, was scooped downward by the wear of innumerable feet. "I should have brought a candle. Can you see?" Julie whispered, with delight in her secret. Lewis struck a match

and saw her face, downward turned and smiling, glow
above him. By a succession of matches they lighted their
climb until Julie, her fingers wrapped about an iron ring,
said: "This is my room," and daylight reappeared.

A screen standing across the door had to be moved before they could enter the bedroom. When they were within,
it was replaced and the door bolted. Lewis saw a room
that closely resembled the library below, having embrasures
in the same position and a like fireplace, at the back of
which—though it was itself used for ordinary fires—the
vent-pipe from the library stove was visible. But the circular
form of the bedroom was broken. An inner segment had
been cut off by a partition which, though it did not rise to
the vaulted ceiling, stood two or three feet higher than the
canopy of the bed. In the partition was an open door and
opposite it another which gave access to the landing.

They went at once into the inner room and Julie shut
the two doors. Here was a second and smaller chimney-
place, evidently cut in recent years, where unkindled logs
lay upon a heap of white ashes. The room was no more
than a slice off the circle of the tower; a small bureau, a
grand piano and a clavichord set upon a low table occupied
the greater part of its floor-space. There was no window.
Daylight came only over the partition from the distant embrasures, and if Julie, when she played, had needed a score,
it would soon have been necessary to use her lamp. But
the music was in her mind; all that she played was deeply
familiar to her until, when the Earl of Salisbury's solemn
dance was ended, Lewis asked if there were anything of
Byrd's that might be said to have, in music, a mystical
quality corresponding to the poetry of Vaughan. Julie
looked at her fragile clavichord upon which traces of elaborate painting still lingered. The poets, she answered, could
develop their own instrument. The musicians were limited
by theirs. Besides, Byrd died when Vaughan was in his
cradle. "But there's a little *Miserere* that might do," she
added. "Listen——" But her memory faltered, and while
she was looking for the *Miserere*, of which, she said, she
had a manuscript copy, Lewis lighted a sconce on the wall

above her. It seemed to him that he had heard nothing more beautiful than this *Miserere*, whispered by the clavichord, and seen no change so great in any countenance as that which the playing of it wrought in hers, for while she played it, and played it again, her lids fell, her mouth drooped a little, and her expression, ceasing to be gay and restless, took on the composure of an enchantment. When she had done she was still, her hands upon her lap; then at last looked up. "Well?" she said, and for answer he begged that she would play the *Miserere* a third time, but she would not. "Some day," she said, and to rouse herself went to her piano. She remained in doubt of what to play, her fingers expectant. Lewis stood beside the chimney, watching the shadow hang beneath her wrists like a sleeve.

CHAPTER FIVE

DURING May, Lewis's view of the activities of the Castle was for the most part that of a distant spectator. At the end of the month there was to be a tennis tournament at Rynwyk to which the van Leydens would drive down each morning. The tennis courts at Enkendaal, laid out near the pavilion on the farther side of the pools, were already busy with practice, and guests were assembling. The cottage, too, had its visitor, a submarine officer named Ramsdell, who had been interned early in the year. A camp-bed had been made for him in the upper sitting-room, and in the evenings, when Lewis had done his work, they would sometimes talk together into the night, but always as yet with constraint as if seeking the subject that should release them into friendship. Their intimacy was slow to ripen, and Lewis thought of Ramsdell principally as the tennis player who was to be Julie's partner in the tournament, a white figure often to be seen from the tower windows. When Lewis heard him speak of Julie, the words seemed to be spoken of a stranger, so remote was the woman whose baffling gaieties provoked Ramsdell's curiosity from the girl whom Lewis knew.

Among the guests at the Castle was De Greve, a yellow lath of a man, said to be the best player in Holland. It was not his custom to play in handicaps, but on the morning of the latest day on which entries could be sent in he asked Sophie to enter with him. Lewis, then on his way to the library, was in the little group at the entrance to the Castle which heard the invitation given, and observed, as they all did, Sophie's delighted and embarrassed surprise. "But why do you ask me?" she said before her dignity had had time to master her astonishment, and when laughter greeted her question she became angry and confused. She did not wish to play, she said then, but her pride telling her that to save herself from ridicule she must laugh with the others, she compelled herself to laugh, and, with a difficult smile at De Greve, consented. There was a colour in her cheeks that Lewis had never before seen in them.

It was in the spirit of a courteous guest sacrificing himself on the altar of politeness—or, perhaps, of pity—that De Greve began to tutor her angular competence. She, in her turn, received him at first as a hired gladiator and no more; she would slash balls at him for three hours continuously, pausing only to ask how her racquet should be held or her feet be placed. "Even when he encourages her," Ramsdell said, "she accepts it as if a barber were praising her hair or a dressmaker lying to her about her pretty figure." But permitting herself at last to recognize that she was indeed a good player and a better pupil, suddenly observing that De Greve, in spite of his youth and her thirty-five years, had admiration for her game and even a smiling friendliness for herself, she let fall one by one her defences of bitter reserve. "It's like a bad-tempered, suspicious, ugly dog that finds itself being patted," was Ramsdell's observation, and Lewis himself, in his brief encounters with her, saw how her defences were melting away. A new sap rose in her; an awkward gentleness, at once eager and half ashamed, entered her life. She could not be beautiful, but she could marvellously cease to be grotesque, and Lewis imagined how, when the tournament was ended and De Greve gone, she would preserve in her heart the dry, fragmentary romance of this time and how it would flower among the secrets that her pride most harshly concealed. He felt that he was looking not at Sophie as she now was but at the old crabbed woman she would become; the woman who would grow into a belief that by these few days her existence was explained and justified.

But even the change in Sophie engaged his mind no

more than some book picked up now and then and in the
intervals forgotten. The intimacy between her and De
Greve, together with the entertainments, the mild rivalries,
the half-stiff and half-lazy good humour of the van Leydens' many guests, appeared to him only in fragments.
Passing through the Castle on his way to or from the
library, he entered for a moment into the life of the place
but with no feeling that he was a part of it. Every day he
worked without interruption until the seventeenth century
became for him a mirror in which he saw, deeply reflected,
the influences of the past, and over which there began to
move continually—a procession of significant shadows—
the philosophic and material changes of the next two
hundred years. Outwardly he was at peace; his work pro-
gressed; his imagination was fertile; he experienced that
high content of scholars in which the mind is felt to
be weaving day and night—for in sleep also the process
seems to continue—a coherent fabric, an emerging pattern,
to which all thought contributes, nothing during these
periods of assimilation being wasted or irrelevant. And he
was tempted to imagine that he owed a part of his mind's
vigour—the colour and pliancy of the fabric, the fineness
of the pattern—to the sensation of joy which in those days
possessed him, an indefinable joy of forward movement, of
release.

Sometimes in the afternoon, more often a little before
dusk when she was tired by tennis and he by his work, he
and Julie went out on to the moors together, or, if the sun
were still high, into one of the nearer woods, and there she
lay upon the ground as she had done in the Harbury
meadows, asking him questions of his work, testing her
mind on his and often yielding to him, in a mood between
smiling and sadness, passages of her deeper confidence, as
if there were a secret intimacy between him and her, as
between friends and exiles profoundly known to each
other in a strange land, which made it natural that thus she
should speak and he listen. Gradually he was enabled to
bridge the gap between his early and his present knowledge
of her, until he felt that all his life had, in a mystery,

corresponded with her life, and that now the mystery had been illumined; and he found it not impossible, when she asked of his own experience, to tell her of Elizabeth—first, lightly, of how it was she that had packed his books for him, then of her gracious wisdom and loyalty and of her parting from him. And at last he added: "I understand now for the first time why I could never love her." But this he had spoken as if to himself, and Julie allowed silence to follow it, lying still with an arm of sunlight across her and one of her hands dipped in sun.

Their being alone together seldom endured long. When their time had passed and they began walking back to the cottage, Julie would put away the quietness of their intimacy, as though preparing herself to re-enter a different world. She told him then of the thousand little incidents that made up the life of the Castle, mocking them in her flying narrative and pretending to mock him for his aloofness from them. Again he became for her an elder brother whom it was her game to provoke. He played to her rule, and she, from seeming to torment him, would return in a flash to their secret mood, and be his penitent with laughter in her eyes. It came into his mind that there was to be written the story—he did not know whether it should be a comic or a tragic story—of a man who, believing a girl to be his sister, had without knowing it loved her all his life, and at last discovered that she was not his sister. He told Julie the story and asked her what its end should be. Instead of answering, as he had expected, with some phrase that blew comedy and tragedy to the winds, she was stayed by his question. As though suddenly disarmed, she began to speak with the impetuosity of a child. "Oh, I expect it would end with——" and there ceased. Her lips closed, her cheeks rushed with colour, her eyes surrendered to him in a deep, swift glance the tremor of her mind; and when, at the entrance to the cottage, they met Ballater, who thrust his arm into hers and said: "Alison has had quite as much of you as he deserves for one day; come and see what's happened in my garden," she had not her customary light, quick answer for him, but released herself, saying that it was late; she must go to the Castle and dress.

But Ballater was without mercy.

"That's what comes of going for walks when tennis is over." He waved his hand towards his flower border. "No time for the important things of life. Or the important people."

"Shall I come and dig in your garden?" she said. "Will that satisfy you?"

"For heaven's sake, no! You're a bit late on it in the middle of May. Although," he added, going into the house, "to save a celibate scholar from interruption, I'll give you a patch to weed after tennis every day."

He kissed his hand to her with a flourish and was gone. The clumsy banter was ended. She stood beside Lewis, staring across the valley.

"It is true," she said.

"What?"

"That I interrupt you."

"No."

After a silence, forcing herself to look at him, "But it might become true," she said, and added, "for both of us, I mean."

Ballater's flowers were bending their heads to a ground-wind and a sharp gust hissed in the foliage overhead. A cloud moved over the sun, which was near to setting.

"Good night, Lewis," she said. "I've been happy to-day."

When she had been gone a little while, Ramsdell thrust his head out of an upper window.

"You'd better come in for your gin and bitters, Alison. There are some dispatches, too, in the *Handelsblad*. Come and translate 'em like a good fellow."

Lewis's work went forward steadily, but beneath the calm of his scholarship was the undercurrent of a secret and opposed delight. Hour by hour he made his way while seated at Dirk's table, but all his being, sleeping or waking,

in labour or idleness, was no longer given to that perfect
continuity of speculative thought which had been his
peace. Once more, as in the days when the tunnel was
being dug in the fort, he was aware of an external world
knocking at the gates of his meditation. His power to work
remained obedient to his will; what was threatened was
that singleness of spirit which, for a purpose more far-
reaching than that of his history, he desired above all else
to cultivate.

When, leaving his books, he went into one of the embrasures of the library and looked down over the lakes
and the garden, he saw little figures moving below, and
saw them now, as he had not before, with a consciousness
of his own separation from them. If they were at the base
of the tower, on their way to the boat-house, he heard
their voices and sometimes their words; if they were on
the upper lake, it was the cluck of their rowlocks he heard;
if they were on the tennis courts, nothing came to him but
their flickering movement, thrown up by a background of
trees. Formerly they had been in his sight and hearing
but had penetrated no further than the outermost fringe
of his thought. Now he seemed often to know Julie's
presence among them before his eyes had observed it
and instantly he was in imagination projected into their
company. As he watched, he began to fancy that he was
invisibly at her side; that her speech was secretly for him;
that in her far-distant figure he could distinguish, not only
the body's supple grace, but the tautening of her limbs
as she ran, the wind's quickness in her hair, and, as
she swung her racquet, the tension of her breasts. From
this external voyage he dragged himself back, in the
instant hating her for having summoned him, in the
same instant filled with joy. A recollection of her childhood and of the different love he had then had for her
quietened his mood, and he began to think of her with
compassion, not with desire, until at last, the sensual
imagination overcome, his mind was for a little while
emptied of her, and he came back to his work. But even
his work was coloured by her. The analogy with her own

life, which both had perceived in her imagining of the
conflicting loyalties of the seventeenth century, persisted
in his memory. In the passages of history she would appear.
In all the pity, the vanity, the tragic beauty of mortal
things, she was present, and the past became her con-
text, from which in her own loveliness she emerged. The
page faded; she only remained; until once more by an
exercise of will he banished her.

A great part of his work at this time was upon Dirk van
Leyden's papers, and every day the Baron visited him to
ask what progress had been made. The old man had been
inclined at first to guard the papers with a jealous caution.
He would bring the keys, open the boxes and display their
contents as an exhibit; he would hand a document to
Lewis and permit him to examine it; but he seemed always
anxious to have the box shut again and, when he departed,
did not leave the key behind him. This family treasure,
Lewis had thought, which has been denied to the scholars
of Leiden, will not after all be shown to me. That is too
much to expect. But it had happened one morning that
the Baron, having heard—perhaps with surprise—that
Lewis was a horseman and that he and Julie used often
to ride together in Harbury Park, had invited him to leave
his work and to ride across the estate with him to visit
a tenant who had been injured in fighting a fire in the
pinewoods. Lewis had accepted, knowing that he was
being offered a privilege that it would be ungracious
to refuse and suspecting that van Leyden had some
reason for inviting him other than a wish for companionship. During the outward ride they spoke little.
At the door of the tenant's cottage, while the Baron
and the injured man were talking like two peasants of the
local past and of the dead worthies of Enkendaal whom
they had known or their fathers had told them of, Lewis
won the heart of the grandson of the house, a lad of eight
or nine, by admiring the little figures of men and animals
that he had carved in wood and by himself trying to carve
a figure of old van Leyden with his gaiters and short coat.
Though the wood was soft and the child could use it with

a rough skill, Lewis's attempt was a poor one, but the attempt was made and the boy, proud of his own work, was even better pleased by his rival's failure than he would have been by his success. When the two figures were finished, van Leyden exclaimed with pretended anger that they were libellous, that he could not part with either of them, and bought the child's with a note that he took folded from his pocket so that none saw the value of it. "It is too much," the grandfather said from his chair, knowing well that it would be too much. "Then I'll take the donkey as its companion," answered van Leyden, and, while the old tenant was laughing and protesting, he and Lewis were on their horses and away. "Devil of a job," he said, "to make my people take money even when they're sick and need it for little things."

He took the wooden figures out of his pocket as he rode and began to chuckle over them. "Sophie has been saying for years that I owe myself a new hat," he declared, and Lewis began to understand that van Leyden tested strangers by their contact with his tenants, whom he knew and loved. By carving this figure, by sitting down to work with the boy and dissolving the grandfather's pride in laughter, he had won the Baron as a friend, and their homeward ride was a journey at ease. Entering the grounds of the Castle, they came up with Julie walking alone and drew in their horses beside her. "Look," said van Leyden, producing the caricatures in wood. "You see how much respect you English have for your hosts!" From the stables, he took Julie and Lewis into the Castle and up to the library. They knew not why, but he would have it so. And in the library, seating himself at Dirk's table, he plunged into the subject which, Lewis now perceived, had long been in his mind.

"Tell me," he said, "you set a pretty high value on those papers—such as you've seen of them?"

"They may be very valuable. They are of three kinds as far as I can judge," Lewis answered. "First, there's a mass of material on the seventeenth century—detailed stuff that he seems to have picked up in English country houses; local, parish history and domestic history of all sorts; copies of old letters—how much of it is new material I can't yet tell. It may be priceless. Then there's material for a history of your own family with his comments—pretty harsh and shrewd sometimes. And there's a third group. The glances I've had tell me little of it. I think he must have had it in his mind to build up, not as a consecutive narrative but in thousands of fragments that made some pattern for him, a kind of spiritual autobiography. There's poetry among it. There are essays in which he seems to have been arguing with himself. There are letters in his own hand written to himself and letters to others——"

"Named people?" said the Baron. "I mean people we know."

"Certainly."

"Not posted?"

"They weren't intended for the post," Lewis said, "any more than the letters he wrote to Dionysus."

"Who?"

"To Dionysus. To half the gods of Olympus for that matter. The point is that these letters were one of his ways of expressing himself. I think he must have had an idea that——"

"I'll tell you what his idea was—one of them anyhow. The fellow from Leiden told us that; besides, it was common knowledge. He thought that for him everyone who ever lived was still alive. He'd say that he was going out for a walk with Napoleon—but I think he said it to rile people and shock them. I don't think he believed it. The Leiden fellow said it was an interesting mental case—in short, that Dirk was mad. That's why I sent him about his business. No Leyden has ever been mad."

"Did you know," Lewis said, "that some of the papers were in code?"

"Yes," the Baron answered. "I knew that. I've had people wanting to decode them. I wouldn't allow it. It was just idle curiosity. They said he was mad. They didn't attach any value to the papers."

He had seemed to be about to say more, but hesitated.

"Would you be glad," Julie said, "if he turned out to be a great writer?"

"Great writer?" van Leyden repeated, as if the idea had entered his head for the first time. "Oh, I don't know about that. The point is one doesn't like to shut away what may be of some value if there's a chance of its being investigated by a man of discretion. I don't want strangers poking about at Enkendaal," he exclaimed, raising his voice and blowing into his moustache; "fellows, I mean, who'd treat our papers as if they were some exhibit in a public museum. And I don't want fools coming here in little black coats and bowler hats, and bowing and scraping to me because I'm van Leyden van Enkendael, and then having the damned insolence to tell me that my uncle was mad."

He rose and, clasping his hands behind his back, strutted to and fro in the great room like a nervous sea-captain pacing his quarter-deck with the enemy in sight. Julie, seated on a high, embroidered stool, her body thrown back, her head a little lowered, her hands clasped about a raised knee, observed him with amusement and, without speech, shared her amusement with Lewis.

"We all know what you're going to say, Oom Piet. Why not say it? You are going to offer the papers to Lewis on condition that——"

"No," said van Leyden, coming to a halt. "That's where you're wrong. That's where a woman would be wrong nine times out of ten—making conditions. Choose your man right and conditions can go hang. There are the keys on your table," he said to Lewis. "You know my mind."

Dirk van Leyden's papers had become a part of Lewis's work. In the latter days of May he was increasingly glad of them, partly because they were the occasion of the Baron's visits to the tower. Simplicity of manner and a stern pride, deep, stubborn prejudice and a fearless originality of spirit, continually revealed fresh harmonies and discords in the old man's character, and Lewis was never tired of hearing his shrewd comments on men and affairs. Enkendaal was his world, but so profound was his love and knowledge of it that, for him, all the world was gathered in to Enkendaal. "A peasant," Dirk had written, "seems stupid to townsmen because, when making a decision, he so often refuses to be guided even by reasonable argument addressed to that decision. But he is not stupid; he is wise. He rejects the particular argument because it bears too closely on the subject to be decided. It is new, raw, human, fallible. He prefers to submit each question, however small, to the sum of his experience and tradition—a method that townsmen find tedious, but one that may well be God's method of judgement. At least, I hope so, for if we have to justify ourselves by reason then we shall be lost, but if we have the benefit of God's experience of mankind there is a chance of salvation. If God is a judge, a statesman, a schoolmaster, a priest or a cultivated woman, we shall all be shut out, but if he is a peasant, he will know that we are fools and give us shelter for the night." "And that little clerk," the Baron exclaimed when Lewis had read the passage to him, "that little black-hat from Leiden, who didn't know a cat from a cow, said that Dirk was mad!"

As the days passed, van Leyden became more and more persuaded that Dirk's papers would prove to be an asset to his family and an asset of a kind to which he attached exceptional value. "You mustn't think," he said to Lewis, "that I despise men of letters. I had a taste for history myself when I was a boy. Might have gone further with it if I hadn't had other things to do. But scholarship and so on has never been much in our line. You know," he added, "that it is not now the custom of the old land-owning families of Holland to take much part in politics? Diplomacy—yes, sometimes. The Foreign Office—yes, perhaps, now and then. But party politics—no. And the *bourgeoisie* in the towns say we are effete. 'We produce the statesmen,' they say. 'We produce the writers, the artists, the scholars.' Of course it isn't true. Van der Wijck and Pijnacker Hordijk were men of family. So is John Loudon, who's foreign minister to-day. But it has an appearance of truth. . . . I'd dearly love to see a collection of Dirk van Leyden's work correct the balance. If it were good enough, it might go through Europe in translation—eh? What d'you think?"

One day, in a tone of challenge seemingly prompted by some vague resentment, Ballater asked: "Why don't you bring in Julie to help you with Dirk's papers? I should."

"You would," Ramsdell interjected.

"Well, why not? She's a bit of a historian, isn't she? Besides it would give her something to do. She needs it."

Lewis answered lightly that Julie was playing too much tennis to care to be shut up in the tower, but the thought that, if he asked her to work with him, she might consent had an increasing influence on his imagination, and he began to be aware of her absence, to feel that there was in the library an emptiness waiting to be filled. They met less often now; scarcely ever was she unaccompanied; but, when they encountered by chance, the presence of others sharpened the intimacy of their private communication, and, though they might part without having exchanged a word, Lewis went on his way feeling that they had been alone together. And yet, how little I know of her, he said, returning to the cottage at the end of a morning's work. Many women are like stringed instruments; they respond to a touch, and we suppose that they have music in themselves. And he forced himself to think that she was what she often appeared to be—frivolous, nervous, vain; powerful only in her power of interference. Was he not living, or attempting to live, a life that was a perpetual challenge to the interference of the world? Every child that sees water lying still picks up a stick, breaks the surface, throws all the reflected images into confusion, and nothing so certainly provokes the curiosity of women as the spectacle of a man withdrawing himself from their company. In women, curiosity may take many forms—hatred, contempt, even love or the semblance of love. But whatever stick they choose, some stick they will seize to set calm swirling, for their fish are all in troubled waters. Calmness of spirit is exclusive of their claims, the deadliest enemy of their nature. And perhaps, Lewis added, the enemy of Nature herself.

Ramsdell was in the verandah before the cottage and, no sooner had his talk of ordinary things broken in upon this jangling argument, than Lewis saw it for what it was—a bitter generalization and no more. A schoolboy trying to excuse himself for the failure of a morning's work might well be ashamed of it, he thought. She was beautiful and very young. Already her life had knotted itself in a way that defeated her hope. It was natural enough that she should use him, who was once her schoolmaster, as an emotional confessor. But while Ramsdell was saying that Ballater had gone to the Huis ten Borgh and would not be back until evening, Lewis could give him but part of his attention. He found that, as the disturbance of his mind was not to be quelled in bitter reproaches, so also it was not to be explained away.

"A good morning?" Ramsdell asked, when he and Lewis were sitting together at their food.

"Not as good as it should have been."

"Why not play tennis this afternoon? You've probably worked until you're stale."

They looked out at a darkening sky and Ramsdell shrugged his shoulders. "I hope the weather will hold. Julie and I are supposed to be playing a single at 2.30 to practise her back-hand."

He looked searchingly across the table, and paused, as if he expected that his having spoken of Julie would provoke Lewis to speak of her. But Lewis was silent and soon Ramsdell went on: "Sometimes she plays tennis like a fiend. When she starts slashing, it's useless to steady her. What's more, it doesn't pay. Sometimes everything goes out and it's hopeless. But sometimes everything goes in— like a twelve-inch on the target. There's no holding her then. The other day we had De Greve against us. He began by giving it easy to her forehand when he could. Either that or something else—God knows what—put her

on her mettle and she began to hit. Sophie van Leyden
was left standing, and even De Greve had to play all out.
She passed him at the net. She plugged him in the back-
hand corner. She could do nothing wrong. She didn't
speak to me for five games and we won them all. Then,
suddenly, after bringing off a drive like the kick of a mule,
she turned round to me with her eyes glistening and
smiled one of her pleasantest, laziest smiles. 'Well, that's
that!' she said. And so it was. She played afterwards like a
lady and we quietly lost the set. . . . There's rain," he
added, looking at a splashed window-pane; "that probably
puts the lid on tennis for this afternoon. It's cold too. I
suppose you'll go back to your library?"

"I expect so. Why?"

"If we're going to have an afternoon in—what about a
game of chess?"

They went into the upper sitting-room when their meal
was over and took out the chessmen, a great ivory set of
German origin, given to the Baron by Narwitz and lent by
Julie to the cottage, a beautiful set deeply carved, cool and
sharp beneath the fingers. The first game was short, for
Lewis allowed a bishop to become entangled and lost his
king's knight in an attempt to protect it. "You ought to
have seen that trap. Your mind wasn't on it," Ramsdell
said. He began to re-set the pieces for a new game, but
before the array was complete his eye fell on a newspaper
paragraph that mentioned the pyramids, and soon he was
speculating on the mechanics of building in ancient Egypt.
Scrambling to his knees on the floor and spreading out
paper there, he showed, with diagrams and slide-rule and
with the poker as model, how unexpectedly small was the
man-power necessary to raise a great monolith. He was one
of those naval officers who temper a keen professionalism
with a passion for argument on remote unprofessional subjects. He would sit down to what he called a "cag" as
eagerly and as patiently as a dog before a rabbit hole, and
Lewis was fascinated by the variety of his knowledge, the
product of wide, scattered reading and an abnormal memory
for detail. He was expert in chronometers and in the his-

tory of timepieces of all kinds; he had collected knowledge of witchcraft, magic and the reading of omens, and was full of an ingenious theory of the mysteries of Eleusis; he was a disciple of Mahan and followed the everlasting problem of sea-power to the Aegean in the fifth century before Christ, showing what effect the periodic north wind had had on the fortunes of Greece and so of the world. "If the Etesians had blown from the south," he exclaimed as a challenge to argument, "the world might never have been civilized."

From the naval power of Greece, it was an easy step to her philosophy, and Lewis wondered whether the conversation had from the outset been led towards it, so willing was Ramsdell to discuss the opposed ideals of the active and the contemplative lives. On this subject they fell into long and tranquil debate. The appearance of the room, the patter of rain on the windows, faded from Lewis's knowledge, and he saw before him nothing but Ramsdell's bony face and the mingled red and ivory of the pieces on the chequered board. These seemed to be enclosed in the compass of his argument. They became, not an individual face and a group of distinguishable chessmen, but the visible focus of his mind.

The qualities that equipped a man for a life of meditation, Ramsdell was saying, were negative qualities; their peacefulness was the peace of death; and Lewis, who was debarred by his own unfaith from using the Christian defence, said that nothing was so vital as thought and nothing so enduring. "But only if it leads to action," Ramsdell answered, "otherwise it is still-born." It was the orthodox attack and invited the general answer that all thought had a continuing effect independent of any action that might spring from it. As there was a physical air that men breathed in common, so there was a spiritual air that, in the processes of thought, they drew upon and exhaled. Some thought purified or enriched it; other thought corrupted it; and in this perpetual struggle there were no divisions of time or place or language. Action perished; thought did not.

As from this outline of their opposed theories they proceeded to the arguments in support of each, and Lewis threaded his way through the evidences for the continuous effluence of thought, there came a moment when he asked whether Ramsdell had not often found himself in a house that welcomed or repelled him, not by its appearance but by some influence of the spirit within it. Did not the thought of vanished occupants linger powerfully in certain woods and gardens? "Yes, that is true," Ramsdell answered slowly. "Certainly it is true of ships." The recollection of a personal experience moved in his eyes, and for an instant the external world flooded in upon them both. Hearing Ramsdell say: "Certainly it is true of ships," Lewis heard also the rain and the trickle of water from the roof gutter; but again, as the discussion went forward, his being was gathered up in it. Through speech and through silence there flowed, like a calm, deep river bearing him away, a persuasion that only in a life of contemplation would peace come to him, such a peace, exclusive of the senses, as now whispered its first secrets in the stillness of this room. Out of the dusk an ivory knight raised a horse's head, the eyes wide and frozen, the throat dully gleaming, and the array of chessmen put off their substance in his mind. They were as spirits that had attained to a final composure; in their world, many battles would be fought of which they were the instruments but they would not be partakers in battle. Listening to the voice arguing against him, he watched the beads of light on the horse's ivory mane, and suddenly Ramsdell's hand came out, plucked the knight from the board and twisted it between his fingers in the air. Soon he set it down in its place. The serrated mane was flecked with a low, fixed illumination; the eyes were again frozen and wide; and there sprang up in Lewis a certainty that this hour through which he was passing would not vanish, that there was an enduring essence in it, that even now its thought was moving out on an unending journey. "Throw a stone into a pool," he said. "Out go the ripples; they don't cease when the stone ceases to move. And if the death of the body does not check the continuous movement of thought, do you suppose that the withdrawal of the body into a hermit's cell will check it?" It was the meeting-point of many paths of argument that he and Ramsdell had searched together—a point from which new paths sprang; and now the pressure of circumstance, which that morning had been so heavy upon him, seemed to have been lifted. When Ramsdell questioned him, answers leaped to his mind. A certitude beyond reason was the impulse of all his reasoning. He felt once more a pulse of the spirit beat in his purposes, and when, in the midst of a sentence, Ramsdell broke off to say: "That must be Ballater coming back," Lewis heard the step on the gravel below as if it were the echo of a life and of a world through which he had already passed.

Though the afternoon was becoming old, light within had been increasing, for only scattered wisps of the storm now remained in the sky; a clearer shadow hung beneath the jaws of the knight; the polish on the ivory throat was heightened. Fine streaks of shade, luminously edged, declared themselves among the tiles surrounding the fireplace, and the newspaper with which the fire had been laid shone behind the bars.

Ballater, who was always busy, would have orders to give to the servants or letters to write before he came upstairs, they thought; his arrival would not disturb them. The argument was taken up where it had rested, and would have been long continued in peace; but while Ramsdell was speaking footsteps were heard on the stair. They were not Ballater's. Lewis knew whose steps they were.

Into the tension of an armed, excluding silence, Julie entered.

"May I come in?" she said, and, something in their appearance striking doubt or wonder into her, she added: "You look like conspirators. What have you been talking about? . . . Secrets?"

They were standing before her when suddenly she dropped on her knees beside the hearth. "They must be deep secrets that keep you by an unlighted fire on an afternoon like this. May I have some matches? I'll make tea for you."

She stretched out her hand for the box and insisted upon lighting the fire herself. Nor would she allow Ramsdell to order their servant to bring up tea. "I know you have stores of things in that cupboard," she said. "Let's make it ourselves. I'm hungry. I walked through the rain and came in soaked. When I was changed I couldn't face tea with mother and Sophie. . . . So I came here."

After her first swerve of uncertainty in their presence, an uncertainty that had set her tongue racing and given an abruptness to all her movement, she began to speak more steadily, but with an air of feeling her way towards their confidence. An intuition warned her that the barrier she had encountered was one that she could not carry by assault, and, as though by some magic she could transform herself, she withdrew the challenge of her loveliness and became quiet and still. Lewis had never before seen her in this mood except when she had been alone with him. It is as if she had lowered a veil over her face, he thought. When Ramsdell began to chatter to her as he always chattered to pretty women, ingeniously seeking for chances to amuse and please her, she with a calm grace passed through his flatteries and drew him little by little into friendliness and ease. Soon he and Lewis were back in their chairs beside the fireplace. She was on the rug between them, the yellow dance of early flames upon her, talking and listening with so final an abandonment of feminine privilege that Ramsdell was tempted to admit her to the dialogue that she had interrupted. "Shall I tell you what our conspiracy was?" he asked.

"Yes," said Julie.

There was a note in her voice that caused Lewis to exclaim: "That's what you've been playing for, Julie, isn't it, ever since you came?"

"Playing for? For what?"

"The key to the 'conspiracy,' the 'deep secret.'"

"Why do you say that I have been playing for it? I have been playing for nothing."

Her eyes told him that she believed her own denial. Within her knowledge, she was speaking the truth. She did not understand why he was angry with her.

"It's Lewis's secret as well," she said, and began without resentment, though with wonder and hesitation, to talk of other things.

"There's no secret about it," Ramsdell broke in. "All we were talking about was. . . ."

She sat back on her heels, seeming to listen gravely to his attempt to show her the course of the dialogue; but though she answered and questioned him with the skill of an amateur who knows how to please her company by caring for what is of interest to them, she was not listening with any depth of attention, and Lewis was reminded of how she had said, of the girl who was to appear in their imagined story of the seventeenth century, that she would listen to the men talking of their theories but would see the men through the theories—a realist, she had added, not a romantic. Remembering this and observing how her hands moved idly from piece to piece on the chess-board, he smiled. She saw his smile and her own lips moved—in mockery, in triumph, in gladness because the tension was at last broken? He did not know. Ramsdell stopped in mid-argument.

"I know," he said, seeing the change in her expression. "It must seem odd to you—our sitting up here and talking and talking. . . ."

"You did hate me for coming in, didn't you? . . . Didn't you, Lewis?"

"Alison's an odd creature," Ramsdell said. "Look at him. He sits there brooding over us like a great eagle. Part of him's a plain man of business; part of him's as wild as a martyr who'd go to the stake singing at the top of his voice. Part of him's a hermit and part——"

"Part of him," Lewis said, "isn't a hermit. . . . No, I didn't hate you for coming in, Julie. But all sorts of other things came in with you."

"Do you know," she answered, turning her head away from them, "I don't think I've ever wished so much that

I was a man as I did a moment after I'd come into this room. You—you two, I mean—weren't in arms against me personally; I knew that. It was because I . . . You see, I didn't want to break in on you. But suddenly, when I was in the Castle changing, I thought of this evening —tea-time, dinner, afterwards—Dutch, Dutch, Dutch— and I envied you all up in the cottage. Someone to talk to. Probably sitting up half the night, the three of you, so intimate that you don't have to think of it—a community all your own. I envied you. So I came. Nine times out of ten it would . . . and even this time, if I'd been a man or if I'd been——"

"If you'd been just a plain woman," said Ramsdell, "we shouldn't have minded? I wonder if that's true."

"You wouldn't have noticed. You'd have broken off for a moment. Then you'd have let me sit down and have gone on." While they were talking, the coals had foundered in the grate and now, lying on the floor, she began to mend the fire with sticks. "Can't you go on now? I'll say nothing if you like. Forget that I'm here." There was a silence. "Lewis, why don't you go on?"

In the evening, Lewis was unable to read calmly, and even Ballater's talkative good humour, when he sought it out, was an irritant.

"They were talking about you and Julie at the Huis ten Borgh to-day," Ballater began.

"Who?"

"Goof and van Arkel. That little devil, with his bangle and his pre-Charlemagne pedigree and his pale mauve tie, is always pecking at gossip. There's no need to listen to him."

"What did he say?" Lewis asked.

"Oh, he had a phrase. He talked about *une amitié amoureuse*." Ballater had evidently given to the adjective a more scandalous meaning than it had had in van Arkel's mind. "Of course," he said, "I know you and I know Julie. And I know there's nothing in it."

Ramsdell stretched out his hand for a French dictionary. *Une amitié amoureuse*, he said, was harmless enough to a Frenchman; at any rate, it didn't call for the instant pistols of husbands. But Ballater would not allow that he had been wrong. "It depends on how it's said," he answered. "You didn't hear van Arkel say it and you didn't hear Goof's reply."

"Which was?" Ramsdell asked.

"He answered in Dutch, which you wouldn't understand," said Ballater, parrying the attack upon his own French. "What it came to was: he'd never be surprised by anything Julie did because she has no roots here."

Ramsdell acknowledged that there was something in that. "You know she came to tea with us this afternoon? Half the time she was all on edge . . . so were you, Alison."

Ballater laughed aloud, and when he had done laughing he too turned to Lewis. "What, in fact, are you playing at?" he asked. "You may not have noticed it—you notice damned little outside your tower—but Julie has changed. She still comes painting with me now and then, and there's the devil in her sometimes; but she's changed—or at least I think so." He had the air of a baffled tactician. "She's damned difficult."

Lewis held his peace. He could not trust himself to answer. And presently Ballater returned to the subject by saying, with the resentful solemnity of a man who had never before known himself fail in analysis of women, that he had supposed she was worried about her husband.

"Not that she's in love with him, or ever has been. Still, when a girl of that age and one with her temperament has been married three months and then suddenly. . . . Anyhow, I thought she might want to talk to me about him."

"Well?" said Lewis.

"She didn't. . . . We were walking over the moors, looking for a place to paint, and for the sake of saying something (she didn't say a word) I stopped on that bit of high ground towards the Huis ten Borgh where there's a gap between two woods and I suggested we might paint

there. She said 'Not here,' and no more. Then suddenly
she began to talk and what she talked about was you."

"Which gap between two woods?" Lewis asked.

"To the east. You can see Germany from it. . . . And
do you know what she said about you?" Ballater insisted.
"She said: after the war, would you go back to your office?
I told her I thought not; you hadn't got a family hanging
round your neck now as you had once; probably, unless
you got tangled up in some way, you'd do your own queer
job. 'What do you mean by tangled up?' she said. I had
been thinking of the fort. I told her how one night, when
you and I were digging in the tunnel together, we'd
suddenly realised that, though we were trying to get out
and would get out if the tunnel succeeded, to escape was
the last thing that either of us wanted. 'Then why did you
go on?' she asked. I said we had to; we couldn't stand out
of it. 'Lewis will always get tangled in something,' she said.
'He's not cruel enough.' . . . Do you know," Ballater continued after a pause in which Lewis made no reply, "I like
her even better when she's serious than when she's pretending that nothing matters or ever will. When she's
serious, she's always half frightened, and that little white
patch in the colour of her cheeks becomes whiter and her
eyes stare at you as if——"

"And then you want to console her, don't you, Ballater?"
Ramsdell asked.

"Well, you know," Ballater said, "it's all very well for
you to laugh, but sometimes she is such a child——"

"Oh, my God!" Ramsdell exclaimed. "We can't have
that story from you!"

"But she is. She is," Ballater repeated. "You don't know
her as I do. Isn't she a child, Alison?"

Ramsdell leaned back in his chair. "Anything less like a
child than Julie was when she was in this room a few hours
ago, I've never seen. She had us at her mercy—I've just
begun to realize how completely. And when she had finally
subjugated us, she lay down at full length on the floor with
firelight all over her and urged us to go on discussing the
contemplative life."

Ballater laughed. "Well, what do you expect? If you shut yourself up and talk philosophy, any woman will play hell with you. And lying on the floor, if you have a figure like hers, isn't a bad way with philosophers."

"I observe," said Ramsdell, "that you are becoming less paternal. You have noticed the shape of her."

"A few hours ago," Ramsdell had said. She had been stretched out in the place where Ballater was now tracing patterns on the rug with the stump of a poker; and so deeply was the vanished scene impressed on Lewis's mind that, while the others continued to discuss her, she appeared again before him. He heard her say: "Why don't you go on, Lewis?" and through his imagining of the silence that had followed her words came Ballater's voice saying: "The thing to judge a woman by is the back of her neck." The discussion of her had not a greater frankness of sensual judgement than commonly entered into discussions of women at the cottage. On Ramsdell's side, it was shrewd and light-hearted; on Ballater's, a mingling of sentiment and forgivable vanities. Open, laughing, unashamed, it yet observed its own restraints. If any other woman had been its subject, Lewis might have joined in it easily enough, but, through his knowledge that resentment of it was unreasonable, there arose in him a hot anger because it was of Julie they were speaking. Not what they said, but that they spoke of her as they would speak of other women, fired and silenced him. For him she was full of secrets hidden from the world. By his knowledge of her, now and in the past; by the years' obscure weaving of her life with his own; by his power to perceive in her what none other could perceive, she was ringed about and set apart.

"The key to almost every woman," Ramsdell was saying, "is her peculiar, personal pride. Find out what that is and you can begin to decode the whole cryptogram. Men run closer to type. Most of us follow more or less a set rule of honour; you can find out pretty soon how far a man will go, and in what directions; apply a certain knowledge of him to the conventional rule, and you can guess just where he'll stop sliding and dig his heels in. But each woman has her own pride. She'll do things that break the convention again and again until you begin to think there's damned little she wouldn't do with persuasion. Then, suddenly, where you least expect it, she stands like a rock. It may be some consideration for her children; it may be some unspoken pledge to the poor devil of a husband everyone supposed she was ready enough to deceive; very often it is some pride of money that no man can grasp. The point is that men have a more or less conventional idea of what integrity means. But a woman's integrity is as personal to her as her own face. It may include chastity or it may not; it may include the keeping of one promise but not the keeping of another; it may lead her into what seem to outsiders incredible contradictions. But there it is—it's her own, within its own limits sacred ground. She'll die defending it. . . . If you can tell me what Julie's root pride is, what is her own view of her own integrity, I can tell you the rest; I can make a fair guess at what she'd do in any given circumstances. It's like a secret ribbon. Find it and pull it; the whole dress falls off. You have her naked.

"I can see her lying there now," Ramsdell went on, moving his hand in the air as if she were indeed present beneath the shadow of his hand. "Nine women out of ten would have thought her in some obscure way immodest because she stretched herself out between us with her frock taut over her shoulders and a great flowing line from hip to knee. They'd have thought her immodest because what she did would have seemed to them a deliberate provocation—so open that it gave away the whole secret game of allurement. It would have been an overstepping of the limits of their pride. But they'd have been wrong. It wasn't in any way connected with Julie's pride. I don't mean that she didn't know our eyes were on her; she did; at any rate it can't have been long before she realized it, and she made no attempt to move. But she hadn't abandoned any fragment of her integrity."

"How do you know?" said Ballater.

"Because if she had, we should have despised her. It's the infallible test."

Ballater stroked his chin and his smile extended. "I wish I'd been here. There was a girl at Goof's with eyes you could sink a ship in—but she was too short and thick from waist to knee. Of all Julie's points that's the best— she has flanks like a racehorse. When we've been painting together, picnicking, I've seen her stretched out, propped on her elbows, eating sandwiches. . . . Probably she's not solid enough for the German taste."

From wild generalization to close, particular comment the discussion moved. In mind and body they searched her, sometimes with cruelty, sometimes with tenderness, often with masculine detachment that was neither tender nor cruel. They searched her with their observation, their surmise, their imaginings, as though she were one of a dozen women about whom they might ingeniously speculate and so pass an evening away. They are searching her, Lewis thought, as though she were not here to listen to them, but, while they spoke, he saw her always before him. The ivory chessmen, still ungathered on their board, were moved by her fingers. The firelight existed in the shadows of her body. When Ramsdell and Ballater were silent, almost he heard her speak. But she is not here, he said within him. She is lying asleep on her bed in the tower, or awake hearing the waterfall. It is my own thought that has summoned her here, not this argument of Ramsdell's. It is my own thought that has enabled Ballater to see her lying before us. But he could escape neither from his anger against Ramsdell and Ballater nor from the charged delight of contemplating her with the eye of his thought. In a determination to escape, he sprang from his chair and moved across the room towards the door. Something in the abruptness of his movement—or perhaps the tension of his guarded silence—must have warned Ramsdell. His words ceased; his eyes came up in inquiry; Ballater's followed.

"Perhaps we've had enough of this discussion for one evening," Ramsdell said.

Ballater was slower to understand. Then, as he read Lewis's face, his expression changed and he became clumsily eager to make amends. "I hadn't the least idea——" he began again.

Ramsdell broke in upon him. "It's odd," he said. "These arguments. They go on; you almost forget that it's one particular girl you're discussing . . ."

Lewis sat down again. "It's my fault, not yours," he said. "If I hadn't been thinking of her and filling the room with her, you'd probably not have begun. . . . Anyhow, now you know what I didn't know myself half an hour ago."

CHAPTER SIX

Two empty chairs, from which Allard van Leyden and his wife had risen, separated Lewis from Julie. He could see Allard moving down the central pathway between the courts, nodding to those who were seated there on scarlet benches or in small wicker armchairs. Allard's greetings were simple—friendly wavings of his slow hand, almost English, as they were intended to be, but his wife, feeling perhaps in some deep recess of her pride that everyone at the Rynwyk tennis tournament was thinking of her as the future mistress of Enkendaal, was affable with a certain regal condescension. When she bowed, her head seemed to slide forward over her short neck, like the head of some matronly, imperial hen; and the movement accentuated the stiffness of her body—a comely but unprovocative body encased in silk poplin of the van Leyden length. Her parasol moved before her, erect like a sword of state. She seemed to be opening a parliament or visiting a slum. And how admirably she did it—for, like a queen, she was not pleasing herself.

"We must go down and watch Goof and Ballater," Allard had said.

"Why? They're sure to be beaten. It's comfortable here. Besides, we get a better view of De Greve."

She had not wished to leave the shady terrace at the end of the ground. The seats there were protected by a little group of planes; they were, too, the Enkendaal seats—her own. But it was her rule not to contradict her husband in public, and she had acquiesced, with no more protest than a sharp click of her parasol as she put it up. Her eye had fallen on Julie. Why should that girl stay on the terrace, coolly at ease, while she herself went out into the glare of brickdust and scarlet paint to watch Goof beaten?

"You will come with us, Julie?" It had scarcely been an interrogation.

"Oh, leave her," Allard had said. "There's no need for her to come"—a comment kindly intended, but exclusive. "You don't want to, do you, Julie?"

She had shaken her head. Allard and his wife had begun their progress alone. Their empty chairs divided Lewis from Julie's silence. She continued to gaze at the court nearest to the terrace—De Greve's court, and to patter the strings of her racquet on the toe of her shoe. The fingers of the hand lying in her lap were driven into a crumpled envelope. Seeing it and the expression of her face, Lewis understood suddenly that she had shaken her head, not answering Allard in words, because something contained in that envelope had caused her to distrust the steadiness of her voice. His lips, which had been about to speak, closed again, for the tension in her was strange to him, and he looked away across the courts at the diminishing perspective of white lines, at the players and their short, clinging shadows, at the shifting, speckled colour of the onlookers, moving to and fro against a background of heavy trees and blue sky and the thin, distant spires of Rynwyk. This, and all that was akin to it, the historians of the war would forget—this lazy prettiness of a continuing civilization, this insulated comedy of another world, in whose illusion the actors themselves were enwrapped. And I shall forget it, Lewis said—even the dulled twang of the racquet on the toe of her shoe, and the knowledge that, if I turned my head, I should see, with uncomprehending shame, even with joy in their beauty, the controlled struggle of her clenched hand, the rigidity of her shoulders, her terrible stillness, her dry eyes. If she would cry! he thought; and the imagination of her tears—a yielding, a confession of herself—flowed through his mind until he began to think that, if he and she were in England, he could comfort her, though he knew not how. If they were

in England, the leisure he now had, the blissful leisure of
escape from the world, would not be his, but such leisure
as was granted to him would be free of the taint of exile;
and she, too, would be in her own place, which had
nourished her childhood. She would discover, even in the
midst of personal unhappiness, that reconciliation of the
soul with its environment, that unspeakable sympathy of
earth and sky which, in a man's native country and there
only, accompany his joy and grief, informing the one with
light, quickening the darkness of the other, so that his inheritance seems to rejoice and weep with him, and he,
though stricken, is neither lotless nor forsaken.

A figure, towards which Lewis did not look, had come
up from behind Julie and seated itself on her farther side,
asking her permission with a slim bow.

"*Ist es erlaubt diesen Platz einzunehmen?*"

"Of course, Alex." She answered in German, since it
was van Arkel's affectation to speak it. The movement of
her racquet ceased and when van Arkel's thin voice said
that they were thinking of giving a theatrical entertainment
at the Rynwyk theatre during the autumn in aid of some
charity and asked whether she would perform, she answered:

"That's a long way off, the autumn," and added,
"What charity?"

"Oh, any charity. It will have to be neutral, of course."

"You think people would come? Are you going to have
professionals? If Uncle Pieter entertained them at Enkendaal, they'd cost nothing."

"They'd want to play all the leading parts."

"So much the better."

Van Arkel hesitated. "Oh, do you think so?" he said
unwillingly, seeing honour depart from him. Then he hit
on an unanswerable argument. "But we couldn't act with
professionals, could we? In Holland they haven't the same
. . . the same social status as. . . . Not that that would make
any difference to you or me, but there are people who . . .
and in an affair of this kind. . . ."

Whether in the end Julie consented or refused to take

part in van Arkel's theatricals Lewis did not know. He was
listening, not to their words, but to the hiss of good
German well spoken, and, when their meaning came to
him again, it was not of acting that van Arkel was speaking
but of the war. Soon, he said softly, it would be ended, he
was sure. The folly of it couldn't go on. The German army
(and Lewis imagined his smile of ingratiation) was a professional army, magnificently commanded—but magnificently! And the English fleet of which so much had been
expected, what could it do?

"You think the Allies will be beaten, then?" Julie said.

"Not beaten. Not precisely that . . . but I think they
will make peace. Perhaps separately."

"They are sworn not to," Julie replied. She had been
speaking, had been forcing herself to speak, out of a deep
preoccupation into which she fell back when van Arkel
was silent.

"You have good news of your husband, I hope?" he
said politely, as a man might say, "I hope you had good
weather for your holiday," and Lewis, hearing Julie catch
her breath like a sleeper in the shock and crisis of a dream,
turned. It was in his heart to cry out: "Go away! For God's
sake go away! Don't you see how you are tormenting her?"
but he was silenced by the discovery that van Arkel knew
well enough what he was doing. The blue eyes were open
wide, the pale lips parted and curled; the whole face,
ordinarily without life, was quickened and pointed by
curiosity. Every word of his had been a deliberate flick of a
whip; and now, the envelope she had been holding having
fallen to the ground, he darted for it. But it was within
reach of Lewis's hand, the angular German writing and
the marks of its origin evident upon it. She took it from
him with fingers that for an instant touched his own,
folded it and thrust it into a little bag that was in her
chair.

"Yes," she answered, "Quite good news, thank you."

"De Greve leads 5—1 in the second set!" came from the
umpire in the court below.

"De Greve is winning his single easily," Lewis said, but

his attempt to cause a diversion was unavailing, for now
Sophie and the Baroness appeared.

"Was your letter from Rupert earlier or later than mine,
Julie?" her mother asked. "Mine was the twenty-first."

"Mine was written one day later."

"Does he say anything of coming here?"

"He always says he wishes he could come. I don't think
this letter really amounts to more than that except——"

"Except?"

"Well, I think he was excited when he wrote it."

"Do you know where he is?" Sophie asked.

"Of course not." Julie's lips moved before she added:
"On the English front, I think."

"Well," said the Baroness in the tone of a hostess who
announces a welcome addition to a party she is contemplating, "I believe Rupert means to come as soon as he can
get leave."

"But will that be possible?" van Arkel inquired. "A
German officer to come to Holland and return?"

"As a civilian, of course."

"Even so . . ."

"I think," said the Baroness, "most things are possible
to Rupert. He has great influence. The only difficulty that
I foresee is that he may feel it his duty to stay at his post.
Once he had a quixotic idea that he and Julie ought not to
meet until it was all over. Wasn't that sweet of him?
Queer. . . . Sweet, too. . . . But now the war has lasted so
long, so very long. . . ." She sighed, and smiled a knowing
smile over young lovers parted. "What do you think,
Julie?"

"I think he'll stay at the front."

"If you asked him——" her mother began.

"I'll not ask him—never, never."

The note of passion in her voice made it inevitable that
van Arkel should intervene. If her control was near to
breaking, he must, in his shrill, innocent voice of a schoolgirl, ask:

"But why?"

"Because he would never forgive me," she answered,

speaking now in her own tongue. "Because I'm English. . . . And, to his honour, he's a fanatic."

She weakened when she had spoken and leaned back in her chair.

Sophie tossed her racquet from one hand to another. "There," she said, "De Greve has won his single." And then, as if the idea had in that moment lightly brushed her mind: "But if there's nothing more than usual in the notion of his coming here, why the 'excitement,' Julie? You said he wrote as if he were excited."

"I think he was going into battle," Julie said, and repeated in a fierce agony of constraint: "I think he'll stay at the front."

"You mean——" van Arkel began.

"Does it matter to you what I mean? You are Dutch! You are grey and safe and neutral! You have nothing— nothing on either side."

"We are all Dutch," said her mother. "Is that something to be ashamed of, dear?"

"No."

"Then I don't think, my darling, you should have spoken as you did."

"You don't understand," Julie said, "how all this has been led up to. Alex and Sophie meant to make me speak as I did. Alex has been planning an English surrender for hours. He thinks that if the Germans come into Holland he would become a German Junker instead of a Dutch nonentity. And Sophie——"

"Julie, Julie, you are behaving like a child."

"And you are angry with me, mother, because I said I am English."

"It was not a wise thing to say, dear," the Baroness answered soothingly. "It wasn't even a true thing."

"No, it wasn't even true."

"Well," said the Baron, coming up with Ballater at his side. "What are you all doing here, fiddling while Rome burns? The family's been overthrown."

"We took it to five-all in the final set," Ballater exclaimed.

"And if I hadn't missed that shot at the net——" said Goof.

While they were talking, Julie rose and moved away. She stood alone at the head of the flight of steps leading down to the courts. Lewis could not deliberately join her to thrust blunt consolations into her secret mood. For a moment he imagined himself going up to her and saying— there was nothing now that he might say without blundering; she was entitled to her silences. But presently, having already passed her on the steps, he looked up and said: "Come and watch the tennis, Julie. You can't stand there in the sun."

"I think I'll go back," she answered.

"To the Castle? But you and Ramsdell have a match to play this afternoon. And, when you've won it, a final to-morrow."

"When we've won it! We shan't beat Sophie and De Greve."

Lewis had climbed over the parapet of the steps and was standing beside her. "You don't want to win?"

"On the court, I suppose I do. I suppose I shall want to beat Sophie, anyhow." She smiled for the first time. "But I can't sit here any more, Lewis. This is the third day. People are always coming up and hovering. Then they sit down beside me. I know beforehand what they're going to say. What a pretty ground with the trees round it and the Rynwyk spires looking over the trees! Then: what a successful tournament—in spite of the war! Then: what news have I had of my husband? Then—but you've heard it all. Do you know why they do it? Alex and Sophie have special reasons; some of the others, too. But the rest— they just want to know whether I shall be glad or sorry when . . . They think England's losing. Have you grasped that? Even the steadiest of them. Uncle Pieter doesn't say so. He goes on saying that, in the end, Germany will break. But he doesn't believe it as he did. Dozens of others, who haven't the van Leydens' character, are waiting to applaud. It's a sort of play to them. They're beginning to tell their neighbours what the end's going to be, and how they've known it all along. They want to know how I'm taking it." And, seeing Ramsdell beside her, she said, "Is it true what they all think—that England's beaten?"

"There's the fleet," Ramsdell said with a smile.

"And that's enough?"

"Quite enough."

"So simple?"

"So simple."

"Is that conviction or just blind faith?"

"Oh," he answered, a little embarrassed by her earnestness. "It's just what one feels and knows."

"You're very English, aren't you?"

"Thank God!"

She laughed and broke in her laughter. "Yes, thank God," she said.

Julie did not return to the Castle, for they might be called upon to play their match, Ramsdell said, before tea-time; and he added privately to Lewis that the game was already lost with Julie in her present mood. "What on earth you're waiting for," he said, "I don't know."

But Lewis waited, sometimes joining a group of spectators and yielding himself to the drift of their talk, sometimes encountering Julie as he moved from one court to another—a Julie seemingly transformed, the delight and provocation of whatever company she was in. If he went back to Enkendaal, the library would, he knew, be full of unrest, and he began to feel that the disturbance in him was so profound that it might be long before he could work peacefully in the library again. All his purposes were entangled, his spirit was set on edge, even his will was failing him. The restlessness of the tennis-ground taunted the failure of tranquillity in himself, and when Ballater said: "Let's go out into the town for a bit. I'm bored with this place," he went gladly. But as they approached the gates he swung round as though a hand on his shoulder had compelled him, and looked back towards the head of the steps. It was long since Julie had been standing there; he had met her in other parts of the ground; but he could not cease to look for her where she had last spoken to him, and suddenly, in this barren, glistening place, he found that, though he could not discover her with his eyes, she was in the air he breathed, so close that she pressed upon his thought, so ardent and pervading that there was terror, the dream-terror of a slipping personality, at the core of his delight. "You're very English, aren't you?" she had said to Ramsdell, and he heard again the word "English" spoken in her voice with a lilt of frivolity in it as a gloss upon emotion; heard it near to him, nearer than hearing, a sound within him. He saw the movement of her eyelashes on her cheek as she looked downward, the texture of her cheek itself, the hard, sudden gravity of her lips. The breeze that moved over him was enchanted by contacts with her; he trembled under it as if, by a miracle of communication, its touch were hers.

"I wish Goof and I hadn't lost that match," Ballater said, and their feet were soon crunching in step over the gravel. As they passed the railed municipal garden, where flowers blazed in geometrical patterns and an old man was dusting his boots with a tuft of grass, Ballater spoke again. "The trouble about a Dutchman," he said, "is that he makes his gardens with a T-square and a pair of compasses." And while they sat at a café their talk passed from Dutch gardens to English. "Nobody will be spending much on their gardens this year," Ballater said. "It will be the devil to get them into condition again after the war. They may never be the same again." A steeple near at hand poured its music upon them while they talked. At each quarter the sounds of the street were deadened by its chime, and Lewis, raising his eyes to the steeple, watched the birds take flight from it and return, a little flock of birds drifting in from the startled, vibrant air. At each ringing of the chime, they flew off in the same panic of flight; in each silence they returned. "You'd think they'd learn," Ballater said, "and either stay where they are or stay away. Queer things birds. . . . Probably they're not just frightened. The sound may hurt their ears."

At last, having set his wrist-watch by the great clock overhead, he declared that, if they were not to miss Ramsdell's game, they must go back. "The glare won't be so bad now," he said, as they passed through the beflagged entrance, and on the steps leading down to the courts he added: "I like it, brickdust and scarlet benches and all, at this time of day. Just when the light's changing but hasn't begun to fail. Particularly looking west. Our lawn in Wiltshire looks west over the valley on to the opposite range. There's a white patch in one of the hills, a great gash of chalk, and when you're having a latish tea the glare goes out of the white; it seems grey for a bit; and then gradually it comes up again as if there were a light inside it. That's why painting in England—Alison, what's that—news?"

He pointed to a little knot of people ahead of them, gathered behind one of the painted seats. In the centre of the group van Arkel held a paper in his hand, but soon he was hidden by newcomers. The players on the nearest court had broken off their game; the umpire had turned in his high seat.

"It can't be news," Ballater said. "It wasn't a newspaper he had."

"A separate bulletin," Lewis answered. "It's news all right." And Ballater, gripping him suddenly by the arm, cried: "My God, if it's peace we might be home in three days. Odd that we should have been thinking of it." He was about to run forward when Lewis checked him. Some intuition, some shock of foreboding communicated to him by the swirl of that little crowd, made Lewis say: "I don't think it's peace."

Ballater looked into his face. "If it's bad we'd better go slow—or let the Dutch bring it to us." Then, his eyes lightening again: "But why should it be bad? How do you know?"

He went forward and Lewis with him. Van Arkel's reading was done. The crowd was breaking up. Whoever turned and saw the Englishmen, twisted suddenly, looked away, pretended not to have seen. Lewis reading their faces—a sneer in some, a wondering compassion in others, in all the embarrassment of unspeakable disaster—drew

Ballater aside. "Better wait," he said. "We shall know soon enough."

And as if in answer to him, Julie's voice from a couple of yards away was saying:

"I don't believe it. It's no good telling me again, Sophie, I don't believe it. . . . Where *is* the lie?"

She was facing him, her back to the tennis. Supported by the railing, she stood on the piece of board that rimmed the court, and was raised above those who surrounded her. Van Arkel, a few feet beyond, had hastily thrust the bulletin into his pocket and was uplifting both his white hands to applaud a stroke in the renewed game.

"Mooie slag!" he cried, dancing on his toes. "Good shot, Mimi!"

"It's the Wolff Bureau," Julie said. "It's bound to be a lie."

But it was written in her face that she believed it. There was belief in the steely lightness of her tone, in the bracing of her body as though she had been struck. What Sophie and the Baroness were saying to her, Lewis could not hear. Their faces were turned from him; their words were lost in the mutterings, the questions, the exclamations of the crowd. But van Arkel's voice, high-pitched, excited, triumphant, was not to be mistaken.

"Why should it be a lie?"

"It's the Wolff Bureau."

"Do you accept nothing from German sources?"

Julie turned upon him with so terrible a mingling of scorn and anguish that, though he had not perhaps intended the full bitterness that had sprung from his words, he fell back from her. But she did not speak.

"I'm sure it will greatly shorten this terrible war," the Baroness was saying in a fluttering, conciliatory voice, and she put out her hand towards Julie as if she hoped to draw her away.

"It will. It will," van Arkel cried. "With the English fleet beaten, the war will be over in less than a week."

"What a happy ending," Sophie put in. "Think, in less than a week you may be in Germany again."

Julie was shaking her head. She was smiling and lifting her head.

"Even if it were true," she answered, "it wouldn't end the war."

"Even if it were true! What is the use of saying that? The British *communiqué* confirms it," van Arkel said, putting his hand to the paper in his pocket and patting it. "Do you think the British Admiralty would paint things blacker than they are?"

Whereupon Lewis broke in: "Will you tell me what this news is? I've heard nothing," and Julie, looking beyond the circle that enclosed her, saw him. Her eyes pleaded with him for an impossible revocation of the truth. Then she added, holding out her hand to van Arkel: "Let me see the bulletin."

A rule of honour, that had not forbidden him to triumph over Julie, caused van Arkel to hesitate before Lewis's question. He touched the paper, took his hand from it, felt for it again, and at last with a dry movement of his lips said:

"I've read it once. I'd rather not read it again."

"Give it to me, then," Julie said.

He yielded it to her. When she held it folded in her hand, she saw Ramsdell beside her mother.

"This is for you," she said.

Ramsdell knew nothing of what had passed. Opening the paper, he began to read aloud the British *communiqué* on Jutland, which laid so exclusive an emphasis on Jellicoe's losses that it gave to all who heard it an impression of overwhelming British defeat. He faltered an instant as his understanding of it increased, then, in a hardened voice, read to the end.

When he had finished reading, he folded the bulletin and handed it back to van Arkel. "Thanks," he said. Then, turning to Julie who had begun to speak to him, he cut her short.

"Come on. Our game's been called. I came to tell you." She did not move, seeming scarcely to have understood him. He thrust her through the crowd, almost with brutality. "Come on," he repeated. "For God's sake, Julie!"

"We're to play?" Lewis heard her ask.

"What else?"

She looked into Ramsdell's face, her eyes shining. "Just like that?"

"Just like that."

"Very well," she said.

Lewis stood with Ballater behind one of the scarlet benches, watching Julie and Ramsdell play their match. The Baroness was on the bench; through the mesh of her straw hat he could see her pearls and her fingers playing with them, shadowy fingers like the fingers of one's own hand seen through water. This hot weather always made her think of ice, she said. The skating at Enkendaal. . . . "You must manage to come up for the skating this year," she protested. There was nothing that could charm him more, the thin man at her side answered, "but in the winter I shall be in Hamburg, I expect. This news makes it certain."

"You mean peace."

"Well, but surely. They can't keep it up now. But how your daughter is playing! Look at that! You missed it?"

Ballater's toe was making patterns in the gravel.

"I don't believe that bulletin's complete," he said.

"Yes, I'm afraid I did miss it," the Baroness was saying. "When one has been watching tennis all day. . . . To and fro. To and fro. Tiring to watch, but tell me now——"

Ballater turned his back on the game. "I can't stay here. Why not go out and get more news? I believe the thing's a fake, Alison. Some kind of fake. If Jellicoe had been defeated, the Admiralty wouldn't advertise the losses in that way."

"Ah—a-ha—d'you see?" cried the thin man. "De Greve didn't know much about that. This is a game to watch!" He leaned forward. Ballater swung round to the court again. But the game was interrupted. De Greve was flourishing his racquet in the air and crying, with the angry authority of a champion, the spleen of a *prima donna*: "Send that man away. Send him off the ground. It is impossible to play," and in a moment the newspaper seller was being driven off the central path. Julie served. The game continued. The newsboy went, still shouting defiantly. "Groote zeeslag bij Jutland! Engelsche nederlaag!" . . . . "Great Naval Battle. British Defeat."

Did Julie hear? Perhaps she heard nothing. It's as if she were playing inside a glass tank, Lewis thought, sealed against the world, sealed against all emotion—she is so cold and set. Her successes she did not pause to observe; even a failure was marked by no word, no check, no sign. Her racquet swung, the ball flew. In her face was neither satisfaction nor impatience, only the composure of an accepted ordeal, a fierce ritual that was not a game. "Magnificent, Julie!" Ramsdell said, passing the end of the net as they changed over. She did not reply. She seemed not to be aware of him. She is playing without knowing that she is playing, Lewis said.

The Baron was beside him, gripping his arm, with the other hand gripping Ballater's.

"I've heard the news," he said. "You, of course, have heard it."

"Yes, sir."

"Believe me, I feel it as if it were my own inheritance. I love England." And he added with quiet humility: "But not as you love her. That goes without saying." His voice trailed away, the voice of a very old man. "But I make no doubt, gentlemen, it was a gallant battle."

He stood between them, his arms fallen limp at his sides, his head moving to and fro with the game.

"I could wish for you," he said. "that you were in your own country at this time."

She has no country, Lewis thought.

In Portsmouth, when the surviving ships came in, the crews must have landed among crowds that stood in incredulous, agonized, pitying silence. In imagination, he walked with the crews, his uniform a mark for pity, a badge of failure. In imagination he stood among the crowd, staring at the impossible defeat. "What has happened?" the children were asking—the smallest children even, aware that the world had fallen about them, were asking it with their eyes. No one answered them. No one dared to say with his lips: England has been defeated at sea.

When the tennis match was over and they ceased to stare at it, when the respite of its whipped excitement was spent, its tension broken, they would turn away from the court into a world changed in all things. Voices would be changed and eyes; the air would have a different taste, and time, weighted with dead pride, a different measure. Death is the incredible cessation of familiarity. A cup is a different cup because the dead cannot use it again; a window cannot be looked from because the dead will never again darken it. Strange cup; strange window; strange, persistent, assaulting clock; strange sea and meadows; strange world with empty hands, expressionless eyes. A void suddenly. An emptying away of life. Now in England is the death of the one absolute assurance, the faith of all men's childhood.

But now, with that death in their hearts, all Englishmen are one. The disaster is irretrievable; by a miracle it shall be retrieved. That spirit, which, in the first August, ran through England like the shiver of passion in the blood, moves again in her, a spiritual pulse that victory could never have stirred. "I could wish for you that you were in your own country at this time." Julie has no country, Lewis thought. Even in the hour of death, she is outcast, even from the community of despair.

"Three straight sets!"

"Brava! Brava! Brava!"

"Poor Sophie!"

"But Julie has never played like that before. It's as if . . ."

"Brava! Brava! Brava! . . . My God, what's she doing?"

"She's going on!"

"She's waiting to serve."

"Well, but—doesn't she know the game's finished?"

Ramsdell went over to her and touched her. She looked at him, recognized him, dropped the balls she held in her hand. She was crossing the court. Her face, brilliant with suffering, advanced out of the crowd.

"Lewis, take me away. Take me now—away."

CHAPTER SEVEN

THEY had been so long silent in the car which brought
them from Rynwyk that, when they reached the gate of
the cottage, they seemed to be locked in silence.

While the car had been moving, and the white streak of
road had continuously widened and engulfed them, and
elms, sweeping up from the miniatures of distance, had
continuously stretched at the sky and tossed their heads
and disappeared; while he could see, whenever he looked
down, her hand curled over the edge of the leather cushions,
gripping them, vibrating, lying there always as if it would
never be lifted, Lewis had been reposed in time's little
suspense, which is speed—speed that says: you may rest
until I have done with you; then take up life again. They
had sat side by side without speaking and without knowledge that they were not speaking.

When the car stopped, the trees became still, peering
down, the road stiffened and the birds asked quick, fluting
questions of the air. The air, which had been a rushing
wind that swept thought backward like the long hair of a
runner, lapped gently on forehead and wrist and cheek,
and waited. She stirred in her place; her hand no longer
interrupted the high light on the polished leather, which
lay empty, awaiting another passenger. She alighted and
stood and waited; the driver turned his head to look at
them and at the sky; and silence welled up out of their long
silences and imprisoned them.

She stood near by while the chink of money handed to
the driver mingled with the lisp of the hedgerow; and
Lewis was awkward with the coins, it seeming strange to

him that they should be there now, hard and warm from his pocket, milled on the edge or with the oiliness of nickel, like other coins at other times. The car would drive away with a little spit of rubber and fine gravel—one of those common sounds which, like the slither of a nickel coin, one doesn't notice in dreams—and its going would be his signal. He would turn and find himself alone with her.

When he turned, and the spit of gravel, an echo from a distant past of thought, was in his hearing, she was already advanced up the drive. Her back was towards him and her shadow was curling over the pebbles and over the low, grassy bank at the edge of the wood bordering the garden. It was easier to pass her than to walk into the cottage at her side, so heavily would their silence hang over them if they went in together, and he strode past her, saying in his mind: I'll go first. I'll lead the way, but saying in words nothing. "I'll lead the way"—as if they were going into a dark place, as if the passage and the stairs were dark. Below him, when he was on the stairs, he heard her say: "I'll leave my racquet here, Lewis. Remind me when I go?" and he remembered that she was in a white frock and a soft white coat and carried a racquet like other women at other times.

In the sitting-room he moved a chair for her, but she went beyond him to the window and stood by it looking out, a being, in her white dress, of more substance than his imagining of her, of more substance than her surroundings in this familiar room, grown now unfamiliar and ghostly; and he trembled in the thought that she was indeed present with him in the body, that her mind also was filled with expectation of what their silence must yield, that she too was feeling, with his own incredulity of the senses, the touch of sleeves on her arms, the weight of her clothes upon her, the thousand fragmentary contacts that were marking for him the tension of those instants. Soon they would sit down and try to talk calmly together. She would sit with her elbows on her knees, her hands clasped before her, her eyes looking out over her hands—the familiar

attitude which, though not distinguishable in form from
the attitude held by a thousand others who had the same
trick of clasping their hands before them while they
talked, was yet her own, having upon it the mark of her
character, the unique imprint of her grace. Thus she had
sat long ago, when she was a child. He saw her long, black-
stockinged legs, her wrists thrust forward out of buttoned
cuffs, her long hair, divided at her neck, hanging vertically,
a double curtain to her face. Thus she would sit now, he
thought, but while the image was in his mind she said
without turning:

"Now we've escaped, Lewis, there's nothing either of
us can say." And when he had crossed the room and was
standing behind her, she added: "It's because we haven't
really escaped, isn't it?"

"Yes, Julie."

"But if it weren't for me, you might escape. It's possible
for you—even now."

"To become indifferent?"

"To the casual things—yes. To make a world of your
own that the world can't touch. O Lewis, my dearest one,
if you knew how little I want to burn and torment and
destroy you," she said, turning towards him but not looking into his face. "I want peace, for you and for me,
and, if not for me, then still for you. Do you remember
that night at the Castle—Sophie's birthday—going in to
dinner. I felt suddenly that because you had come into
Holland I wasn't alone any more. It was all peaceful in me,
then. And in the months since, it has always been easy to
pass to and from you—to you when I needed you, from
you again when I chose. Perhaps because I'd known you
ages ago, I had set you apart from other men—and I loved
you in a way, and I teased you, and I loved and I teased
you because you were aloof, partly—a challenge, I
suppose."

She was trying to laugh, to speak easily, as if of easy
things, and Lewis touched her shoulders to check and
steady her. "Why should you tell me this now?" he said.
"It's useless, Julie."

"Because it's true," she answered, "as true as I can tell. And because I'm telling myself while I tell you. . . . Even up to this afternoon, I was—what I've told you. At least, I think so. And when I came off the court, still I didn't know. I was frightened; everything had crashed. I was cold and frightened and I came to you. But in the car I knew that not you only but I—my God, Lewis, my dear, my beloved one, I never knew that I could be mad as I'm mad now." Her voice had fallen. "And even while I'm saying it, I know I don't love you as you might some day love me."

"As I do love you, Julie," he said.

She raised her eyes to him. He saw fierceness and hunger in them that transformed her, making her at once so terrible and so beautiful that the little space between them seemed not to be a space; she seemed to be already in his arms and their bodies to be one body. But he could not take her to him for she was aflame, as if he had struck her and she were waiting with fear and longing for him to strike her again.

When she had moved from him and sat down, clasping her hands before her, she continued in a new voice: "Half of me is worthless, more than half, I think, and you could never love me until you had made me anew." And she smiled: "You stand over me, watching me, as if there were no evil in me. You think there is none in me, because there is none in you. I could kneel down and worship you, but while I was kneeling I should be quivering for the touch of your hand and, if I hid my face in your shoulder like a child and took your strength from you, in my mind——"

"Julie," he cried, "you are telling lies of yourself. Be quiet. Say nothing. You are saying things that will make you hate me for having heard them."

She would have spoken again and he lifted his hand towards her mouth as though to cover it; but his hand swept upward and he covered her mouth with his lips. Far below him, he saw the whiteness of her dress break in the floor's shadow, and he became still, searching for her individuality beneath the fiery cloud that had enveloped her, seeking his love and knowledge of her within the agony of sensual confusion by which he was possessed.

With a low cry of the breath she fell from him and knelt upon the ground and sheltered her face in her hands.

"From the beginning, I knew. From the very beginning I knew. From the very beginning," she said, after a long silence.

She lowered her hands and stared before her, feeling that in some way which her most secret heart could not express she had lost the only companion of her life, and that the man standing above her was a stranger; that henceforth only his body could be familiar to her; that she had driven out a spirit and was alone in the room and alone on earth. She did not accuse herself; she had passed beyond accusation and judgement. She was cold. And into her coldness, like the run of colour in a tempering metal, there flowed the thought that while she was kneeling he would stoop and touch her, and hearing him move she shuddered, until at last she was lifted up.

Now, seeing that he was no stranger, that he had neither contempt for her nor pity, but love only such as she knew nothing of, she suffered herself to be gathered coolly into his arms and lifted her mouth to him in a wondering innocence that was to herself a mystery. So gentle was he and so silent that tears came into her eyes, and when he released her and would have her go from him, she gave him her hand and was led out like a child.

But in the Castle, alone, she saw, or thought that she saw, the truth, and she took a pen and wrote—in cruelty or renunciation or compassion or love—begging that he and she might never again meet, that he would go from Enkendaal. She sent the letter by a servant instantly, that she might not recall it.

III

THE FLIGHT

But O alas, so long, so farre
Our bodies why doe we forbeare?
> DONNE: *The Extasie.*

CHAPTER ONE

"THEN Alison won't come back," van Leyden exclaimed when Ramsdell said that he was taking Lewis's place in the cottage. "What is the meaning of it? What's he going to do with himself now?"

"He is taking lodgings at Groenlingen, three miles from Leiden," Ramsdell began to explain. "When he wants to; he can get in to the University."

Van Leyden swept his explanation aside.

"I know. I know all about Groenlingen. A cousin of mine has an estate near by. . . . But taken lodgings, has he? Settled down? In his letter to me he said he was going to Leiden to get in touch with the University—there were books he wanted, scholars he wished to consult. A few days in a hotel, I imagined; then back to Dirk's papers. But this sounds as though——"

"I don't know about that, sir," Ramsdell replied hastily, taken off his guard and eager to support whatever excuse Lewis had given. "Perhaps he does mean to come back."

The Baron greeted this with the whinnying noise that was provoked in him by all unreason. There was not, he knew, comfortable room in Kersholt's cottage for more than two officers with their servants. He turned on Ballater. "If Alison had meant to come back, you wouldn't have taken a new partner in your *ménage*, eh? What have you done—quarrelled? You knew he would never come back— never. Did *you* know, Julie?" The onrush of his irritation saved her from need to answer. "All his work thrown away because of some silly quarrel between you young men. I hate to have work interrupted. I hate waste."

His word "never" tingled in Julie's mind as the return-ing blood tingles in a limb that has been dead; and stand-ing at her mirror one morning, still flushed by her waking dreams, she saw her face, so long impassive, so long remote from her like a stranger's face, crumple, and tears grow in her eyes and overflow. In an instant the tears were hot on the hands in which she hid her face; over the throbbing of her naked shoulders she could feel her hair's movement. She sank down beside her bed. The floor was hard under her thigh, the scent of blanket in her nostrils.

That Lewis was gone, not to return, was of her own will, which was unchanged, she had said again and again. The word "never" was of her own choice, and her reason did not revoke it. But the idea behind the word, independent of will and reason, had now a terrible fertility in her imagination. Shaken by a deep, slow sobbing, she seemed to herself to be crying aloud, but she made no sound and at last the convulsions of her body ceased. Emotion was emptied from her, her limbs slackened, she began to know her own paroxysm, and criticize and be ashamed of it. Lifting her head, she saw the shadowed clefts and bulging whiteness of the pillow above her, the tapestried hangings of the bed, the flattened vaulting of the roof, and for an instant observed with wonder and anger the girl crouched at the bedside whose abandonment was a denial of the control traditionally hers. She rose, commanded herself, bathed, dressed, and went down to breakfast with her mother and Sophie.

"What are your plans for to-day, dear?"

"I shall ride after breakfast," she decided, and, having rung for Jacob, ordered her horse.

"You will ride with a groom, Mevrouw?"

"Alone."

"Good, Mevrouw."

Her mother, who was reading a letter, said without looking up from it:

"It's hot to ride, dear. Don't tire yourself."

And Sophie added: "You look pale, Julie. Didn't you sleep well?"

In the hall, while she waited for her horse to be led round from the stable, she moved her toe within her boot, invisibly tapping her impatience. She had sent out orders while she breakfasted, and now nothing was prepared. She remembered how once, in Prussia, Rupert had been compelled to wait for his horse, and with what a sudden outbreak of fierceness he had turned on the groom. "They expect it. It is necessary," he had said to her afterwards, "because they expect it. For no other reason. Violence is as distasteful to me as to you—more distasteful, perhaps," he had added with a shrewd smile and a glance that searched her eyes. "The English are not so mild as their polite manners suggest." He had tapped her shoulder and kissed her. "Particularly English women." Remembering this now as she looked out over the garden and the lakes, she felt behind her eyes and in her throat and breasts that stabbing of needle points which was, in her, the prelude to anger, and she knew not whether she was angry with the groom for his delay or was whipped by the memory of her husband's custom of tapping her shoulder. How serious he had been! How serious with her always, though with others he could be gay and light-hearted. If he had played at love, she too might have played and been happy. "But you are not pretty as other women are," he had said once. "You are beautiful, Julie, and for me you are sacred." Sacred! She had mocked the word when he had first spoken it. "Sacred——!" He had taken her hand and kissed it with a tender embarrassment, and had frightened her by saying: "Into thy hands, I commend my spirit."

She remembered how the deep, still passion with which he spoke had made even these extravagant words seem simple and unextravagant, and with what gentleness he had for her sake tried to smile them away. They had smiled at each other and she had turned from his eyes, for she had felt that his love was making of her what she was not. She had feared his worship of her and his gentleness more than she would have feared any brutality in him; they had seemed to demand that she should outgrow her nature and be by his need and his imagination transmuted against her will.

Now, at this distance of time, when he had become for her a phantom, and their life together, though it might some day be resumed, a fragment of experience separated from her present knowledge of herself, she was able to obscure the power he had once had over her by thinking: I was a child and his solemnity overawed me. She could let him slide away from her mind. She could read his letters as though they were letters found in some old drawer, not written by a living man or addressed to her.

Why, then, am I made angry by recollection of his touch? she said, and, hearing the scutter of a horse's hoofs in the gravel, she remembered that it was the groom's delay that had roused her impatience. But the horse was so beautiful when he stood before her with the sun flowing over the silk of his flanks, and the stooping groom who mounted her grinned with such friendly complacence, that her anger was disarmed, and, seeing the man stand back to admire her—cap in hand, she felt even his admiration glow in her as she rode away.

At last, she thought, when she reached the moors and a scented breeze came to her from the pine-woods, at last I am myself again. She was glad that she had sent Lewis away. She was even a little contemptuous of him for having so readily obeyed her. What she had intended when she wrote her letter was still clear in her mind: to put from her the madness of the body that had beset her beneath his touch and in the shadow of his touch. Neither conscience nor fear nor the rule of her marriage had impelled her to write, but an intuitive resistance to an invasion of herself. Her decision had had as much and as little reason in it as the struggling thrust with which she would have striven to liberate herself from a hood drawn down suddenly over her head. In the cottage she had been powerless to resist. The thing had possessed her; for that reason she had driven it back when she might. It was stronger than she; therefore she had put it from her. Now she was free of it, she thought.

But above the rhythm of the horse the rhythm of her emotion continued, and she could not resist asking herself whether, if she had been free, she would have consented to marry Lewis. In the idea of herself as his wife there appeared (under her smile) an incongruity which—but the thought sped away from her. There had been no question of marriage; the love between them need have been no more than a shared interlude in their separated lives—a delicious game of love without real consequence, without solemn commitment, like the love in a play which is enchanted by its isolation. Without commitment, she repeated, and began to think of it with guiltless, almost frivolous, delight, as if the pleasures promised by it were the irresponsible pleasures of a dance or a kiss, sensual, gay, of their own hour, to be taken, enjoyed, passed over, forgotten. The imagining, because it was at once guiltless and sensual, caressed her as the sun caresses a naked body. Her eyes brightened, her lips parted, she was possessed by a sense of well-being and lightness of heart.

In the sparkle of impulse she had forgotten Lewis. Now she saw him before her as she had seen him in the cottage, and knew that, between him and her, love could never have been as she had been imagining it—a brilliant interlude without commitment. Recognizing the depth and pregnancy of his love for her, she was suddenly pierced by an enraptured fear such as she had never before known. Her husband also had had power to transmute her, to demand that in him she should surpass her own nature, but against his evocative influence she had fought stubbornly. She did not wish to resist Lewis but to yield to him, to increase to the stature of his imagining of her, to become his peace and reconciliation, not his torment. For an instant she permitted in herself recognition of this desire; then, with glittering eyes, repelled it. She was glad that he was gone, glad to be free. When, in the cottage, he had held her in his arms, he might, if this had been their destiny and his will, not have released her. But the instant had dropped into the past; she beheld it sinking as a stone, with diminishing gleam, sinks through clear water. The

instant was gone; she would think no more of it; but would
think—the edge of her rein bit under her fingers, deep
shadows of the pine-wood through which she was riding
wheeled and bowed and parted before her with sedate
mockery, and she remembered how the wayside elms, on
the road from Rynwyk, had stooped and danced while
he and she were driving towards the cottage. But she
would not think of the cottage or of how her arms would
have fallen to her sides as she swayed under his compulsion, and the window behind his shoulders have slid downward beyond her seeing until—— Her imagination was
reversed in anger against him. Her horse, emerging from
the pine-wood, swung from trot to canter, from canter to
gallop. She felt his body stretch under her. The wind of his
movement streamed in cool rivulets under the lobes of her
ears and swirled upward into the edges of the hair on her
neck. She drew rein gently, allowing the rhythm to break
like the dying of a sea, and when the horse was trembling
under her and his steam was spurting between the gloved
fingers with which she stroked his neck, she began to say
that she would write to Lewis so that there might be no
more expectation in their silence. She would say—but it
would be better not to write, for, if she wrote, he would
certainly reply, and to receive a letter from him. . . . She
drew herself up in the saddle and rode leisurely homeward.

One evening of mid-June, about a fortnight after the
battle of Jutland, Allard and his wife and the burgomaster
of Rynwyk dined at the Castle.

Before going down to dinner Julie read a second time
a letter that had been delivered to her during the day:

RUSTOORD, GROENLINGEN,
NEAR LEIDEN, 16th June

MY DEAREST JULIE,

Since I came here I have been telling myself that
we must leave each other in peace. That is why I haven't

written. But I can't endure that our parting in the cottage, which we did not know was a parting, should be followed by no word but your little note asking me to go. To-day I thought: perhaps this cold, blank silence eats into her as into me. I imagined you alone in the Castle, wondering why I had gone without saying good-bye, thinking perhaps that I went in a mood of bitterness or because I believed love between us to be a sin. None of this is true, Julie dear; it is the opposite of the truth.

What has been going on in my mind since I left Enkendaal I will not tell you now. If I tried to tell you, I should write what I must not write or, trying to be calm, should become your schoolmaster, floundering in philosophical autobiography—and you would laugh at me. O Julie, to hear your laughter again, even your mocking laughter that used to sting me!

But though, if that is your will, we may not meet again for many years, I want our parting to be a gentle one, clear in our own decision and untormented in memory, not clouded by an embittering silence; and I will say once that I love you—not that in a passionate instant only I was enchanted, but that I love you with all my heart— with a love, hidden in me, I think, since we read of Nausicaa together, that all my knowledge of myself strengthens and lightens and confirms. I am not torn and confused. I have been, but am not now. I love you and must say so, that you, knowing, may judge. What there was in me before is enriched and quickened by you; what has come into my life now is yours always, though you put it from you, because you have given it to me. And I ask for nothing except that, whatever way you take, knowledge of my love may go with you.

Forgive me if I do wrong in sending this letter. It is the last, unless some day, in peace of mind, you write to me. Do not, in any case, answer for a little while. Perhaps, in your own wisdom, do not answer at all.   LEWIS

She put the letter away in a drawer of her writing-table, but its voice remained an undercurrent of her mind. While she dined, phrases from it came to her out of the conversation that surrounded her—a conversation principally in French, for the burgomaster was French by sentimental allegiance, being one of those Dutchmen who are not content to be Dutch. After dinner, in the long room where coffee was served, he lifted his eyes over his cigar and said that Madame de Narwitz—if she would permit an old bachelor his privilege—grew lovelier every day, like the princesses in the fairy-books.

"But to become lovelier implies a change," she said. "What change do you see?"

"Well," he began, "this evening——"

"No, do not tell her of this evening," Sophie interrupted. "You will pay her compliments and that will be dull. Tell her what she was *before* you began to read the fairy-tale. That will be interesting. You dined here on the evening before the tennis tournament. What was she like then?"

"Shall I tell you?" he said to Julie, patting her hand in what he hoped would pass for a fatherly manner. "Then, my dear lady, you were the Sleeping Beauty. Now you are Beauty awake. Tell me what has awakened you?"

"Have you forgotten the fairy story?" Julie said.

"A prince?"

She laughed. "But of course!"

"But where is he?"

"Do you not see him reflected in my eyes?"

He threw back his head with admirable good humour and exclaimed in Dutch: "Myself! Ha! That is good! That is very good! How I wish it were true—if again you will permit a confirmed bachelor his privilege."

"The miracle you see can have been caused only by your presence," she replied, "for I am sure it exists only in your imagination."

"Well said! Well said!" he cried. "Did you hear that, Leyden? It is worth being snubbed with an eighteenth-century grace." He laid his hand to his mouth, and behind it said to Julie in a chuckling, shrewd aside: "If you weren't so clever and so pretty I should almost believe you."

During the long, tedious evening on the balcony, while

she gazed at the glowing tips of three cigars and listened
to a laborious discussion between Sophie and Allard's wife
on the propagation of tulips, Julie wondered whether there
was indeed a visible change in her and whether a purpose-
ful curiosity underlay the old burgomaster's compliments.
But soon her only thought of the burgomaster was that
the light from the room behind him had set a supremely
ridiculous aureole on his bald, tufted head. For his curiosities and for Sophie's keen suspicions, she ceased to care.
The tormented mood of that morning had gone from her;
Lewis no more appeared in her visual imagination; but he
was present in the lassitude of her body, the delicious lull
of her mind, the dreamlike indifference to all external hap-
penings by which she was possessed. When she moved
from the balcony to make the tea that Jacob brought in at
ten o'clock, and held, crooked over her finger, the curled
silver spoon which she found embedded among the leaves,
the scent of the tea and the energy of steam rising like
a pennon from the kettle seemed to be parts of herself;
she was fascinated by their intimacy, by their weaving of
themselves into the texture of her own emotion, and a little
sigh of delight and sadness broke from her which surprised
her hearing and made her smile. Was she delighted or sad?
She did not know. She was alive with a secret life independent of joy and of unhappiness; and when, after the
lights of the burgomaster's car had swept the avenue with
gold, she went to her room in the tower, she began to
write to Lewis with no thought but that he was at her side,
waiting for her to speak to him and touch him. "My dear
Lewis, This evening . . ." But there was a gap to be bridged
between this evening and her last meeting with him. To
see her pen check on the paper was to perceive the gap.
I will leave him in peace, she said. It is better that we
should leave each other in peace. She held the paper to her
candle and let it burn—like an actress on the stage, she
thought suddenly. But in life there is always more paper,
she added with a smile. Nothing is final except——. How
the edges of the paper wrinkled and sparked! A charred fragment rested on her forearm, so light that, when she closed

her eyes, she could not feel it there; and when she opened her eyes it was gone. Was there moon enough to see the water and the island? In an embrasure, feeling the warmth of her blood drawn into the cool stone against which she was leaning, she thought that to-night she would have liked to dance and hear music, not the whisper of her own solitary clavichord, but the sparkle of a harpsichord or the brilliance of violins. She would have liked to dance for long hours by candle-light, and in the morning, when she was tired, with the echo of music growing tired in her mind, strip and swim in the lakes about sunrise, watching the island afloat among straws of golden crystal, feeling the drag of cold water under the thrust of her striking arm.

CHAPTER TWO

IN THE LIBRARY,
ENKENDAAL,
Saturday, 26th October

MY DEAR LEWIS,

Your pen, your ink, your paper, your table, your library, and so there must be a letter to you before I climb my own staircase in the wall up to my own room. Whether you find it or not will depend on how much interest you still have in Descartes by the time he reaches you. Ramsdell told me to-day that, when he visited you, you spoke about the volume of Descartes with Dirk's notes in it, and just now when I was undressing I remembered. So I came down to find it. I don't know if you really want it. Perhaps I'm only using it as an excuse to end this long silence since you went. Sometimes I wonder why you did go. When I wrote, I think I expected you to disobey me. At any rate, though I wished you to go and perhaps expected you to, I didn't imagine you gone, I didn't imagine the summer and the autumn passing without you. Bless you, Lewis dear. My hand is cold and all trembling—this library is like an ice-well. I haven't said anything I wanted to say. I haven't even told you why I didn't answer the letter you wrote in June. Need I? I love you. Bless you and good-night. I'm happy and miserable and shaky. Perhaps you will never find this—and perhaps that would be best. I don't know.

JULIE

GROENLINGEN,
Sunday, 24th November

MY DEAREST JULIE,

Why did you send it in a book? I might never have found it—was that why? I suppose it was.

Three weeks ago I came in from a long walk to find on my table a parcel addressed in Ramsdell's handwriting. Inside it was Dirk's volume of Descartes with a letter from Ramsdell saying he had taken it for me from the Castle library and that I must return it to him when I'd done with it. I wasn't in a mood for Descartes; I had passed on to other books and other thoughts since Ramsdell visited me here, and I put the book on the window-sill, where it was soon hidden in the mass of stuff that accumulates in these little lodgings of mine. Now and then I have a grand clearance. I began one to-night and found Descartes. That was the end of my housemaiding. I sat down to read. Your letter tumbled out on my knees.

Your writing! I remember the first letter I had from you —in the fort. I didn't know you, but even then I could not escape from the mystery of your letter—a letter from a ghost that I could see and yet not see; your hand on the paper; your pen forming the words under my eyes; your eyes looking at them. And now—O Julie, to have lying before me now, on my table within reach of my hand, a letter from you! It's as if you were in the room. More than that—as if the secret of you, the deepest essence, were with me but intangible—the scent of unseen flowers entering an open window suddenly. You wrote from the library, cold, at night. But though I can perceive the cold and the dark, my imagination does not accept them only. I see you sitting on the library floor, the sun on you, while we talked of the seventeenth century; I see you moving with a candle from shelf to shelf with the shine of it in your hair and shadow flowing and leaping at your feet; I see you under the trees watching the tennis; coming off the court; sitting at my side as we drove up from Rynwyk; walking ahead of me up the path leading to the cottage: and all these imaginings are one imagining from which you emerge, the quintessence of a thousand meditations, a reality greater than the reality of one thing seen.

There has been a gap in my letter—three hours and more. I couldn't go on. I have been walking in the meadow outside the house, where the trees are crackling in a frosty wind as though the branches were hung with icicles. And I have been staring at your letter and staring at the lamp and still I can't easily go on. I don't know your calm mind, Julie. I don't know what you would have written if you had written to me—not to Descartes.

I will tell you why I went away more than five months ago. Partly because you were a woman and the choice was yours—a conventional reason; partly for another reason that was my own. I can write of it coolly now; then there was little left to either of us but intuition. Your intuition was to send me away. You wrote your letter at once, without hesitation; you didn't think it out—you sat down and wrote; within an hour Jacob had brought it to the cottage. My intuition confirmed yours. I could not see. I knew that our love had become a greater or a more trivial thing than either had formerly understood—all or nothing. But I could not see or distinguish. I felt, but could not judge.

Love, friendship even, every intimate association between two people has, I believe, an underlying substance— think of it as a separate personality (the metaphysicians, if you'll forgive them, would call it a hypostasis)—which is distinct from their separate personalities, though it has proceeded from their mingling. To betray or confuse or corrupt or belittle it is the unforgivable sin. So I believe. I do not believe that the bodily delight of love is a sin, but that it becomes a deadly betrayal wherever a human relationship is obsessed by the acceptance, or by the desire, of it. Either you and I were by our discovery of each other made gods with power to create, in our relationship, a perdurable essence, higher than ourselves, independent of our delights, or we were animals caught in a trap. Either our beings would grow, and move towards peace and stillness through our love and because of it, or be wasted in a trivial passion. Our love was a predestined force that would create of itself a personality—a hypostasis—more beautiful and vital and lasting than ourselves, or it was a sterile pleasure, no more. I wanted to know and judge of ourselves. I say: "I wanted to know and judge"—*then* I wanted nothing but to be near you, to abandon all thought in desire for you. But my intuition was to go, as yours was to bid me go. Since my going I have understood why I went.

Another gap. I have been in the meadow again, where morning is beginning, and I have read through what I have written—a letter broken into two pieces, your lover's and, you will say, your schoolmaster's. Whatever the consequence, it must go as it is. Without lying to myself and to you, I cannot mend either part of it. Even what your schoolmaster has written your lover has thought; that must pardon its stiffness. I said once that I would not try to tell you what had been going on in my mind, for you would laugh at me. I would rather be laughed at than deceive you, for now, even more certainly than before, I am yours.   LEWIS

> ENKENDAAL,
> *Thursday, 29th November*

MY DEAR LEWIS,

Thank you for your letter—such a strange letter, too; I imagine you writing it in your lodgings with books and papers round you in such heaps that you can scarcely see over them—into the world.

You tell me nothing of your work. I often think of you and the seventeenth century when I sit down to play on my clavichord. I don't play it often now. The evening is generally my time for playing, and often when I come to bed the fire is out, or almost out, in my little music-room. The weather is becoming very cold. Perhaps we shall be skating soon.

Some day, when you have nothing better to do, write and tell me how your book progresses. I shall always be interested in that. I suppose you will be a great man some

day, and that your letter, which I promise to keep, will puzzle your biographer almost as much as it has puzzled
JULIE

ENKENDAAL,
Friday
LEWIS DEAR,
I wish I hadn't sent that silly letter. It seemed so clever to me when I had written it. I was angry. I am always being made angry by you—just because I am so intolerably young, I suppose, and should really be happier if I were being made love to by little men who amused me and excited me and didn't make me feel as you do—and as my husband did in his different way—that the world is so much older than I am. I want to play and be happy for a little while—that's all; so you mustn't think I'm more than I am and must try to forgive me.

Because that isn't really all. That's the part of me that was made angry by your letter. But you know there's another part that was frighteningly proud because it was you that had written it. The austerity and quietness of it were you, really you. That's why I locked it away. Not for your biographer.

My own reply went off by last night's post. Now it's early morning. I crept down into the hall just now to see if my letter was still on the table; I should have taken it back, but it had gone. And it's too early to get up, so I'm writing this in bed, by daylight and candle-light—half and half.

I suppose our lives, yours and mine, are utterly different. Some day I shall go back to Prussia and settle down somehow with enormous dogs all round me, and I shall have to play cards, and we shall go to Berlin for a part of the year and to Munich for music and pay visits in the Black Forest. Of course everything may be different. Rupert has been wounded a second time; I don't know how badly; he says it isn't serious, but he says I'm not on any account to go to him. After the war, he tells me, we shall be much poorer than we were, but I don't know what that means—

he is always very careful to say nothing about internal conditions in Germany except that the "people are bearing everything with wonderful loyalty." I don't know how serious it is for people like us. I should hate to be poor, even moderately poor, in Germany. To me, as I remember it, it's all like an old-fashioned play, and in a play one must have the lead! And you will go on with your own life— Chepping and a dusty, inky office in Fells Square. Or shall you be able to give up the publishing business? I suppose that, like everything else, depends on how the war ends.

My maid came in to draw my curtains and was surprised to find me sitting up in bed. She has firmly taken my candle away. There is economy in candles, she says. Anyhow, I don't need it any more.

And so a new day begins. How lovely it would be if you were here! What came afterwards for me in Germany and for you in England wouldn't matter so much, would it? I should be able to forget there was a future, I think, but you wouldn't—and I love you the more because you wouldn't. Dear Lewis, remember me sometimes when it's all over and I'm in Germany with the dogs and the cards. And try to think that, though it may be the worthless part of me that wants you here now, it's not the worthless part that loves you—perhaps a little as you would wish to be loved. Write to me sometimes—a lecture on metaphysics or a lesson in Greek will do. I'll take it out with me on to the moors, and when I'm an old, old woman I shall unlock it and read it again and remember the smell of this candle-wick and that it's breakfast-time and I'm not dressed.

JULIE

GROENLINGEN,
Monday, 11*th December*

I haven't answered your two letters, Julie, my dearest. I have let them lie for a week—it must be more than a week—for the answer I wrote when I received them I destroyed, and until now I have been unable to write another.

To live alone as I do here, falling into bed after hours of silence and waking to silence again, is to acquire a new perceptiveness. Silence is not silent; you begin to hear and feel the growth of natural things; your finger seems to lie on the pulse of earth herself. Often I went into the grave-yard at Chepping when I was a boy, for I thought: Not this man or that woman, as they were in life, looks up at me through the grass, but beings who, in their long dark-ness and silence, have learned to see and hear as they could not on earth. If they are reconciled with the roots of trees and the bulbs of flowers and have heard the first movement of water under ground and have a community with the swiftness of fallen birds, rotted and buried from the eyes of men, certainly they must hear me, though I say nothing, and understand me, though all my thought is troubled and in confusion. And as I imagined then that the dead felt and saw, so I am beginning now to see and feel. A voice from the outside world stirs me as the wind a harp-string. And I seem less to hear what is said and to interpret it in its own terms than to receive the essence of the speaker. That is why I wrote what made you angry.

You are in this room with me now more closely than you have ever been. Your presence enters into me and becomes a part of me. And if I say only that I love you, I am using language of which my life has outrun the meaning. One loves what is external to oneself and you have ceased to be external to me. Yet there is no other language I may use, and the words arise again and again— I love, I worship, I desire.

I am filled with thoughts that delight and burn me, but I am filled also with expectation of such a tranquillity as I have always dreamed of. The burning thought and the tranquil expectation are enemies now; but they are inter-locked: without one, the other could not be fulfilled, and I would not have it otherwise.

When I think of returning to you, and of your receiving me, and of the miracle of seeing with my eyes the bodily presentment of what you have become within me, all my memories and half-memories of happiness, all my longings for appeasement of beauty, rise up to be fulfilled. It is very strange that I did not know I loved you when you were a child. There was a quality in you then which, without my understanding it, has always stood between me and any love but yours. When first I came to Enkendaal, almost a year ago, I did not know this, but I felt, when I saw you, an indescribable anguish of remoteness and loss. You belonged to a different world; you were very young, very gay, very scornful, with a brilliant arrogance; you made me feel stiff and old; I saw myself in the flash of your indifference; I knew—though the knowledge did not express itself in my thought—that it had become finally impossible that you should love me. And now you love me. In your first letter, in the Descartes, you told me this, but the words were like a song over the mountains: they seemed not intended for me. When you told me again, in this letter written by morning candle-light, suddenly the words were whispered in my ear and I could hear no other sound on earth. They shut out all else. I wrote to you in a madness—from the burning core of my thought; that letter I didn't send—I didn't finish it.

Still the imagination of your beauty is an epitome of every impulse of my senses since I became man. But the flame is not all of me nor all of you. As lovers, we may pass through and beyond it, not by its failure but by our supremacy over it. If this is not true, then love is corruption and there is no truth but in renunciation and no peace but in death; but in this world, truth resides in our perception of it. Our own judgement is our fate, in this as in all else. For those who, as I am, are freed—or exiled—from belief in immutable, divine commands, there is no rule against love, and no absolute duty of love but the duty to discover, and continually re-discover, its quality, whether it be a greed only and sterile or of the spirit and fruitful. That is my belief, Julie. You must judge of yourself as I of myself.   LEWIS

ENKENDAAL,
Wednesday, 13th December

MY DARLING,

I'll write soon. I've read your letter over and over
again. I don't know what to say. It seems to want me to
feel and be more than I'm capable of. It makes me feel
mean and shallow, and whatever I try to write seems useless. So this is just to ask you to wait and not to think that
because I don't answer yet I'm not

Your loving—but rather frightened

JULIE

ENKENDAAL,
Wednesday, 27th December

LEWIS DEAR,

I think I can write now—at least, I'll try to. Such
a long time, you'll say! And it's true, I've been deliberately
putting it all out of my mind. We've had people staying
here for the skating, and then Ramsdell and Ballater and I,
and Goof and Allard and Allard's wife—and Sophie!—all
went to Utrecht and joined up with another party there.
We skated over the canals, miles and miles. Lovely skating! Have you ever used Dutch skates—a very fine knife-
edge and loose under the heel. You get a swing and rhythm
you don't get any other way. It's like playing music on the
air.

We were away for three days, putting up in an hotel
one night, and on two nights in country-houses where we
picked up more people. It's a good winter for those who
have fuel enough. They were short in the cottage—in fact,
they ran out altogether, but Ballater was so proud of his
housekeeping that he wouldn't say a word. They lived
a kind of secret Esquimaux life on an oil-stove until I
found them sitting round it in greatcoats—Ballater ill and
Ramsdell shiveringly looking after him like a hero. I told
Uncle Pieter. Now he treats them as he treats the whole
village, the whole Enkendaal estate. No one there is ever
allowed to shiver or be hungry. Mother has thousands of
eggs in pickle. She gives them away—and much else—and

loves it! And Uncle Pieter cuts down his woods. It's something to live on an estate where the landlord really does regard his landlordism as a sacred duty—or not even a duty, but as part of the natural, inherited obligations of the head of a vast family. He won't hear of subscriptions by other people or help from Rynwyk. The Enkendaal people are his people. When there's need, everything he has is theirs—just as much as if they were his children. They adore him, and the queer thing is that he's scarcely aware that in this world he's fast becoming unique.

All that sounds as if I were still putting off what I have to say. But it's all mixed up with what I've been thinking about—I mean, the difference between your world and mine. For Rupert and Uncle Pieter are linked in a way, though utterly different as men. If we come down to hard realities, I'm linked with them.

I know I'm often provocative and maddening—all hot and cold. Now I'm going to strip myself of all that, as far as I can. I must. We've got to understand one another, Lewis. Your letter, that makes me love you and fear you and fear what I've done to you, has so much more in it than there can ever be in me that it makes me feel little and ashamed. I don't deserve to be loved as you love me—or as Rupert loves me. There simply isn't the stuff in me unless people bigger than myself imagine it in me and draw me up, as it were, to their imagination; there's something in me which responds to that—no more, Lewis dear. But at least I can stop myself doing you a damnable wrong because I've let you misunderstand me. This is going to be a candid letter, on my own plane—perhaps an unlovely letter, I don't know, but a true one, because I do love you.

In the great world—I mean the international great world, Rupert's, Uncle Pieter's, mine too now—you don't marry for love or, if you do, only exceptionally and by chance. It's not the rule, it's not even the recognised ideal, as it is in professional, middle-class England. No one expects you to. That sounds very harsh, but it's not unreasonable and not at root unidealistic. There's a difference of ideal, as there's a difference of tradition, and I always believe that the value of ideals lies less in the nature of the ideals themselves than in the fact that people will suffer and discipline themselves and perhaps die for them, whatever they are, good or bad. Notions of good and bad change from age to age and between country and country. There's little that's absolute except the power to stand firm by what you *do* believe in. That seems good to me.

And you can't keep property together and preserve a privileged and responsible class without always putting the necessities of the class and the family before the loves of the individual. Particularly that's true of a country like Holland, where all the property *can't* be left to one child, but must by law be divided and redivided. The redivisions have to be cancelled out again and again by marriage settlements. If the Leydens had married for love, though their sons might have brought in new wealth of their own making from Java and elsewhere, they'd have ceased to exist as a family. Good or bad, their tradition would have gone. I think it good—socially, morally, every way; but whether good or bad, there it is—it's their ideal. It's what those who believe in it have to stand by, and do stand by, often at enormous sacrifice of their own inclinations. Uncle Pieter married Mother for love; but not until he'd gone through years of self-denial and was a widower *de convenance* with heirs *de convenance*. I've always felt as if I were a bastard child in this place. It has often made me desperately unhappy, but I see their point.

The whole aristocratic tradition would smash if marriages weren't still largely the affair of the family council. It isn't now, on the surface, as arbitrary as it was. It doesn't say: Mademoiselle, you are to be married next Monday to Monsieur Un Tel, though to you he's an ogre. But it still counts the quarterings and the hectares. It doesn't command and bully you any more; you can go to the rabble if you've made up your mind to it; but it makes it pretty clear to its young women that, though they needn't marry a man they loathe, their choice is narrowly limited. People who are not, as Uncle Pieter quietly says, "one of us", may scoff and may be genuinely disgusted. They think of the aristocratic system as an unromantic greed for power and property or as mere empty snobbishness; but it's not that; there's too much sacrifice and suffering wrapped up in it; at heart, it's much less snobbish and selfish than many so-called romantic marriages. I respect it. Anyhow there's nothing mean, and something rather magnificent, about the self-subordination, nowadays much more than half-voluntary, of the younger generation—girls particularly—a kind of tight-lacing of their own impulses. Girls particularly, because love outside marriage, which is an implied balance of the whole system, is still much harder for them—without bringing down the whole pack of cards.

I'm not going to bring it down, Lewis. That's what I've had to make myself say. And it's been hard for me to say because I'm still English enough to know and feel the arguments of the other side—that I won't come into the open, that therefore my love for you must be selfish and contemptible, that I'm willing to deceive my husband and go on living with him afterwards because I know which side my bread is buttered. If you see it in that light, you will despise me and not answer this. That will be the end for us, and I suppose, if I am as hard-minded as I'm trying to be now, I shall call myself a fool ever afterwards for having written this letter instead of deceiving you. But there's the truth for you to judge me by. I love you as I have never begun to love anyone. But I don't mean to break up my marriage. By standards that are not mine, I may be "deceiving" my husband, though I never loved him or pretended to. But I did go into my marriage, with my eyes open, on certain terms clearly implied—that I wouldn't disgrace him openly or let his tradition down. I stand by those terms and I should stand by them just the same if he became poor and had nothing to give me, and I'd stand by them even if I knew that he had taken mistresses.

Oh, my dearest one, I'm saying it all so badly. It sounds so cold and calculating, but I'm trying to do in my own world what you went away to do in yours—to see the whole thing plain, and, though I love you tormentingly and love you with all of myself, and sometimes so much that I'm ashamed of wanting you as I do, I know it's true that, after this interlude—the war—is over, my husband and his world, which are my realities, as this love of yours and mine is a lovely, magic dream, will claim me again. I shall go back, carrying with me one long, deep, happy secret— still the most precious thing in my life. But I shall go back and live in that great castle of his and be not ashamed of my secret but proud of it. There have been secret and passionate loves there before; he knows it; but he's been so proud of telling me that there has never been an open scandal or any slur upon his race. It's a real pride; not petty and personal and jealous, but representative of much more than he is or I am. I'll not break it.

If he didn't love me, I shouldn't have a fragment of doubt. It happens that he does. And—this is harder to say than all the rest put together—that, to me, is the more reason for secrecy. Every letter I have from him shows me —so that I can scarcely read them if I once remember that they are addressed to *me*, and that he's real and not just a far-off, impossible ghost—every letter shows me that he loves me, or something he has imagined in me, more and more. It's horrible. He has suffered so much. And he's built me up into a kind of idol in the midst of all the mess of his life and—but it's all unreal, Lewis. I don't love him. Sometimes I think he's almost mad. Perhaps he'll go mad. I don't know. But because he loves me, I'll not hurt him personally; he needn't know; he can't ever know.

Now you know what I feel about the impermanence of our being together—you and I. There are people who be- lieve that love isn't love that doesn't contemplate an ever- lasting domesticity. And there are people who believe that there are direct commandments from God which make love between us a mortal sin. And there's a whole world in England—your world, Lewis; I remember your mov- ing in it with a queer air of being detached from it and yet of being tied to it—there's a whole world of people

who think quite differently from me about all these things,
and would be far more ready nowadays to forgive a woman
who faced a public scandal in order to marry her lover
than a woman who kept her secret. They think of the
scandal as a badge of courage—anyhow a mark of sincerity.

You have never told me what you feel about this. Your
letter is out of my reach sometimes. I can't apply it to
what's in my own mind. Does it mean that what we do
we are to do openly? Why do you love *me*? I am so different
from you. Do you love me? Yes, but how? Tell me, please
tell me, how we stand with the world. I'm not a goddess,
Lewis. I'm very little of what you think me. I'm a girl
who loves you and wants to know what you expect of her.
Tell me, Lewis dear, and don't despise me. In my own
way I'm trying to judge of myself.

Julie

Groenlingen,
Friday, 29th December

Forgive me, Julie. There was no need to write the letter
you call unlovely; I ought to have made the answer clear
long ago. From the time when you were a brilliant, impetuous child, I have known how far separated our worlds
must always be. I don't mistake myself—or you. It is not
conceivable, unless a miracle were worked in both of us,
that you could be happy as my wife. My existence after
the war, as I imagine it now, would be prison to you, and
I am not made to be the gaoler of you or any woman. If
we are lovers, I shall enter into the legend for a little while,
and a legend may continue though the book be shut and
taken away. Our care will not be an impossible reconciliation with the world. Our love will be ringed about in time,
having a perfection which, when the ring is dissolved, will
change its form but not cease to be.

Why do I love you, you ask, and in what way? It seems
strange to you that I, who have so long cultivated solitude
and austerity, should be able, without denial of myself, to
love one whose life belongs, as yours does, to the world.

It seems stranger to me, Julie, that you should love such a man as I. That you should be interested by some quality of my mind and feel an affection, even a tenderness, for your schoolmaster, so little schooled in your graces, I can at least explain to myself. Long ago you had affection for me; you were willing to be in my company; if you had a question to ask, you were eager that I and no other should answer it; you sought me out continually; though you were a child and I was a man, we were deep companions. As we loved each other then, it is not inexplicable that we should love each other now. But that you should love me in the way you do now love me is a miracle that makes me hide my eyes from thought. It is as if I had suddenly discovered that the waves obeyed me.

How shall I tell you why I love you or with what manner of love? I know this—I know it now, though I did not know it with certainty when we parted—that my love is not a swerving from my purpose, but an enrichment and a balancing of it. Since I have been here, with knowledge of you within me, I have looked back upon my two years in Holland and have begun to understand how often, and in what ways, I have been foolish and arrogant. Often I have been most arrogant when I have believed myself to be full of humility; this is one of the great paradoxes by which all novices of the contemplative life have been beset. Once only, on my last day in the fort, did I attain to a distant perception of the way I must one day follow. I felt as nature must feel in the first death of winter.

You are the death of another winter in me. I looked for peace in solitude; it was thronged with prides and delusions. I looked for truth within myself alone, but the truth, which is in all men, was frozen deep in me and I had no sun to discover it. Now, because you love me, the winter of my soul moves from me and solitude is emptied of great perils. There is no surprise more magical than the surprise of being loved; it is God's finger on man's shoulder. There is no peace equivalent to the peace of loving; it is the sigh of a hated child who, laying his head upon his pillow, has consolation in sleep, passing from the blindness of life into the serene assurance of dreams. The beauty of this world is comprehended in you and the beauty of another prefigured. You are all the seasons of mercy. And because, like the seasons, you will pass from me, each hour that I am with you will have the double bliss of memory and experience.

When may I come to you?   LEWIS

ENKENDAAL,
Sunday, 31st December

LEWIS DEAR, DEAR LEWIS,

I am afraid of this love. I am so afraid—to let it go or to take it. I dare not take it; but to let it go, and then afterwards to look back and remember what might have been—that makes it unendurable to live. It makes a coward of me. I cannot bear to be a coward. But I cannot bear to be so much less than you think me. So much less and yet so eager to be all your   JULIE

Don't write yet. I'm going out for a great walk with Ramsdell. It's raining and sleeting but we shall go. When I'm back I'll write, or perhaps to-morrow. Bless you in the New Year.

ENKENDAAL,
Tuesday, 2nd January

DEAREST LEWIS,

We walked and walked, Ramsdell and I. He's a dear. He knows everything, though I've told him nothing. He talked about you.

Would it be possible, Lewis, for us to be friends? Then I shouldn't lose you altogether and perhaps you'd never know that I am—what I am. We could work together and be together. I'd work with you. You could come back to the tower where you were happy. Uncle Pieter wants you back. I'd work with you on the seventeenth century. I wouldn't spoil your work. We'd be together, and not just starve and starve, writing letters. And I should be hurting myself—which is something, which isn't just blankness and empty time crawling past—I should be alive again. Perhaps we should be happy.

And yet we shouldn't, I know. But we might try. And if it was impossible, you would go away again, perhaps. I can't think. Everything is in fits and starts. I'm crying now—almost; my pen is all blurred on the paper; and yet I'm in a kind of rapture, as if I were listening to music coming up out of the earth.

I'm going away, so don't write here. I'm going to the Hague with Uncle Pieter; he has to see the Minister of Agriculture next Friday, and we shall go to a concert I expect and pay stately calls.

Good-bye, my dearest, for a little while anyway. Everyone is talking round me. I'm writing in the room behind the verandah. Sophie is reading the *Handelsblad* aloud, and Allard is here; he says even cigars are deteriorating. Good-bye. JULIE

CHAPTER THREE

"IT is too cold for ladies to travel," the Baron said next morning, the third of the new year. "The trains are not heated," and Julie heard her mother and Sophie accept readily the excuse he offered them. A maid was summoned; their luggage was not to be brought down, but unpacked; the Baron would go to the Hague alone.

"But I am going," Julie said.

"You can't. . . . Why should you go?"

"Why should Uncle Pieter go alone? He hates being in towns alone."

He was at the window, the yellow skin of his forehead illuminated by the gleam of snow, his eyes screwed up against the dazzle of the ground and the metallic glistening of the sky.

"It's true I hate towns," he said. "But I have to go. Kind of you, Julie. But don't think of it. It's no weather for women."

"I want to go," she said.

"It's always the same with her," Sophie put in. "Anything to get away from Enkendaal."

The maid hesitated, uncertain of her orders, and the Baroness spoke with decision: "Unpack all the luggage." Julie, she thought, did not mean what she said.

"But I intend to go," Julie exclaimed. "I mean to go." The blood came to her cheeks, a tremor ran across her shoulders, and, seeing van Leyden's eyes shift at the disproportion of her emotion to its apparent cause, she understood, as she had not before, that to go to the Hague was not in her a whim but a necessity, the keeping of a pledge which now she knew for the first time she had given. What had she said in her letter? What, precisely? That she was going to the Hague; that Uncle Pieter had an appointment there on Friday; that they would go to concerts, pay calls. But had she said that it was to-day, Wednesday, she should go? She had given no address there. But Lewis would know to what hotel Uncle Pieter went always in the Hague.

The little dispute with her mother, Sophie's trimmed, contemptuous smile, even the lingering gaze of the maid-servant withdrawing from the room, filled Julie with the zest of conspiracy, and, in the hall, while luggage was being carried out, she looked up from a shoe-string she had stooped to tighten and smiled and said: "Shall we enjoy ourselves in the Hague, Uncle Pieter? I feel as if we were eloping."

The old man gazed at her. "That grey fur makes you rosy," he said, and, seeing her ankle: "But you ought to have gaiters. It is horribly cold. Sophie would lend you gaiters."

In the train, because she was with him, he would not smoke. His fingers pulled at his cigar-case and replaced it.

"But why not, Uncle Pieter? You do in the house."

"Not here," he replied stubbornly.

"Because I'm with you?"

He smiled his prejudice, but would not explain it.

"If I smoke a cigarette?" she said, and opened her bag.

"Ah, Julie! Not in public."

"But the carriage is empty."

He dragged his collar about his ears. "As you will, then."

"You forbid?" she said, the cigarette between her fingers.

"I forbid nothing to women. I ask sometimes."

She returned the cigarette, closed case and bag. "As we have only begun to elope, I'll obey," she answered.

A smile, concealed at the mouth by his coat-collar, appeared in the wrinkles about his eyes.

That night, after the guests he had invited to dine with him at the *Deux Villes* were gone, they sat together in the hall, drinking tea.

"What shall you do to-morrow, Uncle Pieter?" and while he told her his plans she thought: To-morrow Lewis will come; perhaps to-night by a late train, and, hearing the door swing, she turned her head in delight and terror.

"What has become of Alison?" Uncle Pieter said.

He began to talk of Dirk van Leyden's papers.

If it had been Lewis that had come in then, she thought, he would have been sitting now on that empty chair and I should have been saying: We will order fresh tea. But I should add: Let us have it in our sitting-room, Uncle Pieter; it is cold here. And perhaps, before it was time to say good-night, Uncle Pieter would go from the room for a moment, and for a moment we should say nothing; then, suddenly——

"It's too cold for you here in that dress," Uncle Pieter said. "You are shivering. Shall we go up to the sitting-room? We might play a game of piquet. Unless you wish to go to bed at once?"

"You love piquet?"

"I am very fond if it."

"So am I. We will play. First I will have another cup of tea. Then. . . ."

But though she sipped her tea until it was cold under her lip, the entrance-door did not swing again.

"You are playing piquet to please me," the old man observed as they went upstairs together.

"Nonsense," she replied with a smile. "It's a game that depends on one's company. It's a perfect game for an elopement."

They stirred a poor fire and drew chairs close to it. He shuffled the cards and, with his eyes on them, said:

"I wish you were happier at Enkendaal, Julie."

"I'm all right, Uncle Pieter."

He shrugged his shoulders. "Cut then, child."

While they played, she tried again to remember what had been the words of her letter. Were they, in effect, an implied invitation to Lewis to come to the Hague? She had not so intended them while she wrote. Or had she? Would she not then have been more precise? She trembled to think that, reading into her words more than they contained, he had yet decided not to come; her cheeks paled in anger against him; then, feeling suddenly that he was on his way to her, that to-morrow his eyes would be on her, she was unable to play her hand and her weight fell upon the back and the arms of her chair.

"Well?" said Uncle Pieter, and she began to play again, but had soon to confess that she was tired and go to her room. All the next day, walking or driving in the snowy streets, listening in a concert hall to Bach whose intellectuality seemed now frozen and barren, visiting in a drawing-room where an *attaché* of the German Legation bowed over her hand and awoke her suddenly by delaying his release of it, she was in an expectant dream, thinking that at the *Deux Villes* there might even now be a message for her. The *attaché* was a musician; he would, he said, play Debussy, for was not music international? The assembly was hushed; the last little golden chair had creaked and was still, when she, who was near the instrument, suddenly leaned forward and begged him in German to play, not Debussy, but Chopin.

"Chopin?" he said with scorn, dropping his hands on his knees, and she was so ashamed of her interruption that tears of humiliation and anger started in her eyes.

"I love Chopin," she said like a stubborn child.

"Ah," the German answered, "that makes of him a greater composer than I had understood."

Her wit had deserted her; she was silent; and the Nocturne he played stabbed her silence. But presently she forgot the gilded chairs and the eyes turned upon her; the music and her love of it prevailed.

"You were right, Madame; he is a greater composer than I had understood," the German said at last, taking a place beside her.

"You mean that? It's generous of you. I had no right to interrupt. You really believe it?"

"His beauty is established in its influence on your own. I can read it in your face."

He left her before she could reply and afterwards would play nothing but Chopin. He held her hand again in farewell.

"You are staying in the Hague, Madame?"

"I return to Enkendaal to-morrow."

"Alas! the greatness of Chopin will shrink when you are gone. He will become a sentimental memory."

She smiled. "Which is what you consider him?"

"In your absence."

"Then you have been the more generous in my presence. . . . But how do you play so well work that you despise?"

"I am a diplomat, Madame." He kissed her hand again. "And a desolate one. *Au revoir*. It is permitted to dream of the Nocturne, if not to play it?"

"If I could command the dreams of diplomats," she replied, "I should have Europe for my empire."

"*Mon Dieu, Madame, le monde entier serait à peine assez grand pour votre empire.*"

She was warmed by his flattery, not because she valued it or because she failed to perceive his underlying contempt for her race and judgement, but because to be flattered was to exist, to feel herself existing, to throw off, if for a moment only, the sensation, which chiefly tormented her, of being a ghost with no place in the world. Sitting in the hotel that evening before going out to dine, she tried to remember the sound of Lewis's voice, but could not; his face also was indistinct in her imagination; she could recall nothing clearly except his grip on her shoulders, the grip of one who had become invisible, who was, perhaps, dead. Dead? Or ill? Or gone away from Groenlingen? Perhaps her letter had been thrust under his door and was lying unopened. She looked up at the porter's desk, thinking that she would ask for a telegraph form, but to telegraph and receive no answer——. Her fingers tightened in her palm, and, having put away from her, in pride and fear, above all in weariness, the project of sending a telegram, she yet began to devise vain forms of words:

"Did you receive letter?"

"Am in Hague. Leaving Friday."

"Disregard letter."

"Please come."

"Don't come now."

She could send no telegram. There was nothing to say.

As though she had come out of a roaring tunnel into daylight and a relative quietness, she was suddenly able to be composed, to survey and criticize herself. I am going mad, she thought. I am behaving as people behave in newspapers and Elizabethan plays. A wry smile moved on her lips, soon banished by a feeling of profound degradation. Love, if this were love, was an ugly obsession, a screaming in the dark, and so far distant was the woman she had become from the girl she had known herself to be that she seemed to have broken adrift from her identity, from her tradition, from all her faiths and aspirations. If this is what I am, she said, I have nothing to offer him.

A man with astrachan flaps over his ears and a woman deeply wrapped in white fur turned their eyes on her as they passed through the hall—looking out of their own world as one looks out of a warm, closed carriage at a figure on the pavement edge.

"Ready?" said Uncle Pieter, standing before her with a pair of sealskin gloves tucked under his arm.

They drove out to a great dinner-party, given by the banker Penninck, whose wife, not his wealth, entitled him to ask van Leydens to his table. She was a second cousin of the Baron's dead wife and had been well widowed in Bavaria before descending to the Penninck establishment. A strange mingling of briskness and languor, Julie thought, looking into the hard, black eyes and hearing the mild voice that seemed incapable of expressing anything but charming indecision. "It's hard not to go there when they know one is in the Hague," Uncle Pieter had said. "But Lien is a dangerous fool, always pecking at politics. Don't believe anything she says."

After dinner, Julie was led by her hostess towards a sofa

set back in a recess beside one of the drawing-room fire-places, where no fire was burning.

"This is the Ruysdael we were talking of at dinner," she said, and when Julie had admired the picture and would have joined the ladies gathered round a fire some ten yards away, she found herself detained. "Let us sit here for a little while," Mevrouw Penninck said, "the room is warm," and she would not move until, when the men entered, an elderly German, with heavy veins in his cheeks and a collar that thrust little loops of flesh forward from his jowl, crossed the room and, halting before her, said:

"Ah! the Ruysdael. What an artist! He had everything except the vibratory quality of light."

Julie could not escape when Mevrouw Penninck yielded her place to him. He began at once to speak in praise of Narwitz, then in a low, intimate voice, of the blockade and its effect on Holland, of Enkendaal, of the English officers who, he had heard, were living there, of the wonderful influence that the Germans and English might have had on the world if they had been allies, not enemies. The pity of it! The English and the French were not natural allies. . . . From that he passed easily to the inconveniences of war. "A lady of fashion," he said, "who is accustomed to have her dresses made in Paris and has also a tailor in London—now, if I may ask, that dress is from Paris?"

"From the Hague."

"You do not go to Paris?"

"How can I? My nationality is German."

"Nor to London?"

"Of course not."

"I should have supposed that with your English blood that was a thing—*not impossible*."

His tone was not to be mistaken. He was inviting her to become a German agent. The elaborate ingenuousness of the manœuvre amused her and she turned her head away to conceal a smile. Might she not lead him on and then——. Speaking very softly, she replied: "Perhaps impossible—certainly costly."

His fingers closed on the sofa-edge and he propelled

himself cautiously forward, seeking her face. The eagerness of a fat man seated is expressed in the angle between
his belly and his knees.

"But means would be provided," he said.

"By my husband?"

A flicker of hesitation. "Yes," he answered, and she
knew that he was smiling over her subtlety and his swift
appreciation of it. "By your husband—if you choose."

Then, from enjoyment of her game, she was drawn into
fear. To lead him on further might be to learn more than
it was safe to know. Already, she thought, I have gone too
far and cannot withdraw without making a fool of him.
She imagined herself saying with unswerving solemnity,
with mock indignation: "Are you tempting me to play the
spy in the country of my birth?" and the phrase repeated
itself in her mind until she seemed to be hearing it spoken
again and again in some ridiculous melodrama of Wonderland. Her shoulders began to shake and would not be
stilled.

"You laugh?" he exclaimed. "I had supposed for a
moment that you were crying. But you laugh?"

"Oh," she cried, "you have misunderstood me! When
I said 'certainly costly'—I didn't, I wasn't thinking of——,"
and she began to laugh, silently but immoderately, with
laughter that racked her body and sickened her. Looking
into his face, she was seized by a new and deeper paroxysm
of laughter. The white satin stretched across her knees
shook and glinted; the pattern of the rug and the toe of
her shoe upon it became a leaping fantastication; the lace
handkerchief screwed between her fingers assumed the
shape of a small pig wearing a vast, frilled night-cap. To
one fragment of clear knowledge she held fast: that none
must observe her; that she must be silent; that, in all the
convulsions of laughter which was laughter no more, her
lips must not be opened. At last, controlled, she looked up
at the man who was standing beside her, gravely observant.
Her eyes were brimming.

"I beg your pardon," she said. "What can you think of
me?"

"That you are overwrought, Madame."

"Yes."

"And not only by what I ventured to say to you."

A parting of her lips, a quick movement of her breast, told him that his aim had been true. He could not resist saying—and watching for the effect in her—"We all pray that Narwitz may be safely returned to you."

"Thank you."

He bowed, and left her to examine the Ruysdael. While she gazed at the sombre canvas, seeing nothing but its darkness and a cloudy image of her own face, she thought how loosely adrift she was, how contemptibly alone, in a world where even a fool could so far misjudge her. She was without root or clan, unrecognizable, belonging no-where—without existence, she added suddenly. She was the wife of a man in whose reality she found it impossible, at that moment, to believe, and when she suddenly re-membered having felt the pressure of his hands and fore-arms on her naked back she shuddered, feeling that this was not a recollection of her own experience but of the experience of another woman who was dead. He would not return to her; she knew, as if the scene were reflected for her in the Ruysdael, that Rupert's body was lying now partly buried by earth; she saw the back of his head pro-truding and the heel of a riding boot. She imagined herself running to his side and kneeling on the loose earth; his head turned; his eyes stared at her. "Rupert!" she said, but he didn't hear her, didn't know of her existence, and, when he had faded from her sight, she saw, where his head had been, the face of the hotel-porter, who was saying: "Von Narwitz. . . .Von Narwitz. . . . No, there has been no message, Mevrouw."

"You will play bridge?" Mevrouw Penninck was saying.

Long afterwards, lying in bed, Julie was awakened, whenever she was about to fall asleep, by the same voice asking if she would play bridge, and in her mind she began to tap the glossy cards with her fingernail. She had not asked for a message as she passed through the hotel on her way to her bedroom, and in the morning there were no letters on her breakfast tray. Uncle Pieter knocked on her door when she was partly dressed. Covering herself, she admitted him. There was, he said, a train for Rynwyk at 4.17; their guests at luncheon would be gone soon after three; if she would have her packing done——

"It shall all be done this morning," she answered.

He looked at her shrewdly; then, picking up a fold of a dress that lay on her bed, asked:

"You are wearing this to-day—this blue thing?"

"Yes. Why?"

"What colour is it?"

"But—blue, Uncle Pieter."

"I mean—the name of the colour, the dressmaker's name."

"Why, powder blue."

"What shall you wear with it? What jewels?"

"None, I expect. Or perhaps my pearls."

"If you are nearly dressed and could come out with me—my appointment is in forty minutes—we could get a piece of sapphire—if you care for sapphires."

As a peasant buys live-stock, with knowledge, caution, a twinkling humour, he bought sapphires, leaning on his elbows across the jeweller's glass show-case, allowing the brooch on which his choice fell to slide from palm to palm.

"For the end of an elopement," he said. "It pleases you?"

"Uncle Pieter," she said, "it's lovely," and kissed him.

"But it makes you happy?"

"It's lovely," she repeated.

"Good," he said doubtfully, and drove away to his appointment, leaving her on the jeweller's doorstep with a little packet clutched in her hand.

Dark clouds, that clung together in stubborn wisps, were being dragged apart, and a pale, silvery sunshine touched the house-tops and floated down into the street. "The vibratory quality of light!" Her grotesque beguiler had known his Ruysdael; Ruysdael could not have painted this scene—the weak flash of enamelled motor-cars, the

low, silky gleam of shop windows, the fine, diamond dust
that seemed to be rising from the snow and dancing in the
air. Monet might have painted it if he had been persuaded
to forsake his open country, but even Monet could not
have communicated the glitter in the air; he would have
made one glitter of it, and have missed the fibrous quality
that gave it an appearance of being composed of innumerable sparkling filaments, swayed and shaken by the light.
She opened the case that contained her sapphires, thinking that they would have a rare beauty now, but they were
embedded in satin and shaded. She took them out and
placed them, at the base of the jeweller's window, on a
ridge of snow accumulated on the sill. The snow was soft
and loose. They sank into it, but, through the powdery
walls of their little prison, beams of light penetrated,
awaking, in the depths of the blue, greenish fires. With a
gloved finger, Julie pressed the snowy walls inward until the
sapphires were covered. "And now," she thought, "there
is nothing to do but dig them out again, and then———."
She took off her glove and thrust a bare, tingling finger-
tip into the snow.

Where now? The joy she had had in tasting the air was
gone out of her; Monet and Ruysdael were dead, the
clouds were drawing together, her finger-tip dully ached.
At her own dressmaker's no material would please her;
she could think only that beautiful dresses, like silvery air
and sapphires embedded in snow, were the pleasures of
happiness. All pleasures are, I suppose, she said. There's
no pleasure on earth that wouldn't be torment now.
There's nothing I want. There's nothing I want ever, unless———. And she saw herself sitting opposite Uncle Pieter
in the 4.17, and sitting beside him in the car that would
take them from Rynwyk to the Castle. "Well, dear Julie,"
her mother would say, "did you enjoy yourself at the
Hague?" To-morrow morning she would awake in the
tower and look out over the lakes. . . . Fool! Tawdry,
empty fool! . . . All books, all pictures, all nature, all life—
was the heart gnawed out of them all? She would go back
to the hotel and read. First she would ask at the porter's

desk—but she would not dare to ask, and to postpone her humiliation she entered a shop and said that she wanted an evening dress. The mannequins were sent for; dress after dress was brought out; she refused them all, then chose suddenly. She tried on the dress she had chosen. It was pretty with a diffuse prettiness that she hated, but the run of the satin under her hands momentarily soothed and delighted her. She paid six hundred gulden into a padded hand. ". . . Von Narwitz. . . . No, not van Narwitz. . . . Are you not Dutch yourself? Did you ever hear of a Narwitz in Holland?"

"*Pardon, Mevrouw. Mevrouw is Duitsch?*"

She drove back to the hotel and left her sapphires. The greater part of the morning lay before her. She looked at the clock behind the porter's head. Perhaps, she thought, if I went to the Mauritshuis and looked at pictures, I should forget that there are clocks; but the idea of going to the gallery did not tempt her, and she was about to abandon the project when a superstition possessed her that, if she went to the Mauritshuis, Lewis would find her there. She would look up from a picture to find him at her side, and she said to the porter: "If anyone should ask for me, say that I shall be at the Mauritshuis until noon."

He bowed and smiled, a distrustful, tolerant smile, but she did not now observe it. Her superstition had become an assurance; she knew that Lewis would find her; within an hour, her waiting would have ended; she was eager to be gone, the desire for decisive action hung upon her. And it was in a mood of elation, which she would not permit her judgement to examine, that she entered the gallery. There she hesitated. It was clear in her mind that the picture she wished to see was Bellini's "Agony in the Garden." She longed to walk past the sleeping apostles and the figure of Jesus kneeling on its little mound, into that unearthly landscape, and lose herself in it. On her way to the gallery, it was this picture that had hung in her sight, and now she remembered that it was in London, not in the Hague. There's nothing else, she thought; her hands fell to her sides; she stood, checked, as though a door had been slammed in her face.

Then she went forward and sat down before "Adam and Eve in Paradise." Her eyes sparkled as they moved with delight from the golden flesh of Rubens's figures to the gracious, smiling countryside that Brueghel had painted, wherein a lion, with grave scepticism, watched the kittenish gambols of leopard and tiger, and all the bright birds, the macaw, the peacock, were showing off their plumage, and the fish, perhaps startled by the yapping puppies at the brink of their stream and plainly determined to be in the picture, were conveniently displaying themselves in water so shallow that it concealed not a scale, not the edge of a fin. Even the owls had kept awake and the tortoise, careless of the guinea-pigs near by, was making what haste he could into the foreground among the flowers, but not so close to the flowers as to mask one of their petals or permit them to hide the pattern of his shell. Only the cats, into whose natures Brueghel must have had a critical insight, remained aloof, one sleeping comfortably on the branch of a tree while another, with happy indifference to the destinies of mankind, was rubbing his head against Eve's bare ankle while she gave Adam the apple.

Julie smiled at the friendly picture, and, when she had been seated a little while, she thought: What brought me to this when the Bellini was in my mind? I came here without intention and here I am—and how happy! Suddenly, how ridiculously happy among the fawns and the elephants and the swans! There was never a moment in which I said I will look at my Brueghel again, but I came to it instantly; and she began to ask herself what was the nature of the remembered delight that had compelled her to this picture without her having knowingly chosen her way. But she was tired in spirit, and soon was glad to accept her pleasure without pursuing the reason of it, and so was refreshed. It was long now since she had given rest to her mind's arguments. Day and night she had been troubled by her actions and the causes of them, which seemed to be working a transformation in herself; for she was still very young, and, believing proudly that her actions were dependent on reason for which she alone was responsible, was not aware how often she must be changed before she was fit to die. She had not yet that escape into humility which, in return for many hopes proved to be vain and in confirmation of different hopes fulfilled, the years gently and nobly give.

Velvet Brueghel's picture opened a different way of escape to her, for, though she might admire other pictures with more eager curiosity, she loved none so well as this, and works of art that men love are a cloister where they may have absolute retirement and a cooling of their fevers in this world.

Every man, who is not a devil, has his own retreat, his intact island, ringed about with the waters of the spirit, where he may live his own life and not be pursued; and from which he may set out on his own voyages. A saint vanishes thither continually; he walks upon the waters; the hounds check, and lose him; while they are sniffing the earth, he is gone. The simple have an island in their simplicity; children, whom our blind knowledge seeks to encompass, in the starry jungle of their imagination; and some find refuge in the natural miracles, in their secret woods and mountains, to which they flee, not to praise beauty that is of the eye, but to reaffirm a fealty of the soul, obeying joyfully in the midst of life that maternal summons of dust to dust which, like death's compassionate trumpet, is a supreme release from all claims. These sanctuaries of art and nature, these profound and vital illusions which, like the illusion of death itself, are preludes to rebirth, are necessary to them that have not the gift of holiness, for in these also there is confession without confessor and an engagement of the spirit with no arrogance in victory.

In every great work of art, Julie thought, an artist dies and rises again, and we, who enter into its illusion, die to this world and are reborn. Considering the work before her, she was aware of being received into it, as if, walking beyond the apple-tree and the coiled serpent

into the enchanted glade where since her childhood a
white horse had been waiting for her to ride away, she
left her former self behind, asleep on the outskirts of the
Garden.

And even when she remembered in how deep a persuasion of Lewis's approach she had entered the gallery,
and understood that he would not come; even when it
became clear that her assurance was delusion, a happy
delusion as her imagining of Rupert's death had been
unhappy, she was at peace, thinking: Perhaps this stillness
which comes to me in the companionship of Brueghel is
of the same nature with the stillness within the world that
Lewis is seeking, and I am nearer to him now than I have
ever been. . . . Perhaps there is in me, after all, a little
of what he dreams of and imagines in me. When I read
his letters again I shall not be a stranger to them or be
ashamed.

She returned to her hotel, put on the blue dress and the
piece of sapphire Uncle Pieter had given her, and sat on
a low stool beside her bedroom fire. Across her bed was
lying the dress she had bought earlier in the morning. On
entering the room, she had taken it out of the cardboard
box in which it had been delivered, and, shaking out its
folds, had let it fall and forgotten it. Now, seeing it again:
It doesn't belong to me, she said; it has nothing to do
with me.

She rang the bell and the chambermaid answered it—
a timid German girl with clumsy feet and hands, but with
the slow gait and simple stance of a countrywoman, and a
startled innocence of expression. Julie asked her now, in
her own language, if she were German.

"*Ja, Frau Gräfin.*"

"From Prussia?"

"*Ja, Frau Gräfin.*"

"I also."

The girl's eyes brightened; then grew dull. "But your
ladyship is Dutch, not German," she said.

"I was not born German. But my husband is Prussian."

"Prussia is a long way off," the girl said slowly; and

Julie, who had been about to question her further, was
checked by her sadness and the privacy of her eyes.

"I rang for you to take away that dress."

"To take it away, my lady?"

"You may have it, if it is of any use to you."

"But it is new, it is quite new, my lady."

"But you may have it."

The girl touched the satin with the fingers of one hand;
then thrust an arm under the folds. She was staring at the
dress with the delight of a child in some marvellous, useless, inexplicable bright gift on a Christmas tree.

"For me, my lady? For me? But I could never wear it."

"Nor I," Julie said.

The girl spoke no more. She forgot even to utter her
thanks. When she had lifted the dress and laid it down,
lifted it again and turned it and stroked and patted it, she
discovered with a wild glance that she was in Julie's room.
She began to apologize in breathless confusion; then,
unable to continue, looked towards the door, as though
measuring her distance from it, and, her cheeks white, her
eyes burning, threw the dress over her arm and went
out.

I suppose she will keep it in a trunk, Julie thought, and
sometimes take it out and stare at it. She will not sell it;
that was not in her mind.

Lewis's letters were in a dispatch case at the bedside.
Julie took them out and seated herself by the fire again,
holding them in her hand. Presently she would read them,
but for a little while was content to enjoy her quieted
mind, a fever seeming to have gone out of her; and when
she began to read one of the letters, the muffled chime of a
clock on the mantelpiece told her that the time had come
for her to go downstairs to receive Uncle Pieter's guests.
In her handbag was a list, in his handwriting, of their
names, known or unknown to her, with brief notes of
their relationships, their callings, even of their marked
prejudices. "You must remember that *he* was very ill in
the summer," Uncle Pieter had said. "His health is his
only importance. . . . And *she* has a nephew fighting with

the French. She is proud of that—but she is extremely
neutral. . . . And this one has been twice married, but she
is still a bride; she will always be a bride until she is a
widow, and then soon she will be a bride again. You cannot
decently speak of her children; one of them has a beard
and has made her a grandmother."

Julie impressed the list on her memory and walked
across her room towards the door. A bare room, she perceived suddenly, and stopped. The packing of her luggage
was almost completed, and, seeing the straps and labels,
the froth of tissue paper, the emptiness of her open ward-
robe in which hung only her furs, she remembered in what
a bliss of expectation she had entered this room three days
ago. In the Hague she would see Lewis again, she had
thought, and the room itself had been illumined by her
joy. There had been in all inanimate things—the curling of
the straps, the bright colour of the labels, the ridiculous
rabbits and acanthus foliage that were the pattern of the
window-curtains—the same absurd and lovable aspect of
adventurousness which had become visible to her in like
objects on days of holiday during her childhood. Now the
same labels, the same straps, the same tissue paper were
before her. The holiday is over, she said, and a phase of
my life is over. As long as I live I shall dread hotels. I
have grown old in this room: and she allowed her eyes to
rest upon it with the curious, baffled, half-ironic melancholy of one who gazes at the tomb in which he knows he
will be buried. Seventy-two, she thought as she went downstairs; I shall remember the number.

In the hall she found it amusing to recognize her guests,
before their names were spoken, by the list Uncle Pieter
had given her, and to test their foibles in her conversation.

"I hope you are now quite well after your illness last
summer?"

"Quite well? Ah, perhaps that is too much to ask. But
better—mercifully better. Do you know, there was a time
when the doctors——"

"What a lovely sapphire! You are lucky in your step-
father! Did he give it to you only this morning? Your birth-

day, perhaps. . . . May I look at it? Ah, no—do not trouble to take it off."

But observing the pride in Uncle Pieter's eye, Julie unpinned the brooch and held it out. How different it had looked in its bed of snow! How mad she must have been to put it there! Now it was being held up for admiration, the centre of a cluster of polished finger-nails, from which Julie raised her eyes to see her stepfather, with white cuff edging the sleeve of his outstretched arm, move forward to take Lewis's hand.

"But Alison, what a chance! You in the Hague! Unfortunately we're just leaving. But you must lunch with us."

"Leaving?" Lewis said.

"And here's Julie. You haven't forgotten her?"

Her hand was in his.

"Are you leaving?" he said. "Not to-day? Not now?"

She moved her lips, touched them with her tongue.

"Thank you," said the woman with the sapphires. "Shall I pin it on for you—there!"

"Shall we go in to lunch?" Uncle Pieter had taken Lewis's arm and was leading him away. "Come, Alison, we must find a place for you," and, as they were moving towards the dining-room, he added: "Why not come up to Enkendaal with us? The cottage is full, I know. Stay in the Castle, then. Is that possible? Stay until Dirk's papers are finished."

"You may be inviting me for years," Lewis answered.

"Well, . . . so much the better. You'll earn your keep. . . . Isn't that a good idea, Julie?"

She saw Lewis's eyes on hers, and answered: "Yes . . . yes"—the repetition being a scarcely spoken secret of her breath, for she seemed to be consenting to a miracle; the word raised her from the dead. She was giddy under the impact of life and she thought: How shall this body die and these limbs be cold beyond the sun? And because the idea of death was to her then but a sheet of transparent glass, holding no image of herself, she saw her body in her grave as a child sees, through the window of a doll's house, a doll lying in its bed. She saw herself lying with open eyes, gazing upward through the turf, and smiled as though she were playing a game, so enchanting to her senses was it to imagine herself dead and to feel the currents of desire within her.

The group in which she moved had drifted on towards the dining-room. When Uncle Pieter asked her what was the number of her room, that he might order their luggage to be brought down, she answered: "Sixty, I think. . . . Or sixty-two," and it was the page-boy who corrected her. She was wondering what she might say to Lewis in the hearing of others, and while the party was gathering at the table she did not look at him.

Two guests separated her place from his; at last she spoke across them:

"What made you come to the Hague to-day, Lewis?"

"But what makes you leave to-day?" he replied.

"Uncle Pieter's appointment was for this morning. There's nothing else to stay for."

"But don't you generally stay a few days if you come to the Hague at all?"

"We have been here since Wednesday."

"Since Wednesday!" he exclaimed. "Then——"

The woman on his farther side interrupted him. Sometimes, out of the babble of conversation, his voice came to Julie. He was talking of the severity of the winter, of Groenlingen, of reading at Leiden; and she herself was listening to the old gentleman on her right who warned her that, in modern conditions of warfare, Holland's power to flood her countryside might not prove to be as effective a barrier against invasion as it had been in the past.

"No," she said, "I suppose there are all sorts of contrivances now for overcoming the difficulty of——"

"Yes," the old gentleman answered. "In the first place——"

After luncheon, Julie was thinking, shall we have a chance to talk together? He must have supposed that Friday was the day of our arrival in the Hague, not of our leaving it. Did I in my letter——

"The Castle at Enkendaal must be very beautiful under

snow," said the young man on her left, a Swede with wide, dark eyes set surprisingly in a blond face, and she began to discuss with him winter-sports in Holland, in Sweden, in Switzerland.

"After the war," he said, "you must come to Sweden. It would please you, I am sure. There is something that would delight you at every season of the year. In the spring, for example——"

"I should like to make my first visit in the spring," she answered, thinking that, when they rose from the table, Lewis would be detained among the men and that when he came into the hall she would be already surrounded. But she was untroubled by the thought, untroubled by the crowd, the chatter, the necessity to divide her attention between the military defence of Holland and the Swedish spring. Her companionship with Lewis was not affected by interruption. Seeing his hand laid on the table, she felt that her own was beneath his fingers' touch. To the world she was sleeping, withdrawn into imperturbable composure, speaking and laughing and listening in a dream; in herself and in him, she was awake.

IV

THE TOWER

A place to stand and love in for a day,
With darkness and the death-hour rounding it.
    E. B. BROWNING: *Sonnets from the Portuguese*

CHAPTER ONE

TO-NIGHT he will come to me, Julie said. Standing before
her mirror with arms raised, loosening her hair, she became
still, gazing first at the receding images of the room behind
the girl whose face she saw, then at the face itself, its
unfamiliar flush and whiteness, its sparkling, fascinated
terror. She did not know herself in this girl whose face
made her think of lilies and diamonds. But suddenly she
recognized the eyes; they were familiar; there was a shaft
of her childhood in them; and she thought: It is I, who
wondered so often what would become of me. It is I, who,
when I was lonely here, hugged my sides with my elbows
to give me courage, and set my mouth and dreamed
dreams. She set her mouth again, seeking to recover the
virginal determination of that remembered child, but her
lips would not assume the old shape. She could but smile
at her failure, a smile, she thought, of farewell.

The instant was gone and the face that had touched it
with magic; though she looked for ever into her mirror,
she would never see that face again. Hair fell over her
shoulders, and what she saw now was the inclination of
her body, the rise and fall of her arm, white against the
tapestry of the bed, and a gleam from her moving brush.
How deep, how silent the room was! She turned abruptly
from her dressing-table to face the shadows that had been
stooping over her. How silent! And soon his voice would
be in it and hers answering him. She spoke his name aloud,
but softly: "Lewis!" and spoke it again. Thus she had
spoken it when he was gone away and she seemed to have
lost him. Often, then, she had fallen asleep with the

237

whisper of his name on her lips and his absence aching
in her body. And to-night, she thought, before I fall
asleep at last, I will speak his name, saying to myself,
He is not here! and shall stretch out my hand and find
him.

And some night, after a few months, a few weeks—who
knows how soon?—I shall stretch out my hand in the
darkness and not find him. It will be ended; he will go his
way and I shall go mine; in all our lives we shall not, as
lovers, find each other again, but all our lives we shall feed
on the hours and days that will begin—she looked towards
the door by which he would enter, thinking she heard his
step, but she had heard nothing, and while she completed
her undressing her fingers were by turns hot and cold
against her, and she would stand long motionless, now
sad that her love held not even that delusion of the everlasting which is our little weapon against death, now in
delight of that very impermanence which made of it, not
an impossible loyalty to be fought for, not a youth that
must grow old, but an immortal thing, as they that die
young are immortal. She was filled with lightness and
exaltation, as though by some miracle she had been made
exempt from the rule of life, from time, consequence
and price, and the joy now approaching her were indeed
magical and detached—scarcely her own joy, interwoven
with the stuff of her existence, but the joy of a song or a
play to which she was audience; and she began to think
not of the actual winter but of the scented darkness of a
summer's night, not of the physical man that was to take
her but of a being that was part of the fire in her own limbs,
not even of herself as she was—a half-naked girl crouched
by the fire—but of an illusion proceeding from within her as
music proceeds from an instrument. But no sooner did
she begin to recognize this aerial independence of circumstance as the illusion of love itself and to whisper in her
mind, This is love, than the illusion was dissipated, fleeing
as Eros fled before Psyche's lamp, and she saw that she
was naked, and was ashamed, and made haste to cover
herself.

To-night he would come, but not yet, not until the household had long been asleep.

The world and its fear and the stimulus of its fear being now upon her, she trembled. Come soon, come soon, she said, and because to wait had become intolerable she imagined that she might kill expectation in sleep. His touch would but half-awaken her; the reality of his coming would be cloaked in a dream. But it would be impossible to sleep, she knew. In the dark, as now in the candlelight, she would remember how this evening, when they had seemed before others to be saying good night, his eyes had asked, and hers had answered, the question that for three days had hung between them; and the remembrance of this unspoken betrothal would pierce her and quicken her breath so that she could not sleep.

Now he was in the library below her room, waiting until it was certain that none would visit him there. Then he would open the door at the foot of the interior staircase, and climb the narrow, broken steps, his shoulder guided by the curving wall. He would knock on her door and she open it.

She lifted away the leather screen that stood across the door and slid back the bolt. Should she go down to him? But she turned away, drew a fur gown closely about her, renewed the fire with peat and fragrant wood; then, mounting the low dais set in an embrasure, drew her feet under her on to the window-seat. When he knocked, she would not move. When he entered and spoke, perhaps she would not answer. He would suppose the room to be empty; his eyes would search it with surprise and alarm; then he would see her, and his exclamation ease their encounter, breaking the silence between them.

She drew the curtains apart, but there was no moon, no glint on the waters nor rift on the heavy sky. When she opened a pane and would have leaned out, January drove her back, but after the window was closed again, the curl and hiss of the waterfall persisted in her hearing, or in her imagination, and a thin, lisping breeze flicked at the outer stones like the run of a lizard. Come soon, she said, pressing her clasped hands upon her knees. Let him come soon, she repeated, laying her fingers on her hot cheeks and rising from her place as though to welcome him. The future may take care of itself—and with a gesture of her hand she thought that she put it from her. Grant that I may not be mean and fearful; give me a single mind for this love that will not come again. Encircle it. Guard it. Enclose me in it. And covering her face, she supposed that she was enclosed from the world. But I am praying, she thought, and, surprised that she had been praying, sank down on her knees, there being for her an ancient comfort of familiarity in the attitude of prayer. But criticism of herself had driven prayer from her mind, and she could say only, without thought of their relevance, words taught to her long ago, which by their rhythm and association, not by their meaning, so commanded her that, when they had been silently spoken and repeated, she remained upon her knees, hearing the waterfall and the low wind as though they were of a world that she would never revisit.

When Lewis knocked on the door at the head of the wall staircase and received no answer, he thought that she was perhaps afraid to answer, and entered. She was in the window-seat, her face turned towards the blank night beyond the panes, and seemed not to have heard him. Even when he had taken her hand in his and she had spoken his name, there was for a moment a wandering look in her eyes, as though she doubted what they saw. Her breathing was long and deep; when she was in his arms, her body was tremulous, like a tree that is not visibly moved but responds to the wind with gentle, continuous vibrations.

"Julie," he said.

Her head, which she had turned away, was lifted to him again and, though her lips did not move, he received an impression of her smiling, of gladness, finality, rest.

"It isn't true—" she began, trying to smile. "It was all to have been for an instant of our lives only. That's what we said. But it isn't true." Her voice failed her and she pressed her face into hiding.

"Julie," he repeated. "Julie——" and he too became silent, possessed by a happiness so great, and so different from any happiness that he had before experienced or imagined, even in his thoughts of her, that there seemed to be a spirit crying within him: I am born! I am alive! I have come out of the darkness! He sat down in the window-seat and she beside him, feeling that all other existences had been laid to rest, that they only were waking; that they were by some miraculous influence set a little apart from the natural world, and were watching it as they might watch a child that, having been in pain, was fallen asleep.

Her fingers tightened on his. She raised her eyes, wide and shining with tears. They were filled with supplication and surrender, not to him personally, but to the new life in her that he represented, and, as she saw him, not as man only, but as a frail symbol, which is all man can be, of powers on whose surface his life is tossed, compassion flowed into her love. She seemed at once to be pitying and beseeching pity. She was his refuge and the being whose only refuge was in him. A flame passed through him; his body became a single pulse, leaping from strength to strength; and suddenly, lifting her hand, he pressed his lips to it. Over him she sighed, as though all life had been given into her keeping, and he felt her fingers move upon his hair. He lifted his head and gazed long into her face, silently and with growing comprehension of the change in her, in himself, in the destiny and significance of their love for each other. How radiant her face was! How lighted with tenderness and acceptance and awe! The fear and hunger, the wild, troubled fierceness that he had once seen in it, were vanished. Desire remained without the terror and anger of desire. Delight shone there, but with a clear, tranquil brilliance. He sprang to his feet, drawing her towards him by both her hands, and so easily did she follow that her hair was lifted from her shoulders by the swiftness of her movement.

CHAPTER TWO

"WHAT have you been doing all day?" van Leyden asked each evening as he sat down to dinner, a question seldom answered. It was no more than a formal indication that he was done with the work of his estate and had become a social being; he did not expect a reply. If Sophie said she had been into Rynwyk or his wife that she had been paying calls, he lifted his eyebrows to suggest that he was interested, and continued to drink his soup in peasant-fashion, his fingers wrapped round his little bowl. If they spoke of his tenants, or of the war in its relation to them, he became animated at once and allowed his soup to become cold while he talked; but nothing else roused him until, after dinner, his cigar was alight. Then he could be gay and shrewd, and his eyes, emerging from his wrinkles like a bird's, shine with delight as he twitted Sophie or led Julie on to talk of vanities.

It was his habit to pretend that young and pretty women could be interested in nothing but adornments and pleasure-seeking—unless it were in money, considered as a means to these feminine ends. When they were married and old, he spoke to them of solider things—of rank, of marriage-making, of family affairs, often of the past when they also had been young. But married or single, they were women. Conversation with them must never be deeply serious. Business was barred; politics, except its polite superficiality, was barred; all gambling, all aspects of love except a flirtation or a matrimonial alliance, all profound grief or hope, all genuine insight into their minds—these were to be avoided or cloaked in raillery. You did not give yourself away to a woman—not more than once in a lifetime. If her eyes shone and you guessed the reason, you made no use of your knowledge; there was pleasure enough in silent possession of it. If there were tears in her eyes, you rustled a newspaper or looked out of the window, and a few days afterwards gave her sapphires—some trinket. . . . Nice things, women; too nice—or devilish; but gentle or cruel, if you gave them a chance they twined themselves. Like ivy on a tree trunk; like serpents, he would think sometimes; like children at play, irresistible, gripping your knees.

Julie understood now, as she had never understood before, that her stepfather's elaborate manners—his geniality and his sudden, forbidding coldness, his little jokes, unexpected gifts, and shaped courtesies—were self-protective. Why, she had often wondered, had he withdrawn into impenetrable silences when she, a child, aching to spend her affection on someone who would respond to it, had gone into his room and curled herself up expectantly in his arm-chair? All her life she had been puzzled by this question, for she had known intuitively that he had not been wanting in tenderness towards her. Now, in the first days of her love's fulfilment, she perceived the reason. Uncle Pieter's life was laid open before her, and she said to him one evening after dinner:

"If I'd been a boy when I came here, should you have taught me how to run the estate?"

"I suppose so, my dear."

"Though I didn't belong?"

"Why not?"

"And you'd have taken me about with you and talked to me—seriously, as an equal?"

He shifted in his chair, tried to ride away on a little joke.

"Ladies, you see, have to be treated with respect."

"No," she said. "Tell me, Uncle Pieter. If I'd not been a girl, when we were in the Hague together——"

"I shouldn't have given you sapphires!" He chuckled. "It cuts both ways."

"Ah," she answered quickly, "that's what I wanted to know," and he looked up, puzzled, uneasy, feeling that he must have said more to this girl than he had intended to say. "Bless you," she added, touching his hand with hers. "You're a dear, Uncle Pieter."

He gripped her fingers. "What is it you want now—more sapphires?"

"No."

"I'd give them to you."

"Why?"

"Don't you want them?"

"No."

"What then?"

"Just to understand."

"Bah! You women are always making mysteries. I can't make head or tail of you."

"Yes, you can," she answered. "That's why you're a dear."

"Then do something to please me."

"Anything."

"Play on the piano . . . Chopin."

But though he might escape into Chopin, she knew that she had discovered in him what had long been hidden from her; she saw him as an inhabitant of the world of new perceptions into which she had but lately entered. Her mother, too, was changed, had ceased to be formidable; the biting affability peculiar to her, which had once had the effect on Julie of chafing harness on a horse of mettle, had no more influence now than the repetitive patter of a comedian. Her hatred of her mother was a surprising memory of another existence, so indifferent to her had she become. And Sophie —Sophie was a suspicious ghost, embittered, pitiable, powerless. It's odd, Julie thought, if Sophie could prove what she suspects, or is beginning to suspect, she could ruin me, and would. Yet I am no more afraid of her than I should be if she were blind and deaf and dumb.

Having come from the piano, she listened idly to Sophie's observations on the winter—that it was good because it was Dutch, so different from the clammy bitterness of an

English January. Soon Lewis would rise and say good night.

"Shall you be working late?" her mother would say.

Meanwhile he sat among them, his hands, which in the past had been restless, lying still on the arms of his chair, his dark eyes lively but at peace. She remembered having read the complaint of some lover—a poet? a philosopher? she could not recall the form of the saying—that the agony of lovers was their powerlessness to surmount the barrier of individuality. Even in love, the writer had said, there is no escape from the eternal solitude of oneself. We kiss but cannot mingle. We clasp each other but come no nearer. We would be one but remain two always. When man and woman lie together in the last ecstasy of passion, making the utmost endeavour of the flesh to pass beyond the division of their souls, they mock themselves; though they endow the act of love with every power of imagination, with romance, poetry and religion, though they identify it, in the begetting and the love of children, with their aspiration towards immortality itself, it remains the physical act of two divided and solitary beings, and they are mocked in it as two birds are mocked that seek each other through a pane of glass.

So she had read and until now had believed. Often, during that long winter, walking alone through the frozen countryside or sitting in the library with Lewis or hearing his breathing when he had fallen asleep in her arms, she asked herself in vain how it was that the consequences of this belief, which reason still supported, were lifted from her—its consequences of fear and doubt and jealousy, the torments of love. There was no answer but the plain one— that nothing was as it had been, that all earth was made anew.

The evidences of change were in her own pride. Once she would have been jealous of Lewis's solitude. He would shut himself up in the library and come from it at last wrapt in thought that could not at once be shaken from him. A haze of meditation was still upon his eyes, and from it his seeing emerged slowly when he encountered her.

"You had forgotten my existence!" she said, and, when he turned to walk beside her, she added: "Dearest, I'm glad it is possible," and said it from her heart, for it appeared to her as an endorsement of their love that his work had a new peace and continuity and that she could be alone for many hours without feeling shut out. But of all her joys the greatest at this time was the discovery of tranquillity within passion itself. The shadeless burning that had tormented her was transformed into the ardour of a benign summer, an ardour of which each quenching and renewal was as natural a miracle as nightfall and daybreak. All the barbs had gone from desire, yet was desire itself continually deepened and enriched. The impulse to resist, the humiliation of being compelled by her own hungers to surrender, the core of resentment in this delight, were gone; to hear Lewis's approach by the tower-stair, to feel her pulses quicken and a current of expectancy leap from brain to limbs, to lose her breath when he uncovered her body, to be caught into a tumult of consciousness without thought when his silence was upon her, was now to her as unstained with misgiving as the stretching out of a hand into the sun.

Because the earth and all men in it were revealing themselves anew to her, and nothing seemed stale or used or finally accepted, but everything, however familiar, came to her with the offer of fresh secrets, Julie was visited by a sense of being at once very old and very young—very young in her eagerness to seize every instant of each new day, to lose none of the sparkle of existence beneath the grey mists of half-thought, very old in her having passed beyond a former life upon which she now looked back with smiling curiosity, wondering how to identify herself with it.

"All men are children," she had heard women say and had dismissed the phrase as a formula of sentimentality, but she understood now that there was a fascination, and a cause of love, in watching a man grow, in remarking the changes in him and his slow awakening to truths that she had already perceived. It seemed strange to her, whose mind was retentive and logical, that Lewis should so often appear to have forgotten, or have strayed away from, truths that he had long ago apprehended. His work on Dirk's manuscripts was steady and consistent; the patient investigation of them satisfied a need in him and, though he was baffled now and then by some historical allusion or roused to sudden excitement by a passage of uncommon humour or wisdom, his struggle with the crabbed writing was an equable one. But sometimes he would turn from his own work on the seventeenth century with a laughing sigh of despair:

"Julie, I wonder if all this is wasted labour?" he said. Do you remember the man in Ibsen's *Little Eyolf* who was writing a fat volume on Human Responsibility. First, he sacrificed everyone, his wife, his child, everyone, to the composition of his masterpiece; then, when he had at last discovered that the task was too big for him, he made excuses for abandoning it, and glorified his excuses and sacrificed everyone to them. These great tasks that men set themselves are always perilous. To go on with them may be hypocrisy and to abandon them another form of hypocrisy. That is true in a way of any exceptional task, great or small, that we choose for ourselves."

"But, Lewis, dear," she answered, "are you wanting to justify your choice to yourself or—to the world? You still wonder whether anyone will read your book when it's done, whether it will be famous or not. And yet, deep inside you, you care for applause less than any man I've ever known. But part of you is a man of business and belongs to the world. He's still alive, isn't he? . . . Isn't he?"

Lewis acknowledged it. "He writes to his mother or his sisters and to his partner every week," he said with a smile. "Do you know, Julie, sometimes when I've put those letters aside for an hour or two and have re-read them before closing them down, they seem to have been written by someone who died long ago."

He was standing at his table in the library, running his hand over the books lying open there. Julie put her arm in his and they began to walk up and down together in the shadows of the great room.

"O Lewis," she exclaimed. "Ghosts! Ghosts! How you live with them! It's that business man, the dead man, you want to please by producing a famous book. So that you can say to him: 'I told you it wasn't just arrogance and a waste of time. You see there was something in it after all.' And if you did, what do you think he'd answer? He'd sneer and say: 'O yes, the book is famous; but it's miles away from the solid bread and butter of life.' And he'd add: 'How much good do you think it did to people? Are they going to be less hungry or warmer or have more leisure or more of any of the good things of life because you've written it?' That's all he'd say. He wouldn't be grateful or satisfied. It's no good trying to satisfy the ghosts of oneself; they're insatiable. . . . And the odd thing is," she added, "that you know it far better than I do. Didn't you tell me, long ago, that this book wasn't an end in itself but a—a kind of——"

"A discipline," he said. "I know."

She glanced into his face. "But you forget—as a child forgets its lesson."

"No, I don't forget," he answered. "But some lesson farther on in the book suddenly attracts me, and I turn on, and then I lose my place. You have helped me to find it again." He laughed and drummed a knuckle on the snowy window. "There's no index. That's the devil of it."

"To what?"

"To the inner life—the life of the spirit."

"Isn't every religion an index?"

"Is it? Jesus and Plato may write the book, but they leave you to find your own way in it. Their followers try to write the index. Isn't that why men accept the discipline of churches? . . . You see, Julie," he added, "I'm miles away from being a philosopher. I talk and try to learn, but still in effect I'm a pupil who's scarcely begun to find his way. I thought I was so damned secure, and that little else mattered but the development of my own ideas. And now—there's you—like sunshine and wind after a stuffy room. You teach me more than I should ever have learned from books."

"What can I teach you?"

"Not to mistake day-dreams for meditation—that's one thing. And to laugh at my solemn self—that's another."

"That's why I love you," she said.

"Because you can teach me?"

"Because you think I can."

CHAPTER THREE

WEEK after week, the frost held. The angles of the Castle were blunted and every undulation of the moor was flattened by snow; over the little village a thick covering was spread from which proceeded wreaths of smoke that seemed to be the issue of subterranean fires. Vertical walls had the appearance of rents in the general whiteness and window-panes gleamed like ebony within their encrusted frames. The eye, entranced by the mysterious deadness of the countryside, which seemed to lie under a spell, and by a reflected pallor within doors that gave to high noon the ghostly semblance of early morning, began to accept at last, as though it were everlasting, the bleak, neutral glitter of a shrouded sun. At dusk, when the skaters were gone, birds swept down in hungry clusters to the edges of the lake, hoping that the villagers might have left food there; and soon, if there were to be stars, the first constellations appeared, not as serene jewels hung on the domed surface of the sky, but as fierce origins of light profoundly embedded in it, their rays piercing its blackness like needles of crystal.

So few were the changes in weather during those days that each change was memorable, and Lewis long remembered an evening on which, while he was walking home with Julie, the wind moved southward and clouds thickened in the sky—promising a thaw, she said.

"Perhaps the last of the snow," he answered. "There may be a sudden spring."

She paused to watch the sunset drive down the sky like a ship in flames. The frozen floods in the distant valley,

250

which all the afternoon had been grey and dead, were now a running fire; the black, huddled pines in the foreground glowed and stood apart, divided by tawny gleam and shadow of sapphire; the snow of the moor, which had appeared to be of unvaried smoothness, exhibited to the flattening rays each billow of its surface, each roughness of its texture, but did not shine; the colours it received were dim and watered, as though seen through frosted glass.

"It will freeze again when the wind shifts," Julie said, "even if the frost breaks to-night." And suddenly she exclaimed: "I believe you are glad!"

And he answered, glancing at her with delight: "I am! In winter, time stands still. To-morrow is always the same as to-day as long as there's snow on the ground. I don't want time to move."

"You are as happy as that?"

"And you?"

She nodded and walked on, drawing him with her.

"I know what you are thinking," she said, "because I too am thinking it. You are thinking what neither of us has dared to say—but it's only folly, Lewis dear, to say it now."

"That there needn't be any end for us?"

"That we might have all our lives together, if we chose. . . . Let's imagine, Lewis, that it's true. Everything we said and thought before we became lovers isn't binding on us any more—we've broken free of it, and of all the circumstances of our lives—let's imagine that. And imagine," she added with a hardening of her voice, "that marriage with me wouldn't ruin you and make all the hope of your life impossible and that I am not married and pledged—even more important, that I'm not the kind of woman I am. That's the barrier between us, Lewis. Not that you are poor and I—on other people's money—rich; not that you are ten years older than I am or that I have a husband. All that we could break down. The barrier is that I am I and you are you—not made to live in the same world."

"Here we do," he said.

"Yes, in a kind of enchantment that shuts out your world and mine."

"But Julie," he cried, "we love each other. Something that is neither yours nor mine has arisen out of our love—something independent of us. Aren't we pledged to that? When I see you as you are now——"

She took his hand and pressed it.

"But this winter can't last for ever, Lewis dear," she said, looking away from him to the west where already the deeper colours were fading in the sky and great fleeces of cloud were drawn out into primrose shreds. "Spring will come, and summer; then autumn and winter again. Unless we ourselves are changed, we shall become members of separated worlds."

"Do you hear from Narwitz?" Lewis asked suddenly.

"Yes."

"It is on your mind? . . . Julie, you aren't unhappy or guilty or sad?"

"Not guilty, or unhappy. . . ."

"But sad?"

She did not answer at once. "Sad, only because I love you as I didn't know I should," she said after consideration. "I suppose, deep down in my mind, was the thought that if you were my lover I should become satisfied, and that, when the time came for us to part——" She raised her voice in defiance, not of him, but of herself. "I wanted you, I suppose. And now," she added, "it seems intolerable to me that there should ever be a time when we shall not walk across snowy moors, scarcely speaking for hours, or sit in the library together, debating some line of Quarles or a passage from Fénelon or a fragment of the Timaeus.

Fénelon led them to Bossuet, Bossuet to Molinos, and from Molinos the way was easy to Inglesant and the seventeenth century in England, a subject of which they never grew weary. Darkness had fallen when they entered the grounds of the Castle, but the clouds were drawn away to the north and stars were out. The reflected glow of lighted windows seemed to be rising from within the snow.

"Stop for a moment and listen," Lewis said.

They stood in silence, hearing the wind flow among the branches of the avenue. Julie's face turned to his; she was about to speak; but, seeming to decide that what she had intended to say might not be spoken, she put her two furry gloves on to Lewis's shoulder and hid her face in them until he, bending back her head, kissed her lips and her icy cheeks and her closed eyes. She moved and clung to him.

"Don't let me go," she whispered. "Never let me go."

"Never?" he said. "Is that your promise, Julie? Your will?"

Instantly she slackened in his arms and released herself.

"Yes," she answered, "it is my will—O Lewis, it is all my being—in this enchanted garden."

Swiftly, at the word, as though it had in her ears a fatal sound, she touched him.

"Listen," she said. "Do you hear the voice of God among the trees?"

He searched her face in the darkness, questioning the seriousness of her mood. There was fear in her eyes but her lips were smiling.

"The last lines," she said. "Say them to me."

"My dearest—of what?"

"Of the Milton. Say them. When we hear them again we shall remember."

Still he did not know of what she was speaking, and she began in a low voice:

"'They looking back all th' eastern side beheld of Paradise. . . .'"

She could not continue. The wind of the avenue was in her silence while she waited. And Lewis said:

> "They looking back all th' eastern side beheld
> Of Paradise, so late their happy seat,
> Waved over by that flaming brand; the gate
> With dreadful faces thronged and fiery arms.
> Some natural tears they dropped——"

Her fingers tightened abruptly on his arm. "Soon," she said, "so soon for us!" But in an instant she had thrown her darkness from her. "Now," she exclaimed, "let's go in. Lights. People. This evening I'll come down to you in the library. Shall I? Read to me. All night we shall be together. And to-morrow and to-morrow."

They went on, having forgotten the world. In the hall they found Goof, Corrie, Allard and Sophie, with the Baron in their midst. The Baroness came with Ballater out of the smoking-room. Behind them Ramsdell's face appeared.

"You're late," Goof said. "We thought you were lost. You know the news?"

Allard rounded the phrase for it.

"The Russian Empire has fallen. The Tsar has abdicated."

"Then Russia is out of the war?"

There was an outbreak of confused comment. "It may strengthen her," one suggested. "The new Government is pro-ally," another exclaimed.

"But will the new Government last?" Ramsdell said.

"If you ask me," Ballater put in, "it may bring the re-organization that Russia needs." His smile was comforting but the disquiet of the group persisted.

"Change! Change!" van Leyden said. "Even the Romanovs." And he added incredulously: "It will be the Hapsburgs next."

He clasped and unclasped his hands behind his back. "At least," he said, "England will save the Tsar and his family. He is your King's cousin. There is no need that England should be too late this time. There's a breathing space."

Ballater cleared his throat. "Don't you think, sir, that perhaps you're taking too gloomy a view? After all, the Tsar appears to be in no danger."

The old man flung out his hands. "No danger! No danger! When the wolves have him down! Ah," he cried in exasperation, "that is the English all over. You never recognize a revolution when you see one. You always hope to convert a pack of wolves into a Liberal party and gener-ally, in your own country, you succeed. But Russia is not

England. You will be too late. I see it. You will be too late!"

"What matters," said Ballater, intending no more than a conciliatory diversion, "is that Russia, whoever rules her, shouldn't make a separate peace."

The Baron stared at him. "That's English too," he exclaimed. "That is very English. That is the reason of your greatness——" and Ballater, not understanding, smiled affably and shook his head.

Lewis and Julie observed the old man's emotion without sharing it. "The Russian Empire has fallen!" They had listened to the remote words and to the excited, nervous discussion that had followed, as though, two passers-by, they had overheard through an open window the exclamations of a group of strangers.

CHAPTER FOUR

ONCE in each week the English officers went into Rynwyk to report at the office of the district commandant. Ballater was often absent with his car, having leave to visit the Hague or stay with Govert van Leyden at the Huis ten Borgh, and Lewis and Ramsdell would then go into the town by the tramway that passed within a mile of Enkendaal, returning on foot across country. A new intimacy between them arose from these long, regular walks.

Saturday after Saturday at the same hour of the morning they came by the same way. Sometimes they took up an argument where it had been left some days earlier. More often, having received news of the war in Rynwyk, they would discuss it as they came through the prim outskirts of the town and be led on to speak of what might follow the compromise that both now believed to be inevitable. Suspense? Disorganization? Another war? The tide of revolution would not stop at the Russian frontier: all foundations were shaken—badly shaken in Germany, Ramsdell added.

"You believe that?"

"Julie believes it."

"What reason has she?"

"But hasn't she told you," Ramsdell asked, "of her husband's letters?"

Lewis answered that she had not, and a silence fell until Ramsdell, feeling that having said so much he must say more, continued: "Though he never speaks of revolution, he gives her news of their estates. From words here and there about their servants, and local people, and a

256

cousin of his who is a social democrat, she thinks—and is sure Narwitz thinks—that there are rocks ahead."

He had chosen colourless phrases, hoping that Lewis's interest in the subject would fail, and Lewis pressed him no further for Julie's confidence.

"She said nothing of it to me," he repeated.

"Probably because she didn't want to worry you with it?"

"Worry me? Was she genuinely worried?"

Ramsdell hesitated. "I think she was. After all, her own future is tied up in it."

"Yes, I had almost forgotten that," Lewis replied. "It is easy to forget in this place that there is a future in which all of us, you and I—and Julie, will become different people, sailing off like paper boats on different streams. Soon after we part, we shan't be within hailing distance, and all this—my work in the tower, yours in the cottage, these walks together—will seem to have been a false interlude. Things remembered from a dream. Unless in the end, we come to think of them as the only reality and all else as a dream."

He went on to speak of Julie with anxious tenderness, as if, Ramsdell reflected, she were a child who was soon to be cast adrift upon the world; and so different was this view of her from Ramsdell's own—for her clear intelligence of men and her power over them seemed to him her sufficient defence—that he thought: No one could fear for Julie who has not already transformed her in his mind, and he searched Lewis's face. It was, indeed, the face of a one under a spell. Its expression, while Julie was being spoken of, was that of a deeply sensitive man entranced by a play, by a poem, by some profound and excluding enthusiasm, and Ramsdell remembered how Julie had surprised him by saying: "Isn't it perhaps cruel to make anyone very happy in this world?" She too is changed, he said. She too is under a spell, but she sees beyond it as he does not—or will not. From the words "will not" and his understanding that, while Julie was still four-square with the world, knowing herself to be a creature of infinite adaptations,

Lewis was cherishing an idea of an impossible permanence, there emerged a sudden fear for both of them, and to test Lewis he said: "To think of what is past as the only reality is to deny life itself, to be dead. You are not looking forward to that?"

"I am trying to carry this dream into the future," Lewis answered. "To establish it. To make it so much a part of myself that whatever the circumstances of my life may become——"

"But that is to tell yourself a fairy tale, and even in fairy tales the spells are lifted at last—the good as well as the evil."

"That's one of the great mysteries," Lewis said. "In all the fairy tales there are miracles, and the miracles are in conflict, the good with the bad, and it is only when the miracles have ceased and the prince and princess have come together as man and woman that the storyteller dares to say, 'And they lived happily ever afterward.' There's very seldom any suggestion that there will be new miracles to help them in the future. Yet the miracles and spells and enchantments were not put into the stories as meaningless decorations; they are built into the conclusion. An evil spell is worked off by the performance of tasks—generally they are impossible tasks, such as the carrying of water in a sieve, which are made possible by the intervention of benevolent spirits in the solitary struggles of man. And even the beautiful spells, the happiest enchantments. . . ."

He broke off and walked for a little while in a silence that Ramsdell did not break.

"Even the happiest enchantments," he continued after reflection, "end at last, when they have served their purpose. One of three brothers misses his opportunity because he does not recognize a fairy in the beggar-woman beside the road; the second misses it because he is in such haste to be about his business that he doesn't pause to look into her face; and the third, the fortunate one, who recognizes and serves her and receives her favours—even he would lose his reward if he had not wisdom enough to assimilate it. When he leaves the enchanted place, carrying his reward with him, he must not look back. He may take with him only what he carries within himself—that is, what he has become—and he may not look back. He must go straight on into whatever world may be. Then the story-teller dares a happy ending which is also an ironic one; he brings us down to earth. 'And they lived happily ever after,' he says. It's always the beginning of a new story as well as an end of the old. It is the key with which he takes us from one world into another. 'And now,' he says, 'a new chapter of their lives began in which they related imagination with experience, and illusion with necessity; and this they were able to do because they had been taught by wonder and suffering——'"

"By suffering?" Ramsdell said, and Lewis, slackening his pace which had increased while he spoke, answered laughing: "But if you ask me about fairy tales, you must expect a lecture. I'm sorry. The subject is full of mysteries —as Dirk van Leyden knew."

How far they had wandered from their discussion of the war! So it was always during these walks. Habit had determined a route for them and the changes in its landmarks were tokens of the passing year—the softened shape of a copse against the sky-line telling of winter's departure, the movement of colour in a cottage garden proving the approach of spring. The owner of the garden, a frail Belgian in black suit and straw hat—the costume of the *café* in Namur from which he was exiled—shambled down to his gate as the Englishmen drew near. He wanted, he said, to set his watch by theirs; but there was little fault in his watch; he wished only to chatter of the war with allies and to say: "The English are just. They will restore my property to me, will they not? They will see justice in Belgium. We, after all, have done our part." To escape from his querulousness, they would ask of his garden, but he could not praise it without adding that in any country but Holland—his contempt for Holland was all-embracing. "They think the Belgians fools for having fought and they expect us to be grateful to them for their charity!" When there was a heavy snowfall in the second week in April: "What a country!" he cried. "How can a man live in it!" And the sudden heat of early May pleased him no better. "Look," he said, squeezing the sweat from his wrists, "here is the summer. But in Holland they have summer before the leaves are out on the trees. The season is a month behind."

Lewis and Ramsdell were always glad to leave him, but they did not avoid his cottage, a visit to it having become part of their routine. When Ballater was with them, the visit was prolonged, for Ballater was irritated by the Belgian's horticulture, which no persuasions would change, and argument would be continued in fierce French until the Belgian's daughter appeared by chance from the back of the cottage and, having shown by little flutterings of her hands how surprised she was to see the Englishman, stared at Ballater with the eyes of a child outside a pastry-cook's shop. His daughter? "Nonsense," Ballater would say, "I don't believe she's his daughter. She'd escape sometimes if she were. . . . Not that I've any real interest in her. Her neck is too short." Often they left him in the Belgian's garden, for he never tired of inventing ruses to trick the man into leaving him alone with the girl. Neither failure in this nor her short neck discouraged him. She was a woman and she admired him; that was enough.

But as summer increased, Ballater's absences from the cottage became longer and more frequent, and Ramsdell, being often alone with Lewis or with Julie, began to know them, through his intuitions of their relationship, with profound knowledge, and to guess, as one guesses of people in a tale, what they were discovering, or might discover. One morning when he and Julie, having met by chance in the little wood that divided the upper lake from the road, were walking there together in sight of the Castle, she looked across the water to the tower and said:

"You know—don't you?—what Lewis and I are to each other?"

"Yes."

"How did you guess? Tell me how you guessed!"

What a child still in her eager voice, her unguarded impulse!

"You are both changed," Ramsdell began, "in a way that——"

"Well? In what way?"

"There's a repose between you when you are together, and when I meet you singly, you speak of each other."

"But to you only," she insisted, defending herself against a charge of guilelessness. "I never speak of Lewis to anyone but you, except in a casual way."

"Then no one else guesses, of course," he answered with a smile.

Instantly the childishness left her. "It doesn't matter to me who guesses," she said.

"Someone does?"

"Sophie. But she can prove nothing. She prowls about the passages at night. I think she's half mad. Once she came to the door of my bedroom and knocked, hoping to find Lewis there, and found nothing. And once, guessing that Lewis wasn't in his own room, she crept into the library. If she had found it empty, I suppose she would have locked the door on the tower-staircase; then have given the alarm. Lewis would have been trapped. But it happened that Lewis was in the library, sitting there in the dark. She was as frightened as if she had seen a ghost, and when he spoke to her could think of nothing better to say than that she had come for a book. But she knows," Julie added.

"Then why does she say nothing?"

"Because no one would believe her. Uncle Pieter least of all."

Ramsdell understood now that, though she was frightened, it was not Sophie she feared.

"Tell me," she said. "You see things plain as Lewis doesn't, as I don't now." She walked away from him a few paces, turned and came back. "Tell me what's best to do." And before he could speak, she added: "I believe that—I believe that my mother knows."

In the midst of that sentence she had changed her mind.

"That isn't what you were going to say," he answered; and she smiled at him, the disarming smile of one discovered in a trick.

"My mother does know," she said. "It's more than suspicion with her. She has made that clear enough—to me, not to Lewis." And she added with pleased quietness: "But my mother will say nothing. That would break my marriage, which was of her making. She would say nothing—except to me—if I had twenty lovers."

The brutality of that phrase surprised him. No girl is quite sane, he thought, when she speaks of her mother and her lover in a single breath.

Julie was laughing at him. "Now I have shocked you!"

"No, but you are playing with me. A moment ago you were asking me what it was best that you should do. Now you say that Sophie guesses and you don't care; that your mother knows—and will never speak. And yet you are frightened of something——"

"Frightened? I—frightened?"

"So frightened," he answered, "that you are trying to deceive me—and yourself."

She compressed her lips and did not reply. A sharp imperious movement of her head declared that she would not be scolded; a flash of her eyes that she was calling anger to her aid. Then, the barriers down, she confessed: "My husband knows."

"He has been told?"

"He hasn't been told. . . . But he knows."

"Certainly? He has written it."

"He has written nothing."

"You mean, then, that he suspects—that you believe he suspects?"

"I know that he knows."

Ramsdell perceived that it would be vain to reason with her.

"If he does," he said, "—you care?"

"Desperately."

"Why? Do you love him?"

"No one but Lewis."

"Then?"

One of the gardeners had come down to the boat-house and, taking a boat, had launched himself on to the upper lake. He was standing over his oars, facing for'ard, and as his body swung to and fro its reflection danced on the rippling, sunlit film of the water.

"I wonder what he is going to do on the island," Julie said, standing to watch him, and not until the boat was concealed by the island's trees did she turn to Ramsdell again and say:

"You like Lewis?"

"Yes."

"More than you did? You doubted him once."

"Not now."

"Why, I wonder?"

"Never an easy question," Ramsdell said, "but I can answer it, I think. You see, in one aspect, he's a solid, ordinary man. That links him with me; I'm solid and ordinary. He's a good man of business; he's capable of standing up to the world and doing his job; that made me want to like him. I was willing to give to his ideas the respect one gives to another man's religion—rather a cold, negative respect. And then I found that you couldn't be cold and negative about his ideas any more than you can be cold and negative when you're standing by a blacksmith who is hammering white-hot metal on his anvil. The sparks fly and touch you. Lewis is disturbing in the same way. He doesn't interfere with anyone else, but it's not possible to be with him and aloof from him. What I doubted in him was his humanity. I thought he was playing with barren theories——"

"I know," Julie said. "But it's not true. I remember I used to think: If Lewis is anything more than dry-as-dust, then he ought to be a leader of men. I imagined him as a founder of a new religion—a new way of thought. It was that kind of greatness I looked for in him and because he hadn't got it—well. . . ."

"You despised him?"

"No. Never that. But I tormented him. I wanted to drag

him out of his solitudes. I wanted to make him acknowledge— And then," she added, "I wanted him. I tried to laugh myself out of it. I tried to break myself. But I had come too close. . . . And afterwards I began to love him as I love him now. That's all. He's not a leader of men in the open. He will never have a mob following him. If he finds his own secret it will remain his own secret, but after he has gone and is forgotten the world will be changed by it."

"You have answered your own question for me," Ramsdell said. "Once he and I began to talk about fairy tales. He said that, though life was empty without enchantments and miracles, no enchantment had any meaning until it had been assimilated in common existence. A miracle is a seed and no more; you must plant it in earth and cultivate it if it is to bear fruit. When he said that, I think he was understanding it for the first time, and perhaps I was understanding him for the first time. And in the last few months—this winter and spring—I have learned more and more of him. I don't doubt him now."

"And I love him," Julie said quietly. Then: "Do you think me a fool? What *do* you think of me?"

"Need I tell you?"

"Do you think that I am a woman who takes a delight in confusing men's lives? Am I Lewis's enemy?"

Ramsdell stood uneasily, twining blades of grass over his fist.

"Are you taking a delight in confusing a man's life at this moment?" he asked.

"I? Now? Your life?"

"Good God!" Ramsdell exclaimed with a smile of self-mockery. "Four syllables—and what destruction! Nothing is more dangerous than a beautiful woman who happens to forget how beautiful she is."

"Do you mean——"

"No, Julie, I don't mean that I love you. More than the romantics suppose, love is a thing one permits or denies to oneself—after the earliest attacks before which we are all helpless. . . . But it makes me happy to walk here with

you. It's an odd privilege, half-agony and half-delight, to
see you so aglow with your own life that you can say to
me ‘*Your* life?’ as if the possibility of your confusing it
had never entered your mind. And to hear you asking my
advice as if you intended to take it—that's good too. But
I'm in no condition," he added, looking into her face, "to
tell you whether you are Lewis's enemy."

But she would not cease to be serious. It was in her
mind that she was bringing disaster to Lewis.

"Why?" Ramsdell asked. "He has never done better
work than he is doing now. He has never been happier."

"That's the danger," she said.

"To be happy?"

"As he and I are now."

"You believe in fate and the jealousy of the gods?"

"It is happiness that compels belief in them."

"Because enchantments end?"

She nodded and echoed: "Because they end."

"Or are assimilated," Ramsdell said quickly, and, pausing again to watch the boat return from the island, she
replied:

"But ours can never be assimilated. On earth, Lewis and
I are opposed beings—anywhere but here. What would
happen to us, do you think, as man and wife?"

"It wouldn't be easy," he admitted.

"Impossible. Just a loyal, hopeless, loving lie—until we
could deceive ourselves no longer."

"Is that why you are afraid?" She nodded again, her
white teeth on her lip. "Is that what you were thinking
of when you said that your husband knew?"

"Did I say that? I meant—it is as if he knew. As if he
were here watching us, a ghost. Every letter I have from him
now seems to be beseeching me, to be saying that I am all
he has left in the world and beseeching me not to leave his
world empty. It's horrible. It's horrible because, though
I'm sorry for him and for the suffering he's going through,
I don't feel it in myself. It's as if he were writing to some
other woman and I were stooping over his shoulder,
reading her letter. He writes to me in English and,

though his spoken English is nearly faultless, his written English is—just fluent, no more; he can't put himself into it. At the end of each letter he falls away into German. He writes it beautifully. He says wise, tender, desperate things—always as if deep deep in his mind, hidden even from himself, was a knowledge that it was all in vain; that I didn't love him and never could; that he was writing to someone irretrievably lost."

"Are you lost to him?" Ramsdell said. "You will go back to him."

"Yes," she answered, "if he lives, I shall go back. But the woman he loves is lost—if ever she existed."

Ramsdell had picked up a handful of pebbles and was tossing them one by one into the lake. There was a question in his mind that he hesitated to utter, and it was a relief to him to turn away from Julie and watch only the intersection of the rippling circles on the water. What would Julie do—what would Lewis do?—if Narwitz were killed? "If he lives," she had said: the chance of his death was present with her. And she was so happy that she believed in fate and the jealous gods! He emptied his hand of pebbles with a single, angry fling. It would be a pretty trick of the jealous gods to destroy Narwitz and, by removing that convenient obstacle to another marriage, thrust, with all the forces of honour and convention and sentiment, a freezing permanence on Julie's and Lewis's enchantment. Could they part then? Would not he stand by honour and she by sentiment?

"And if your husband is killed?" he said over his shoulder. "What then?" He would not look at her, for then he would cease to observe, with self-protective irony, a victim of the jealous gods, and would see the girl whose every mood, even when it angered, yet beguiled him.

"He must not be killed," she said.

"How can you say that—'*must* not'?" He turned on her, his anger blazing. "Must he live for your convenience?"

She drew back, her eyes wide, the colour gone from her lips. And, as though she were drawing a sword, she said:

"He must live for my——" and stopped.

What word? She would not speak it. Instead she touched Ramsdell's hand.

"We will not quarrel," she said. "Never mind what I meant. It wasn't as base as you thought."

They went down to the bridge and crossed between the lakes. In front of the Castle, Lewis met them, his morning's work done, and Ramsdell returned to the cottage alone. "He must live for my——" What word? My pleasure? My concealment? My comfort? All were impossible. No word would fit her sentence and her mood and her character. But as he stood in the verandah of the cottage the word salvation appeared in his mind and he stood to ponder over it, there being no other less unexpected, and none, he began to think, more illuminating.

CHAPTER FIVE

DURING this summer, Lewis consistently attempted to define his philosophical position in its relation to the contemporary world. All his study urged upon him that there was a great division of method, though not of principle, between Christian and non-Christian contemplatives. The principle of detachment was common to the two groups; each sought the establishment of a citadel within the sensible world; but whereas the Christians desired, in varying degrees, identification with God, or communion with him, or, in the extreme instance of St. Juan of the Cross, an absolute submission to a god having no resemblance to any living creature, the non-Christians had no such external focus of their endeavours and their idea of contemplation impelled them to mastery, rather than to hatred, of the nature of man. To them the body was a child that must grow in self-discipline, not a fiend and an instrument of the fiend.

And though there were certainly few, even among Catholics, who to-day accepted in its fullness St. Juan's doctrine of a journey towards an incomprehensible god through a night of the sense and a night of the intellect, there were many who, beneath the remote, unsuspected but still powerful influence of mediaeval Christianity, associated the contemplative ideal with asceticism and the abandonment of reason in faith. It was the fierce negative of St. Juan, not the courage of St. Clement or the profound independence of Eckhart, that gave colour to the thoughts of men ignorant of the teachings of them all. That this was so was the outstanding weakness of the Reformation. It had failed to implant in the minds of its adherents an effective distinction between the contemplative ideal itself and the extreme practices with which, in the Middle Ages and even more closely in the period of the Counter Reformation, that ideal became associated.

As time went by, this distinction became more and more clear to Lewis. It was, he saw, the link between the conditions of the modern world, wherein faith in revealed truth was no longer predominant, and the philosophic mysticism of the pre-Christian era. To establish a citadel within the sensible world without first annihilating the senses, to build the spirit not with the deaths of mind and body but with their selective and disciplined vitality, to lead the whole man, fearless and undivided, into that peace which is invulnerable and requires no immortal armour—these were his purposes; and he knew that to achieve them a man must be stronger than the Christian saints. Not only must he be wedded in spirit to nothing mortal and conquer that fear for the loss of earthly pleasures which the saints also overcame, but he must be without terror, as they seldom were, of the impact of earthly forces, and, as they could never be, of the loss of immortality. They were bound to the fulfilment of their faith, as a rich man to his riches, but a modern contemplative, excluded from Christianity, must be, like Socrates, bound to nothing, afraid of no encounter, capable of no loss but of his own integrity. Though he were persuaded by reason or intuition of the immortality of the soul and this persuasion were indistinguishable in effect from faith, yet it was not faith won from revelation; he must be prepared for reason to unmake what it had made; and though he believed in God, he must carry his god within him—an eye to see all lights, not an external beacon which, if he were to miss his view of it, would leave him blinded.

Under the compulsion to these thoughts, Lewis's own life revealed new aspects to him. There were periods in which his pleasure in the detachment of his present existence ceased to contain any element of fear. Instead of feeling, as he had, that there was an impassable barrier

between himself who was secluded in the tower and the
dutiful man of affairs who wrote letters to his partner in
business, he became aware of a unity between them, as
though each were a necessary complement of the other,
and he looked forward, not with resignation, but with an
acceptance neither eager nor distressed, to the day when
he should re-enter the world. I shall not, he thought,
return to Alison and Ford, for I have other work to do, but
while he was in these moods of reconciliation he felt no
revulsion from his former tasks. He could even be free for a
little while of knowledge that time was passing and that
an interlude in his life was slipping away. The wheeling
shafts of sun and moon on the library walls, the sound of
the waterfall, the mysterious sense of a multiplied blessing
from the hours themselves, which arises in one who hears
the night and the day chant through his solitudes, armed
him against time and misfortune; and when, during August,
Julie was absent for a week, she seemed often to be present
with him, so woven together were her life and his. The
parting, which he had feared, was not a parting in effect
until, on the eighth day, the day before her return, the
mood of security forsook him. Its protection gone, he became as he had been in the past. He could not work; he
could be calm neither alone nor in company; he could think
of nothing but that when Julie laughed, a little triumphant
laugh full of malicious gaiety, she would look up under
eyebrows that she made seem severe—then raise her eyebrows to mock him and lift her face to be kissed. More
than a year ago, he remembered, she had thus tantalized
him, for then, though he might not kiss her, the quick
upward movements of her head and the rounding of her
lips had always been her last thrust in an unspoken duel
between them. He felt again the jealous, eager tingling of
his body that he had felt in the past, and was possessed by
his former illusion of the senses, contrary to reason, that
she, so lithe and firm, was little more than a child, and
virginal. It was an illusion that charged his being with
opposed adoration and desire, and, while he was trembling
in a conflict of images, it seemed to him suddenly that

what had appeared as memories of her shape and warmth and movement were but hallucinations, and that a being at once so remote, so beautiful, so feminine as she could never have been his in the flesh. In that instant of fear he lost her—not as if she had come, been possessed by him and gone, but as if she had never lived except in his imagination, and, looking wildly round the library, coming to a desperate halt and staring into its spaces, he drew his breath in a panic of loss.

"Did you miss me?" she whispered when she returned, and before he could answer she was away among the others, pouring out a tale of her adventures. And next morning, awaking in the first gleam of summer dusk, feeling, when he moved, the weight of her beside him, he lay still and gazed at the fluted post of the bed nearest to the light and the lion's head under the canopy. He would not wake her, but watched the morning increase upon her pillow. Her lashes lay darkly on her lower lids; her lips made so soft a contact that they were neither open nor closed; her hand, lying beside her head, with white palm exposed and fingers gently curving, seemed to be on the point of movement. If she should wake, he would become aware of that stress of will and consciousness, that struggle to communicate, which is inseparable from all human companionship, even that of love. Their relationship, like a ship cast off from night-moorings, would move out into the current of experience; but while she slept, while her own consciousness of him was suspended, he felt himself to be part of a single being in which he and she were included.

It was not necessary even that he should look at her, and he lay apart, thinking how great a miracle it was that without sight of her, without touch or any communication of the senses, he should yet be mingled with her. If she died in her sleep, the consciousness of their mingling would persist while he gazed at the carved manes of the lions and the tall windows turning to gold; and if I died, he said, would this stream of consciousness cease, should I be aware of loss? It seemed to him then as impossible that he should lose her as that his consciousness should be emptied of his own being, but the insatiable curiosity of love caused him to look at her again. She stirred in her sleep; her hair fell back from her temples; her lips moved; she lifted her hand as though warding off an approach in a dream; then, with a gentle sigh, let her hand fall on the sheet, where its ivory fingers lay extended. The idea entered Lewis's mind that in her dream she had been afraid, that her sigh was of relief, her fear being past, and all his thought was of how the day of their separation was falling upon them like a sword. It was intolerable now to be parted from her even by her sleep; he longed for her eyes, her voice, the swift grace of her limbs; and he was stooping down to awaken her when her lips moved again and, as though she were whispering into his ear—for now his face was near to hers—she said: "No. No. Rupert, it isn't true. It isn't true." And after an interval of heavy, troubled breathing she repeated the name, and sighed deeply, and awoke.

No memory of her dream remained with her. She drew Lewis's face down to her and kissed him; then, seeing how far the sunrise was advanced and that the hour when Lewis must return to his own room was approaching, she folded herself close to him and begged him not to leave her.

"Shall it be a holiday to-day? Let's picnic on the island among the trees." And she added: "If we knew that within a week we must die, how should we spend to-day, Lewis?"

"If it is to be a holiday," he said, "let us go far away on to the moors. How you love your island!"

"And you your moors! O Lewis," she said, "what does it matter where we go? This is the last summer we shall spend together." She moved away from him and, turning on to her face, hid her eyes in the darkness of her hands and her hands in the darkness of her pillow. Her bare shoulders were glossy under the honeyed glow of the sky; her side was golden above the pallor of linen; and when, thinking she wept, he would have comforted her, she whispered.

"Wait. . . . Wait."

Suddenly she sat up, threw back her hair, looked at him under eyebrows she had drawn down with her old severity.

"I was hiding in the dark—the deep, private, secret dark. Do you know why? Because there will be sun all day and——"

"And all day we shall be together," he said.

"And it is summer still. The leaves have not begun to turn on the trees," she answered. "Have you seen a yellow leaf? Shall we look out of the window together and see whether September is coming?" But she stretched out her hand and laughed and seized his wrist. "No," she said, "why should we look out?"

But the days were fast shortening, and Lewis, who had been accustomed to spend one or two afternoons in each week riding with van Leyden over his estates, heard him grumble that the summer was over. "I hate the winter," he said, "it ties me to my desk and makes a clerk of me." The foliage of the avenue was the first to change its colour, but autumn spread to the little hills surrounding the lakes, and one day, while Lewis and Julie were standing near the boat-house, a fierce gust brought down a torrent of leaves and the surface of the water was lively with a golden fleet. The gold vanished, the sodden leaves drifted on for a little while, a mottle of black on steel.

As though even the seasons were in haste, storms blew through the sunshine of that autumn, and soon the pattern of branches stood everywhere naked against the sky. Nothing remained but the dark glitter of evergreens which clacked and hissed as the breeze jostled them. At last the winds ceased. The lakes were grey and dull and motionless, speckled with a sleety rain. In the early weeks of December the earth was saturated by snow and thaw, the sky, whether dark or pale, was unluminous, and all the interior of the Castle—the rugs, the polished tables, the gilt frames, the silver—seemed to have sunk into a lethargy. Colour itself had fallen asleep. Shape was emptied of its vitality. Furniture stood, dead, among sombre shadows; one remembered its weight—neither its beauty nor its strength; and a figure seen in sickly illumination at the end of a long corridor, or touched by the white gloom of windows at the head of the great staircase, had the appearance of a wraith which advanced and vanished and appeared again, formless in that struggling fantasy of light.

Lewis had completed his first sifting and annotations of Dirk van Leyden's papers. The translations, with Julie's aid, were done. In a couple of months, perhaps—certainly in the early spring—his selection and final ordering would be finished. "And I shall have no more reason then to live in the tower," he said.

"Then you must play Penelope," Julie answered. "Uncle Pieter will never know how near you are to the end. Besides, where should you go?"

"To the cottage," Lewis said.

"And I?"

They let the subject drift away from them until one morning Ballater came in through a blizzard to say that his uncle was dead. His cheeks were pink, his eyes sparkling; he stood by the stove in the library, warming his hands and rubbing them; he did what he could to seem grave and mournful but could not conceal his joy.

"That means the Ballater acres for you?" Lewis asked.

Ballater grinned. "It means more than that. It means leave to England. They granted it to Jerram when his father died; they'll grant it to me. And once in England, it's easy enough to get parole extended and extended. If the war ends next spring, I probably shan't come back."

"Then you'll leave the cottage—for good?" Julie said. "What will Ramsdell do?"

"Hasn't decided. Probably live in the Hague or join up with the people at Haarlem." He looked round him at the long windows and the crowded shelves, at the table spread with Lewis's pipes, at Lewis himself and Julie; then searchingly at the door that barred the walled staircase to her room.

"It's odd," he said. "Next spring I should have been in Enkendaal two years. Now I'm going away and I haven't been in this library a dozen times. . . . Do you like sitting and working here? I should never have thought Julie would."

"But I love working with Lewis," Julie answered. She had intended to make no more reply than this; she would disarm Ballater's curiosity with her candour—then be silent; but there was that in her mind—a sense of the breaking-up of beloved associations, a shiver of farewell— which touched her with sudden madness, and she said to Ballater: "I shall always remember this moment. The books grey and cold; the top shelves in darkness; this light every- where, pearly and opaque—as if we were all living in an oyster shell; and you standing there by the stove like a vast, grey giraffe. I suppose some day I shall come back. You never will. When you go out of this room, you'll never, never enter it again. But I shall come back years on. And I shall see you quite easily as you are now, standing by the stove. I shall wait and struggle, and perhaps I shall see Lewis again—there, at that table, with his long fingers running up the edge of a book. But I shall not see myself."

After a silence, because he knew not what else to say, Ballater said:

"The waterfall makes more noise now than it's ever done —the lakes are so swollen with snow and rain. Doesn't it worry you, working here?"

"No," Lewis answered, "you forget it. Only if it stopped you'd remember."

Ballater went out. Julie had seated herself on a stool near to the shelves and her head was turned away.

"Julie. Tell me what you are frightened of?"

She rose and stood beside the table. "Lewis, dear, I'm ashamed when I—when I've broken down like that. It's these dark skies, day after day, like a tomb. That—and my own weakness—and time sliding away under our feet—and your strength. That more than all."

"My strength?"

"You have changed," she said.

"Not towards you, Julie."

She smiled. "Sometimes, when you think of the end,

you are afraid, as I am. But there's a part of you that isn't afraid—not even of losing me. A part that's independent. It is what you have been fighting for—your tranquillity, the seed of it. And since I have loved you, it is what I have wanted for you. O Lewis, it's true; I have wanted it for you, but it divides you from me. Not now; you love me; perhaps, if we lived together all our lives, you would love me always, but every hour of every day, we should become more and more different beings." She sank down beside him and pressed his hand against her face. "And so," she said, "when we part, though it will kill something in each of us, still it will be best. When we began I thought so, now I know it. Here we are close together, but in the world we should grow further and further apart. I believe that is true, but it seems a waste of life, Lewis; I don't understand it."

"Perhaps it is not true," Lewis said.

"Perhaps!" she repeated. "But you too believe it. "Listen. I'll prove it. If Ballater and Ramsdell leave the cottage, if you finish Dirk's papers and go from here—you could live in the cottage *alone*, without loss? If I died, then——"

"Julie!" he exclaimed, lifting her up. "These months with you have been more to me than all my life without you. I came here cold and proud and ignorant and blind. Now——"

"But you could live alone," she insisted. "Not perhaps without loss; there's a part of you that would suffer. But there is a part that would be stronger because I was gone. It's true. And there's a part of me," she cried, throwing up her head and speaking as though her words were being dragged from her, "there's a part of me that would be freer—more gay, lighter, harder, more brilliant—if you were gone. But it is the worst in me that would profit and perhaps the best in you. Lewis, what is it that we are learning of each other? We shall part with the lesson half learned. You will go on. You stumble; you are blind sometimes, but nothing in your life is wasted. For you everything comes together in the end. But for me everything is broken into little pieces. I love you, but it's all like a story half told. As if the book with the story in it were to be shut suddenly and carried away. I don't know how the story ends—or why it was begun."

"But the book isn't shut yet," Lewis said. "We are listening to it now and——"

"Soon it will be," she answered.

"Why do you say that?"

She hesitated. "I know it. I tell myself over and over again that we have time. After the winter the spring; after the spring another summer—who knows? I tell myself that. But it's not true," she cried, "it's not true."

And Lewis heard in her voice the same accent of fear that had been in it when she spoke her husband's name in her sleep. "It isn't true. It isn't true." But again she passed beyond the terror that had possessed her, and said:

"Perhaps I'm being a fool, dearest one. I will go up to my music-room and play myself into reason and leave you to your own work."

He seized her hand; it was trembling; and in her eyes was a secret that she could not share with him, an intuition which swung as yet beneath the surface of her mind so that sometimes it was brightly visible and she shrank away from it, but sometimes she could forget that it was there.

CHAPTER SIX

At the opening of the new year, the fourth of war, Lewis became certain that there was a burden on Julie's mind that she could not share with him. When he spoke to her of it, she would elude him by saying: "Perhaps it's only something I imagine," and, if he pressed her further, would so beseech him with her eyes and the tones of her voice not to force her concealments that he felt he was hurting her by his urgency, and allowed himself to be led away to other subjects. She will tell me in her own time, he said.

In her own time she told him. He had been across to the cottage and had spent an afternoon there. Soon after Ballater's leaving for England, Ramsdell had gone to Haarlem and the English servants had been sent away, but Ramsdell might return if Lewis ceased to live in the Castle, and the rooms they had occupied in the cottage were still full of their possessions. Among these Lewis had been searching for a pipe that Ramsdell wished to have sent to Haarlem, and, though the pipe was soon found, he had stayed long in the cottage, talking to Vrouw Kerstholt. It was already dark when he returned to the Castle.

He went to his bedroom and prepared for dinner. As he entered the drawing-room, voices that had been uplifted were suddenly, though but for a moment, hushed. Then the Baroness said:

"But how long have you known? You must have known before this. Why didn't you tell us before?"

Julie, with her back to a table, was clutching its edge with her fingers and leaning against it. Her heels were raised from the ground and she had the same air of defiance that had been hers long ago on the tennis-ground when van Arkel had challenged her with news of Jutland. So strong was the association in Lewis's mind between the two scenes that he supposed for an instant that the German spring offensive—"their last shot when it comes," the Baron had said—was already begun, and he asked: "Is there news?"

"Yes," Julie answered, flattening all tone out of her voice in her effort to control it. "Rupert is coming here." She was pale and stern, with eyes feverishly bright. "He is hurt almost to death—invalided out—useless to them any more. He's coming here—" and she added, with a twist of terror and pride that tautened the words, "here—to me."

She looked everywhere but at Lewis—at the Baron with a sliding, negative glance as though he were of no interest to her, at Sophie with violence and contempt, then at her mother fixedly. The Baroness was in a flutter of annoyance because she had not been informed and because Narwitz, in his letters, had evidently deceived her; her irritation over these trifles obscured at first every other consideration in her mind and she poured out questions in an angry stream. Julie replied with unnatural calm, though a little breathlessly, as women often do in the witness-box. In the autumn, after Rupert was wounded a third time, he had known that he would never return to the front and had expected to die. She had never believed that he would die. . . . Why? She didn't know why, but she had not believed it. Then, after a long time, he had written of the possibility of his obtaining leave to come to Holland. That was long ago—well, several weeks ago.

"But why didn't you tell us then? Why didn't he tell us?"

"Because I didn't believe he'd really come," Julie said, leaving the second question unanswered. And she added: "He is only coming here to die."

"To die!" her mother exclaimed.

Julie replied in a hard, bitter tone: "His right arm is amputated. His right shoulder and his back are terribly injured. The earlier wounds remain. And gas . . ." she continued to tell them of his sufferings in such a way that a stranger might have supposed her to be without pity for them; she seemed to be reading from a document. At the end, after a stifled pause, she said: "He has what one of the orderlies called 'the frozen sickness.' He meant by that just dying—dying—worn out—not having the will to live—wanting to get out of the pain. But here, Rupert says, he will live." She repeated it as though she had been contradicted: "He says—here he will live."

"Is it on Friday he comes?" her mother asked.

Julie counted the days, a smile moving over her face. "Three days," she answered. "He will cross the frontier on Wednesday and stay a day and two nights at the Legation. He is formally attached to the Legation and will be granted leave from there."

"Then we must meet him. You, at any rate."

But Julie shook her head. "He says, No. He wants to come here alone. He says he is not an easy travelling companion."

"But not to meet him——" the Baroness began.

"Ah, leave him alone. Let it be as he chooses," her husband interrupted. "Journeys are hard for sick men. We must have nurses here."

"I will nurse him," Julie said.

"But if there are wounds to be dressed?"

"I think he is past that."

"Perhaps. . . . But there must be one nurse to relieve you."

While this conversation proceeded, Lewis had been silent, the counting of the days, the argument of one nurse or two, ringing in his mind as the disputed detail of common life rings always through the deepest silences. Jacob announced dinner and they began to move out of the drawing-room.

"It's as well I've finished Dirk's manuscripts," Lewis said. "You won't want me here, sir."

After dinner, he went early to his bedroom, then to the library, putting his papers together. Julie, carrying a candle from which the grease had overflowed on to her hand, came up the stair from the empty banqueting-hall.

"Where shall you go?" she asked.

"To the cottage. Vrouw Kerstholt will look after me until I can get a Dutch servant in."

"Not to the Hague, then?"

"Not yet. Ramsdell may come back."

She sat down quietly.

"Lewis," she said, "I don't think I can bear this. He's a stranger to me. I don't know him."

"How long have you known that he was coming?"

"In my heart, a long time. . . . It seems now as if I'd always known."

"You wouldn't tell me?"

"I wouldn't tell myself."

Because he did not intend to work that evening, Lewis had not remade the fire in the open stove. The colour was almost gone from it, the peat was crumbling into ashes; the room was growing cold. But a little blaze sprang up, a primrose tongue blue-edged, and Julie stretched out her fingers to it.

"You will be here, in Enkendaal, though you can't stay in the Castle," she said, seeming to explore her own thought. The light of the fire flowed up wrist and arm to her throat and cast deep upward shadows on her face— a face which, as Lewis watched it, began to wear a closed and secretive expression, like a flower that folds itself at the approach of wind or darkness. As though by repeating a lie she might persuade herself to believe it, she said, "He's a stranger to me. I was a child when I married, and now——" But the lie would not serve and she let it fall in silence, drawing herself up in her chair, leaning her head backward, forcing herself to look into Lewis's face. When he bent down to kiss her, she encircled him with her arms, whispering: "This isn't the end for us, Lewis dear. Right or wrong, I can't bear it now. Not yet. . . ."

His silence and his trembling assented.

"For a little while after he comes we shall be parted. But afterwards," she said, "in the spring, in the summer——"

She was struggling to speak lightly. Against her nature and intuition she forced a hard carelessness upon herself, as though by her husband's coming nothing was of necessity changed between them; but her defiance snapped in her like a tautened string; she knew, and had long known, that the future held for her a challenge not to be averted by any contrivance—the inescapable challenge of self to self, and she would not face it. Was she now saying farewell? A terror, wordless and almost without thought to give it form or substance, travelled upon her, like a hand over her body. She was emptied of the passion that an instant before had been reckless within her and, releasing Lewis, she sat still, like a lost animal.

V

THE BOND

He has outsoared the shadow of our night;
Envy and calumny and hate and pain,
And that unrest which men miscall delight,
Can touch him not and torture not again.
From the contagion of the world's slow stain
He is secure. . . .

SHELLEY: *Adonais*.

CHAPTER ONE

SOPHIE came in from the verandah, where she had been on watch for more than half an hour, to say, exulting: "Here it is! Here's the car, Julie; it's past the lodge!" and Julie without answering went out on to the steps before the front door, where she found her mother and Uncle Pieter.

The trees of the avenue were tossing their heads in a March wind that had freshened since morning, and a rug, which had partly broken loose among the baggage on the roof of the car, was inflated like a balloon, tugging lopsided.

It was something to watch as the car drew near, and Julie gazed at it, pressing her skirt down against the swirling gusts.

Jacob at the bottom of the steps opened the door of the car but no one came out. "Catch that rug," Uncle Pieter shouted, "it will blow away," and when Julie looked down again from the rug a broad-backed woman at Jacob's side was leaning into the car. "Go and help the nurse," Julie heard her mother say, but she could not move, and indeed the figure that emerged appeared to need little help or to be unwilling to accept it. Uncle Pieter and Sophie began to speak in German and Rupert's voice answered them— a voice which had the distant and mysterious familiarity of a scent that, suddenly re-encountered, fills the mind with unidentified memories. Nothing but the voice was familiar; and the strangeness of the man from whom it proceeded—the shaggy whiteness of the moustache and the bared head, the bony pallor of the cheeks, the twist of the body to the left, like the droop of a stiff rope not stiff enough to stand erect—deepened the voice's incision into the past. When he had climbed the steps, he came to Julie, releasing himself from the nurse, and wrenched at his body that he might straighten it. Pain drew down the side of his mouth. "My glove," he said. "There!" and, when the nurse had taken his glove, he lifted Julie's hands in his one hand and tried to stoop to them.

"Rupert!" she cried and moved forward half a pace, thinking he would kiss her, but he held fast her hands, his fingers folded over them, and said in English: "My English name! To hear you speak it—that is what I wanted. Nearly four years now I haven't spoken yours—not aloud—not once—Julie." He checked himself, dropped her hands. "Let me lean on you. I will not be heavy. Let us go in." He entered the hall with her, leaving the little group on the steps as though he had forgotten it.

"You are in pain?" she said, searching his face.

He nodded, silent.

"Always?"

"A little." He stood and waited. She felt his arm stiffen and heavy tremors pass through his body. "But to see you," he said, driving the words from him, "alive, visible, tangible—to hear you—it's like sunlight in a grave." And suddenly with greater ease: "Would you have—should you have known me? Which is good English?" He smiled for the first time. "I could never learn that in the interrogative—'should' or 'would'. You must teach me. I have been reading English—always, but I haven't spoken it."

When he had lowered himself into a chair, he said again: "Should you have known me?"

"But Rupert——"

"No. The truth. The truth. I'm not afraid of it."

"Your voice—and now when you smiled, yes. And now, of course, near you, more and more——"

"My voice and my smile." He turned his head away "It matters not very much—the body."

The nurse came in from the hall, the others following her. He must go to his room and rest, they said. They spoke to him in the brisk, facetious tone of nurses, as though he were a child. Yes, he answered, presently he would go to his room; the journey had exhausted him; but for a little while he would stay where he was, would rest in his chair. It was said with a calm finality that could not be disputed.

Tea was brought in. The external world seemed to be of little interest to him except when Julie alone represented it, and he spoke seldom; but none was embarrassed by his silence, for it was a silence neither of nervousness nor ill-temper but of repose. Nothing stirred emotion in him but Julie's voice and movement. His eyes followed her as though he could never have proof enough of the wonder that she was alive and within his reach. She found his look hard to interpret. The plain interpretation of it—that to-night he would claim her—filled her with dread, and some-times she imagined that behind his blue eyes, which were certainly paler than her husband's eyes had been, was knowledge of her fear, an agony in her shrinking. When in the past she had refused him, or had yielded unwillingly, she had seemed to strike him in the face with a whip, and had not greatly cared; but to strike him now——

She met his eyes, went near and spoke to him. Perhaps he would not claim her. But she found that to interpret his manner, his deep preoccupation with her and her only, in any other way, was to be enwrapped in a different fear—an awe of something unknown and terrible. Like sunlight in a grave, he had said: and she began to think of him as one who had arisen from the grave and was discovering in her, in her life, her being tangible, evidence of his resurrection. When he put his hand on her, there was no greed in the touch but an awful faith which was confirmed by his finding that she was indeed no creature of his imagination, but flesh and blood.

"Now I will go to my room," he said, "and I will say good-night. I shall not come down again." A room had been prepared for him in the passage leading to the tower; it was within a few yards of Julie's door, and leading out of it was another smaller room where his nurse would be within call. "You may sleep quietly to-night," he told the nurse. "I shall not have an attack. I know when they are coming." The nurse began to tell how he had had an attack last night in the Legation, "the first night I spent with him," she added, "and I knew nothing of the case. It isn't asthma, you see, Mevrouw, though it looks like it at first. It's this gas. And he has no position of relief."

"What did you mean," Julie asked when the nurse came out of his room, saying that he was in bed, "what did you mean—'he has no position of relief'?" And the nurse explained that asthmatics generally knew by experience of some position of the body that eased their suffering, "but this," she repeated, "isn't asthma. It's the lungs themselves that choke him. And it is made worse because he can't use the great muscles of his back as asthmatics do when they're having their fight. His muscles are twisted and shot away and his spine is touched." She looked at Julie, thinking: the girl's heartless, she'll stand anything I say; she was professionally angry because Julie had not cried out. "Asthma may not be dangerous to life," she said, "but this—it's just how much he can stand—then there's the heart."

"Do you mean he can't live?"

"One never says that."

"But you think it?"

The nurse hunched her great shoulders. "He's a queer patient," she said. "Was he always like that? Why, the doctor said in the Hague, you might think it was happening to someone else—and so you might. He don't seem to care, not for all he's going through."

"You mean he's brave? . . . He *is* brave."

"Well," the nurse answered, "brave you can call it. It's as if there was a great noise going on—and he wasn't listening. . . . Oh, and I was to say he wants to be alone now. But this evening, before you go to bed, Mevrouw, you will go in, last thing?"

On her way to bed Julie paused at his door but could not enter. She went on to her own room, began to undress, hesitated, thrust her feet back into her shoes. She must go to him now, as she was.

He was propped high on many pillows, his eyes already on the door by which she entered.

"Have I kept you awake? Have you been waiting for me long?"

"Very long, Julie."

There seemed to be nothing of the arm he stretched out to her but the protruding bone of the wrist and a flat forearm which gave an edge to his sleeve as though the silk were hanging on a plank of wood. But his fingers had strength in them. They took, not her hand but her flesh near the elbow, and his little finger moved on the inner curve of her arm. She was to sit at his side, leaning against his pillows.

"Are you afraid of me, Julie?"

"My dear, of course I'm not afraid. Why should you think that?"

"You were always a little afraid, even in the past," he said, and lifted his touch from her.

But she could not cease to tremble, for it was on the inner curve of her arm that Lewis's hand would linger, and her mind was suddenly inflamed by thought of him. The lamp on the table before her became a furry ball of radiance in her sight and the sheen of the coverlet was sliding like a waterfall into the floor's darkness. "I can't move. I can't reach you," Rupert was saying. "Let your head come down to me," and she lowered her head. Her thought, straining away from him, came back to the discovery, which ran through her like the drag of a brier across her throat, that this kiss, the first he had given her, was for him a miracle. He had stretched out his hand and touched the hem of a garment; he had kissed her, who was lifeless, and life itself had risen in him, shaking him with a sacred joy. She spoke to him, faltering, empty, lying words, and he held her to him and kissed her breast and her knees and the palms of her hands, silently, always silently, as though his salvation were in his contact with her. She was frightened by his silence and by the beads of sweat that the unregarded agony of movement had thrown up on the bones of his cheeks. Not now, not now, not to-night, she cried within her, but she could not speak; she was imprisoned in his ecstasy, and if he had bidden her strip and lie down beside him would have obeyed. She began to loathe, as an assault, the gentleness, the adoration, the blind humility of his love. Her tongue ran over her lips. In an instant she would have spoken any words of cruelty to break his power over her and let her be free. But his movement ended. On her breast, his head lay heavily and she saw that he was falling asleep. After a little while he stirred and said in German, "You are crying, my Julie. You must not cry. All the world. . . ." But already he was sleeping.

One of her fingers was clutched in his hand and, if he sighed, she felt his grip tighten. When he began to moan in his sleep, he was quietened by her arm's pressure. Perceiving these things, she began to tremble again that so much power was confided in her; her mouth was dry and when she closed her eyes tears clung to her lashes. An hour passed. The candles stretched their flames and steadied; the fire was set; even the shadows moved no more. She had only to hold him, that he might not slip from her breast.

Next morning Narwitz was awakened by pain, a customary summons. Though an agony of back and shoulder and a cord-like binding of his diaphragm were part of life, he had, in waking, less mastery of himself than at other times, and he cried out. The nurse did not come at once. When shall I learn control? When shall I learn? he thought while he waited for her, repeating the phrase inwardly until it became part of pain's rhythm.

She raised him from the stiffness in which he had been lying. When she spoke in her own language he did not answer, for his Dutch had been learnt long ago, before his marriage, and while in pain he could not command it; but when she used German, asking what he felt, he forced himself to reply, not wishing to alarm her by silence: "As if I'd gone to bed in a suit of armour and it had contracted on me. But it will——" It will pass, he would have said, but the armour choked him. It was necessary to be silent that he might not cry out again.

"It will soon be day," she said.

"Leave me then. I'm more comfortable now," he answered at last. "I shall take care not to fall asleep again."

She was easily persuaded to return to her bed, leaving him to watch the unlighted candles borrow, inch by inch, a gleam from morning. Pain slackened and he was lulled by the softness of relief—a joy he had learned to distrust. If he yielded to it, he would be led into a languorous meditation on the body, his own broken and condemned body; and to think of the body, even in relief from pain, was to yield to it more than he dared yield. Pain was like rising water. In the past he had walked painless, on dry land. Now the water had risen. Sometimes it was very deep; sometimes it flung its darkness over his head and he descried only finality in the darkness. But it was possible —wasn't it?—to float on this water, disregarding its ebb and flow; to recognize it as a necessary condition of life and, however its depths might increase, to float still, aware but unaffected.

To compel his mind was not easy in the dusk of morning, and he had to wrench himself continually out of a despair in which all effort seemed vain. With daylight, Julie will come, he said, but he found it hard to believe. He had so often stayed himself with imagining of her that there seemed now to be some trick in the thought of her lying asleep almost within call. She had sat last night on the edge of his bed; he had kissed her; but he could remember nothing of her going away. She had faded from him as his visions of her had always faded in the past.

But morning came and she with it, carrying a tray. "If you go to your breakfast," she said to the nurse, "I will stay here," and he told Julie that to see her with a tray in her hands had given him extraordinary pleasure; had endorsed her reality, dividing the present from the past. "I never imagined you with a tray," he added, smiling. "This is real."

He tapped the silver with his finger-nail and she replied suddenly: "What is real? The silver? Why, of course."

She had not been listening, and he was about to explain to her that it was she, she herself, who had emerged from a visionary into a real existence, when he found that explanation was useless and foolish. "What were you thinking of?" he asked.

"I was wondering what you would do all day," she answered. "You could sit in some sheltered place in the sun, and we might walk together a little if you feel strong enough."

How could he tell her with what delight her use of the word "we" had pierced him? It was recognition of a unity on which his courage and hope depended. One by one, during the last four years, his ambitions and faiths had been taken from him. Some he had outgrown; some that were substantial once had been made wraiths by his suffering; many had been broken by death. Even the passion that had swept him into war was spent. Loyalty stood, but it was an endurance now, not an exaltation; and when he thought of his country, his Prussia, and of its struggle against a world in arms, he felt that he was watching the last act of a tragedy in which he himself had perished long ago. She only remained, a vital epitome transcending loss, an immortality beyond all the deaths within him. He could not tell her this, but he took her hand saying: "Yes, we will walk together, Julie," and she looked at him, surprised, almost frightened that he should be so deeply moved by so light a promise.

CHAPTER TWO

OFTEN during Rupert's early weeks at Enkendaal, while she was still a stranger to his secrets, Julie was alarmed by his profound response to words or acts of hers to which she attached no particular significance. It was his sentiment, she thought at first, remembering him as he had been. It was a habit among Germans, a form of courtesy, to pretend that a woman who picked a flower for them gave them the world, and Rupert had always been a German of the old school. But the truth, she perceived, was deeper than this shallow explanation of it; there was no formal pretence underlying Rupert's emotion; nor did it suffice to say that, being an invalid and a man who loved her, he was naturally made glad by any kindness of hers. It was not gratitude that moved him, not a sick man's pathetic dependence; nor was it love, as she had formerly understood his love. No man could be more independent than he. To all who came near him in the Castle he was charming and gentle and courteous, but he was separated from them as though he and they inhabited different planes oi existence. In the same way, he was separated from the war. Though he asked for bulletins and studied them with great maps pinned to a table, he made no comment and seemed to be engrossed in a historian's narrative, not in a campaign that had power over his own destiny. Only from Julie was he not separated and, in his imagination, inseparable.

When she went out to the place where he would sit and gaze over the lakes, he seemed scarcely to know that she had been absent from him. Was he lonely? she asked. Had she left him too long alone? "But you are always here," he answered. "You are the lakes and their quietness; you are the sun and its warmth; you are the spring, and the summer that's coming. You are my last throw, my Julie, on the table of this world. The past and the future are included in it."

"Your last throw? Why do you say that?"

"But for you, I should play no more."

"You mean you would die? But why should you——"

"No, my dear, I'm not trying to frighten you with the heroics of suicide," he said, "though suicide is a journey like another which reasonable men are entitled to make. I mean only that to all else but you I am already dead— or shall be when I am fully master of myself. I know that, except in you, the world can give me nothing comparable with what I have lost, and a world that has nothing to give has nothing to take away. I am a German and a landowner. After this war, my land may still be mine and hold its value—perhaps the only thing that will hold its value. But the greater part of my wealth not in land will vanish if we are beaten. If I die, there will be nothing for you; the land will stay in my family; there will be nothing else. And if I live—the whole tradition is gone, or so I believe. In generations, we may build it up again. The Prussian ideal will prevail at last because it is necessary to civilization. But meanwhile——" He moved his hand towards her. "I shall see nothing of it. Only greed and indiscipline and selfishness and the throttling of the best by the many that is called democracy. Why should I share in it or have any part in it? I believe in nothing but that it will some day be superseded, when the world has learned at last what Prussia tried to enforce too soon. I would work and fight against it if I had my strength and my friends were living, but I have none and they are dead. But you are alive, Julie, and in you, perhaps, my children and their children."

"Who are to be revenged on England?" she said.

"To be revenged? O Julie, I have made nothing clear. It is not of England or France or Germany I am thinking. Not of this war or another; they are all put away from me.

But of an aristocracy of mankind that has the will and courage to rule, to breed a tradition and preserve it. Revenge on England? I do not think in those terms. The flower of the two great peoples of the world have choked each other; that is all. We shall pay for it. The great peoples will be ruled by their own degenerates. But some day, if civilization does not perish, the world will begin to think again.

"You revive old heats in me that I thought I had outgrown," he added after a pause in which he looked attentively into her face. "I don't wish as long as I live ever to feel hatred or anger again. Read to me——"

"The newspaper?"

"No, not the newspaper. . . . You can't read Goethe?" She smiled. "You never liked my German verse."

"Prose then. Let's have a book, a long book, that you shall read to me when you have time, little by little. Shall it be Wilhelm Meister?"

"But it isn't a good book to read aloud," she said, "particularly to one who knows it as you do. If you were reading to yourself you would pass over yards of it, but if I am reading you will sit there listening——"

"To your voice, Julie. You don't understand. You will never understand. You think of yourself as a girl like another girl—perhaps more beautiful, perhaps——" He broke off; then continued with fanatical intensity. "But to me you are my life, my hold on life, my reason for it. You hold all that the world has spilled—you have it in the cup of your hands. That I should sit with you beside a great, still lake while you read Wilhelm Meister. . . . Think, there will be new colour on the water with every chapter, and for every sentence a little shifting of the sky. . . . I shall be still, listening; that is the core of sanity in the heart of madness—to listen and be still. But you are right," he added in a changed voice, "Wilhelm Meister is not the book. It is too German—in a way, too close. Some books are absolute—absolute as art or absolute as philosophy. They are no more changed by the circumstances in which we read them than a lake is changed by the moving images of ourselves that we perceive in it. The Odyssey is such a book; the Phaedo is another——"

"The Odyssey! the Phaedo!" she exclaimed, and, when he asked her why she had been astonished, she could answer only that she had not been astonished by his choice, but that it had reminded her——

"Of what, Julie? Do you love the books so much? I haven't heard that ring of wonder in your voice since—I think I have never heard it until now," he added musingly.

"I read the Odyssey when I was a child," she said. "It was that, I expect, the old memory."

"In Greek? Were you a scholar of Greek as well as of Latin?"

She hesitated before answering that she had learned a little Greek, but that for the most part it had been trans-lated——

"Ah! I remember," he said. "By the Englishman who was a prisoner here. Is he still in Enkendaal?"

"In Kerstholt's cottage."

"Alone?"

"There were two others with him. He's alone now."

"Alone by choice?"

Julie nodded. "What you said just now—to be still, listening—that is what he is after. He calls it the stillness of an axis at the centre of a wheel."

"I understand that," Narwitz said. "It is a good meta-phor. The axis that moves forward with the wheel but never revolves. It is a beautiful metaphor. . . . Why does he not come here?"

"How can he, Rupert?"

"Because he and I are enemies?"

"You are officers at war."

"You mean, he would not meet me?"

Again Julie hesitated. "He wouldn't refuse," she said.

"Then? . . . Julie, my dear, he and I are not enemies. I am not the enemy of such men. Ask him to come. He is a scholar. He has a mind and a tradition. . . . You like him?"

"Yes."

"Ask him to meet me then."

Julie did not answer. She had not visited Lewis in the cottage; perhaps, if he were to see her husband, he would know why it had been impossible that she should go, and in what way, beyond her expectation, she was bound by Rupert's imagining of her.

"What book shall I read to you?" she asked. "I will bring it from the library."

"He worked in the library, didn't he?"

"Who?"

Narwitz sought for the name. "Alison. You said in a letter——"

"Yes. But his work there is finished."

She thought that he was listening for the tones of her voice; but he said: "I know the book—Turgeniev's On the Eve. That is an absolute book. I read it last in Vienna before we were married. Read me that."

"In German? There is no German translation here."

"In French then," he said. "Or in your own language. Let it be to-morrow. And when I wake in the night, or if I can't sleep, I shall say: To-morrow Julie will read Turgeniev to me, and I shall hear your voice and see your head bent over the page."

CHAPTER THREE

NEXT morning Julie went down to the Enkendaal post-office with the possibility, perhaps the intention, in her mind of going afterwards to the cottage. If she had met Allard or another walking up the hill towards the moor, she might have gone with him, and, reaching the lane that led to Kerstholt's gate, turned into it; if she had met Lewis, she might have said: "Rupert wants to see you. Come to the Castle and meet him." But when she came out of the little shop, she was alone; the avenue, from which the last few days had withdrawn the freshness of spring, was empty and still. She gazed down the great aisle, barred with May sunshine, and thought how exciting it would be to stand like Samson between two trees and break them. Then she returned by the Castle lodge and the avenue that skirted the first lake. Rupert was in his accustomed place. She felt that it was cruel to stand and watch him as though he were a stranger. She might almost love him if she could but confess, if she could break his eternal repose by leaning over the back of his chair and whispering that——

Instead she seated herself beside him and began to read Turgeniev, but her thought was not in the story. Its distant melancholy came to her as the throbbing of stringed music comes in the night to one who lies awake far from the violins. Her own mind, beset by intuitions of loss and peril, tossed in wakeful fever between remembrances of her love and an eagerness to fulfil her husband's imagining of her. Looking up from the book, she saw that Rupert was in pain; the compression of his mouth was her evidence; but his eyes were calm as the lake itself and she wondered whether it was indeed possible, while suffering bodily pain, to remain altogether aloof from it. Her heart leapt in admiration of this self-mastery, which was more than courage; but from admiration she fell back into a cold, separated awe.

While continuing to read, she wondered when, and in what circumstances, she would meet Lewis again. Every day that passed would give to their meeting, when it came, an added emphasis of intervening silence. How, when they met, should she explain that her silence—but there would be no need of explanation. Lewis would perceive that not failure of her love, but a growth of herself, had withheld her, and that the desperate mood in which it had seemed natural and easy that she should pursue her love in secret was fallen into her past. She remembered Lewis's power of discovering aspects of herself which she did not at first believe in but was afterwards compelled to recognize, and, laying down the book, she said: "Rupert, how does one distinguish between what the mind perceives and what it creates? I mean——" She heard him struggling to answer her and raised her head swiftly, in alarm. She sprang up; so terrible a change had been worked in him that she, who knew nothing of death, supposed him to be dying. His face was twisted and charged with blood as though there were a cord at his throat; his eyes were swollen and staring; the intervals between his breathing were so long that during them it seemed impossible that he should ever breathe again. She would have run for the nurse, but he seized her hand, held it, would not have her go, and while the attack endured he held her fast. Through his struggles, she saw the lake and the great drum of the tower and the sky where no cloud moved; even when she was on her knees beside him in helpless anguish, filled with an obscure shame for the ease of her own body, the fantastic quietness of the scene lapped at the edges of her mind as a still sea laps at a ship blazing.

His breathing eased at last. He lay with head thrown

back, drawing in the unspeakable luxury of breath and expelling it with little vibrant sighs.

"You give me more strength than their remedies," he said. "I didn't know——"

The abruptness with which he let fall her hand warned her that the release had not been voluntary. His fingers had lost their grip; his body had slackened and fallen loose; a pallor, stained at the lips and nostrils with dull purple, grew in his face, and Julie, supporting him, began to cry for help. She could not be heard; nothing answered her but a puppy, yapping in the sunshine; nothing moved but the spiral smoke of a chimney-stack until by chance the nurse came down the verandah steps and began to throw pebbles to the puppy. Julie continued to cry out. The woman turned her head, stared, shaded her dazzled eyes, and came lumbering across the gravel with the puppy dancing at her heels.

For a night and the greater part of a day, Rupert lay in exhaustion, his features visited by the shrunken refinement and the tranquillity of death. The doctor, who knew him less well than the nurse, feared that he might die, but Rupert gazed up at him with a silent challenge that caused him to say when out of his patient's hearing: "There's death in his body, but he has life in his eyes."

"If he hadn't something to live for," the nurse answered, "he might be dead in an hour."

"And what has he to live for? Precious little that I can see."

"His wife."

The doctor was coaxing the lock of a small bag that he had propped on the banisters. "Och! An affectionate couple then," he said with a chuckle, and the nurse, beginning to explain, checked herself and shrugged her shoulders. Julie was walking towards them down the passage.

The doctor shook a playful, encouraging finger at her, wishing to show the nurse that he was at ease among these aristocrats. "D'you know, it's you he needs, Mevrouw, more than me."

He was disconcerted when Julie answered, "Yes, I know," and for his own consolation, more than for hers, he patted her shoulder. She smiled and withdrew, entering the bedroom.

"English," he said, knowingly, and the nurse, making a funnel of her lips and cocking her head, drew in breath with a hiss that committed her to nothing.

When Rupert had gathered strength enough to leave his bedroom and sit in the verandah, he remembered the Englishman. Now that the attack is over, Julie will bring him here, he thought. First we shall talk of subjects that have no nationality; that will be easy enough, unless he's a fool; but when we begin to speak of the war or the destiny of peoples—then we shall have our work cut out. Not to keep our tempers—we are not savages; but to speak our minds, to break down polite barriers, to go, as German and Englishman, to the heart of our subject.

He wondered what Alison was like; Julie, whose letters had a caricaturist's trick of suggesting a likeness in some extravagant phrase, had never described him. He would ask her when she came; meanwhile, Sophie or the Baroness would tell him, and he opened his lips to ask. But, looking at the two women, he hesitated; their silence was pleasanter than their speech which, once begun, would not easily be checked. They were seated in wicker chairs to his left and right. The elder had a frame of drawn-thread work lying on her knee, but her needle had long been inactive; she was gazing at the verandah railings with the dulled unseeing eye of a passenger in a waiting-room. The younger had before her an open book of which she turned a page now and then; once, Rupert thought, she turned two pages without noticing it; she was not reading with continuing interest—perhaps not reading at all.

Only when Julie was not with him did Sophie come; only when Sophie came did the Baroness appear, inevitable as a shadow. Now for the first time he perceived that there was system and connected motive in their coming and going. In his presence they were on guard over each other, though they seldom exchanged a glance or a word; and, looking suddenly into Sophie's mind, he said: What is it that she wishes to tell me but dare not? What is it that the Baroness is determined that she shall not tell? He wondered if there was in Sophie a cabined unhappiness for which she sought relief, and though there was something complacent, almost exultant, in her manner that did not invite sympathy, he was sorry for her. When she and he were alone, she was talkative in vague, timid approaches, skirting the subject, whatever it was, that lay upon her mind, but when the Baroness appeared, she fell into a resigned and stubborn silence, sitting hunched in her chair, her knees pressed together, a book balanced on them, her fingers plucking at it. The Baroness made no more than a formal pretence of being occupied in her sewing. Sometimes she spoke to him, but it was of Sophie that she was thinking.

"Tell me," he said now, "what does the Englishman look like?"

"The Englishman?" the Baroness answered as though she did not understand.

But Sophie understood. Her slack body became animate. Her book closed on her finger. "Mr. Alison," she said, "he is—he is—oh, dark and tall."

What a spray of hatred sprang from those little words, deliberately commonplace!

"That tells me little," he said and waited.

She swallowed and wetted her tongue. "Have you ever seen those statues," she went on, "those statues cut out of wood—French, fifteenth century? Flat cheeks, ridged bones, deep eyes in deep pits so that often you scarcely know whether they're shut or open. A long neck, long hands and——"

"And what?"

"Brown, too—like wood," she said.

"Sophie!" the Baroness put in. "Don't be fantastic. . . . He's a very ordinary Englishman. A publisher of some sort. Why do you ask, Rupert?"

"I should like to see him."

"Yes, yes," Sophie cried. "Do see him. He'd come if Julie asked him." She sprang from her chair, letting her book slide to the ground and lie unheeded. "He and Julie were such friends. But since you came, they haven't seen each other. Not as far as I know, at any rate."

The Baroness, too, stirred in her repose. "It is very natural. An Englishman and a German—here! Of course it's impossible."

"But he is in Enkendaal?" Rupert said.

"He was living in the Castle, working at some papers in the library," she replied with the air of one cautiously opening a long and difficult narrative. "When we heard you were coming, he went—very rightly. No doubt he will soon leave the cottage too. Meanwhile, he won't trouble you. He is very proud, very English. If we asked him here now——"

"If Julie asked him he would come. You know he would!" Sophie exclaimed.

The Baroness disregarded her. "You need quiet, Rupert. Not quarrels and excitements. Not to be reminded of things best forgotten."

"But you would not object to his coming?"

"Object? Why, no. Certainly not, but——"

"Ella hates him," Sophie cried. "She's afraid of him. She——"

"Afraid? Who is afraid?" It was Julie's voice behind his chair. He stretched out his hand to her.

"I don't know, my dear," he answered. "We were talking of Alison. I'm afraid your mother doesn't wish him to come here."

"I have no kind of objection," the Baroness replied in a tone of sweetened anger. "Why should I have? I was thinking of you, Rupert. It will be impossible for you to meet an Englishman who——"

"Is a student of Plato?"

"Plato or no Plato, he's your enemy." Her tongue began to run away with her. "He knows as well as you do that now, after Ludendorff's failure, it is only a question of time before. . . . A meeting could not be comfortable for you or for him."

"Ludendorff's failure," Julie repeated. "Is that final, Rupert?"

"It is not the end," he answered. "We shall struggle on to back the diplomatists and try to save face. But, in a military sense, it is final. No one who has been lately in Germany can doubt it." He spoke with regulated calm as though of some profound emotion belonging to the past. "But am I for that reason to be shut off from this man? We may be of the more value to each other."

"He would come if you asked him," Sophie said, looking at the ground, and Julie replied swiftly: "Yes, I don't think for a moment he'd refuse. Shall I ask him, mother?"

"Certainly, if Rupert wishes it."

He knew that the Baroness's consent had been wrung from her; he perceived the dry smile at the corners of Sophie's mouth; the tension between them was not to be mistaken. Julie would explain to him; and when they had withdrawn—as they always withdrew when she found him—he raised his eyebrows and asked: what was the mystery? "Mystery?" she said, and, when he told her how her mother and Sophie had done battle, she shook her head, saying that he must have imagined it. "Imagined!" he exclaimed. "Didn't you see Sophie's face?" But Julie had taken up the Turgeniev from the table at his side. "How far had we read before your attack?" she asked, sliding her fingers between the leaves; but when she had begun to read he found himself searching her expression as though he suspected her of concealments, and she had read several pages before his reason quieted him with the thought: But naturally she would not wish to insist upon differences between her mother and the Leydens.

"Julie," he said, interrupting her sentence so abruptly that her eyes came up to him in protest and her lips remained parted, "this thing—whatever it is—between your mother and Sophie—it's nothing serious?"

"They have never liked each other."

He nodded. "Nothing fresh, then—nothing to make you unhappy?"

"Nothing."

"That's all I wanted to know."

She moved her face abruptly away from him as though she were afraid that tears would spring into her eyes; then returned, smiling a wry, tender smile, and, with the generous ardour of a schoolgirl, very different from her smile in its quality and significance, took his hand impulsively between hers. As if she were a younger sister, he thought.

"You are good to me, Rupert."

"I love you, my dear."

"So much? . . . It must need the charity of the gods to love me as you do."

"No," he answered, "my love is not at all godlike, Julie. It is the love of a man for a woman. Though I have been an invalid, it is that still. Often I think: Perhaps the time is near when I shall hold you and see you as I used to see you. And forget that bodies are grotesque, poisoned, festering things. And have children—who knows?"

She had released his hand. She was rigid beside him, her teeth pressing her lip, her breath held.

"That frightens you?" he said.

"No."

"But in that way you do not love me?"

"Oh Rupert. . . . Perhaps it matters less than I think. And will change. Before, years ago, I wasn't awake. I couldn't be. Now——" She added with an agonized eagerness in her voice, ruling herself, persuading herself. "In the past, I know, though you were gentle and patient, sometimes I refused you. I will never refuse you now. Do you understand, Rupert, that whatever I say, whatever I seem to fear, even if in some kind of madness I can't control I seem to hesitate, shrink—I'm yours. And it won't be sacrifice or duty—never think that. I shall never wish to refuse you again. Be at peace, my dear; you shall have all the peace I can give. It is yours already. Yours finally."

But while she spoke, tears filled her eyes and began to flow down her cheeks, denying all her will.

"Where is the place?" she said. "Let's read," and she stumbled into the scene in which Bersenyev describes Insarov to Elena. When she had read a few sentences, a single, uncontrollable sob took speech from her. She was silent and ashamed.

"It will all come right," she managed to stammer out. "It shall. It shall, Rupert. I promise. Don't despise me."

"I have never despised you less or loved you more," he replied.

For answer, she hid her face in her hands. She was not weeping; her shoulders were still. Soon she took the book again and, without looking up, began to read—very quietly at first, then with natural liveliness.

CHAPTER FOUR

On the day after his return to the cottage, Lewis had walked on to the moors by a path through Kerstholt's garden. It led him across two rising meadows to a belt of pine trees beyond which the country opened out into a vast, undulating tableland. Afterwards he chose this way always, for it touched none of the approaches to the Castle. From one edge of the tableland he could look down on to Rynwyk, with its river stretched across it in the haze like a ribbon of watered silk; from the other, the Castle lakes were visible, gleaming among the valley woods; and a wide circuit over high ground would take him in the direction of the Huis ten Borgh.

He chose to go out at dawn or in the evening dusk and to keep the house by day, for Julie, if she came, would come in the daytime. Often, while reading in the upper room, he imagined that she was on her way to him and listened for her footsteps. But the silence continued; she did not come; and returning to his book he would be lost in it and look up after many hours to realize with wonder, even with a sense of betrayal and loss, that for thus long his mind had been emptied of her. The images of her beauty would break in upon him as though music flooded through a silent house, but would recede at last, leaving him his own stillness.

Sometimes all his being was held in stress by Julie's silence and by his imaginings of her life separated from his; sometimes this tension of personal longing was superseded by the higher tension of solitude, that tuning of the mind to perceptions beyond common range which, at once terrible and full of delight, enables men to transcend for a little while their loves and fears on earth.

Once he wrote, asking news of her. "Nothing is as I thought it would be," she answered in a letter that bore the postmark, not of Enkendaal, but of Rynwyk. "I can't explain now. Wait until I can tell you. Meanwhile, don't come here, Lewis. But, my dearest, don't go away." She had repeated the command and underlined it. "*Don't go away*. I'll make everything clear soon." He crushed the letter in his hand and started up. Though night was falling, he would go to the Castle at once. The need to cut through her wavering contradictions to some finality, some enduring peace, inflamed him. He set out, but, as he went, the vanity of his own wrath appeared to him; he hesitated, and stood beside the lakes, gazing at the lighted windows of the Castle.

Dread and longing, he thought, are identified in love, and, turning from the glow of light, he saw the trees on the hill behind him lay their quiet branches against the sky. They reminded him of the elms in the fort, as he had so often seen them, through the open window of his dormitory, when all but he were sleeping, and he perceived a profound continuity between that happy isolation and his present solitudes in the cottage. His hand touched a letter in his pocket, not Julie's but his mother's, and he remembered the letters that she had written when his internment began. Then and now she wrote in the same tone, eagerly recalling him to the world. Mr. Ford had died early in April, and she wrote continually to complain of his death; it seemed to her the crown of his neglect of the firm that he should have died at this time. His trustees, as far as they were able, would withdraw his capital; the firm, weakened by him in his life, would be deeply impoverished. "Perhaps beyond all hope of recovery," Mrs. Alison wrote, "unless you ask the Dutch for parole and come to England at once." She was deliberately an alarmist, but Lewis knew from figures he had already received that the work of ten years was to be done again. His mother assumed that it was worth doing and that he would do it; his suggestion that after the war the publishing house might be sold and she and Janet live on the proceeds was resisted by her with all the persuasions of sentiment. "Remember," she said, "that if ever you have a son, you can leave him nothing so valuable as a flourishing business."

Lewis smiled, remembering her vehemence. Perhaps it would in the end become inevitable that he should return to Alison and Ford, but he did not now deeply consider the future. He knew only that to choose between one routine of existence and another was not to choose life itself. Life, he thought, as he walked up the road among the trees, does not consist in outward acts and is little affected by them. It is an inward and secret experience which those who become aware of it—and they are few except in childhood and perhaps in great age—seek to intensify, for to intensify is to protect and sustain it. In this encircled consciousness, on this secluded ground, wisdom flowers from the seed of the mysteries, of which the most fruitful are love and death. Here they yield their immortal fruit, but in the field of action, which men call life, they yield only pleasure and fear, emotions that perish. Therefore they who dwell in the outer field, aware in a sick distress that though they seem to live they are not immortally alive, seek always to drive contemplative spirits to corruptible action and emotion, using every instrument of pride and desire to goad or allure them. And as men are thus divided into those who would live inwardly and those who, in the name of action, are the enemies of life, so each man is divided against himself, being of the flesh as well as of the spirit, and his desires cry in his silences, calling him to betray his own citadel.

His desires cry in his silences, Lewis repeated, remembering with what heat he himself had set out into the night. In the upper room of the cottage Julie's letter was lying on the floor, crumpled, as it had fallen from his hand. He picked it up and gazed at it under the lamp, feeling now neither resentment nor hunger. It was as though the wind had dropped in his soul and she were the calm succeeding it.

Owls hooted in the wood above the cottage. While first
reading her letter, he had been aware neither of their
melancholy complaint nor of the intervening silences.
Now the anger that had been a storm within him was an
anger recorded in a tale and, spreading his books under
the lamp, he was flooded with the joy of integrity recovered, the delight of one who wakes from a thwarted
dream into the power and freedom of daylight.

So day by day he withdrew within the circles of consciousness towards the centre of his being, little disturbed
even by the knowledge that the solitude of his present life
could not endure. Nights of dreamless sleep were followed
by the vigour of the morning, given always to new work,
for his history moved forward now, swift and smooth. In
the afternoons he revised old pages, allowing an interval
of several days to pass between writing and revision; and
in the evenings, among his books or on foot across the
moors, he allowed other men's genius or his own experience to flow in upon him, not compelling himself to learn
from them purposefully or in a way prescribed, but happy
that they should teach him as they would, like wise
travellers encountered fortunately who walked with him
a little while until their road parted from his.

Beneath his happiness in this seclusion was the knowledge and memory of a different bliss, present in his mind
like the sound of a sea from which he was moving away;
and as one who dwells long inland remembers at last not
the turbulence of waters, their fret and change, but only
their rhythm, their everlasting force and splendour, so
his thought of Julie was coloured always by those qualities
in her that were enduring and beautiful. The representation of love as a movement through hunger towards
satiety and indifference, he perceived now, in his own
experience, to be false. It was possible to love in peace;
to desire, and remember desire, without the jealousy of
possession.

The thought of Julie rose continually within him, but
as an endorsement of his tranquillity. Its warmth was the
warmth of the sun, a source of energy and natural delight,

not of a flame, edged, biting, uncertain; and as at night
he would pass through dreams of her into that whiteness
of spirit from which remembrance of this life is abstracted,
so by day his vision of her would fade, not into forget-
fulness, not into love's death, but into a dreamless suspense
of its aching and travail.

By such a mood was he enwrapped when, coming downstairs one morning, he found on a table a letter from Julie.
It had not been there when he went to the upper room on
the previous evening. His Dutch servant could tell him
nothing of how it came; there had been no messengers; and
Lewis remembered that the windows on to the verandah
had stood open all night. Thus Julie had entered and gone.
A few hours ago, in the darkness, she had been in this
room, laying down this letter, secretly, with what expression of fear, of adventure, of excitement on her face?

LEWIS DEAR,

Rupert has asked to see you. I was afraid at first—
not of him but of seeing you again. But he has set his mind
on it. So have I—now. I will tell you why, some day. Please
come. It is best that you should. If I wrote explanations all
night I should say no more than—please come.

JULIE

He could think only that she had been in this room
where he now stood, that her hand had lain on the paper
he was touching. Afterwards she had gone down the gravel
slope towards the gate, looking back, perhaps, to his lighted
window above her, and had returned to her husband. For
the first time he struggled for an image of this man who
claimed and possessed her, and everything before his eyes
was agitated and transformed by the struggle. Even the
wooden table had a bleak, angry gleam. Silence and isolation became suddenly intolerable, and his work so distasteful that, when he went upstairs and seated himself at his
table, striving to pick up again the thread of his argument,
the quiet sentences he had written had a mocking sound
in them as though they were not his own but the composition of some satirical writer aping him. His pen lay idle

at his side and when a gust of wind scattered his papers he did not move. It reminded him of how on the ramparts of the fort the wind would bluster in the pages of his book and rip them from beneath his finger. The fort is empty now, he thought; the barbed wire is dangling from the poles; but every evening the children on the opposite bank turn to watch the train as it passes and wave their caps. Soon this room, also, will be empty. I shall be on my way to the Castle. When I return to sleep here to-night, I shall be entering a strange house. It is already strange to me, he added, raising his head, as strange as the fort would be if I went back to it.

CHAPTER FIVE

THE breeze that disturbed his papers had fallen when Lewis went out of the cottage; even the cord of the verandah-blind did not sway or tremble, so heavy was the air. As he walked down the hill towards the Castle, no shadow moved but his own, and the lakes had the appearance of being covered by a glistening film. At the gates he paused, reluctant to enter, and, as Julie had done nearly a week earlier, he looked down the great avenue that stretched from Enkendaal towards the main road into Rynwyk. The regularity of these elms and of their diminishing intervals of sunshine, their soaring strength wearing anew the quick green of early summer, which had taunted her by an aloof and imperturbable repose, delighted him, and he turned away with regret, for he saw in the endurance and renewals of Nature and her superb independence of men's passions, not a threat or contemptuous challenge to the shortness of human life but a pattern of what man might aspire to become. To go into the Castle grounds and accept Julie's summons was, he knew, to abandon an inward security that was precious to him; but to go back would be to shrink from life in a pretence of transcending it, and he went forward.

His heart quickened at the thought that soon he and Julie would be face to face. The lapse of time would have taken away the ease of their association and each would search the other with an almost sensual curiosity, surprised, a little embarrassed even, by seeing in the flesh the companion of an intimacy that was already becoming a remembered, rather than an actual, delight; and he, shaken by her beauty, would begin to think his old thought, that there was something arbitrary and fantastic—as though Oberon had squeezed juices on her eyes—in her bodily love for him. He remembered how, in the past, this thought had been the subtlest of his pleasures, preserving always a miraculous element in their love so that each evidence of her passion, each rapture of her breath and movement, was to him a fresh wonder never finally credible or established in his mind as a thing known and accepted. It had evoked in him a sensation of brilliant impermanence, not of possessive and personal right, and there arose within him now, not physical jealousy of her husband but a profound repudiation of the being by whom a personal right in her was assumed. The idea of marriage, of exclusive and enduring possession, had never been a part of his own and Julie's love; it had been of the essence of their life together that this idea was excluded from it; and now its entry in the person of Narwitz worked in Lewis's mind like a sudden poison, calling up a succession of brutal and sensual images so loathsome to him and contrary to the natural organization of his mind that his thought violently rejected them, spued them out as the body also vomits a poison. For an instant his consciousness was blank; and when, emerging from bewilderment, he saw that he was still walking under the shadow of the trees at the edge of the first lake, his memory, thrusting aside what was unendurable to it, presented von Narwitz to him as a name only, an idea without association, and his thought was confused and puzzled by it as by some indeterminate terror surviving from a dream. In this moment during which, for him, Narwitz had only a shadowy unreal existence, he saw on the grassy bank at the edge of the drive the man himself, who turned his head and stretched out a delaying hand and spoke.

"You must be Mr. Alison. I have long hoped to see you."

"Yes, I am Alison."

"I am Narwitz. . . . You will forgive my not rising to welcome you? It is hard for me to move quickly when I have been long in one position."

Lewis said in a low voice that he must not attempt to

move; then was silent, even this formal courtesy having required of him an effort of will; but Narwitz seemed unaware of constraint between them.

"That chair is Julie's," he said quietly. "Take it for a little while. Soon she will be coming out to read Turgeniev to me." And he added, when Lewis had taken the chair: "She says that you have been working on Dirk van Leyden's papers. Tell me of them. I have always been curious about that old man."

Though Lewis told him of Dirk's papers, and they fell into argument on subjects arising from them, his impression of Narwitz was at first less of his words than of his eyes and of the extreme frailty of the face in which they were set. It seemed that this was not a man met for the first time, but another long known to him whom he ought to recognize but could not, and, struggling for a key to this mysterious familiarity, he gazed at his companion with deepening intensity until at last Narwitz broke their discussion to say: "What is the question you are trying to answer in my face?" and Lewis apologized for having stared.

"No, no," Narwitz answered. "You were looking at me in a way one does not resent—not in empty curiosity but as if the answer to your question, whatever it is, would be of some genuine value to yourself."

"The question? I suppose I was asking myself: Where on earth have I met that man before?" Lewis said. "Of course we have never met; I know that. But I feel that the few minutes we have spent together are—are like a little island sticking up out of the water. You see an island floating on the surface and you say, There's an island, as if that were all. Then you remember that it's only a fragment, the topmost peak exposed by chance, of a vast sea-mountain, perhaps of a range of mountains rooted in the ocean depths."

"Or rooted in yourself," Narwitz interrupted, throwing out a keenly interrogative glance. "Perhaps what makes me seem deeply familiar to you is that we have one profound interest in common? Isn't it so?"

An interest in common? For a moment, thinking of Julie, Lewis recoiled before the possibility of her husband's suspicion, but Narwitz's expression was gentle and calm.

"I mean," he added, "our desire so to control our lives that we are invulnerable within the world. That is, certainly, a universal desire, but you and I are conscious of it, and that's rare; it's a link between us. Contemplation is one of the words that unite men in Turgeniev's sense," he added, after pausing to pick up from a small table at his side the book that Julie was to read to him when she came. "Do you know this story?" He raised it in the sunlight.

"Yes, I know it well."

"In the opening—and there isn't a lovelier opening to any story; it's the character of Insarov, when he comes, that prevents it from being a masterpiece—in the opening, when the two young men, the philosopher and the artist, are lying in the shade of the lime tree on the river-bank, discussing ants and beetles and beauty and women and love, do you remember how Bersenyev declares that happiness isn't one of the words that unite men? The words that unite are Art, Country, Science, Freedom—so he says; it seems a strange choice to us, over-coloured with liberal optimism. Still, Bersenyev was young. . . . Then he says that love, too, is a word that unites—not the love that Shubin has in his mind, but the love that is self-sacrifice."

"That's a bad phrase," Lewis interrupted.

Narwitz considered it, lifting his eyebrows and lowering them, as though he were tasting a wine. "Yes," he admitted, "smudged. Nineteenth-century liberalism again; even Turgeniev couldn't escape it." He laughed. "No wonder Shubin answers: 'That's all very well for Germans!'"

"If I remember, Shubin had French blood in him," Lewis said, smiling.

Narwitz's eyes sparkled. "Yes. You are right. Shubin wants love for himself. He wants to be first. Then, suddenly—and this is what I've been leading to—suddenly

Turgeniev writes his autobiography, or rather his explanation of himself, his *apologia*, in a phrase of Bersenyev's—'it seems to me that to put oneself in the second place is the whole significance of life.' When Turgeniev wrote that, love was in the foreground of his thought; it was of love Bersenyev had been speaking; but the saying is a universal one—or so I understand it," Narwitz added, gazing before him. Slowly he turned his eyes on Lewis and awaited his answer. But Lewis could not answer at once. He felt that he had been engaged in this dialogue before, long ago—perhaps in his own mind—and his reply, when he spoke it, seemed to have been given him by some prompter whom he was powerless to disregard.

"It seems to me that to discover what to put before oneself, in the first place, is the whole problem of life," he said.

"It seems so to you now. So it did to me—for years. But it is not a problem that any man is under compulsion to solve."

"An artist has his answer, I suppose," Lewis continued, "and a saint. But most of us have none. We snatch at any answer that comes—Freedom, Country, and now, in Russia, Class. Is there any answer that endures except Art and God?"

"Death is the answer," Narwitz said. "No," he added swiftly, "not in the sense in which men say stupidly that 'death is the answer to all things,' meaning only that they are tired of thought. When we are young children, we know nothing of death. Then we become aware of it, recognize it, fear it or conquer our fear of it, seeing it always objectively as something outside ourselves, a final pit perhaps, or a pit we shall climb out of, as some believe, into another life. But there is another stage in the knowledge of death. A man who ceases to regard it as something outside himself and, so to speak, draws it into his consciousness and assimilates the idea of it is completely changed. He is in all truth born again. He sees himself now in a second place absolutely—not relatively to something else in the first place. What occupies the first place he may, or may not, learn some day, but that is not of present importance. The arrogance, the delusion that I have found it hardest to overcome," he said, leaning towards Lewis as though this aided his confession, "the fatal delusion is our belief that we are entitled to first place until we have discovered in our own experience something that transcends us. So we set up idols, our country, our creed, our art, our beloved one, what you will, and pour all our spiritual possessions into the idol's lap. We call that humility or love—Turgeniev would call it self-sacrifice. Except to the gods we make out of our experience or dreams we will not kneel down. But the true saint and philosopher," Narwitz concluded in a tone not of assertion but of longing, "is he who can kneel without an image because he sees himself in a second place absolutely, and to kneel is an inward necessity to him. Fate cannot touch such a man—or, rather, though it rend his mind and body, it cannot affect him."

While they talked, the breeze of the early morning returned. The still gleam of the lakes was changed into a sparkling ripple and Lewis felt the air move coolly on his forehead. Among the trees on the opposite bank, the domed roof of the pavilion was shining in the sun, shining and occulting as the shadow of branches swayed over it, and the little waterfall streamed in brilliant froth from under the darkness of the bridge. Life had never held a gayer or more delicious quietness than at this moment. Lewis found that his mind moved strongly and at ease, as though he had been given new insight into whatever subject they discussed; he had the same pleasure in argument with Narwitz as an artist has in a drawing which simplifies and declares itself before him, flowing with such a rhythm of inward power as he has never perceived in any work of his. Even when speaking of his history of the contemplative life, Lewis found that in Narwitz's presence he understood it more fully than in the past. "The difficulty," he said, "is to make clear the distinction between the inward stillness and balance which is the genuine purpose of contemplation and the indifference to life or the fear of it which has many of the outward appearances of contemplation, but is the product of a lazy or a cowardly mind."

"The distinction is difficult," Narwitz replied, "only because the genuine contemplative and the indifferent or lazy man have certain superficial actions in common, and it is hard for us to distinguish between men except in terms of their actions. Ascetic forbearance may be a genuine discipline or a form of cowardice, and calmness in joy or suffering is easily confused by an external observer with insensitiveness to them. So it happens that many suppose contemplative stillness to be a kind of death or suicide. 'The man isn't alive,' they say. 'He has chosen to go down into the grave before his time.' And of those who shut themselves away from the world and mortify themselves, the saying is in part true. But shutting away is not essential to stillness. The supreme stillness is achieved in the open. We suffer and enjoy; we fight and love, win and lose; but, in the midst of it all, are still. Is that a contradiction in terms? How can a man who delights in victory and suffers in defeat yet be still? Can you, in your history, make that paradox comprehensible?"

"I can think of a childish parallel with it that everyone will understand," Lewis answered with a smile. "When we play a game, we love to win and hate to lose; we don't stand aside in cold indifference but struggle passionately with every energy of body and mind; yet the struggle is unreal; another and deeper life continues independently of the game, and survives it and is not affected by it."

Narwitz answered with a chuckle that this was a very English metaphor. None but an Englishman would attempt to explain the contemplative ideal in terms of sport.

"Socrates wouldn't have hesitated if it had served his purpose," Lewis retorted.

"You are right," Narwitz said gravely, "and you are a better scholar than I am."

"I am not a scholar among scholars."

"That matters not very much if your scholarship helps you to give an idea to the world and saves you from the

folly of supposing that what is old is new. We are working
over very old ground, you and I, searching for treasure
that was currency once but has long been buried and by
most men is forgotten. The world has become so poor
that its ancient treasures of the spirit are necessary to
it. It has formed a habit of thinking in groups, classes,
masses; and civilization is breaking down under the burden
of that error. It is an error because masses are contrary to
nature; they are not born, they do not die, they have no
immortality; the poetry of human experience does not
apply to them. Birth and death are solitary; thought and
growth are solitary; every final reality of a man's life is his
alone, incommunicable; as soon as he ceases to be alone,
he moves away from realities. And the more he is identified with others, the farther he moves from truth. Lenin
is aware of this. He knows that the nearer any human
association is to spiritual solitude, the more damaging it
is to what he believes to be mass-truth. Therefore the
love of man for God or of man for woman is counter-
revolutionary and he would destroy it. It can't be destroyed. When Lenin can merge two consciousnesses into
one consciousness, when he can enable men to yield up
their secrets which now they cannot communicate even
to those they love, when he can break down the isolation
of the human spirit, then he will succeed. Not until then.
Men can share their possessions but not themselves. That
is the mystery and the power of love," he said, his voice
falling again into the tone of personal confession, "it
approaches more nearly than any other human experience
to the impossible sharing of self. Like every other supposed sharing, it is an unreality, but it is the supreme unreality—the last that we recognise as unreal. But it is a
part of your game, Alison; we play it with heart and soul;
all other gains and losses are poured into its loss or gain."
After an interval of silence, he added: "I have not learned
how to transcend it. If that too were lost, should I not,
for all my lessons, be like an angry child who cannot
distinguish between the unreal game that is over and the
continuing reality?" And, having rested long in thought,

he said, with his eyes on Lewis: "I don't know why I ask you this. It is a question I ask of myself."

The tone of intimacy and frankness in which these concluding words were spoken made upon Lewis an impression so deep, sudden and overpowering that he did not reply and was even unaware of any need to do so. He had from the outset recognized in Narwitz an exceptional candour and strength, but had remained, in some degree, an external observer of them, admiring but with reserve, and asking himself, without being able to discover an answer, whence arose his feeling of familiarity with this man whom he knew to be a stranger. Now, with that abrupt and inexplicable transition with which one's thought of a woman changes from "I like" to "I love," a transition which makes of her a new woman and of the world a new world, he said within him: Here is a great man, here is my master! and, looking again at Narwitz, he added almost with terror: To betray him is to betray myself. When he tried to recall the words that had produced this effect, he could remember only the confessional simplicity with which they had been spoken, a simplicity that had seemed to lay open his own as well as the speaker's heart, and he was filled with the shame of one who receives dumbly, because he dare not respond, the affectionate confidence of a child upon whom he has secretly worked some great evil.

But Narwitz's strength was in his capacity to transcend suffering, whether it gripped him now or lay in wait for him. He was not to be pitied. As well pity the triumph of the Cross. All values of the past were changed by being seen in the proportion of his spiritual stature, and, in his presence, Lewis ceased to blame or to defend his own conduct, arguments that would have been applicable if Julie's husband had been a different man seeming now to have become irrelevant.

"That's Julie's step!" Narwitz said, unable to turn far enough in his chair to watch her approach.

At sight of Lewis she hesitated. Her eyebrows went up for an instant and her eyes shone. Then she ran forward and, leaning over her husband's chair, placed her hands on his shoulders. She looked over his head towards Lewis and exclaimed: "So you have met, then!" and waited.

"In a sense, we have known each other a long time," Narwitz answered as though he had power to look into Lewis's mind.

She would not take the chair she was offered, but curled herself on the grass, plucking little shreds of green and scattering them idly on her white dress.

"It's good to see you again," she said to Lewis. "You have deserted us. I didn't dare to come to you. I thought that when you were working——" The bantering untruth would not be completed, and though Lewis covered her hesitation with the first nonsense to enter his head they could not be at ease. Narwitz, whose habit was to speak his thought without ceremony, broke in upon them.

"Do you know, Julie, that he and I have not spoken a word of the war?"

"A good subject to avoid."

"I don't think so. Neither of us deliberately avoided it. It was by chance we talked of other things. But we shall talk of it, and must, unless we are to shut away a great part of our minds from each other, like polite old ladies at a party."

"If we talk of it," Lewis said, "for heaven's sake let it not be with 'tolerance'. What we think, we say."

But Julie was nervous of the subject and led them away from it. What she wanted to say to Lewis she did not know; chance and mood would decide that as they decided so much for her; but she wished to be alone with him, and to find herself now within reach of his hand but divided from him was to her an intolerable penance. It drove her, in an attempt to cloak her feelings, to conversation of a kind that she might have held among strangers. She was already in a highly nervous condition. An hour ago she had gone upstairs, rung for servants and given orders that Rupert's bed was to be moved out of his westward room into her own great bedchamber in the tower. Standing by her dressing-table she had watched the alteration made,

forcing her mind to consideration of its detail—the avoidance of draughts, the direction of light falling from the
embrasures. At night, she thought, I will look after him
myself; the nurse will be within call if she is needed. While
the bed was being wheeled into position she went into her
music-room and seated herself at her clavichord. "Listen,"
she called to the servants through the open door in the
partition. "Tell me, can you hear when I play?" "Ja,
Mevrouw." "Clearly?" "O, ja, Mevrouw." "That is good,"
and she had returned to the bedroom and had walked
restlessly to and fro, refusing to allow her eyes to settle on
the screen that concealed the door leading down into the
library. She had been impatient of the servants' presence,
of their clumsy movements and heavy breathing as they
lifted the furniture. They went at last, looking over their
shoulders, and left her alone, her cheeks flaming. What
would come of this change she did not know. At least
Rupert should not believe that she separated herself from
him.

After sitting for a little while in her window-seat, for
her limbs were shaking and she needed rest, she had gone
down into the garden, thinking that she would find
Rupert alone and wondering whether and in what manner
she should tell him of the change she had made. To see
Lewis had sent a freezing thrill through her body which
checked and confused her. She had been able to overcome
it only by running forward and saying emptily: "So you
have met, then!"

Now, tearing the grass at Rupert's feet, she saw him
fold and unfold his fingers in the sun as though he were
allowing an invisible fabric to run between them, and
heard him say: "This is a day to be happy on."

She jumped up and laughed and stretched herself and,
stooping suddenly, kissed him on the lips. She had not
before done this of her own will and knew not now why
she did it, except that it seemed a part of the determination
in which she had come from the tower into the garden. He
caught her hand, but she could not leave it to him and
drew away, laughing again to cover her withdrawal. As

she did so and her eyes met Lewis's, she knew that Rupert had intercepted their glance. And had perceived its significance? It was ridiculous to believe this; he had not a key to their minds. Suddenly she was possessed by an impulse to kneel down and hide her face in the rug covering his knees and to tell him the truth. She imagined herself behaving in this way and the contact of the woollen rug with her cheek.

A clock over the stables began to strike and far away in the village a bell was ringing.

"I must go back to the cottage," Lewis said.

She watched him go.

"Well," she asked, "what do you think of my Englishman?"

CHAPTER SIX

THE Baron's liking for Narwitz had always been reluctant and a trifle surprised, for his wife had chosen Julie's husband and he distrusted all her judgements. He was, moreover, impatient of invalidism; people should live or die, like animals, he said, and nothing in contemporary legislation angered him more than its sentimental preservation of the unfit. "Run a farm on the same principle and you'd be bankrupt in a couple of years." In the application of his doctrine, he was pleased, with a smile, to be inconsistent, making an exception of women, particularly of elderly women, who were entitled to be cosseted in armchairs and to remember, with him, their youth. As for the illnesses of young girls, he didn't believe in them; marriage was his remedy; but because even young girls were feminine and therefore in his eyes privileged to have their follies winked at, he did not wish them to be humanely killed when they fell sick; they were to be shut away and sent flowers and books until they were sane and presentable again.

But invalidism in men, except in tenants of his who had the grace to die not of sickness but of old age, appeared to him as a contradiction of Nature. Wiry and vigorous himself, with a light in his eye, a spring in his walk, and a seat on a horse that young men might envy, he recognized Rupert's illness as a fact, and even the probability that he would not recover from it, without being able to overcome in himself a feeling of anger against the worn features so often twisted by pain, the crooked walk, the single, emaciated hand. In spite of this, he liked Rupert and often stood beside his chair, cautiously avoiding sight of that hand, and told him that he would soon be better. It was not a fruitful seed of conversation; never had there been an invalid less willing to talk of his health; and they passed on abruptly to speak of other things—of stock and crops, never of politics. So often had he said, without believing it, that health would return with summer, that when the face became less grey, the movement more elastic, and even the skin of the fingers less brittle, it was easy for him to persuade himself that he had been a prophet. "Always said so," he told Julie. "Getting fit is just a question of making up your mind. You live if you want to live; die if you want to die." She repeated this to Rupert, who said: "It's true."

She knew that it was true of him, and the truth frightened her. By his will, by the working of unceasing miracles in his own body, he was establishing his hold on life because she had reappeared in it. In a month he suffered but one attack of asthma, after which, instead of lying like a man in a trance for twenty-four hours, he had rested two hours only, then had risen and, unaided, walked into the sunshine like a ghost. She was beginning to understand that his sensuous perceptions had little force except in association with her. When she was present or when, in her absence, he thought of her, the flowers had scent and the sky colour as they had not for him at any other time. He told her this; it was an amusing freakishness that he had observed in himself: "You see," he said, thinking to please her, "even Nature's your servant." And once, at the edge of the island in the upper lake to which he often asked her to take him, he made her stoop down and dip her bared arm in the water. "That's worth living for," he said.

If these things had been in him a refinement of a passionate lover's sensuality, she would have received them as she knew how to receive like refinements in other men, quietening them with the ease of her glance or turning them aside with laughter. But they were in Rupert stages in his rediscovery of life itself. She could

not interrupt them though she knew that they were leading
to a demand which she could accept but never fulfil. To
accept all things from this man whom she did not love
became for her a passionate vocation. In concealing the
past, she was no longer protecting herself. Neither pity
nor fear nor remorse compelled her. To withhold herself
from confession was part of her expiatory resolve.

Only at night, as she lay in bed listening to the sound of
his breath across the room or, when he was unable to
sleep, waiting through stiff, enduring silences for his next
movement, only then did she have relief from her obsession and allow her mind to drift away. It approached
with timidity, almost with disbelief, the rapture of her
days and nights before his return. He had seemed then to
be unreal, and powerless to affect her illusion of encirclement. Now the joys of the past, which had seemed protected, untouchable, absolute joys, existed only as a
prelude to expiation, and when she and Lewis were together, Rupert stood in their thoughts like a giant by
whose shadow their own love was changed. Changed,
made older, cast down to earth; but not destroyed, she
said. Not destroyed? What remained but their secret and
a profound gentleness towards each other in the sharing
of it? Her lids began to sting and she closed them against
the darkness. She curled her body between the sheets,
aching for a ghost, as she imagined old people must ache
in whom passion, but not the memory of it, was dead.
Then, as though even this thought were a denial of the
pledge she had now given herself, she crept out of bed
and crossed the room to Rupert's side and kneeled there,
staring at the gleam of his high forehead and the pits of
his eyes.

In the morning he remembered that she had knelt beside
him.

His evening meal was always taken to him in the tower,
and except on rare occasions Julie dined with him. He sat
propped on a sofa with a tray beside him on a low stool;
she at a little table with a hand-bell on it. When the meal

was done she rang the bell, and two servants, whom he would not have in the room and who waited therefore in the passage, cleared away. Before going, they lowered the shades on the tall candles and saw that the wood-basket was full, for though it was past the season of fires, and in Holland, but not in Enkendaal, fuel was scarce, Julie would sometimes set a few logs blazing when Rupert was sleepless. To watch the flames was better than to stare into the dark.

At nine o'clock the nurse came to prepare him for the night and settle him in his bed. Julie would go to her music-room and undress; then, putting on a silk wrap and loosening her hair, sit at her piano or her clavichord, waiting for the nurse's withdrawal. When the woman was gone, Rupert's voice would call: "What are you going to play to-night, Julie?" and she would play, sometimes by his choice, sometimes by her own. She had offered to have the clavichord moved into the bedroom itself. "No, please leave it," he said. "I like you to be invisible when you play. Do you know, Julie, what gives me more pleasure than anything in the world? Imagine it. Here I lie on my bed. You ask me to choose music and I choose it. Then, there's silence. Then, suddenly, the first notes—sometimes of the piece I chose, the music that has been waiting in my mind; but sometimes it's not my choice but yours, a clash with my expectation, something that for an instant I don't recognize. Then recognition comes, like a flood. And in the excitement of recognition, the music seems to rise from nowhere—to flow in from no human origin; then, because I can't see you, the imagination of you appears through the music like a face out of a stream, and when the music ceases I think: She will come through that door. I shall see her. After all—she is alive!"

When she returned to the bedroom, she would talk to him a little while, often in German for he loved her to speak it; then stoop over him and kiss him. He kissed her lips and her hand. "Some day," he had said once, "perhaps—a child—at your breast," and had cupped her breast in his hand, as though he held his fate. He would close his eyes while she was stooping over him so that her face might be the last thing seen before he slept, and she, leaving him rigid and with eyelids compressed, would go from candle to candle, extinguishing them.

One night when she returned from her music-room he was not in his bed but seated in an embrasure, looking out on to the lakes—the same embrasure in which she had awaited Lewis's first coming. He turned his head to speak, and she knew instantly what he would have of her. A streak of soft terror like the fluttering of a moth's wings ran up her spine, curling over the backs of her upper arms. She felt the air swing between her body and her nightdress, and drew the folds taut to quell the prickled uprising of her flesh. Then, tilting her chin, she answered him, with a flourish of gaiety like the waving of a flower. She would pluck out fear from herself by a brutal wrench at her own thought. It's nothing, it's nothing, a little thing, she whispered within her. She would treat it lightly as a physical incident to be passed over and forgotten. All her life it must be that, not suffered to become an extravagant martyrdom, and she mocked at herself as she sat beside him for having allowed the word martyrdom to enter her mind. "Well," she said as though she were reproving a child, "why aren't you in bed, Rupert?" and when his hand moved up flank and side, when he laid his mouth over hers and tried to hold her with one arm behind her shoulders, she drew away, but not beyond his reach, concealing her reluctance in a blind, unwilled coquetry that flooded her with self-contempt. Her cheeks burned and a pulse leapt in her throat. She knew that her beauty was inflamed by the burning of her cheeks. He drew back from her as though from a sudden light, gazing in blinded wonder and awe; then, seizing her hand, pressed it against his face and spoke her name again and again in a low voice. "Julie, my dearest, my Julie, my beloved"—again and again, quietly, in the receding voice of one withdrawing from her into the caves of his own mind.

She could say nothing but foolish broken things: and because all that she could say was meaningless and without power to check his illusion, she fell upon her knees at his feet and wrapped his hand in her hair as if she were binding and imprisoning him. While she knelt, with the darkness in her eyes and the knowledge of him stooping over her, she became aware that never, never since his return—never in my life, she added suddenly—had she said to him: "I love you." She would look up, and seek his face and say those words. In the shadows of her hair they seemed true, being made true by her compassion and the reflected gentleness of his love for her, and she began to untwine his hand, believing that she could then raise her head and speak.

She could not. He saw speech upon her lips and waited, but she could say nothing, and he, interpreting her silence by his own longing, took her by the upper arm and led her from the embrasure. As they passed the screen across the door to the library, her shoulder struck it. It rocked but stood; she drew in her lower lip, clipped it for an instant with her teeth, her imagination springing into the past, to Lewis's figure framed in the open doorway, to the candle in his hand throwing the cheekbone shadows upward over his eyes. And to-day, she remembered, when the heat had gone from the air, she had walked with him across the plateau behind Kersholt's cottage and looked down on to the thickening mass of Rynwyk. Though they were silent on the edge of the plateau, Rupert was in their minds. Suddenly she had said: "If I hadn't been married when we met, Lewis, or if he had never come back, if he had been killed——" And Lewis had answered: "We might have been poorer than we are. Whatever comes now comes to us with our eyes open," and he had taken her in his arms and kissed her as he might have kissed a child. They had not kissed since they ceased to be lovers. A tremor had shaken her—not of desire itself but in question of desire—and she had reached up to his lips, wondering how it was that what had once been theirs abundantly was theirs no longer. And she had thought: If Rupert died and Lewis and I were left face to face—a thought that could not be completed.

It rose again in her mind now. With Rupert near her and his power upon her, she understood that even his death would not recover the past; she and Lewis were changed, whether they went on into the world apart or together; and, incapable of looking into the future, she submitted her thought to the pressure of the instant, seeing, as if they were not hers, her breast raised and tautened by the curling of her arm over her head, and, cutting the line of the breast, the curve of her hip, and beyond the hip a naked foot, silvered by candlelight as by being dipped in water. The stumbling awkwardness of his maimed approaches drew her lips into a smile, pitying but cruel in its pity, a smile of which she was as much and as critically aware as an external observer of it would have been; and to banish it from her mental sight, to extinguish finally the cold, solitary flame of individuality that licked at her like a whip, she threw her arm over Rupert's shoulder and turned to him and nuzzled her face into the hot pit of his throat.

Clamped in darkness, she could be still; an absolute passivity quieted the tremors of her flesh; a whiteness, like the shimmer of an opaque mist, stood between her and thought; nothing existed but the blur and sparkle under the fast-closed lids of her eyes. But when Rupert forced up her head and the boundaries of her consciousness rolled back and back in the fierce panic of clouds before a gale, when his breath was on her cheek and his ecstasy included her, she was seized by terror lest he should die, should die upon her breast; and the desire to submit herself to him was all her desire—to be his as he believed her to be; but she could not recall herself from the drift of impersonality that bore her continuously away from him. I am not here, she cried within her, I am not here, and she knew suddenly that all her limbs were stiff, her muscles in stress, her body stone.

At last he lay beside her, deep plunged in silence, his breathing inaudible, seemingly at peace. She waited long; then spoke to him softly; he did not stir. Was he fully asleep? She lifted him high on his pillows into the position in which he must sleep, leaned from the bedside to extinguish the last candle; then lay still. Time's drum beat upon her wakefulness its muffled and everlasting rhythm.

At last, from the edge of sleep, his hand was blindly extended towards her as though he would be assured that what he dreamed now was indeed the fulfilment, and not the repetitive mockery, of his dreams. She held his hand in hers and gazed at the canopy above her—a soaring wedge thrust into the shot pallor of the ceiling, a swerving bulk against the watery flicker of moonlight cast up by the lake; and hot tears, flowing back across her temples, grew cold and stiffened among the roots of her hair.

The memories and consequences of that night hung like a cloak upon her mind. She knew that she had failed and must always fail. When Rupert became aware of the finality of the division between them, his intuition would lead him to its nature and cause. To accept his love and with her own forced responses to renew his patient expectation was to add betrayal to betrayal. In his imagination of her, he was still blind, but his eyes would be opened and he would see the pit to which she had led him, to which, in dread and adoration, she was now leading him day by day. Every tenderness of hers, every act of confidence or affection, seemed to her base and hypocritical, for he was inevitably her victim who received these outward signs as evidence of what was not and could never be. And to escape from this torment of conscience and from her desire to confess, she would go out on to the moors alone and walk until thought was deadened in her; then return and stoop over her husband and kiss him with tears in her eyes.

During these days she refused Lewis's companionship. He and Rupert spent many hours together; then she could see him, but not alone. She could listen to their conversation, not pursuing the detail of it but yielding herself to its strength, its intimacy, its commanding freedom and impetus, and could feel with wonder and delight the pressure of circumstance that bound them and her together. But when the group broke up and Lewis, perceiving the new stress in her, begged her in words or with silent pleading to share it with him, she could not. "Not

yet . . . least of all with you. . . ." They were divided from
each other and frozen, every communication suspended,
and in each mind was the thought, known to the other,
that, though divided, they were bound as they had never
been in the past, secretly dependent as prisoners are who
in their solitudes tap and tap on the separating wall.

One morning, when he came to the Castle, he brought
Ramsdell with him, and, after luncheon, Julie walked a
little ahead of the others towards the boat-house with
Ramsdell at her side.

"Have you come back to the cottage for good?" she
asked.

"For as long as I am wanted."

"Lewis asked you to come? . . . I'm glad. It's good that
we should have you there."

"'We'?"

"Lewis and I," and she put her arm in his.

They crossed the little bridge between the lakes and
stood in silence on the opposite bank, looking across the
water to the island and the tower.

"What is it you are trying to say?" she asked.

"Things that can't be said."

"But to me?"

He put his hand on hers for a moment; then, breaking
the touch, said:

"It's harder than you know, Julie. You see, though it
doesn't affect you one way or the other, I'm an interested
party. But we can forget that or try to. . . . If I talk to you,
I shall say things I don't want to say. You had better talk
to me if I'm to be of any use. What do you want me to
do?"

"Look after Lewis."

"And what of you?"

"That's my own battle," she said. "You can't help me.
You can help him. He's doing no work?"

"Not to any purpose. I have tried to make him come
away."

"Away from Enkendaal?" There was fear in her tone.

"Away from you. Even more—away from your hus-

band," Ramsdell answered. "If Lewis hated him or was
jealous of him, we should know our ground. But Narwitz
has thrown a spell on him as he has on you. My God,
Julie, if you and Lewis were just separated lovers hungry
for each other, it would be plain enough. . . . I know that
sort of torment when I see it, but this——"

Sophie and Allard's wife were advancing towards them
across the bridge, but paused, leaning on the rail, with
white dresses blazing in the sun.

Julie kept her eyes on the two distant figures.

"What drew me to Lewis first of all was——" She
clasped and unclasped her hands. "It's not easy to say,
even to you—even to myself."

Ramsdell waited. "Go on," he said.

"It's just a coward who can't bear her own secrets—
stripping herself of them," she answered. "It's damnable
for you."

"Julie, my dear, say what you have to say. I'd rather
hear it than watch the stifled look on your face while all
this is baffling and choking you."

"It seemed easy at the beginning," she said. "I thought
that, if we became lovers, after a little time the madness
would pass; I shouldn't be thirsty any more; I should be
able to be happy with him again, working and talking—
just being with him; and I imagined that when the time
came to part——"

"My poor Julie!"

"I was mad," Julie said. "So was he. . . . And yet,
looking back on ourselves as we were then, ringed round
in this place, it seems reasonable enough still. So easy to
return to our separate lives outside the ring—some day.
Now we are caught in it."

"Still loving each other?"

"Loving?" She was asking that question of herself.
"Passion is dead—or asleep," she said, speaking calmly
and without bitterness. "No, not dead and broken; not
worn out and frayed and ugly; but once, you see, it was—
the colour of a world we had made for ourselves, and
now. . . ."

"Now the world has become real? The fate of Adam and Eve when they were driven out of Paradise," Ramsdell said. "Not exceptional, Julie."

She smiled. "No. Not exceptional. That doesn't make it easier. . . . And the odd thing is that the world hasn't become real yet. If it had, either we should have parted and put it all behind us, or we should be meeting secretly and leaving Rupert out of our thoughts, or we should be waiting for him to die, wanting him to die so that we could be together. But Rupert has become the most powerful influence in my life—and in Lewis's. What we are now we are because of him and what we become we shall become because of him. I can't tell you why, but it is so. When you know him, you'll understand. I don't love him, except as one loves a god. His love for me, his bodily love I mean, has a kind of terror in it for that reason; it is horrible to me because I worship him—*because* I worship him, do you understand?" She was breathless. "I can't overcome that shrinking. I can't. It's a kind of paralysis—like a dream in which you're turned to stone, no will, no power of movement, just helpless. And he thinks that it's because he is maimed. He thinks, with a dreadful humility that's an agony to me, that he is repulsive. I don't know how to kill that idea in him. I can't. I do everything. I——" She turned her head away.

"Is it a true idea?"

"That he is physically repulsive? No."

"Truer than you will admit, Julie?"

"No! no!" She faced him, her eyes hard and shining. "Don't you understand? I am far beyond that—caring what happens to my body. All I care for is to let his imagination of me fulfil itself. He has lost everything else; everything he has ever loved or honoured or hoped for is poured into me. There's nothing earthly left to him but his idea of me. If I broke that, if he knew the truth, he'd go mad. But he shan't know. He has a power of seeing and understanding everything, except that one thing. He sees through a thousand shams and pretences; you can't lie to him; he has a light in him that shows him his own truth through all lies. But not about Lewis and me. It's a kind of protective blindness. He shall never know; neither through me nor through Lewis."

"And Sophie?" Ramsdell said.

Julie flinched and gazed at the white figure above the waterfall. "She hasn't the courage. She would have told him before now. She will shrink and shrink from it whenever she looks into his face. . . . We must go back," she added. "I promised to take Rupert across to the island."

"Why to the island?"

"He likes to be there."

"Alone?"

They had begun to walk down to the bridge. Julie stopped abruptly. "It's only lately that he has wanted to go there."

"Escape?"

She shook her head. "No. He doesn't need to escape. That's the difference between him and Lewis. Lewis's motive has always been escape—deep down. Rupert has almost passed through that to a final stability. He doesn't need to be physically alone. He's not earthbound as we are except——" She broke off, perhaps in doubt of her own thought, perhaps in hesitation to express it.

"Except in you, Julie?"

"Perhaps."

"Then why the island? Does he let you stay with him there?"

"I row him there and leave him. Then fetch him again."

"Often?"

"Almost every day now."

"Have you ever offered to stay with him there?"

"Once," she said. "He didn't want me," and she could say no more.

Ramsdell saw that she was trembling and gripped her hand. "Tell me, Julie, what you are afraid of?"

"I can't tell you. I don't know myself. There's no reason in it." And she repeated: "No reason; just vague fear." But he continued to hold her and at last she said with the impulse of thought new to her own mind: "What I said

was untrue—about his thinking I shrank from him because
he was maimed. It was true at first. He did think that. He
doesn't now. He's feeling in his mind for the reason. And
one day, when I bring him back from the island, he will
know."

Narwitz felt his peril before he was aware of its nature,
and when at last he knew that Julie was lost to him the
knowledge seemed to be at once sudden and old. He was
walking towards the Castle from his chair by the lake,
leaning on Lewis's arm. "We shot our bolt last spring,"
he was saying. "Since then the French reserves have been
reorganized and Americans have been poured into France.
Our summer offensives . . ." and while he continued to
speak of the war the knots of his deeper thought were un-
ravelled. Julie's shrinking from him when she was off her
guard, her propitiatory gentleness when her will commanded her, the strained reserve and the swift, yielding
intimacies of her behaviour towards Alison—all these evidences and many others, which had long seemed contra-
dictory and puzzling, were reconciled in his mind; and the
truth came to him with indisputable authority as though
an inner voice had spoken it. His fingers tightened on
Lewis's wrist and an agony like tongues of flame licked at
his knee-caps and ran up the back of his head. His sudden
understanding that the man whose wrist he held was Julie's
lover provoked in him no sort of revulsion; but he did not
wish to look into Lewis's face, for a curtain would have
been lifted from its secret, its familiarity would have become unfamiliar, the dark intelligence of the eyes would
be poisoned, and in its calm, which was the mirror of their
friendship, would appear the turbulence of fleshly images.
He would not look into his face, nor anywhere but at the
brown and grey and blue of the shining gravel and at the
gleaming toes of his own boots that flashed and receded
above it, for when he lifted his eyes beyond this little circle
of vision he would encounter a world that had become
barren with the barrenness of insanity—a despair full of
the appearances of joy.

At the steps of the verandah, hearing voices above him, he was compelled to look up. Van Leyden and his wife were propped against the railing; Sophie stood beside them with a basket of flowers on her hard, sallow arm and a pair of scissors hanging by a cord from her wrist; and Julie herself was on the steps. She took his arm from Alison's and crooked it in her own.

"Now," she said.

The ascent of the verandah steps exhausted him. "Let me rest," he said, when she would have led him indoors, and, seated in a wicker-chair, he gazed at the pairs of eyes looking anxiously down upon him, gazed at them with curiosity, wondering how it was that these people with known features and voices were unaware of having become grotesques; and he saw before him the routine of this day, and of all the days that must follow it, as a series of dead experiences, aping life and mocking it, leading to nothing but an everlasting and vain repetition of themselves. He shut his eyes. "My dear, are you ill?" said Julie's voice, and he beheld in imagination the twist of her shoulders as she stooped over the body of a man lying in a chair. With what tenderness she had spoken! With what warmth of affection her hands enclosed his hand, rubbing it between her palms so that he could hear the movement of her flesh on his dry skin! He began to suppose that the knowledge which had visited him as he came across the gravel was part of a dream from which he would awake, and once more he said within him, as he had said a thousand times during the years of fighting: Nothing is lost while she remains; all that perishes is reborn in her. He opened his eyes, reliant upon this faith, which was the rock of his soul. But his eyes showed him her beauty sterile of consolation. He was a child whose mother's breast was entwined with adders; he was the dead summoned to resurrection whose saviour spat upon him and choked him with cerements. His head fell over on its cheek and a long shudder contorted his body. So he lay, smelling the hot odour of Sophie's flowers, and screaming in his throat soundlessly.

CHAPTER SEVEN

THAT evening there were guests at the Castle and Julie dined with them. Upstairs, Narwitz lay in bed, and near to him, at Julie's small table, his nurse ate her meal. His eyes did not move from her, and when she asked him with a determined smile why he found her so interesting to-night he made no answer. To be stared at in this way she found embarrassing, until she understood that he was staring not at her, but at the place at table that she occupied. Then with professional curiosity she returned his gaze.

When Julie entered the room his expression changed. He looked at her with surprise as though he had not expected her to come or had imagined a different appearance in her, and the nurse, who had no great liking for young married women, particularly if they were the wives of her patients and rich enough to live at ease, nevertheless felt for Julie an obscure sympathy and spoke kindly to her, saying that she looked tired and that she must not be troubled for Mijnheer; he had been lying very quietly and there seemed to be no danger of an attack of asthma; the heat at noon must have been too much for him—no more than that. "And now I will be leaving you, Mevrouw, if there's no more I can do. I will look in again at ten."

When Julie advanced to Narwitz's bedside and said that she had come up to play to him, a wave of uncontrollable emotion broke upon his mind—such emotion as had often tormented him when he was a child and a pleasure had been offered to him which, in ordinary circumstances, would have been a great pleasure, but was made intolerable by its contrast with a wild mood of loneliness or despair.

339

He remembered that on the days before his returns to school his mother, who hated his school as he did, would spend the evening with him and allow him to choose their pastime. In the summer he would say, "Let's walk in the garden," and they would wander beyond the garden to the edge of the sweet-smelling wood and return by way of the fruit-garden, where he plucked apricots from a wall and munched them slowly in the dark. In winter, he would say, "Let's sing together," and would stand at her side while she played songs of his choosing; but the delight of each song was an agony to him, and it was a test of his courage to keep his voice clear, a test of his chivalry not to let his mother guess how his heart ached. Those songs, those apricots—their poisoned melody, their tragic taste! How ridiculously he had suffered then—but how deeply! No child of his should ever be made so raw by suffering that each touch of happiness was unbearable.

He had made this resolve long ago and confirmed it a thousand times. Now he knew that he would have no child to whom he might show pity, and he looked at Julie as he might have looked at her if she had been dead.

"What shall I play?" she asked. He tried to answer but could not. He wished to answer because he felt no enmity towards the girl at his bedside but only grief for the vanished being of whom she now represented the bodily shell, and he saw in the movement of her mouth that his silence frightened her. But to choose the music she was to play had become impossible for him and he was glad when she said: "Then I shall choose and you shall listen," and turned away.

There was a long silence. In her music-room she was undressing and letting down her hair. She had been accustomed, while she did this, to chatter to him through the open door. Now he heard only the waterfall until suddenly the melody of a trio of Mozart's cancelled all life external to itself, framing imagination by its own fulfilments.

When it was done, she called out: "Do you remember?" and began at once to play again. For more than an hour she played, now on her piano, now on her clavichord; then returned to his room, her face childishly anxious and eager, desiring, he knew, nothing so much as assurance that, as in the past, her music had soothed him, made him happy and "washed the dreams out of his sleep." He remembered the spring evening on which she had first used this phrase, stooping over his pillow and moving her fingers in his hair. "You are very gentle with me," he had answered, and now, when he made himself repeat the words, she looked searchingly at him as if she were half aware of listening to an echo.

Next morning, when he awoke, he had slipped low in the bed. The old grip of an ingrowing armour was on his body and the nurse had to be summoned to help Julie lift him. All day and for many days afterwards pain continued, until it appeared to him as a thing having life in itself, combative, wilful, unsleeping, a cruel enemy, and he began to imagine, as he had in the past, that it had a face and hands and observant eyes that pursued him. His agony was sharpened by knowledge that this pain, which might be said in loose phrase to have returned, had in truth never been absent from him; for a little while he had been its master, shutting against it the door of his inmost mind, which now stood open, submitting him to invasion and recapture.

He could resist no more. The sustained determination, which had enabled him to establish over himself a rule of conduct and spirit, sufficed now to control his conduct only. He would not confess that his sickness had increased; he would not speak to Lewis or to Julie of what he knew; he would cling to the outward forms of his association with them and of his life in Enkendaal. But within him was anarchy. The spirit is ruled by expectations and memories, of which the first were gone, the second unendurable.

His defence being down, he lay open to every attack—above all to the torments of pleasure in a heart forbidden peace. As the sound of music, summoner of ghosts, had become the enforcement and cruel accent of his desolation, so were all his former delights of sense and thought changed to serpents about him; and beyond the range of his will—as though he were indeed possessed by a succuba, alien to his knowledge of himself—he burned with perceptions of female shape and texture; desire, having ceased to spring naturally from personal love, assuming, in the mind's pit, a vile anonymity of limb and muscle and mere attitude. Yet, when he might have taken Julie, for she would refuse him nothing, he felt that he was divided from her by a wall of glass; and by the same barrier he was cut off from different pleasures, even from the tranquillities of Nature and meditation.

The sound of water, so long interwoven with a faith now perjured, was a perpetual remembrancer of loss; and from the warmth of the sun he would withdraw his hand sharply as though it had been dipped into an irrecoverable past.

From his conversations with Lewis, which he bound himself to continue, reality was emptied out. It seemed, indeed, a kind of hypocrisy to debate the theory of contemplation after he had become incapable of practising it, and in the midst of argument, remembering that behind Lewis's eyes was knowledge of his own secret, he became suddenly weary and fell into drifting silences, aware only of the pain eating his body and of the little patch of sight— the arm of a chair, the knot in a tree branch, a twig bobbing in the water—immediately before his eyes. This was his only relief—to confine consciousness to a gleam of varnish or the wet glistening of an inch of bark; to enlarge his thought was to stumble madly over a desert without limit in space or time; and to remember who he was and to what single folly of love he had confided his being was to be filled with shame for the failure of all his purposes. Against the orders of his doctor, he insisted that Julie should again and again row him to the island and leave him there. He wished for nothing but to be secret, hiding himself from the inquisition of memories, and when, in the late afternoons, he heard the low clack of rowlocks and the spray of approaching blades, he would come down to the island bank and, keeping his gaze fixed not on Julie but on the

slack plume of the bow wave, struggle to ask himself who
it was that came for him in the boat. Who is she? he
said, reaching out towards an unattainable impersonality,
and until she spoke, twisting her shoulders towards him
and allowing the shimmer of the water to flow upon her
throat and breast, he could hover on the edge of delusion.
"Are you ready?" she would ask and, leaning on her oars,
exclaim softly: "Don't move, Rupert. Listen." Her oars
ceased to drip; the ripple at the bows flattened and shone;
time waited, mild and golden.

Lewis was aware of the change in Narwitz and had little
doubt of its cause, but he did not speak of it to Julie. She
was clinging still to her hope that the past would be
swallowed up. She would not look beyond the saving of
her husband's body, which she had set up as a limiting
symbol of her task, deadening thought and setting bounds
to her imagination by nursing him, playing to him, making
herself more and more a slave of his infirmities. That
she had already failed in her struggle, Lewis could not
bring himself to tell her. She would know and suffer soon
enough.

Meanwhile, during the last weeks of August, Narwitz's
guarded knowledge hung over all their lives. He behaved
towards Julie with a mingling of tenderness and pity and
curiosity that made Lewis turn his face away and, when
he could, move out of earshot; for this was the tragic
curiosity with which a man might observe on the stage
an actress's representation of a woman he had loved,
marvelling at the outward vitality and resemblance,
stricken by the lack of inward likeness, perceived by him
only. The same look of incredulous investigation Lewis
found turned upon himself. Narwitz did not regard him
with bitterness or reproach, but as a man might regard
his friend whom fate had chosen as the instrument of his
destruction. On the surface was the same gentleness and
patience, the same rule against pain, the same heroic
reticence by which Narwitz had always been distinguished;
but the spiritual passion which had made him seem godlike

and invulnerable was gone. He was haunted; and sometimes in the evening, when he returned from the island,
he wore an expression of loss and despair, as though, looking down into the waters of his own soul, he had found
there no substance and no image.

Julie became more and more afraid of his visits to the
island, and would invent arguments to keep him in the
garden, on the verandah, in the library—anywhere but in
the encirclement of the dark trees and the lapping water.
On an afternoon of early September she pleaded the extreme heat of the day and the approach of a thunderstorm.
The island was dangerous, she said; he would be wet
through before she could reach him; the trees drew lightning down; only within the thick walls of the library might
he be cool and safe. Her words came from her in nervous
disorder. She could not choose them or govern their stress;
she cared only that he should not go away into the solitude
that had become terrible in her imagination. He looked
at her as though she were a child whom he wished to
humour; then, with a smile at the corners of his lips,
consented. He and she and Lewis went together into the
library.

Day after day for nearly a week the sun had blazed in an
unclouded and windless sky. This morning it had become
a honey-coloured disc seen through a shroud of thickening
atmosphere; the heat had dampened and increased; little
fierce gusts followed by an expectant stillness had set the
trees hissing and had shaken the surface of the lakes; the
air had been alive with flying insects. Now the library was
filled by the white glare that awaits the sudden darkness
of storm, but the storm did not break and the heat
continued.

Seated on a stool, with her body pressed against the cold
wall, Julie listened to the men's voices. This triple association, which had once seemed to her beautiful and miraculous and flowering, was dying now as certainly as a poisoned
flower. She was lonely and afraid. She was filled with an
aching desire to tell Rupert the truth, to tell him now, in
Lewis's presence, so that their frozen relationship might

become fluid again and life, however bitter, return to her. But she remained in the shadow, her eyes moving now and then from one to the other of the two faces above her. One man she loved as a god who in his mind had created her and whom she had betrayed; the other with a profound, mourning, sterile tenderness as one loves the irrevocable dead. From each she was finally separated; to each eternally bound. She gazed at Lewis's eyes, deeply set above hard cheeks made angular by the fall of light, at his lips which long ago, when he was sleeping beside her, she had touched with her fingers that she might feel the shape that the darkness partly concealed from her, and at his hand, lying spread upon his knee, which had once been the core of her desire. Was she finally separated from him? The neutrality of her senses, the power she now had to examine and to ask, fell upon her mind like a blight, and turning away from the beloved features, as she might have turned, in the exhaustion of barren love, from contemplation of the dead, she looked out at the staring sky, her ribs thrust against the stone.

And when there came up from the village the ringing of the church bell, the sound seemed at first to be falling to her out of the metallic sky; she received no meaning from it. Then she stiffened, sat erect, her head raised, listening. The ringing was even and regular; there was persistence but no urgency in the beat.

"What is it?"

"A fire in the woods," she said. "Listen. There'll be a break in the ringing soon. Then single strokes, slowly, to tell the direction," and, the single strokes beginning as she spoke, she counted them. "One—North; two—North-East; three—East." There was a brief interval. The continuous ringing began again.

"That's the virtue of the Dutch," Rupert said. "Even their alarm bells haven't the panic of alarm. Nothing excites them."

"Three—East," Julie repeated. "In the woods between here and the Huis ten Borgh. . . . Lewis, you and I ought to go. Uncle Pieter expects the whole countryside to go. . . .

We'll tell the nurse that you're alone here, Rupert. Or shall I stay?"

"No," he said, "go, both of you. And don't tell the nurse."

"She must be told."

He moved his hand. "Very well, then. If she must."

CHAPTER EIGHT

OUTSIDE the Castle the air stirred, warm and soft, against their faces, not in distinguishable gusts, but as though the whole atmosphere were rocking a little to and fro. No single tree moved perceptibly, but now and then a shudder of autumnal yellow passed through the greenness of the high wood as the edges of innumerable leaves were curled upward into the light; and on the surface of the water beady patches formed and vanished as though a giant were breathing on his shield.

In the sky, cloudless but opaque, the sun was embedded, its rays seeming to spurt out upon the earth as from a molten pit. Beneath its influence the dry heather of the moor and the late gorse close to the ground received a silken gloss. Every rounded stone was magnified by the violence of its own shadows and each chip of pebble that held a facet skyward cast up a piercing splinter of light. Though her shade was thrown in front of her, Julie walked with her eyes narrowed, listening to the slip and crackle of the turf under her feet.

"If the fire is far away," she said, "Goof's people from the Huis ten Borgh will be there before ours."

They talked for a few minutes of the fire, then fell into silence. Ahead of them was Kerstholt, both his legs hanging loose on the on-side of his shambling pony, with pick and shovel and axe clutched to him, and Ramsdell, now walking, now trotting, near at hand. The Baron and Allard, mounted, with four others, passed them, the Baron turning in his saddle to wave to Julie and again to shout to Kerstholt, who raised his hand in acknowledgement and let his teeth gleam in the sun. Across the low undulations of the moor, figures in blue smocks, some on ponies, some carrying tools, some with children at their heels, appeared, vanished and reappeared.

Long silences shared with Lewis steadied and comforted Julie as words could not have done. Their companionship before they had become lovers floated into her memory, a strange companionship in which she had often teased and provoked him, partly in mischief and partly, though she had not known it, in defence. He arose from the past as he had then seemed to her, and such was her power of accepting illusion that she began to lose herself in the past and to recover, as though they now came to her for the first time, ideas and hopes and misgivings which had been hers more than two years ago; to recover and to experience them afresh, to perceive as delicious uncertainties questions to which, in fact, the answer was declared. Her mind was lightened—perhaps for no more than a fragment of a second —of its present burdens, and recaptured the brilliance, the seemingly inviolable isolation, of her first joys—her joy in his freedom and in her own, her rapturous sense of translation to a world in which time and consequence were without effect, there being no inhabitants of it but he and she.

Not venturing to look at him, she took his hand, thinking: Whatever comes, that ecstasy can never be again; and they walked on hand in hand until a rise of the ground brought them within sight of a group of woodmen who were resting their tools and mopping the sweat from brow and throat.

During their walk there had hung in the sky before them, alternately revealed and hidden by folds in the moors, tufts of smoke like grey wool which appeared not to move and to change shape but slowly. Now, as they paused on high ground, they saw that this cloud had become paler and was drifting away in thin, trailing wisps. "The fire's under," Lewis said, but they went forward for another couple of miles until they met the Baron returning. "No great damage," he cried and rode on, beckoning them to turn and pointing to the western sky where the storm so long expected had brought up its forces at last. The sun was swallowed in its pit; sullen clouds, ridged here and there with an angry yellow froth, were growing downward upon the earth, and beneath them the moor had sprung into a hard-edged illumination against which each shoulder of ground, each hastening figure, each tree and copse stood up as though clipped from iron.

"There's a chance it won't last," Lewis said. "Let's make for that wood."

Before they reached the wood, heavy drops had begun to fall and soon the rain was hissing among the branches above them. They found a hut set up last year by woodmen who had felled a neighbouring copse; it still had value as a shelter but was dark and so low-roofed that they could not stand upright in it. They crouched silently, listening to the rain. The temperature had changed suddenly as though heat were being sucked out of the air. Wherever the rain penetrated, the pine-needles and the undergrowth threw up a thin steam.

"I suppose it's useless to stay here," Julie said. "Shall we go on through it?"

He did not answer, but took off his jacket and wrapped it about her shoulders, his action saying plainly that he wished her to stay with him, and she acquiesced, glad that they should be together and that the pressure of her anxieties should be lifted if only for a little while by the chance which held them in the ribbed gloom of this hut.

"I don't want to move," she said. "The rain is a curtain that shuts everything out. I should like this minute to go on and on. Never to have to go back."

"Are you afraid, Julie?"

"Tired," she answered, "of fighting and deceiving. If he had been a different man, or had thought differently of me, it would have been bearable to deceive—and to undeceive him. As it is . . ." She interlaced her fingers and for a moment pressed the backs of them against her forehead, closing her eyes as though her head were aching. "I am failing," she continued. "I know that. I don't know why.

When he came and I saw who he was and what he was, I was afraid. He was so different from anything I had imagined. He made what I had done seem terrible. His life stood up suddenly between yours and mine, like a mountain risen out of the earth. That frightened me first—losing you. And the suspense of secrecy frightened me. Mother knew; Sophie knew; and, worst of all, when we met—you and I—there was this concealment freezing us. And nothing of what was in the minds of us four was ever spoken of. It made all life like an animal waiting to spring. . . . And I wanted to make good, Lewis—to him, I mean. Something in me"— she looked at him, shy before the word that was in her mind—"my salvation depended on it, my integrity." She paused again, listening to the patter and hiss of the wood. "And, after a little while," she said, "something in him made me cease to be afraid. Everything seemed possible—except that I should ever love him fully, as he wished to be loved. Everything else seemed possible. And he became happier, stronger. He suffered, but he passed through suffering as one passes through rain. Now, he's changed. In some dreadful way, he's breaking up. It's not just that he has more pain but that pain affects him more. The news from Germany and from the front—he reads it now with a kind of bitter despair. He had written off his losses; he is counting them again. You, too, know that, Lewis."

"I know he is changed," Lewis answered, "but whether he is breaking up or will become more than he has ever been, I don't yet know."

"Why do you say that?" she asked, and, her thought drifting away from her own question, she added suddenly in a low, agitated voice: "What I am afraid of is that he may kill himself. I'm sure it's in his mind, Lewis. He endures; he doesn't complain; he has an outward calm, still; but his tranquillity is gone. Always I am afraid that there'll be no answer when I go out to the island in the boat. At night, when he lies awake, sometimes I speak to him; he doesn't answer. He's like a prisoner lying in chains, waiting."

"But he will not kill himself," Lewis said.

Her breath was quickened. "Once he said to me that it was a way a man was entitled to take."

"But he will not take it," Lewis replied. "He has out-grown violence, even to himself."

She looked at him as though his refusal to be persuaded to her own terror of suicide were a harshness against her. For an instant he asked himself: Did she desire Narwitz's death? Was her fear of suicide a means of cloaking that desire, of protecting herself from it?

"Julie," he said, "if Narwitz were dead—what then?"

"Don't you understand?" she answered. "I should have killed him. . . . We should have killed him." She clasped her hands in front of her and stared through the opening in the hut at the trunk of a pine tree that was creaking and whining in the upper wind, and Lewis perceived that the idea of Narwitz's death hung over her like a sentence of death upon herself. Her arms were stiffened and her shoulders weighted by the terror of an unendurable finality. "When we loved each other," she said, "we didn't know, Lewis. We didn't know what we were doing. And the joy we had then is turning into thirty pieces of silver." The hysterical violence, the ugly theatricalism of that phrase filled her with shame as soon as she had spoken it, and she threw up her head, her lips hardened and her cheeks twitching under tearless eyes. Then, the tension in her breaking, she sighed and sat back on her heels like a desperate, unhappy child, and stretched out her hand.

"Lewis, what are we to do? What can we do? If he finds out the truth now, he will kill himself."

Again, again this obsessed fear of physical death, Lewis thought, this jealous clinging to it! And, casting about in his mind for words to comfort her, he understood that her fear of Narwitz's death was forced upon her by another and greater fear that her imagination dared not encompass. She was speaking, in terms of the body, of the death of the soul.

He held her hand fast in his own and said: "I think he knows the truth, Julie."

Her fingers jerked in his grasp but he held them. Her

eyes widened, her lips parted, the colour ebbed from her face.

"He can't know," she said, and repeated it slowly and softly. "He can't know." Then, in a flood of words, like the beating of fists against a door suddenly closed: "He can't. He can't, Lewis. Why do you say that? If he knew, he would have spoken to me. He would have been angry. He'd have been wild and mad. And you—could he go on seeing you, saying nothing, doing nothing?"

"You forget who he is and what he is," Lewis answered.

A long silence was broken only by her saying in a vague, light voice: "The rain is stopping." But the rain, unaccompanied by thunder or lightning, continued to fall. The undergrowth steamed no more. Dusk, stretching its web over the trees, drew Lewis's thoughts into a wood outside Chepping wherein he and she had been caught by a summer storm years ago. Nothing but the grave music of rain and foliage distinguished this walk from the many others in which he had been her companion when she was a child; during all the intervening time it had not risen out of his memory; but now the scent of the Chepping wood was in his nostrils and her slim figure pressed against a tree was before his eyes. It had been the backs of her hands that she pressed against the bark; the tendons of her wrists had stood up beneath the tightly buttoned cuffs she was wearing. She had lifted her chin so that the drops from the branches above her might splash on her face; and, laughing, had cried out with a note of disappointment in her voice: "I believe it's stopping, Lewis. I believe it is."

"What are you thinking?" she asked now.

"About Chepping."

She drew in a slow, deep breath. "You will go back there," she said, looking at him as a child might look into the face of some legendary traveller, and he asked her whether she would ever come to him in Chepping.

"To visit you?"

This had been his uncertain thought, but now, challenging his own doubts and hers, he said: "To be with me."

She smiled. "Even if that ever became possible, I

should be a poor ally, Lewis. We knew that long ago," and she added—"even when we loved each other."

" 'Even when——' Is it done, Julie?"

"Is it?" she repeated. "Once it was my blood, my light, my madness. Now, though you are more dear to me than ever before, when you touch me, I feel old. There's no madness left." She faced him. "You, too. If I were free to be your wife, if Rupert were dead, still—between you and me—O Lewis, you know it's true!"

"That we are separated?"

"That I should break your life as I have broken his. Even now," she said with deliberation, "I stand between you and all that's best in you. You are doing no work. Ramsdell told me that. You sent for him—you, who were always content to be alone. You are on edge as I am. This place, which was once solitary and encircled, your peace, the foundation of your peace—you let me into it—you see what it has become."

"Not through your fault, Julie."

"It is the consequence that matters," she said, "the consequence—not the intention. I didn't intend what I have done to him or to you. I loved you." She picked up a handful of pine-needles and let them stream over her palm. "The pardonable becomes unpardonable independently of us. The sin, though it seemed not to be a sin, grows to the stature of what we sin against. Its spiritual consequence leaps up and grows and burns like a forest fire. I see that now. There's no escape from it. None for ourselves; none for those we sin against."

"Unless we pass through the fire."

"Through it?"

"Unburned."

"That is for the gods," she said. "Even Rupert is failing. It was to have been the miracle of his life that he should pass unscorched through every fire. He has passed through so much. But his love for me has trapped him. . . . Now at any rate," she added in a voice of anguish and relief, "we need not be silent. We can go to him and say——"

"Not now," Lewis answered. "Give him time not to fail, Julie. He has transcended every other loss. He is beyond any help we can give or any reparation we can make."

He said this so quietly and with so profound a passion that Julie, hearing again in his voice that ring of devotion and exaltation which had first set him apart from other men in her eyes, turned to him in sharp wonder, in the delight of rediscovery. "You love him," she exclaimed. "You could not speak like that if you did not love him."

"As a pupil loves his master," Lewis replied, and, going out of the hut, he looked up through the branches to the sky, seeing that the storm had passed. The branches, even the highest, moved little. The wind had dropped and between the western beeches a reddened sun was slanting into the wood. Julie also came out, and stood beside him.

Through showering sprays they went on to the moor. As the gloom of the copse fell back and the great expanse of the evening sky shone upon their faces, they were touched by the blissful awe of those who, in the instant of beauty or love, are bound in a common wonder and look deeply into one another and speak silently as they cannot at other times. For the spirit of man is blind and dumb except God touch him, and awake, in the winter of his flesh, the spring of his immortality.

The air, cooled and polished by rain, had that transparency with which at sundown on wet evenings it is sometimes invested, as though the substance of it had been drawn away and there remained between earth's floor and dome only a lucent emptiness edged with crystalline fires. Soon the crystal would be stained by dusk, the forms of earth thicken and night flow on; but for a little while the trees dreamed above their shadows and time slept. Lewis and Julie waited. At last, when the heather had begun to darken, they set out towards Enkendaal.

CHAPTER NINE

"SOON after you had gone," the nurse said to Julie, "I gave him his tea and sat with him in the library while he was drinking it. He didn't speak, but that's not uncommon."

"He wasn't more silent than usual? I mean," Julie asked with hesitation, "did it strike you that he had anything . . . special on his mind?"

"Either a man's silent or he's not, Mevrouw. . . . No, I thought nothing. . . . Afterwards, when he had finished his tea, he held out his cup for me to take. He'd have dropped it, I believe, if I hadn't taken it quick. Then he said he was tired; he would go to the bedroom. 'A pity,' he said, 'that wall-staircase isn't open. We shall have to go down into the hall and up.' He went over and tried the handle of the door. 'Why,' I said, 'that staircase hasn't ever been open as far as I've heard.' 'I know,' he said, but he went on worrying the handle as though he was afraid of the climb down into the hall and up again. 'Come,' I said, 'we shall manage it easily.'

"Well, it was hard going down," the nurse continued, "harder than it's ever been, and before we got up to the bedroom we had to stop several times—not that he wasn't ready to go on, he'll stand anything, but he was heavy on my arm."

"You put him to bed?"

"On the bed. He wouldn't let me undress him, Mevrouw. He lay down and shut his eyes. In two or three minutes he seemed to be asleep."

Putting a hand-bell by his side and leaving the intervening doors open so that she might hear if he rang, the nurse had gone to her own room. She was tired with much standing and had put her feet up. There was thunder in the air and, a heaviness coming upon her, she had slept. The sound of falling rain awakened her. In his room she could not find him. "The little table where you have your dinner sometimes, Mevrouw—it had been knocked over as though he had fallen against it; that was what frightened me."

Julie perceived that the nurse had been genuinely frightened and confused. The panic peculiar to stolid natures when imagination begins to blow hot and cold upon them had awakened in her, and she had hurried through room after room searching for the man she did not hope to find in any of them. He had gone out. Where? He was incapable of going far. The emptiness of the Castle—even the Baroness and Sophie having gone out to the fire—added to her alarm.

While she was telling how she had questioned the maid-servants who, "being of that class, Mevrouw," had stood "like dummies, gaping and wagging their stupid heads," Julie imagined Rupert's secret struggle, his climb down-stairs unaided, his dragging step across the hall, his march into the air; and she tried to plumb his mind. The nurse's voice broke in with an exclamation of extreme self-content. "Then I knew. Of course, he had gone to the island!" Through the rain she had gone down to the boat-house. "What a rain! The lake was all boiling and spitting with it and the gutters on the roof wouldn't carry it; it was froth-ing over them and clattering on to the laurels like slides of snow." The boat was gone, but she had taken the red dinghy. No one to help her cast off the painter; it was slimy and its knot stiffened by disuse. No one to help her row or bail. She had sat there with water lapping at her shins. The rain spurted off the backs of her hands between her knuckles as she rowed.

On the island she had called out but received no answer. She had searched and found him—"deep in under the bushes as though he'd crawled there." At first she had thought he was dead. His toes were driven into the earth, his face was twisted upward and, though his eyes were open, she couldn't see the pupils of them. When, having felt him, she knew that he was alive, and had straightened his body, laying him on his back and propping him with leaves and branches, she had understood that his weight was more than she could hope to lift down to the boat, and, running to the water's edge, had begun to shout for help. Against the slash of the rain her voice would not carry; anyone not away at the fire would be sheltered indoors. There was nothing for it but to return as she had come and fetch help. "I didn't think to find him alive again, Mevrouw," but when she reached the island a second time with Jacob and a stable-boy, the stiff, propped figure had shifted, the eyes expressed consciousness, the lips moved.

Julie knew already the little more that the nurse could tell, but she did not know in what mood Rupert had undergone the ordeal of rowing himself across the upper lake. The boat's helm had been found lashed over. Pulling against it with a single scull, he had landed on the island and allowed the boat to drift away, as though he had intended it to be of no more service to him.

Of the determination that had drawn him to the island he said nothing, and little of what had passed there. An attack of dreadful severity had been suffered; the rain had chilled and stiffened him; he had lost consciousness in the belief that he would never recover it: this was acknowledged to the doctor. More he would not say, the subject appearing to have no interest for him. Day and night, between sleeping and waking, he lay still, like an effigy on a tomb, seeming to regard all who approached his bedside as inhabitants of a plane from which he was withdrawn.

In his own mind was an assuránce that, upon the island, he had made a great part of the voyage of death and been recalled from it. It was strange to him to hear it said that he had been unconscious, for, though the experience through which he had passed would submit to none of the forms of thought and could not therefore be described even to himself, it had not been forgotten; the spiritual impression of it remained, as the impression of a poem may remain of which the words are no more remembered. That it had been active and continuous he did not doubt, and, though his thought could not now encompass it— thought being an emanation of sense and this experience a conclusion from different premises—it was for him a reality so far transcending the appearances of his present state that he felt himself to be indeed a visitor from another world.

A desire not altogether to lose contact with this supreme experience from which he had been recalled dragged at him like a vanishing memory and produced in him, during the following days, a low delirium which was attributed by others to the pain and fever that he endured. In fact, the pain and fever had little part in it, they like all else of this world being to him now in a manner fictitious, as though they were the sufferings of a body not his own; and he took no account of them until he found himself, as his doctor said, rallying, or, as it appeared to his own consciousness, slipping back into life. To slip back finally, to forget what he had known and that he had known it; to accept delusion again and be no more possessed of that farther reality to which he felt himself to have been admitted, became the fear of his heart, and he asked Lewis, who visited him often, whether he supposed that Lazarus, raised from the dead, was in complete oblivion of what, in death, he had seen and known, or continued upon earth in the bliss and torment of unseizable memories. He asked this question in many forms, continually reverting to the subject of it, until Lewis, who had at first supposed it to be the afterwash of delirium and had not seriously applied his mind to it, at last perceived its personal significance.

But Julie, when she saw that Rupert's former will to live was gone from him, supposed that he despaired bitterly of this life, not guessing that he hungered for another as an exile for his own remembered country.

"You must rouse him," the doctor said. "He is a great fighter, but he is fighting no longer," and one night in the third week of October, having lain awake until she could no more endure the burden of silence, she rose and went, as she believed, to her necessary confessional, and kneeling beside his pillow stretched her arm across it, and took his head in the crook of her arm gently, and with her fingers touched his face.

"Rupert," she said, "don't shut me out."

She was warm from her bed and his face so cold against the softness of her arm that his silence filled her with sudden terror, but he answered her: "You will make yourself ill, Julie. You are uncovered. The night's cold."

"It's not winter yet."

"No," he said, "not yet."

The bleak futility of their words, the ungovernable, inconsequent words of a dream, stood across her mind as a barrier between her and the confession she would make, and she said: "You know what I have done, Rupert. Is there nothing I can do now?"

"My dear, all that is far away. I am dying."

"No, no," she whispered. "Your voice sounds as if you were already dead. You must not go in that bitterness."

"Not in bitterness," he answered. "In eagerness and in hunger."

"For death?" She laid her cheek upon his pillow. "Though you know it already, let me say what I must say, Rupert. I have been silent so long. When it began between Lewis and me, it seemed——"

"No," he said. "You are telling me of this world and the body."

"Yes. I——"

He put his hand upon her in restraint. "Julie, do not make me remember you."

From that she fell away and knelt beside the bed, not touching it.

"Is even the memory hateful?"

A little dark cry issued from his throat as he perceived in what way she had misunderstood him.

"It is not hatred that makes me wish to forget," he said. "But my love for you—which does not cease to be love, Julie—love in all fulness by this world's reckoning—is among the things I must leave behind. It held me to life; now it must consent that I go."

"Because I betrayed you?"

"Not as you mean it, Julie. Do not blame or hate yourself for my death. There was a time when it seemed that you had been false and cruel. I could see nothing but your falseness and cruelty. I wanted to destroy the life that held the knowledge of them. It was in that mood I went to the island. I did not mean to come back. In what I was changed I cannot tell you; that is the last secret, which I cannot tell even to myself. But the breath of that change is upon my eyelids, bidding my eyes open, and the warmth of it in my soul like the sun in an apple yet upon the tree, and the taste of it on my lips like the taste of salt waves in the inland air. And what I have tasted shall not be denied me. What I leave behind—suffering and love—is becoming a shadow. You are becoming a shadow and my love for you a story that was told me long ago. Let it be so. If I am to have peace and not fall back utterly into the despairs and raptures of that story, you must consent, and willingly let me to go, without remorse or weeping or condemnation. For even now, Julie, you might recall me. With you, I might read all that story again and believe it true. Even now, while you kneel beside me, the memory of it flows up. Do not compel me to remember you."

"What shall I do to give you peace?" she asked.

"Let this be an end between us. Afterwards, for the time that remains, think that I am already dead. Let me be moved from here to the little room to which I was first taken and where, one night, happier than I have ever been, I fell asleep with my head upon your breast."

"You mean that I am not to see you again?"

"No, Julie, I do not mean that. But when I am able to die, I would go freely and alone, not held by the one farewell that has power to hold me. Let us say good-bye now and become again separate beings without call upon each other. In our own hearts let this be our parting, that we may not be torn apart in the last agony or the last failure of the body."

He paused and said: "I married you without your love. That was a great wrong."

She was speechless, and he spoke again: "Now, Julie, good-bye. May God keep you."

And she drew herself up to him and took his face between her hands in the darkness. "Come back to me, Rupert. I shall not betray you." Though his hand seized her wrist, he made no reply and, a finality greater than her desire for pardon shrouding her will, she could no more entreat him. "Remember a little, then, in this moment," she said, "before you forget for ever."

He drew her down and kissed her. "I remember that without you there would be no world to leave." Holding her shoulder, he asked: "We are at peace?"

"At peace, dear Rupert," she said, struggling to see and remember his face.

"Then let us kiss once more, as travellers setting out."

When she had done as he asked and knew that her lips would not touch his again and that between them the recognitions of love were ended, she felt him take her hand and kiss it. Then, knowing herself released, she turned away and lay down upon her own bed apart from him. She believed that all night she would listen to the waterfall, but, in an instant, sleep with a sigh had taken her.

CHAPTER TEN

In the smaller room to which he was now removed,
Narwitz lay in peace, his eyes resting for long stretches of
time on a little clock, framed by interlaced ribbons of gilt
and covered by a convex glass, which was attached to the
wall above the lintel. The clock was an old one; its hands,
like Chinese eyebrows, stood always at eight minutes to
two; and, because it had so long ceased to give out any
living command or stimulus, it had become, like the face
of a priest experienced in confessions, deeply passive,
receptive and impersonal. Upon it his thoughts might
converge without disturbance. He could, moreover, when
the night had been long, estimate day's approach by the
broadening gleam of that rounded face. A white slip above
the door, like a paring from a new moon, was the earliest
hint of morning.

Even when struck by his agony and fighting for breath
like a twisted animal run down in the street, he would
compel his eyes to the gilded ribbons, as though there were
help in them. He wished to detach himself from the pain
which his flesh endured, and often he succeeded; he was
able to look back upon a writhing body, which was no
longer his own, and to experience, above pain, a bliss
proceeding from it—the bliss caused by a cool hand laid
upon a fever, the hand being in this instance not an
earthly one. During the intervals between attacks he was
without fear of their return. They were of no more significance to him than the common processes of the body,
and his desire for death was not now a desire to escape
from them or from any affliction or wrong, but an eager-

362

ness for that perfecting of the contemplative life which, he was persuaded, was almost within his reach.

His strength was to look forward continually and to feel upon his lips that air of another world which, while he was unconscious on the island, he had seemed to breathe. His peril was to look back; and to fortify himself in the way he was going, to teach himself to die, was his single purpose. He found that, even now, an avoidance of earthly contacts and knowledge was contrary to his discipline. To shut out the world was to begin to long for it with fears and hopes and curiosities not to be stilled, and he could not be at peace, or make any advance towards death, until certain facts were known, accepted and overpassed. For this reason, when countrymen of his came from the Hague to visit him, he received them gladly and would allow them to conceal nothing from him. He asked for news and received it nearly always in silence, from which he would emerge at last to speak of other things. But there were occasions on which his guard was broken down. "Now it is too late," he exclaimed once. "We should have fallen back and fought on the Rhine. We might have had terms there," and when it was objected that this would have been to prolong the war without changing its result, he replied with a flash of anger: "It would have saved the *régime*." Disturbed by his wrath, he allowed his mind to return to the past, and, while the two Germans at his bedside argued without conviction that all was not yet lost, he remembered the September day of heat and storm on which, when Lewis and Julie had set out for the fire, he had remained in the library, overwhelmed by a solitary blackness of mood. Bapaume had fallen and the line of the Somme was being abandoned. Since the failure of Ludendorff's offensive in March he had known within him that victory was impossible; now, while the nurse was bringing him tea, he had understood for the first time that defeat was certain. But he had not guessed that the struggle would end before Christmas.

The fire had spread fast while he lay sick. Now Bulgaria had gone; Scheidemann and Bauer were in Prince Max's

government; a request for an Armistice had been dis-
patched to Washington; the captured territory was to be
abandoned. His visitors had told him that the army itself
was crumbling; to-day they had brought news that under
a political amnesty Liebknecht had been set free.

His mind flamed with grief and indignation from which,
after the Germans had gone, he was still unable to escape,
and Lewis, entering the room, heard him exclaim: "Moltke
sent two corps to the Vistula on August 25. If they had
been on the Marne a fortnight later to close the gap between Kluck and Bülow, Paris would have fallen. Even
without them we ought to have stood." And he repeated:
"Even without them—the flank couldn't have been rolled
up. Bauer was wrong. I was at headquarters in Luxem-
bourg. It was clear enough that Moltke and Bauer were
wrong. Moltke lost his head. He sat there with his face
white and his hand stretched over the table, curling and
uncurling his fingers. We others—who were we?—we
could say nothing. We couldn't overrule him. No one but
the Emperor. My God, what fools—and now. . . ." He
opened his eyes and saw, first, his own fingers curling
and uncurling themselves on the coverlet, then, above him,
Lewis standing in silence.

He considered the Englishman with dawning curiosity,
thinking how strange it was that the face looking down on
him should be, indeed, that of an Englishman, and that
this face, more than any other, was welcome and had
power to recall him from such heat and bitterness as had
just now possessed him. No secret divided them; their
intimacy was far-reaching and tranquil; they could sit
together for hours, sometimes talking, sometimes drifting
away from speech into silences which, when they ended,
seemed always to have been an agreed preparation for
what had yet to be said.

"Will you tell me," Narwitz asked, "what it is that
makes you wish to be with me? I am glad when you come
—always glad. But you have another life outside this
room."

"Yes, I have another life, but you have changed it."

"In what way?"

"It is hard to answer that," Lewis said. "But wouldn't——" He hesitated. "Wouldn't any student of philosophy have come to Lazarus?"

"To Lazarus? Because he was raised from the dead? But I can tell you nothing of the next world, Alison. If you had been taken into a strange country before daybreak and dragged back from it at the first hint of light, there's little you could tell. Some of that light has entered into my imagination, changing what I see——"

" 'Changing what you see?' " Lewis repeated.

"Yes," Narwitz answered. "I can tell you a little of that. Do you remember how, in Italy, early in the fifteenth century, the infusion of the Greek into the Christian vision changed the eye of certain painters, so that in the faces they painted, in the faces of Botticelli, for example, there appeared always a sadness which seemed to spring from a desire to participate in two separate and opposed existences? The women of Botticelli are beings of divided mind or, I would rather say, of divided spirit. Into their knowledge of earth, their love of it, their wish to cling to its sensible beauty, there enters the disturbing breath of aspiration. They are aware of, but dare not accept, their kinship with the angels who whisper to them; and with reluctance, but under necessity, they turn away their heads. They are saddened by visible beauty, even while they rejoice in it, because they perceive, shining distantly through it, another and absolute beauty, calling to them, but by them unattainable. In the same way the infusion of the heavenly into the earthly vision changes the eye of him that experiences it, and he sees men and women, not as empty vanities, as some of spiritual pretension have claimed, nor as self-sufficient and responsible in reason, as the materialists will have it, but as beings whose dominating character is uncertainty—uncertainty of where they are and of what may be their true relation to their surroundings. Seeing them thus, he can neither condemn nor pardon them; indeed, pardon and condemnation are ideas that have origin in human uncertainty and are without final substance; nor, except as one pities the joy and energy of a child, can he pity them. He is in a condition, as Botticelli seems to have been, in which pardon and pity and condemnation and all the judgements of philosophy are fused in wonder."

"In wonder?" Lewis said. "Not in knowledge or understanding?"

"It seems to you vague and indeterminate?" Narwitz answered. "It would have seemed so to me a few weeks ago. I too wished then to know and understand; I supposed that ignorance was what chiefly separated the mortal from the immortal state, and believed that death would be a door to secrets—that after it everything would be made plain. Nor do I suggest now that greater knowledge and understanding are not attained to in the immortal state; but that they are the distinguishing essence of God I no longer believe. What we have hitherto called omniscience is better thought of as an infinite power of wonder. Knowledge is static, a stone in the stream, but wonder is the stream itself —in common men a trickle clouded by doubt, in poets and saints a sparkling rivulet, in God a mighty river, bearing the whole commerce of the divine mind. Is it not true that, even on earth, as knowledge increases, wonder deepens?"

"Then the purpose of a contemplative is to develop the faculty of wonder?" Lewis asked. "Is that the imitation of God?"

Narwitz smiled. "Are you disappointed, like Naaman, that something more difficult is not required of you? It is, I think, difficult enough. The soul hardens like the mind. The mind, becoming set, excludes fresh knowledge; the soul excludes the wonder which is in God and in children and in the gentler saints. The doctrine is not a new one."

And Lewis said: "'Whosoever shall not receive the kingdom of God as a little child, he shall not enter therein.'"

He asked no more that day, but, feeling himself to be in the presence of one who was the bringer of gifts, he returned often to the subject and asked for guidance. Narwitz answered that each man must find his own way, that there was none prescribed. "But what you have in your mind," he added, "is the choice, always uppermost in the minds of men, between the acceptance and refusal of earthly love. You know, as I have long known and as has been sufficiently proved to me, that all spiritual achievement is, in essence, solitary. Women, when we lie with them, look into our faces and ask what we were thinking of in the moment of sensual climax and in the succeeding moment of release. They have seen isolation in our expressions, but they wish us to answer that it was of them we were thinking. We may answer so, but it is not true. The fact that we love them excludes them momentarily and gives us freedom, not from them only, but from our own bodily shells. It is a very simple paradox that though, in that instant, we might remain conscious of a woman to whom we were indifferent—that is, remain earthbound by her flesh and our own, we escape in inexpressible wonder from a woman we love. She has power to release us, that is all; it is a miraculous power.

"You see, just as we teach children to have good manners and to give place to others—in a word, to be courteous and self-denying—so we, while we are in our philosophic childhood, must be self-denying and must love. But self-denial, though a great and necessary virtue, is a virtue to be transcended and left behind, and love also, for love is a distraction from personal unity—it prevents the coming together of the soul. Yet—and this is a deeper paradox—it is on earth necessary to the growth of the soul. To reject it, while we are in a condition to require it, is to stunt ourselves with asceticism and to grasp at spiritual independence before our time. Love, a form of suffering, is, like pain and ambition and loyalty and all profound emotional experience, a form of discipline, being a part of life, itself a discipline; and like all earthly gains it is a designed prelude to loss. When we know intellectually that loss is freedom, then we are philosophers; when loss has become freedom, then we are baptized in wonder and are fit to die. Has the death of Jesus any other significance that is unchanging, whether he was human or divine?

"But I am tired," Narwitz added. "I shall be able to speak little more with you."

It was the last of his conversations with Lewis on the subject which had interwoven their lives. Henceforward, though Lewis visited him often, Narwitz spoke little, having fallen back into himself. His nurse and doctor had become hands and voices. The Baron he could still welcome, for the old man would talk to him of sport and the affairs of Enkendaal as if the blaze in Europe were of little account in the van Leyden generations; but the others—Allard; his wife, Marietje; Goof; the Baroness herself—were of a hopeful, persistent and ardent neutrality that was for him the clink of words. The war, they assured him, had not been fought in vain, for there would be no more wars; Germany, reconstituted, would enter swiftly into the brotherhood of nations; the years to come would be years of healing and peace. They added with the air of schoolmasters that the world had learnt its lesson.

Among them Sophie was an exception. She was without complacency and did not speak of war. Standing at the window, with her face turned away from him, she would talk of trivialities, twisting her hands; then go abruptly, always without having said what she had come to say. But at last, unable to abandon the task she had undertaken, though suffering agony in the discharge of it, she did not go, and he became aware of her voice at his pillow, her agitated, frightened desperate voice, and of the sound of her breath. She was pouring out her secret—that Julie had betrayed him, that she could prove it—could *prove* it; that she had known for months; that Ella had known. "They have all lied to you!" she cried. "All! Lewis as well." There was something pitiable in her agitation; she seemed to be confessing a sin of her own that had sickened her conscience and corroded her mind; and when Narwitz, having brushed her tale aside as a thing not to be believed, laid his hand upon hers as though she were a frightened child, he knew that she was glad of his disbelief. But she snatched her hand away and fell into reiterated accusations, which he continued to disregard. Suddenly she broke off and, covering her face, fled towards the door. There she turned and confronted him, her eyes distended and her lower jaw moving laterally to and fro. "Do you know what else they have hidden from you?" she cried. "Do you know what else? Ludendorff has been dismissed. There's a mutiny at Kiel. And now the Emperor has run away. He is going to the Bentincks at Amerongen. He has left your army to fend for itself. Do you disbelieve that? Do you think I'm lying now?" She swayed, watching him, waiting for the effect of her words; then, all the fierceness being suddenly emptied from her, she was filled with remorse, and tears began to flow down her cheeks. At last, in terror of herself and of what she had done, she pressed her knuckles into the sides of her mouth, and twisted her head and shoulders away from him, and went out.

It became plain to Narwitz on the evening of that day that he had not long to wait. On the lassitude following the next attack, he would go out as on a tide, and would go out alone. The thought of frightened and embarrassed people gathered round his bed to watch him die was deeply repugnant to him. He said this to Julie, and, when she asked whether she might not be with him at the end, he replied that they had already said farewell to each other and that he wished, if the nurse and doctor could be excluded, to endure the final pang in solitude.

While the November days went by, it seemed to him that he lay in a womb, eager for the summons of birth. His mind, though streaked with premonitions of the life he was about to enter, was deeply coloured by memories of the past. Still he asked for news, and the spread of revolt, first to Hamburg, Lübeck and Bremen, then to Leipzig and Munich themselves, was admitted to him. But the names of the Centre and the South fell away. He had returned to the country and the marshes familiar to his childhood. He was astride a great horse of his father's, feeling the stretch of his legs and rocking in the saddle because he could get no grip on it. He was out in the woods, startling and delighting himself with legends, and making of each tree an adventure, endowed by his imagination with terrors and wonders. Over his bed stooped again the promise of life; everything was fresh and shining; Nature had been made for him, the hush of evening and the last flight of birds were his, the hours, the days, the years were waiting for him only. Even in sadness—and his childhood was not free from it—there was a springing emotion, an evidence of life, a pulse; and this pulse moved again in him now and he ached with longing for he knew not what —for an enchantment that was being woven for him alone, for a music that would be poured upon him from the air. And there appeared before him a girl whose beauty charged him with power. She gathered into herself his childhood and his old age; she absorbed his being and released him, as prayer released him, from the prison of his own individuality. Gazing at the lamp beside his bed, he found it impossible to know whether she was of the past that he was leaving or of the future, into which, out of the darkness of this womb, he was to be born; in her, past and future were inseparable; she was his origin and his redemption. And when, on the evening of November 9, the womb in which he lay contracted upon him, and there was neither light nor breathing, and shrewd eyes were thrust into the core of his agony, he saw Julie among the eyes, and recognized her and stretched out his hand to her, for he and she were running together from pursuers through a brilliant wood. She took handfuls of darkness out of a bag swinging at her hip and threw them behind her. Soon they had shaken off their pursuers and were alone in the wood. They fell asleep and, while he slept, he knew that she rose secretly and went away, but when he awoke she was beside him and her going away seemed to have been a dream.

But he was not in a wood and the curved slice of light on the clock-glass above the lintel told him that morning had not yet come. The nurse was lifting him in his bed; there was a hiss from the cylinder of oxygen, and a smell of rubber and vulcanite was stronger than the soapy smell of

her hands. "You were dreaming," she said, and he answered:
"Whatever it was the dream has done me good," for his
mind was clear and he knew that very soon, perhaps before
daylight, he would die. But time passed. The gilding on
the clock began to glisten and footsteps passing his door
told that the Castle was awake.

From a light hovering on the edge of consciousness, he
awoke and asked the time. It was eleven o'clock. He asked
where Julie was and was told that she and the doctor had
just gone from the room. He wished his wife and the
English officer to come to him, he said, and to be left
alone with them a little while.

When they were beside his bed, Julie on her knees with
her face hidden in the coverlet and Lewis standing
opposite her on his right hand, he touched her and said:

"You have loved each other?"

She answered: "Yes."

"With more than the body?"

"With more than the body."

He breathed heavily and was silent. Lewis searched his
face in anxiety, but the long silence seemed not to be of
exhaustion but of thought. His head was unmoved but
his eyes turned from one to the other.

"But not evilly—not evilly towards you. Can you
understand that?" Julie cried, looking at him with entreaty
and interlacing her fingers with his. "Neither he—nor I—
knew you until you came back."

"It is true," Lewis said. "We did not know ourselves,
I think, until your endurance taught us."

Narwitz withdrew his hand from Julie's grasp and laid
it upon her head, weighing down her head, as though he
could not endure to look into her face and would have it
hidden from him.

"I am not asking these questions in jealousy," he said.
"From that agony I am absolved." And afterwards, looking at Lewis he said: "Nor do I hate you, Alison; indeed,
you are the last friend I shall make in this world. Hatred
and jealousy and possessive love, perhaps all earthly love,

belong to the childhood of the soul, as you know. You are among the few men living who understand that they are to be outgrown." He drew in his breath with pain. "And I have learned that there are experiences which quell them. There are experiences," he added with a smile, "which take the place of philosophy."

Julie stirred at his side, urging him to rest.

"I shall have time to rest," he answered, "and I would not rest in doubt. Give me a few minutes in silence. Then let me speak."

"Tell me one thing," Julie said.

"What is it?"

She straightened her body. "Rupert, do you remember, long ago you said—long ago, in Germany, when we were first married, you said——" She could not speak. Her fingers were locked in the coverlet. At last, in a voice shrill but very small, she continued: "You said to me: 'Into thy hands I commend my spirit.' Have I betrayed you in that? In that, too?"

"It was a charge," he answered, "that you could not accept, for you never loved me."

"Until now."

A light entered his face. He raised his hand a few inches, unsteadily, perhaps to cover his eyes, but the movement defeated his strength.

"Even that—is it possible—now," he whispered and, relaxing the weak tension of his limbs, lay in an ivory stillness, an enchantment of memory being upon him. At last he roused himself and for the first time moved his head, drawing down Lewis's eyes to his own.

"I must be brief," he said, "and say crudely what I have to say. I shall not spare your feelings or my own. Julie never loved me in the past with mind or body. Since my return, she has pitied me and she has adored my suffering, as though I were other than I am and raised up on a cross. You, too, have felt—friendship towards me for the same reason? Is that true? . . . But it is you, not I, who have made her capable of her pity and adoration. She has loved you, not me. Often she has lain naked against

me, thinking to give life to me. But it has been her torment
and penance. It has been my torment also and my penance." He closed his eyes and continued: "I see the past
and the future clearly. There seems to be no division
between them. Whether I shall continue in my own
person—a separate consciousness—in another world, I do
not know. As to that, I have no faith to guide me. But I
shall continue here in your thoughts and lives, not as a
cause of guilt——" He hesitated. "Not as a cause of guilt
but as an inevitable consequence."

"O Rupert," Julie cried, "can you not forgive us?"

"Forgive you and set you free? My Julie, forgive is a
word for the gods, and freedom an attribute of the gods.
Here nothing is certain but fulfilment and consequence.
We sow and reap; and if we fail to reap our own harvest
when it is ripe, then afterwards we reap it when it is
poisoned. While we live, we must live our dreams. There
is no other way of passing beyond them into reality. . . .
Come nearer to me. It's hard to see you. Nearer, Julie,
nearer. And you, Alison, nearer."

A silvery pallor had touched his eyelids and was spreading like a curtain over the middle and the lower parts of
his face. "Do not leave me," he said. "It will pass." Julie
gave him water silently and waited.

"My dream," he began, "was one that couldn't be lived.
You were to replace every loss. While you lived, nothing
could die. My friends, my country—all were poured into
you. When no help was left, you were my help. Now——"
A rigor shook him. "I must make haste," he whispered,
and lay still.

Then, in a stronger voice, to Lewis:

"You love her. You have made her. She is the bridge
to your own truth. Will you guard and keep her?"

And to Julie: "My beloved one, there is no other way
that is not barren. We forgive ourselves in this world by
working out our forgiveness."

And to both: "Give me your hands. That shall be your
oath."

His hand lay upon theirs.

"It is your betrothal," he said. "You are not pledged to the dead but to yourselves. Your own vision must confirm it."

He lifted his hand to Julie's face and felt it, like a blind man. "You are crying. . . . I shall not see your face again. It is strange, I hope that I may forget your face before I die. . . . Now, leave me. Call no one. Say that I am asleep."

She would have kissed him, but when he felt her touch upon his shoulders, he said: "Leave me. I wish to forget even your kiss. . . . I wish to be alone."

When they were far from him, he asked:

"Am I alone?" And after a long interval, he said: "My Julie. . . ."

She did not stir, nor Lewis at her side.

And he cried aloud and said in his own language: "Into thy hands, I commend my spirit," and when he had spoken thus, he gave up the ghost.

VI

THE END

CHAPTER ONE

IT was expected in Enkendaal that the Gräfin von Narwitz would travel with her husband's ashes to Germany. Allard and his wife, with Goof in support, shared this expectation and urged that Julie should be made to fulfil it. "In Prussia they will expect her to go. Certainly she must go," Allard said. "If we give way to her now, we shall always give way."

Julie, in a stupor of shock, neither consented nor refused. She knew that by Rupert's death she had been made worthless to the van Leydens—to all of them except, perhaps, to Uncle Pieter; she had become for them their governess's daughter, Julie Quillan, no more; and she watched their cautious encirclement of her with an apathy that irritated them because they could not believe it to be sincere. They could not hunt if the quarry would neither run nor fight, and they assumed resistance where there was none.

Julie was blinded by the flash of the past and the deep mists of the future. For the present she did not care, nor for what became of her. When she thought of her husband, she felt no grief, but only, as part of the emptying of her life, grief's absence, a tearless void; and Lewis, in her thought and in her brief encounters with him, was for her a being to whom she felt herself bound by ties the nature of which she dared not and could not consider. "Give me time," she said, "I cannot think or decide."

The contest over her going to Germany was fought out in her hearing on the day after the body had been cremated in Rynwyk.

"It makes no difference to me," she said, "whether I am here or there. I should have thought that Rupert's people would have been better without me. They cannot want an Englishwoman."

"How can you say now that you are English?" Sophie demanded. "Can't you forget that stubborn, wicked arrogance—even now, when he is dead? In ashes, in this house. You are wicked. You don't know the meaning of loyalty."

"But it is true that I am English," Julie replied. "Above all, to them. And it was Rupert himself who sent me away from Germany."

"The more reason that you should have courage enough to return."

"I must say, I agree," said Allard.

"It would be———" his wife began, and, failing to find the impressive phrase she was seeking, she concluded awkwardly: "It would be the least we could do."

She looked at Goof who, staring first at Julie's straight figure, upright in a chair, and afterwards cocking up his chin towards the ceiling, pronounced: "The very least, I must say."

The Baroness, having perceived clearly since Narwitz's death that all her battles for her daughter were to fight again, chose not to fight on this ground. The journey into Prussia would be intolerable; she imagined the box containing the urn among Julie's baggage; there would be disorganization everywhere, no porters; the girl would have to carry the thing herself. The Leydens were fools; they had no imagination; but they were evidently determined. Besides, to get Julie away now from Lewis Alison. . . .

"Julie has not refused to go," she said. "I'm sure, Pieter, that if you feel she ought to represent the family———"

"Represent the family!" Sophie cried.

"Be quiet, Sophie! I was talking to your father."

"I will not be quiet. I will not be ordered by you. If you think that now, Julie———"

"The thing is plain to anyone not mad," the Baron

said. "There is revolution in Germany. And look at the child—she is worn out."

Sophie's eyes were narrowed by her indignation. " 'The child!' " she exclaimed. "Why must you take her side against your own family? Because you are a man, I suppose. All men are fools and gluttons with her." Her neck was thrust forward, the veins distended by passion, and her fingers were plucking at her black dress. "Or are you so old and blind," she cried with little clusters of bubbles forming at the corners of her lips and her voice rising at each word, "that you don't know what she is and has been——"

The Baron strode at her with both hands uplifted. She withered like a stiff tree touched by lightning.

"Go from the room!" he cried. "Go!" And when she had gone, he said to the others: "There will be no more of this, you understand? Why must you hate her so? She has done you no injury."

"They hate her," the Baroness said to him privately that night, "because they hate me." She wished to be assured by his reply that Sophie's words had been for him no more than a raving, that suspicion of Julie's fidelity to her husband had not been aroused in his mind.

He shuffled out of his slippers and climbed into his bed.

"You women must learn to live in peace," he answered and thrust his face into his pillow.

She was long awake, considering wearily the battle she must fight. Hearing her husband stir, she asked if he were awake.

"Yes," he said. "That affair goes on in my head. Women's voices should be quiet always. They become devilish when they are raised."

"Sophie was beside herself. You must not blame her too harshly."

He chuckled. "It's not often you plead for Sophie, my dear."

"But this is serious."

"Serious?" he echoed. "I know . . . but in what way particularly?"

She had his attention now. Through the gloom she saw his head raised from his pillow, that he might hear better with his right ear.

"Just now, Sophie is scarcely responsible for what she says. Particularly about Julie. I don't think you've ever understood how it is between them. Men always forget that plain women can be hot-blooded too. You see, Pieter, Sophie has been passed over and passed over."

"Nonsense. She could have been married half a dozen times."

"For your name and money—yes. She knows that. That makes it the more bitter."

There was silence in the dark room. Then she heard him fiddling with the watch on the table beside his bed. Not wishing to appear urgent in her persuasions, she waited for him to speak.

"But that has always been so," he said at last. "Why this outbreak now? What concern has Sophie with Narwitz's death?"

It was the question she had hoped for.

"If he had lived, Julie would have been out of the way," she answered. "Now she is marriageable again."

"Then when Sophie said——"

"There is nothing she may not say now to damage Julie," the Baroness interrupted quickly. "We must be prepared for that. Fantastic things." She held her breath, hesitated, decided. "I believe Sophie has it in her mind that between Julie and Lewis Alison——"

"Nonsense. Nonsense anyway. Besides," he added thoughtfully, "Narwitz's behaviour to them both puts that story out of court. The three of them were deep friends. That would have been impossible."

"Still," his wife said, "there are people capable of saying anything."

The old man turned over. Across the gap between their beds she heard him drag the blankets round him and re-settle his pillow.

"They'd better not repeat such things to me."

She waited until he sighed the heavy, contented sigh

that told her each night when he had put his troubles from him.

"If Sophie speaks rashly, we mustn't be too hard on her, Pieter."

"No, my dear."

It was wise, she thought, that Sophie's name should be in his mind as he fell asleep. She could lie more quietly now, listening to his harsh, regular breathing; the danger that Sophie's story might find him unprepared was warded off. Insistence now would serve only to increase his unbelief. How strange it was, she thought, returning to a subject which had long puzzled her, that Narwitz had never known! Couldn't he read it in Julie's eyes and more certainly in her touch? Perhaps because she had never loved him—perhaps, anyhow, the wretched man was so racked and obsessed, so desperately ill, that he was easily deceived. But she despised him for having been duped.

She put the problem away from her. It had ceased to be of importance, for the man was dead. Enough remained to be thought of. To get the Englishman away. He and Julie had never had any intention of marrying, she felt sure, as long as Narwitz lived; they had been elaborately secret; they had taken their pleasure—she smiled tolerantly in the dark, inwardly applauding their worldly discretion—without any wild ideas of challenging the world and attempting an impossible match. Now she was less certain of their wisdom. The match was still impossible. It would burden him, harass him in his work, and it would take her—the Baroness imagined Chepping, almost a suburb now, she supposed. Walking through mud to the station. Mrs. Alison grown old—sisters, vaguely seen; callers, the parish, the tradesmen's books; she imagined Julie going into the kitchen every morning at ten o'clock. An intolerable life for both of them, and if there were children. . . .

Julie herself would have almost nothing; her settlement, after the revolution, would probably not be worth the paper it was written on and her dowry—there was a little in Rentes and Consols, but for the most part it was in

German land mortgages or in City of Moscow Bonds. Nothing. But for that reason the more, he might offer to marry her, and after such a scene as there had been to-day she might, in a fit of madness and loneliness, consent. Anything to get away from Enkendaal! Sophie had always said that Julie would do anything to get away. And once, without loving him, she had married Narwitz. Now. . . .

Still, the Baroness reflected, there's one safeguard—passion must have lost its edge. Passion, money, position—she felt more secure when she had discarded the incentives of which she recognized the power. Loneliness and dislike of Enkendaal, though they might make a child lose her head, would not be enough to blind a girl of Julie's experience to the doom of an English middle-class marriage. But though her reason quieted her fears, she herself had enough experience to distrust her judgement of Julie's emotions. She had never understood them. She had wished to love the child and had failed; an everlasting division between them was the penalty of her failure. There had been, moreover, something in Julie's relationship with Lewis that had baffled her. None of the blowing hot and cold, none of the violences that were to be looked for in those who, with a cautious eye on the world, were taking their pleasure secretly! She had said nothing, for there had been no other way but silence to guard the marriage; but she knew now intuitively that there had been a truth which had eluded her.

For a little while, she allowed the mystery to trouble her, turning it over and over in her mind, and wishing with all her heart that now—now with more urgency than ever before in their lives—she could break down the barrier between herself and her daughter. If Julie would confide in her, would lay aside for a little while her steady hostility, then she could help her. The Baroness, thinking of herself now as Ella Hoek and not as the great lady she had become, looked back upon her life with mingled sadness and triumph. How she had fought for Julie—with what cleverness, with what success! And now, when Julie had failed and lost everything, how she would fight again—if only Julie would play her part! But Julie had always been ungrateful. There had never been love or intimacy between them since Julie had passed beyond a child's understanding. But perhaps, the Baroness thought, warmed by her own forgiving spirit, I may be able to soften her heart and guide her even now. First, I will win her to me. That I have never spoken of what I have known will prove to her that she can trust me. Then we must be rid of the Englishman. In any case, now that the Armistice is signed, he cannot stay in Holland long, and he must not loiter in Enkendaal. . . .

Until she was re-established in the Castle, Julie must bide her time. Bide her time, the Baroness repeated, but it must not be put to her in that way. That would fire her. She must not even be allowed to understand in what way I am working for her good.

She sighed over Julie's unreason and the ingratitude of children, but as she was falling asleep she remembered with satisfaction that, though Julie had lost all else that had been won for her, her youth and her beauty remained. Germany now was useless; nor was a French son-in-law to be thought of; but in England Julie's slimness would be more appreciated than in Holland and, though she was a widow, there were Scottish noblemen who . . . Now that the war was over it would be possible to travel again. Claridge's would not be changed. In dreams of London and Scotland, Ella Hoek passed hopefully into unconsciousness of the ingratitude and unreason of the world.

Inaction had served her well in the past, and for a week she relied upon it. Soon the Englishmen would go from the cottage, though how soon neither she nor they could certainly tell. Meanwhile, Sophie was hugging her knowledge, aware that to attempt to use it in her father's present mood would be to waste it. If she waits too long, the Baroness thought, and the Englishmen leave Enkendaal, Sophie will miss her market.

Seeing this clearly, the Baroness was patient. But she

itched for action, and every day that passed, every meeting between Lewis and Julie, enlivened the itch. Their meetings were outwardly harmless and could not damage them in the eyes of the world, but what decisions were being made, or had been made, between them, she dared not guess. She imagined that, without her knowledge, the ground might be crumbling under her feet. Fear presented to her Sophie's and Allard's derision if Lewis were to go suddenly and Julie with him. Julie, restless, weary, dully expectant, was capable of any folly.

"In the spring, Julie," she said at last, "when it is possible to travel, shall we go abroad together, you and I? It will make a break before settling down in Enkendaal again."

"I don't think I can ever settle down in Enkendaal again," Julie answered.

"But this is your home, my dear. You have no other. . . . Now, let us think where we should like to travel. I haven't planned a real holiday for five years. You shall choose. I want to do what pleases you."

"I know, mother. You have always thought of me—too much perhaps. We may never have got on together; we're differently made. But I'm not ungrateful."

"Then, my dear——"

"What, mother?"

"Won't you let me help you again?"

"In what way can you help me?"

The Baroness sighed. "I can't help you at all if you will not trust me. You have reason to trust me, you know. Another woman, who cared less for her daughter's point of view—for her independence—might have behaved differently when she knew that——"

"That Lewis was my lover?"

"It was natural and forgivable in the circumstances of the war." The Baroness touched her daughter's hand with groping affection. "I have been young myself." She smiled, though she had little heart for smiling.

Julie withdrew from her. "It was not for that reason you were silent, mother."

The Baroness made a little gesture of despair. "My

dear Julie, do you blame your mother for safeguarding your marriage?"

"No, but it does not bring us nearer as human beings with understanding of each other."

"You are hard, Julie."

"We are both hard, mother, when we are together."

The little silence that fell between them included all their past. Looking into it, the elder woman saw her struggle and her justification.

"You forget," she said, "that I fought the Leydens, alone here, when you were a child. To establish you. To gain recognition for you. To make you Sophie's equal. You forget all that."

Julie was standing by the mantelpiece in her mother's own sitting-room—the room, she remembered suddenly, in which she had been taught Dutch when she was a child.

"No, mother, I don't forget. That's what I'm grateful for. But you were fighting the wrong battle as far as I was concerned. And you'd fight it again. You *are* fighting it again—now?"

"If you have sense enough to help me."

Julie turned from the fireplace and looked down on the trim, proud figure seated on the sofa's edge, striving to identify it with the mother she had known in England— the mother of her early childhood whom her father had worshipped. Perhaps, she thought suddenly, as Rupert worshipped me—and with as little cause. And her eyes filled with tears. She tried to check them but could not; she had no wish to shed tears in her mother's presence, but they overflowed from her eyes; her lip trembled and her throat burned. And she saw the expression in the face before her change from astonishment to a flurried mingling of tenderness and gratification. Her mother rose and took her in her arms. The falseness, the absurd theatricalism, of her weeping in her mother's arms struck her; but, though she was aware of the stiffness of her own body— the stiffness of a dressmaker's dummy tipped forward on its stand—she had no power to resist. The warm drops were drying on her cheeks. Her mother was making low, clucking noises in her ear.

She broke free with a wrench of her shoulders and an instant later was regretting the petulant violence of her movement.

"O Julie!" her mother said, twisting her ringed hands together as a cottage-woman twists her apron in embarrassment and grief. "Julie, dear, what have I done that you can't bear me to touch you even when you cry?"

"I wasn't crying. I wasn't crying," Julie said, and, sitting down, curled her body away, hid her face in the back of her chair and sobbed as though her heart would break.

The Baroness also sat down, took out her handkerchief, and waited.

Soon, dry-eyed, they were gazing at each other, while a great Persian cat twined itself to and fro between them.

"I'm sorry, mother. I didn't mean to be brutal. I——"

"Now, listen, Julie. Since, as you say—and as you prove, we are hard when we are together, let us at any rate see things as they are. You say like a schoolgirl that you can never settle down in Enkendaal again. Where else are you going, tell me that? You have pocket-money that came to you at your father's death. Apart from that you have little—probably nothing. You are a pensioner here whether you like it or not."

Julie did not answer. The Baroness went on: "Very well. You must make your bed if you are to lie in it. Apart from myself, you have one friend in the world—your step-father. You have been nothing but trouble and expense to him, but he likes you; there it is. But if he knew what you had done, he would wash his hands of you. Mr. Alison was his guest; you were under his protection; your husband was at the war. You know your step-father's code of honour well enough——"

"If it is true," Julie said, "that he would 'wash his hands of me,' it is useless, mother, for you to fight any more. Sophie will tell him."

"He will not believe Sophie. I have seen to that," the Baroness answered with pride. "I am not a fool, my dear. . . . But there is one thing," she added, "that might lead him to believe Sophie. Mr. Alison——"

"He is going," Julie said.

"But when?"

"Soon."

The Baroness leaned forward. "It is folly—the deepest folly—to keep him here, Julie. To be seen with him. To walk with him publicly. Your step-father isn't quick in his suspicion. Still——"

"But we have walked and ridden together for nearly two years," Julie said, suddenly roused from her listlessness by perceiving, in her mother's argument, an illogical twist which suggested that she was not speaking all her mind.

The Baroness also was aware of the weakness in her own case as she was forced to present it. She could not confess that, in getting rid of the Englishman, she was less concerned for her husband's suspicions than for her daughter's rashness. Too late, she began to regret that she had spoken to Julie of Alison's going. She should have tackled the man himself. But something in Julie's face, quickening her fears, impelled her to continue. At least, Julie herself might be tested.

"It is different now that your husband is dead," she said vaguely. "In any case, it is wise to be on the safe side. You would lose nothing by his going. All that was over long enough ago."

"In a sense, it was over," Julie answered.

"In a sense? It was over or it was not."

"If you mean that we have not—that he has not been my lover since Rupert came back—that is true."

"Then what did you mean—'in a sense'? There is no other sense," the Baroness persisted with deliberate stupidity, and waited for the confirmation of her fears.

Julie rose. "I don't know what I meant, mother. Does it matter so much? I suppose we were in a kind of enchantment—and this is the real world, that's all."

Her mother hesitated, searching the girl's face, alarmed but wishing to discover reassurance in it.

"Then remember that it *is* the real world," she said. "And in the real world a penniless widow needs a background."

"A background?"

"Ah, Julie, do not pretend to misunderstand me. What else can you do—be a secretary? A governess? You would despise that. You cannot live here, a single woman, for ever. And if your step-father should die and Allard succeed to Enkendaal—besides," she added, softening her voice, "there is no reason that you should not some day be happy again."

"Or make you happy again," Julie said, stung to bitterness by the nagging futility of the scene she had passed through.

Her mother rose beside her. They stood facing each other, while the cat still fawned upon their shoes.

"You are a fool," the Baroness declared, her tone rough and stifled. "You are the kind of fool that will not know herself. Have you the idea in your head that your marriage was all of my making? You were ready enough to take the profits while they lasted."

Julie was silent.

"You think you were a child, coerced," her mother exclaimed, shaking with indignation now as she had long ago over the stubbornness of a pupil, and breaking away, in her anger, from the control she had by careful training imposed upon her voice. "You tell yourself that now—to flatter your romantic vanity; but the truth is——"

"I was not coerced," Julie answered quietly. "But I was a child."

"Child or no child, coercion or not, you would do it again," the Baroness cried. "You *will* do it again when I have prepared the way. There is nothing else you can do. And when you want a new lover, you will blame me for having forced you into a rich marriage. And be glad to blame me. And be glad to blame me!" she repeated.

She walked across the room to the window and looked

out, her hands moving on her hips. Then, as though a
weight had been lifted suddenly from her mind, she
turned and laughed—a short, low-pitched laugh:

"You will never marry a poor man," she said. "Never."

When Julie was gone, she sat down, trembling, and
pulled the cat on to her lap. She rubbed her cheek against
the fur of its head, feeling outcast and ill. I meant to help
her, she thought, and began to cry. The cat flicked its
ears and sprang free on to the hearth-rug, where it lay
washing itself.

CHAPTER TWO

THE Baroness came downstairs next day with her decision made. At ten o'clock she walked over to Kerstholt's cottage. Ramsdell admitted her and took her to the upper sitting-room where Lewis was.

He was leaning against the window-frame with a book in one hand. With the other he was crumbling bread from a platter that stood on a low bookshelf. The eyes he raised from his page when Ramsdell spoke to him were bright and animated—so bright that she wondered for an instant whether he was in a fever. After a slow recognition—for the light of the window had been in his eyes and she was in shadow—he came towards her.

"I hope I am not interrupting your breakfast," she said.

He seemed not to be aware that there was anything unusual in munching dry bread at ten in the morning or to be embarrassed by the disorder of his room, which was burdened with books and papers.

"I was reading," he answered, looking about him. Then, seeing the bread: "I eat when I'm hungry."

Ramsdell left them together and the Baroness, observing Lewis, thought with satisfaction: He is all books. I needn't have come, but she pursued the purpose of her coming. He listened to her in silence, giving her no assistance by any comment of his, and before she was done she had changed her opinion, though not her dislike, of him. Never before had she encountered so formidable a silence. There was neither threat nor defiance in it—only an impenetrable composure.

"When do you wish me to go?" he said at last.

"I am sure you will understand, Mr. Alison, that it is better for Julie's sake that you should go at once."

She knew that she would have been wise to press him no further, but she heard herself rattling on into hints—delivered with an admirable tact and discretion—that the Kerstholts were not owners of the cottage, but tenants and dependants of the Castle, and that in so small a community as Enkendaal, the Castle—but her implied threat of eviction produced no effect on Lewis. It was as if she had attempted to beat down or divert a flame by throwing pebbles that passed through it. She looked round the room, feeling that she would long remember having visited this Englishman whom nothing touched.

"Does Julie know of your coming here?" he asked.

"I did not think it necessary to tell her. She is troubled enough, poor child. What is past is past. She has to begin her life again. That is what I wanted to make clear to you, Mr. Alison. I felt sure that you would not be so selfish or thoughtless as to make her way more difficult. You see, while you were living in the Castle, while the war continued, everything was exceptional." Her voice ran on, beyond the rule of her will. Watching him, she understood, with an unwilling understanding that wrenched at her self-respect, why Julie had accepted him bodily as her lover, and she found herself wondering whether in this disordered room, this cottage room where the window-light shone upward on to the triangular planes of the sloped ceiling, Julie had ever permitted—— The word "permitted" gratified her. While she spoke to Lewis, she allowed it to echo in her mind. It was a contemptuous word that might be used of a lover who was a peasant or a footman.

"You see," she was saying in a tone of shrewd, mincing affability, "we must accept the world as it is. Your position and Julie's——" Under her words, the thought persisted that a man who could sit up all night over his books, and read standing, and eat dry bread like a serf, who yet had beauty and repose and power, was a menace, a pest. She hated him because he would not defend himself. He did not care for her argument, though he attended it, or for her taunts, though he understood them. He seemed not to be within her reach.

Going out, she said: "Well, Mr. Alison, we are agreed, I hope?"

"Whether I stay or go," he replied, "is of no importance to me and probably of none to Julie."

"If you will take my advice, you will put Julie altogether out of your mind," she answered; and, the words coming to her from the past, she added: "That was a kind of enchantment, shall we say? This is the real world."

Instantly his expression was altered. "Julie herself might have said that!" he exclaimed eagerly and she knew that he was searching her face for resemblances to her daughter, searching it with a compelling, fiery tenderness that made her feel that he had passed through and beyond her, as though she herself did not exist.

"The man is mad!" she said to herself, as she walked down the lane outside the cottage. It rankled in her mind that he did not eat regular meals like normal people but munched dry bread, standing, at ten o'clock in the morning.

Seeing Kersholt in the lane, slowly returning home, she said:

"You will not have your English tenants long, Kersholt."

"Now that the war is over, Mevrouw. No, I suppose not," he answered, standing cap in hand. "They will be glad to be home, poor young gentlemen."

"Mr. Alison will be going at once," she said.

He opened his eyes at that. "But they told me only last night, Mevrouw, that——"

"I have seen him this morning," she insisted, wondering even as she spoke, why she had paused to speak to Kersholt. "I think he will be going at once. The other may stay a few days perhaps."

She enjoyed the puzzlement in Kersholt's eyes, knowing that her power was the key to it, and her joy was sharpened by seeing across his shoulder, near the entrance to Allard's house, Sophie's narrow figure, wrapped in fur and moving across the muddy road like a fastidious cat's. There was a handkerchief rolled into a ball under her fingers and to her own surprise she let it run in the breeze and waved to Sophie. Sophie's hands stayed in her muff, but the thin oval of her face twisted in her coat collar.

When she reached the Castle, the Baroness was tired. In the hall she met Julie and was envious of her. There was colour in the girl's cheeks, and her body, under its black dress, moved with spring and suppleness. They did not speak and Julie went upstairs—to her own bedroom, no doubt. The Baroness watched her go. Well, she thought, he won't go that way again! She ripped off her gloves. Her nails were blued by cold and, there being in the hall no one to observe her, she dipped four of her finger-tips into her mouth and began to suck them.

CHAPTER THREE

SOPHIE, not unobservant of signs of panic in her step-mother, had been content to wait. The possibility that Julie might run away with Lewis was present in her mind also, and she was unalarmed by it. Julie would ruin herself and be gone; her mother would be humiliated; three birds with one stone. Sophie's ambition had swelled with time. She wanted not so much the ruin of the governess's daughter, for whom she had indeed an obscure, envious admiration, as the humiliation of the governess herself. She wished to rule Enkendaal for her father as she would have ruled it if he had not married a second time. To persuade her father of Julie's intrigue was not enough; she must persuade him that his wife had known of it and protected it—that she was, and that the world knew her to be, a procuress in effect. "A procuress," Sophie whispered in her obsession. The word would cut when the time came to use it.

Why had that handkerchief been brought out and waved? Ella was not accustomed to wave to her. There was no other cottage but Kerstholt's in the lane at the entrance to which Ella and Kerstholt had been standing; it led nowhere but into sludgy fields; therefore she had been visiting Lewis. She had not awaited his coming to the Castle, whither he would certainly come during the day, but had gone to him before eleven o'clock in the morning. She disliked him; she had said often enough that the Englishmen in their cottage lived like peasants, though they dressed up and pretended to be gentlemen when they came out of it; the call was not made for pleasure or without purpose.

Sophie sought for this purpose in vain. She felt that it must be clear enough, but so eager was she to discover it that she could not. Her head ached that afternoon with such violence that she whimpered on her bed and pressed the mountains of her thumbs into her eyes. The darting agony in her temples and crown was so intense that at last, unable to be still, she rose, trotted across the room with the childish toddle that came naturally to her when she was alone and in distress, and rubbed her forehead and even the top of her head (pulling the hair apart) against the cold window-pane. This comforted her a little, and she began to wonder, as she often did when her head-aches were bad, whether she might not turn into a child again instead of becoming old.

While, in her mind, she was choosing the clothes she would put on if she awoke one morning and found that she was a child, she saw Ramsdell cross the bridge between the lakes and approach the Castle. In less than ten minutes he came out with Julie at his side. They went to the boat-house, crossed the bridge, and disappeared, through the thicket where the pavilion was, in the direction of the cottage. Lewis had sent for Julie. Why had he not come himself?

"Leaving Enkendaal? Not to come back?" Julie had asked when Ramsdell delivered Lewis's message. He replied that Lewis would go to the Hague, or perhaps to Rotterdam, in readiness to take ship for England. "Then this is the last time I shall see him," she said.

As they walked through the grounds of the Castle, they spoke little, and when Ramsdell asked her: "Is it to be the last time, Julie?" she turned her face from him and could not answer.

Lewis took her into a room downstairs, for the upper sitting-room, he said, was littered with his packing, but it was the upper-room that was familiar to her and she felt isolated and chilled, as though he and she were on a stage, ignorant of their parts, or had met by chance in a waiting-room with nothing they could say to each other. The same constraint was upon him, and though he spoke tenderly and touched her with the same gentleness which long ago had struck fire into her, there was no fire now between them—only the burden of a frozen intimacy, the ache of an emotion emptied out.

When he told her of her mother's visit, she replied: "What my mother does can make no difference to us. Go, Lewis; it's easier. We have nothing to gain by fighting her, and nothing to lose that she can take away."

"But you, Julie, what shall you do?" He was standing near to her and, though she did not look up, she saw, beyond her interlocked hands, that he was rigid and trembling. Then, suddenly, in a jet of decision, he said: "Come with me, Julie. Together we can work out our lives, not apart." To check the wild unrest in his own mind and to cover her silence, he allowed his words to run on: "You are legally German. It won't be easy to get you to England at once. But through the Legation it could be done, and shall be. Come with me."

"To England, as your wife?"

"Yes, Julie."

She smiled. "Why do you ask me, Lewis?"

"Because I love you," he said. "Whatever may have happened between us, we are part of each other's lives. More than ever now by. . . ."

"By a kind of necessity?" she answered. "Yes, say it, Lewis. Why should we be afraid of each other—to tell each other the truth? It is a necessity that binds us. As though everything round us had died. As though there were no one left in the world but our two selves."

"Is it no more than that, Julie? It is more to me. Our love may be out of our reach now——"

She grasped his hand. "It is out of our reach," she said. "It is out of our reach—like something lying at the bottom of a deep pool. We can see it and know it. But we can't move towards it. We can't recover it."

"And yet," he answered, "we cannot leave it. Cut off from each other, we shall never live again in this world. . . .

O Julie, you and I—talking here, chilled by a memory of
what we can't feel—afraid to go forward, unable to go
back. And yet," he continued, letting her hand fall, "we
are what we were—you as beautiful—and I. . . ." He
walked across the room and returned to her. "Nothing is
dead, Julie, but sleeping—undergoing change. What was
shining and secret, our own, has become his, until we
make it our own again. The joy and the brilliance have
gone from it. It is bound up in suffering—his and yours
and mine. It's dark and heavy—but it is alive. Without it,
you and I are thrown away."

"I believe that," she said, "but I feel nothing."

"Then——"

But she would not let him continue. "You are making
yourself speak of love for my sake, Lewis. You have
burdens enough. In England you have your own struggle.
I have no decision left. Perhaps, some day, we shall be
together again. I don't know."

"Come now," he repeated, "come now, or give me your
word to come."

She was silent a long time.

"Lewis," she said, "try to believe and forgive me. I
know that I love you and shall not cease; but now I feel
nothing. For so long we have thought of him only, of
saving him. And we have failed. It is as though you and
I had been struggling and struggling up a mountain and
had fallen back suddenly into the valley. And you say:
'Come now. Climb again. Another mountain. Climb it
blind.' We are to set out, with no illusions, starved and
tired, to struggle again. I can't Lewis. I can't now. I can't
think or feel."

"But when time has passed?"

"I can't even give you my word," she said. "I love you
—that's true still. But I'm cold and tired. I don't trust my
own word. Something has died in me. . . . And in you it
has died," she added, "in you too. The enchantment has
died."

"All enchantments die," he said. "Only cowards die
with them." He lifted up her face, and into his she saw

the old calm returning. "Come when you will, Julie. Life will begin again."

He released her and walked with her towards the Castle. Suddenly she looked towards him, hesitated, and said, as though all her inarticulate truth might be expressed in the words:

"It's just that I'm numb—and frightened, Lewis—that's all. Not a coward."

The curbed pleading in her tone and the failure of her words to match the dumb passion within her struck deep into his memory.

"You might have said that, Julie dear, when you were twelve years old."

She gave a little laugh, almost of happiness. "It is true, then, that you love me," she said. "You wouldn't have remembered."

When they reached the pavilion and were drawing near to the lakes, he stopped. "It was here we met, Julie. Shall we part here?"

She gazed at him, feeling only the shutters of the past closing in upon her mind. She was stiff, without tears. They dared not touch each other, and she turned away and went on towards the bridge, determined not to look back, incapable of it. Then, hearing him follow her, she turned. He took her hand and bent and kissed it. Her body began to tremble in ice and fire, and she exclaimed: "But I made you kiss my hand when Ballater was here!" For an instant she was stung with wild shame and joy, but when he was gone she could think only of the sound of the water flowing beneath the bridge and of the emptiness of her words. There will be snow before night, she said, for she could read the skies in the colour of the water and the shrewd bleakness of the air.

That night, after dinner, Lewis came into the smoking-room of the Castle, not in evening dress, and wearing a rough overcoat powdered with snow. Sophie pressed her knees together, curling her toes in her slippers. Julie rose,

and stood without moving. Her mother, elaborately unaware that there was anything unusual in this visit, continued to sew and asked Lewis to sit down. "Tea will be
coming in a moment."

"A cigar," the Baron said. "These are light. Or a
Havana?"

"I've come to say good-bye," Lewis answered, "and I
mustn't stay. I still have packing to do."

The Baron was nursing the cigar-box. He looked
up. "Good-bye? Why so suddenly? Are you off to
England?"

"Possibly not at once, sir, but I have to go down to
the Hague. When I sail depends on ships and transport
arrangements. But I start from here early to-morrow
morning. I wanted to say good-bye and thank you for all
you've done."

"Ah, nothing," the Baron said. "You've done more for
me than ever I've done for you. You'll take your translation of Dirk's papers with you to England and arrange
publication there?"

"Yes, certainly I will."

The Baron stood up and took his hand. "Well, Alison,
you've learnt something of how the Dutch run their
estates. I shall miss you. It will seem queer, always riding
alone. I shall have to take Julie with me. . . . She'll miss
you, too, reading and so on. We shall all miss you. We
shall often meet again no doubt. Still, it's always a trifle
sad when something ends. After all, it has been an interval
in life, eh? Things may be as good or better, but they
won't be the same again."

"No," Lewis said, and pressed the old man's hand, and
could say no more.

There was silence and a clink of decanters.

"Is Mr. Ramsdell going too?" Sophie asked.

"Not at once. He'll stay and clear things up at the
cottage. There's more packing than I can do."

"Strange that they should send for you and not for him.
Aren't you on the same file so to speak?"

"Probably not," Lewis answered. "I'm Naval Division.

He's a submarine officer R.N. We didn't come into Holland together."

That was clever of him, Sophie thought.

The Baron turned away from the side-table, a glass and a brandy decanter in his hands, holding them up.

"Telegraphed for you, I suppose?"

For an instant Lewis hesitated. "Yes, from the Hague this afternoon."

They talked for a few minutes, Lewis being persuaded to take off his coat. "I shan't publish Dirk van Leyden myself," he said. "I scarcely know whether my firm's alive or dead till I get home."

"Yes, I see that," the Baron answered. "You'll have a tough struggle. But it will come right, you'll see. It will come right when you have settled down to it."

"I hope so," Lewis said. "It will be a fight with precious few munitions."

He rose to go. He shook hands with the Baroness.

"Good-bye," she said. "I hope you have a pleasant journey."

He came to Sophie herself and when he touched her she curled her toes again inside her shoes. He went to Julie.

"Good-bye, Julie, until we meet again."

She had not moved while he was in the room. Suddenly she leaned forward, put her hands on his arms, and kissed him.

"Good-bye, dear Lewis."

She was smiling as she stood away from him, holding out her hand.

The Baron chuckled. "That's the way for old friends to say good-bye," he exclaimed, and drew her arm into his own.

Next morning Sophie went into the post-office, bought some stamps and a bag of sweets that she gave to the postmistress's child, and began to spin the weights of the balance on the counter.

"That telegram from the Hague yesterday for the

English officers at the cottage—it was long in being delivered. Wasn't there anyone you could send up with
it?"

"Telegram? What telegram, Freule?"

Sophie went from the post-office to the cottage, which
she approached from the meadows behind it, and found
Kerstholt working in his back garden.

"You will be sorry to lose the English officers, Kerstholt.
Mr. Ballater made the front look pretty with his flowers."

"Yes, Freule. But we still have his flowers. You'll see
next spring. . . . The others were nice gentlemen too. My
wife was only saying last night how quiet they'd always
been. She was nervous at first at the notion of having
them. Strangers—Englishmen too. She didn't take to the
English after the affair in South Africa. But she was sorry
to see Mr. Alison go. We were out, both of us, to wave
him good-bye."

"It was very sudden, wasn't it?"

"That it was, Freule. We didn't rightly understand it.
Only the night previous Mr. Alison was saying: 'It will be
some time yet, perhaps a fortnight and more.' And the
next I knew was in the morning Mevrouw van Leyden
met me in the lane there. Mr. Alison was going, she says.
So I asked him. He'd let me know, he said. Then the
Freule Julie came up, and afterwards he came asking for
his packing-cases that we had stored in the shed."

"He had a telegram during the afternoon," Sophie
suggested. "That was it."

Kerstholt looked at her. Evidently he didn't know what
the English officers had been up to. He would be discreet.

"That must have been it," he agreed.

Sophie went down to Allard's house. He and his wife
were doing accounts together by the fire, and were irritated by her coming. It pleased her now to waste time, to
watch their bored faces.

"Well, Sophie," said Allard, his patience deserting him.
"You see we are busy."

How it delighted her to see their faces change when
she began to tell them what she knew! Julie had been

Lewis's mistress—for months, for more than a year. And Ella had known, had allowed it.

"But why did you say nothing if you knew?" Marietje asked.

Sophie had expected this question but was annoyed that, when nothing but eagerness for action was in her own mind, she should have to pause to answer it. There were so many answers, and to the chief of them—that she had been afraid of humiliation and ridicule—she would not confess. How often, she remembered, had she laid plans for trapping Julie, and how often had she failed to carry them out! Though she had been convinced beyond all doubt in her own mind that Lewis went often to Julie's room, she had never been certain on any particular night that he was there. He came and went always through the library and it was his known custom to work at night. To meet him at any hour between the library and his bedroom was proof of nothing. Once she had knocked at Julie's door, and after a time a sleepy Julie had opened it and led her in. What had she wanted? Her explanations had stumbled and fallen; a smiling Julie had led her out. A dozen times, having crept into the library and found it empty, she had stood before the door of Lewis's own bedroom and failed in courage to knock. Once, softly turning the handle and finding the door locked, she had tapped gently, persuaded that the room was empty, but had not dared to force the alarm. And she remembered, with a fluttering of her heart, the night on which she had found the door ajar. Ah! at last he had forgotten to lock it. Downstairs she had crept, through the drawing-room, through the ante-rooms, through the banqueting-hall at the base of the tower, up the staircase to the library. No light showed under the door. She had raised the latch and entered. Inside—darkness and silence. She had been certain then; she had her proof. All that was necessary was to bar the door leading upward to Julie's room so that none might return by it, then to go to her father; and she had been groping her way across the library, for in her wanderings through the Castle she carried no light, when Lewis himself had risen up in the faint gleam of an embrasure and had asked what she did. She was looking for a book, she had said; and had been unable to think of the name of any book but the Bible.

Her tormented memory of these things ran on while she was telling Allard and his wife, with what assurance she could command, that she had been biding her time. She told them, in terror of provoking their laughter, as much as she dared tell of her nocturnal flittings. "It was useless to try to prove anything while Ella was on her side," she concluded. "Who would have believed me? Father would have been too surprised and angry to believe. You saw how he behaved the other day."

"You might have told us," Allard said.

"Not until I was sure. . . . Not until I was sure," Sophie repeated. "I was waiting." And she added in proof: "I did tell Rupprecht."

"You *did* tell him!" cried husband and wife together. "Well?"

"He smiled."

"He didn't believe you?"

"That's what's so odd," Sophie answered with a sigh, running her fingers across her forehead. "I have always felt that he did believe me—secretly. And yet he can't have done, I suppose. I don't understand. . . . But it's different now," she added, speaking rapidly and with decision. "Ella sent Lewis away. She concealed it from father. She let the lie about the telegram pass in father's hearing. Why did she send him away? Because he had been Julie's lover and she knew it. Because she knew Julie might become his mistress again—or his wife. There can be no other reason."

Sophie was disappointed by the effect of her story on Allard. He believed it but was cautious. "You ought to have told us long ago," he said, "instead of hugging it to yourself. You're hysterical, Sophie—running about the house at night alone. It's just a question now whether we can surprise Ella into giving herself away. She's made it awkward for herself. We'll get Goof over from the Huis ten Borgh."

But Goof was in the Hague and did not reach Allard's

until the night of the third day. Meanwhile Allard ploughed through the snow to question Kerstholt and the post-mistress. He sat late with Goof on the night of his coming; in the morning Sophie visited them and they went over the ground again. After luncheon, at a time when they knew the Baroness would be sitting in the smoking-room, toasting her feet and reading the *Handelsblad*, Allard, a little nervous because he was attacking his former governess, and Goof, a little embarrassed to find himself a guardian of morals, were led by two women, who laboured under no such handicaps, across to the Castle. The snow was thawing fast. They heard nothing as they came but the squelching of their own feet. Goof was irritated by the weight of his sister-in-law's boots and the determination of her legs. Why Allard had married so much muscle, he had never understood. Like a great mare in a cart, he thought, walking behind her.

Julie had lunched with her mother alone—the Baron having ordered cheese and claret in his office—and had afterwards gone with her into the smoking-room. The long, high-ceilinged room was darkened by its verandah which, though pleasantly used in summer, was now but a shoot for the thawing snow. From time to time a wedge of snow would become detached, rush with the sounds of a broom and a muffled drum over the roof, and fall, hissing, into the laurel bushes.

"Don't roam about, Julie. There's nothing to see from the window that we haven't seen a thousand times before. Throw some logs on the fire and be comfortable. . . . Would you like a sheet of the *Handelsblad*?"

Julie seated herself at a little distance from the fire, in a position from which she could see the silvery sky and the bare tree-tops above the laurels. She heard the moisture whistle in the logs and their bark peeling away, tranquil sounds that plumbed her own tranquillity. The shining of the laurels and the afternoon twilight of this familiar room had fallen into the past. Nothing that happened here could ever again affect her, and she looked at her mother as though at a portrait on the wall, part of a vanished existence.

After a little while she rose from her chair.

"Where are you going, Julie?"

"To my music-room."

"Isn't it bad for you, dear, to be alone so much, cooped up in the tower?"

In the hall she encountered the four who had come from Allard's house, and, looking down upon them from the staircase, was reminded of the mixed choir that had visited her home in Chepping at Christmas-time. The little group in black, facing inward in consultation and—for some reason that she could not guess—embarrassed, might have been about to sing a carol. The idea that Sophie and Allard's wife would lift up their chins and voices amused her. Goof caught her smiling, smiled back, sheepishly, and looked away. Before she was at the head of the staircase she had forgotten them, and in her room, with a quiet mind, she began to play her clavichord.

CHAPTER FOUR

AT the sound of the opening door, the Baroness withdrew her feet from their comfortable extension before the fire and looked over the back of her chair. This was her hour of ease; soon she must go upstairs to rest, an exercise which, beneath the repairing hands of her maid, was more strenuous than its name; meanwhile she enjoyed the fire's warmth on her outstretched legs. She enjoyed, too, the twilight of the room which at about three o'clock had made her reading of the newspaper difficult. Since then she had lain in her chair for a quarter of an hour gazing at portraits of her husband's ancestors, the need for effort lulled to sleep in her mind.

But she did not expect to be disturbed during this time of unguarded peace wherein all memories were softened and all ambitions laid away. The appearance of Allard's bulk round the leather screen by the door irritated her. When she saw by whom he was accompanied—the full Leyden muster—a streak of fear ran through her body. Perceiving danger, she called up the reserves of her pride and skill, but they also were lulled to sleep and did not answer. Allard's wife would trap her into some trifling display of social ignorance—the families of Holland and their connexions through Europe were so hard to remember. She had learnt them once, but they were for ever changing. And Allard's wife would smile and correct her: "Ella, dear, surely you remember——" Or they would chatter among themselves of books she had not read, and turn to her suddenly for an opinion, knowing she could not give it—they whom she had taught. "There is

no need for you to teach me!" she exclaimed once—
foolishly, she saw afterwards, for Sophie had been quick,
quick. "Well, you had your turn when we were children,"
she had answered. . . . They would tease her and taunt her,
she knew. Generally she was a match for them all. But
now she was tired. They would laugh at her, and so have
her at their mercy. There was nothing she could do but
escape, and she rose with careful slowness, that they might
not guess she was running away, and said that she had just
been going to her room. A little flicker of humour prompted
her to add: "Are you going to play cards, the four of you?
You must ring for candles and have the fire made up."

"Could you spare us a few minutes?" Allard said.

"Why, yes." But her voice would not ring with surprise.
"I hope nothing has happened."

"I'm afraid something rather serious has happened."

"Nothing to Pieter!" she made herself exclaim, but
again her tone was false. She knew that Sophie had shot
her bolt.

"Oh no, Father's all right," Allard replied.

He and Goof seated themselves on the fender. His wife
—always to be thought of as Allard's wife, never as
Marietje, a diminutive that sounded ridiculous whenever
it was applied to her—took a chair and planted a hand on
each knee. Sophie stood apart, a thin black tree growing
out of the carpet, swaying a little but rooted.

Allard cleared his throat. "No doubt you'll be able to
explain," he began. "But it's very unpleasant—extremely
unpleasant for all of us. In all our interests—not just our
own, I mean, but the family's—it is absolutely necessary
to clear her character."

"Oh, begin at the beginning, Allard," his wife exclaimed. "There's no going back on it now. You can't say
what you have to say and be polite. Besides, Ella knows all
about it. You're telling her nothing she doesn't know and
ought not to be ashamed to know."

"Say that again." They looked up like foolish children
to see the Baron a few yards within the room, his crested
hair and white collar breaking from the distant shadows.

"Say that again please, Marietje. Whose character is to be cleared, Allard? What ought my wife to be ashamed to know?" He came down to the fire and stood in its glow, his shoulders up, his arms stiffened, like an angry wooden soldier. "What are you all doing here? What's it all about?"

Allard and Goof rose; Allard's wife pursed her lips and began to rub her hands together.

"It's nothing, Pieter," the Baroness said. "What brought you in here? I thought you were working away. . . ."

"My box was empty," he answered, a boy with a grievance. "I came in for a—I came in for a piece of string."

Whereupon Goof gave one short, nervous laugh, like the hoot of a solitary owl, and was silent.

"Yes, sir, you laugh. You laugh like a fool——"

"But why didn't you ring your bell, my dear?" the Baroness said. "Look, we'll soon find you a piece of string. In that brass box, Allard—behind you—on the mantel-piece."

"It's always the same in this house!" his father said, patting the leather of an arm-chair to ease his impatience. "You want something. 'Tisn't there. Then——" His petulance overcame him. "I couldn't ring my bell because it's broke. *Kapot*."

This was too much for Goof. He slapped his hands on his thighs and threw back his head as if he were about to enjoy the laugh of his life.

"Oh, don't laugh, don't laugh, don't laugh!" Sophie cried with impassioned seriousness. "Have you all gone mad?"

Allard was holding out a twist of string. The Baron stared at it as if he did not know what it was, but he knew now that he had been led away from his track. His eyes moved slowly from face to face.

"What is all this?" he said, enclosing the string in his fist.

After a long silence, Allard's wife began: "It has come to our knowledge——"

"Excuse me. I should like my son to speak. Now, Allard."

"All the time," Allard said reluctantly, "all the time that Englishman, Alison, was supposed to be working in the library——"

"He *was* working. Why—'supposed to be'?"

"Very well, sir. All the time, he was—well, going up to Julie's room."

The Baron had control of himself now. "Go on," he said.

"Isn't that enough?" said Allard.

"You are saying that she was——"

"Yes."

"You must say more than that, Allard. This touches me. He was my guest. She is my daughter."

"Your daughter!" Sophie cried.

"Yes, Sophie. I choose my own words. I said, my daughter. And you, Allard, mark that."

"Very well, sir. I'm sorry. But the truth's the truth."

The Baron smiled, looking from Sophie to his wife. He was not unprepared for this story. Beneath his anger, he was a little pleased that Allard, and particularly Allard's wife, had been fooled.

"Now look here," he said. "Let's not say what we may all be sorry for. I know the origin of this lie. No matter how I know, but I do. Sophie told you—now didn't she?"

"Yes."

"And you accept that?"

"Why not?" Sophie intervened. "I was here. I know. I have known for months and months. While it was going on——"

Her father over-rode her. "If she had come to me with it, I should have known how to treat such a tale. But you, Allard—you have your head screwed on—and you come here——"

"It doesn't rest on Sophie alone."

"Then, perhaps you'll tell me how—how what you say —was possible? Och! But it's not worth talking of!"

"But it was very possible and very easy," said Allard's wife. "You think the staircase from the library to her bedroom has been closed up for years. It hasn't been. You can look for yourself."

"Yes," cried Sophie. "Look for yourself. The latches and bolts of both doors. And the hinges."

He did not know how to answer that.

"That can be explained," his wife said, but not before his confidence had been shaken. "Julie opened up the wall-staircase when she came here at the beginning of the war so that she could go to and fro from the library to fetch books."

"I knew nothing of that," he said.

"No, Pieter, nor did I at first. But you know how reticent she is about her own affairs—a kind of game. She told me later."

"When did she tell you?" asked Allard's wife.

"Really, I don't remember."

Sophie broke in. "Was it after you knew what was going on?"

"No. It was——" She recovered herself, again too late. "It was some time this year, I think."

"And did she close the staircase again when Alison began to work in the library at nights?"

"I am sure she did."

"In June, two years ago!"

"I suppose so."

"Look at the locks and hinges!" Sophie exclaimed. "Anyone can see they have been used more recently than that. I will tell you when she closed the staircase again— when her husband came back."

The Baron had been waiting. "Now, Allard," he said, when Sophie was quiet, "anyone malicious — anyone malicious and hysterical—can monkey with locks and hinges. What else have you?"

Allard, who was himself beginning to wonder whether he had been duped and now wished with all his heart that he was at his own fireside, said nothing.

"Will you allow me to speak?" his wife asked.

The old man looked at her angrily. "If you have anything useful to say."

She drew herself up in her chair. "Allard has made a very serious accusation," she began with formal calm.

"For some reason he is tongue tied; he seems to have forgotten everything. Very well, then; I must make it good. This, as he said, doesn't rest on Sophie alone or on hinges and bolts. In the first place, you can use your own memory. The way they went about together—riding, walking, always together. In the library too. No one else went there when he was working——"

"I went continually," the Baron remarked.

"Perhaps, but perhaps you were thinking of something else. Perhaps your eyes are not very sharp for these things."

"Pray God," he said.

"None of your eyes seem to have been very sharp," Sophie put in scornfully. "You must have been blind, all of you. Every time she looked at him or touched him——"

"Let me go on, Sophie. You do no good now," Allard's wife interrupted. "But I will say this. Sophie was living in the house. We were not. I thought it a disgraceful flirtation but I never dreamed of more. I wouldn't let myself. But Sophie was living in the house, and although—well, although she may not be reliable in everything—she observed; she went about the house at night, she says; she's not likely to have invented——"

"Now listen, Marietje," the Baron said, irritated beyond endurance by her precise, explanatory sing-song. "As for their going about together—they were both English; they'd known each other all their lives; he'd taught her as a child; they thought the same way—music and history and so on; and they were shut up here together. D'you expect them to behave like strangers? Why, when he came in here to say good-bye to us, she kissed him in front of us all. That doesn't look like——" But, remembering that little scene, he saw it afresh, with new eyes. I wonder! he thought, but he said swiftly: "And as for Sophie's being in the house—wasn't her mother in the house too? You've all made a mistake and a shameful one. That Allard should be shipped in this galley is what beats me. Still, what happens in these four walls is our own. There's nothing gained by shouting and railing——"

"That's the worst part of it," Allard put in suddenly.

"What is?"

"Well, Ella, you see——"

"Now wait a little," his wife said. "Will you tell me something, Ella? You, of course, knew nothing of this?"

"Nothing, of course." The Baroness looked at her husband. She felt that he was ceasing to believe her. "But I have no intention of being cross-questioned by you, Marietje, about this or anything else. The whole suggestion is shameful." She began to rise from her chair, wishing only to escape.

"She's afraid—afraid to answer," Sophie jeered.

After all, the Baroness thought with hot indignation, there is nothing to fear. I have only to deny everything. They have no proof. Her strength returning, she was filled with a desire to defeat and humiliate them. They had no proof, none.

"This is enough," the Baron began, evidently to protect her, but she would not have his protection now, while doubt remained in his mind. She would not run for shelter before them all.

"What more do you want to know?" she asked, and observed with satisfaction that even Marietje seemed to be moving stealthily towards conciliation.

"There's very little more I want to know. It is of course possible that Sophie was mistaken. Were you never even suspicious?"

"Never. There was no reason to be."

"Apart from—the final thing—did it never strike you that their being together so much was, perhaps, indiscreet?"

"Perhaps that was foolish of me," the Baroness said, feeling that she could now afford to concede so much. Then her anger flashed. "If I had known there were so many lying tongues even in our own family, I should of course have warned Julie and Mr. Alison."

"But you didn't speak to either of them?"

"My dear Marietje, why should I? They were friends and no more. The possibility of their being anything else never entered my head."

At this her husband intervened again, eager to make an

end. She smiled and acquiesced. It pleased her to think how near they had come to success, how they had stumbled and fallen short of it. When they apologized she would be magnanimous. Magnanimity would cut as anger could not.

"Now," Allard's wife said, "I can prove that you are not speaking the truth, Ella, and have not been from the beginning. It was you who sent Mr. Alison away. We can prove that."

It was a bow drawn at a venture, the Baroness thought. They were trying to confuse her. Alison would not tell, nor Julie, nor Ramsdell. It was impossible that Marietje should know.

"I did nothing of the kind."

"Then how did you know before any of us that he was going?"

"I did not."

"But you told Kerstholt. You told Kerstholt on the morning before."

She remembered now—Sophie in front of Allard's house, picking her way through the mud. She had taken out her handkerchief and waved.

"Oh yes," she said with a vague, frightened smile. "I had forgotten. Mr. Alison did tell me he had been recalled."

"So you did visit him?"

"I was passing the cottage."

"One goes to the cottage or one does not. The lane leads nowhere."

"Across the fields," she said desperately.

"I see; it must have been an interesting walk across the fields. It was strange, wasn't it, that he should tell you he was going before he received the telegram—before he knew himself?" Marietje turned to the Baron. "I was not here that evening. But you were. You heard him say that he had a telegram from the Hague in the afternoon?"

"Anyone may—may make a slip in conversation about the time of a telegram. Obviously he did, if he knew in the morning. A few hours," he added weakly. "What do a few hours matter?"

"What matters is that there was no telegram. You will find that out at the post-office. Alison was lying to cover Ella, and Ella kept quiet to cover him. It was she who sent him off because she knew that he had been Julie's lover; he was poor and useless; she was afraid that Julie might run away."

"Now," said Sophie, "perhaps you will believe that I have eyes."

The Baroness, looking up, saw that they were in the dark; only the firelight illumined their faces and hands.

"It is true," she began without knowing what she wished to say, "it is true that—in a sense—after Rupert died and Julie was a widow, I——"

"I will not endure this," the Baron exclaimed. "You are like bloodhounds, all of you. . . . I will not listen—now. . . . You will go, please. . . . I must see you all again when——"

He turned away abruptly that they might not see his face. When he had been gone a little while, the others moved. Goof went last, having paused to throw a log on the dying fire. All wrong, all wrong, he thought. We've hurt no one so much as the old man. And hearing Sophie in the doorway say to Allard in breathless eagerness: "Let me have tea with you! Let me come over to tea with you!" he hated his sister.

The Baron had climbed to the head of the stairs and was seated in a little alcove there. Opening his hand, he found a twist of string and began to unwind it. He wondered where the stuff had come from and what to do with it. You couldn't drop it on the stairs; someone would trip and fall. . . . The sound of voices below recalled him. The front door slammed. Well, Allard had done his business. Not Allard—he was led by the nose—but the women. Mischief-makers! Liars! he added suddenly. This stuff about telegrams. Questioning poor old Kerstholt! Questioning Juffrouw Steen at the post-shop! You can find out at the post-office, that woman had said—as though he'd go asking Juffrouw Steen whether Julie, the minx, had . . . Mixing servants in van Leyden affairs. . . . As for Ella— his thought choked there, and he watched Jacob walking across the hall with two branched candlesticks in his hands, spilling the grease, the idiot. . . . Julie, she wouldn't do that, not she. Not hole-in-the-corner, with her husband at the wars. She wasn't French! But my God, he thought, the library and that staircase and her bedroom up above —I suppose even the English are cold on winter's nights! And what a pother she was in at the Hague that time! Had to give her sapphires. Then down to the Hague he came. Why to our hotel? Was that the beginning—under my nose? No wonder he took so much interest in Dirk's papers. . . .

Then, suddenly, he could see nothing but the shame and dishonour of it. His guest. His Julie. . . . She wouldn't lie to him. Never had. Best have it out with her.

As he approached the tower, he heard the sound of her clavichord. Half an hour ago, he thought, how I should have loved to sit quiet and listen, and there I was in my room, grubbing money. She may have been playing then. He went in without knocking so that he might not disturb her, but she looked over her shoulder, her eyebrows went up and she smiled—glad to see me, he thought. He made a face at her and signed with his hand that she wasn't to interrupt music for him, and down he sat, crossed his legs and clasped his hands about a bony knee. Byrd, was it? and he forgot that there were spiteful women in the world. But his eyes, staring out into the music, perceived that the door leading to her bedroom stood open; his purpose came back to him and, ceasing to enjoy the music, he wished only that it would go on and on. She stopped at last and turned round in her seat.

"Well, Oom Piet, it's not often you come to the tower nowadays. Shall we have tea brought up here—for a treat? Then I'll play again. . . . My fingers are cold."

She knelt at the fire to warm them and reached for a log from the basket.

"Let me, my dear."

They were kneeling at the fire together, he stiff and upright, she comfortably back on her heels with hands stretched out, rosy and golden.

"This is a devil of a business," he said.

"What, Uncle Pieter?"

"D'you know what they're saying of you—that all the time Alison was staying here, working in the library, you had that staircase open and—well, you see how it is? Sophie's at the bottom of it, but the others are in it too. They say your mother knew."

He was shaking.

"Tell me what has happened," she said. "I don't understand yet."

He stared at the flames and told her.

"All I want is your denial, Julie. I don't want explanations. Telegrams, Kerstholt—they don't touch me; I'm not an attorney. You're my daughter; I count you so; you tell me it's a lie and I'll wipe the floor with them. . . . I don't want even that," he added. "If you'll allow me to forget I ever came to you with this dirty thing, I'll take it generous of you. You go on playing your clavichord. That's enough answer for me."

She moved her hand towards his but did not take it. "It is true, Uncle Pieter," she said.

He stumbled up from his knees and looked down at her. "In this house!"

"Yes."

"For how long?"

"Does that matter? Soon after Lewis came here until—until Rupert came back."

"Julie, it's impossible in you. Shameful."

"No," she answered steadily, "not shameful. But for you, Uncle Pieter, I'm sorry. There was no reason that you should have known. I wasn't going to disgrace you or break up my marriage. It was to be—what you called it—an interval in life. Now. . . ."

"But, Julie," he said, "I'm not a preacher—God knows. But here you were, sent here by your husband, under my roof, under my protection. And he was at the wars—not his own fault he left you. I was pledged for you. You were doubly pledged. You were my daughter—I've always seen you so. And, my God, more than ever I see you so now. I told them that, when they were blackguarding you. Am I to go back and say——"

"You must."

"And afterwards—how am I ever to stand in with you again?" He looked at her as if she were vanishing from him. "It can't ever be the same. I used to enjoy whipping them off. . . . I thought I knew you better than any of them and that though you were"—he picked the word—"high-spirited, still . . ." After a long pause he added: "You've let me down."

"I'm sorry, Uncle Pieter."

"What's to be done now?" he said. "I'll have to face them. There's nothing I can say." Then with a little movement towards her that was not completed: "You'll have to face them too."

"It makes no difference to me," she said, "what they say or do or think. That's true. I'm sorry you should hate me, that's all."

"Not hate you, child. God forbid."

"Despise me, then. Feel that I. . . ."

He did not deny it, but walked across the room without looking at her and let two of his fingers rest for a moment on the keys of her clavichord.

"Well, there's no more to be said, Julie."

And he went out.

At the door of Allard's house, his collar round his ears and his nose buried in a muffler, he made the bell peal wildly, and, when the manservant opened the door, shouldered past him without a word. A lighted window had told him in which room they were sitting.

They had finished tea. Allard had a cigar alight and his slippers on. Marietje and Goof were playing picquet. Sophie had taken a fan out of a case on the wall and was fanning herself—flutter, flutter—why couldn't she be still?

"Come in, father," Allard said, and began to make room by the fire.

"I'm not staying."

He loosened his muffler and remained standing. This was what Julie had brought him to, this humiliation—to come here and confess that she was rotten. Marietje, he knew, imagined herself to be a tactful woman. She would keep her eyes on the cards and be careful not to smile.

"Well," said Sophie, reading his face, "what do you think of your daughter now?"

His daughter; the word was like a spur.

"Allard," he said, "I'm speaking to you now as my eldest son."

"Very well, sir."

"You will succeed me here. You will be head of this family."

"I understand that."

"Then please understand this—all of you. I have not abdicated. Is that plain? . . . Good. Now, I have seen Julie. What you say against her you say against me. Whoever says it does not come into my house while I live. That is all I have to say. You have wronged me. It is forgotten."

"We have not wronged you!" Sophie cried. "You know it is true! Why should it be forgotten?"

"Because I have forgotten it," he said.

When he had left her, Julie did not move. Soon the heat of the new logs he had thrown on the fire began to scorch her face and she put up her hands to protect it. Whenever he sees me, he will be ashamed, she thought, and, remembering how his mouth had worked, rumpling up his moustache, while he stood beside her clavichord, and how his eyes had held the look that came into them always when he was speaking of one whom he had loved and who was dead, she said aloud, "I shall hurt him less by going than by staying."

She went into her bedroom and put into a suit-case a

few clothes, her jewels, her personal papers and German passport, what money she had and three books. Then she wrapped herself in fur and for an instant was still, not in hesitation.

If the wall-staircase had been open she would have chosen to go down by it, but the lower door was bolted; she would not see the library again; but one doesn't look back going out of an enchantment, she said, and as she crossed her music-room, did not look at her clavichord.

The hall was empty. A glint in the upper lake reminded her that she had not extinguished the lights in her room, and suddenly she thought: How strange it will be to come into a town where the advertisements are written in English! She passed the tennis-courts and through the wood by the pavilion. The lane to the cottage was very dark, but she was thinking of it as it had been in the sun-light of the afternoon on which they had received news of Jutland, and, when she reached the gate, the darkness of the cottage against the sky, its black roof and the wintry stillness of the trees, shocked her by their unfamili-arity. There was no light to be seen in any window. Was Ramsdell out and the place shut? If she walked round the cottage she would meet the Kerstholts; they would look at the case she was carrying. She knocked at the front door softly, afraid that, if her knock sounded through the house, Kerstholt would come. There was no answer. She thought: Ramsdell too has gone to the Hague. . . . I can't go back. I can't go back. I can't now. She knocked again.

The door opened and Ramsdell's voice said in Dutch: "Who is it?"

She laughed. "Julie!"

"Julie! . . . Why, what have you there? Not more papers of Lewis's?" They were in the little passage now, in the gleam of a candle he had set down on a bracket. It was in that corner, she thought, under the bracket, I put my tennis racquet when I came here with Lewis after we had had news of Jutland. "Why, Julie," Ramsdell exclaimed, suddenly putting his arm under hers, "what's wrong? You look like death."

"I thought you weren't here," she said. "I thought you'd gone."

He put down her suit-case and took her to the upper sitting-room. It was littered with wooden boxes and packing straw.

"Are you all right," he said, "while I get you some water? There's none here."

"I don't need water. I was only afraid you'd gone."

"Such a loss, Julie?"

"Yes . . . Ramsdell——" She stopped. "I always call you that. So did Lewis. I don't know why."

"People do," he said.

"But you have another name."

"Not that matters."

"Tell me."

"Well, oddly enough, it's the same as his—spelt differently, though. Louis."

"I see," she said.

He lifted a packing-case off a chair and lowered a pile of books into it.

"What's wrong, Julie?"

"I oughtn't to have come to you," she answered.

"And why not?"

"Because——"

"Because I feel about you—as I do? That's a reason for coming if you're in a tight corner." He added, looking at her: "I'll do what you want—anything on God's earth."

"Take me to the Hague," she said.

"To-night?"

"Now. You still have Ballater's car?"

"I have. But why car? It's a long way."

"I want to go by car. We can talk—and move. It will be exciting. There'll be a moon later."

"Very well," he said. "I can take in more petrol in Rynwyk. If you'll give me five minutes, I'll put some things in a bag."

She held out her hand. "You're good," she said. "No questions?"

He smiled. "That's the advantage of coming to me."

And before she had need to answer, he added quickly:
"There's one question, though. I take it no one knows
about this or you wouldn't have come here. What are they
going to say in the morning?"

"They can say I've gone to the Hague. That I'm going
to England when I get passports. I'm known to have relations there."

"You'd better leave a message," he said. "Write it while
I pack. My one remaining servant is out, but I'll leave it
to be delivered in the morning. It can be addressed in my
handwriting. Kerstholt needn't know you've been here."

Soon he came in again, bag in hand. The envelope was
ready for him and he addressed it as she told him.

"Now . . ."

"Oh," she said, "thank God, you were here. Thank God
for that. . . . Can you manage my passports as easily as you
manage me?" She was making plans and did not pause for
his answer. "Do you think," she said, "if I stay at—at the
Deux Villes——"

He looked at her. "Are you still so rich?"

"Until I leave Holland I must be."

He nodded and blew down the chimney of the lamp.
"Right. You must. . . . Well?"

"If I stay there until the time comes, do you think we
could sail together?"

A spasm of pain twitched his mouth. "You and Lewis?
. . . It might be. Depends if he has to take men across.
They're mostly gone, I think."

He opened the door for her, holding the candle up. She
took it from him and looked round the room. The shadows
leapt and, because her hand was unsteady, would not be
still.

"You'll come back here," she said slowly.

"I shall have to. . . . This infernal packing is scarcely
begun."

VII

THE BEGINNING

The world was all before them, where to choose
Their place of rest, and Providence their guide.
They, hand in hand, with wand'ring steps and slow,
Through Eden took their solitary way.

MILTON: *Paradise Lost*

THE BEGINNING

"Don't go," Julie said. "Not yet," and Lewis, turning his head to look at the clock on the wall of the chart-room, touched Ramsdell's arm and added: "Stay another quarter of an hour."

Ramsdell's lips began to smile. It sprang into his mind to say: "But I should have thought you'd have wanted to be left alone!" But he could not mock them; he was too near in sympathy to their undertaking; and, saying nothing, he stared down with them from the bridge-rail on to the quay, and the bleak expanse of the dockyard, and the dark, tangled background of Rotterdam.

The *Starling* should have sailed early in the afternoon watch, and Ramsdell, having said good-bye, should have been on his way to Rynwyk. But a later train would bring him home that night, and, when the sailing had been postponed, he had waited, perceiving that the delay and their confinement in the little ship were intolerable to them. Now he said:

"I wish you could have been married before you left."

"Why?"

"Over and done with, I suppose."

Julie smiled. "It's clear in our own minds," she answered. "That's what matters."

Silence fell over them again, and when they spoke it was of the affairs of the journey—the stowing of the baggage, the three other passengers who, the Consulate had decided, were to cross the North Sea in this little merchant ship, the probable time of arrival in England; or of the final arrangements that Ramsdell must make before he left

Enkendaal. Lewis remembered a debt of eight florins and took out the money with which to pay it.

"No more walks up from Rynwyk on Saturday mornings," Ramsdell said. "I must call on the Belgian and his daughter before I go."

"And you must come to see us in England," Julie answered.

"I will."

"But at once? At Chepping?"

"Shall you be at Chepping?"

"Why not?"

Ramsdell hesitated. "You will be going away for a bit together?"

She turned to Lewis. "It will be better to settle down at once?"

He put his hand over hers, gripping the rail, but he answered Ramsdell. "Chepping at first. Then London. There are rooms over the publishing house that we could live in. They'll have to be cleared of stock."

Ramsdell knew that, while he remained, they would continue to play the rigidly unemotional parts they had assigned to themselves. When he was gone—he who was their last contact with the past—they would be compelled to face each other and the future; and the very fixity of their determination made him think they were afraid—were steeling themselves. While Julie was insisting that he should laugh at two Dutchmen seated on a bench, with their two dogs beside them in the same conversational attitude as their masters and with bullet heads and planted feet that were a caricature of the human pattern, he looked carefully at her face, asking himself what chance she had of living as she now intended to live. She turned her head suddenly, caught his gaze, interpreted his question and the tenderness of it towards her, and, seeing that Lewis had crossed the bridge to speak with one of the ship's officers, she said:

"You're afraid for us?"

It was hard to reply. He trusted them; he believed that what they were doing was right and inevitable; but he saw darkness ahead.

"Not if you are unafraid for yourselves. But you have told me nothing, Julie, since I brought you to the Hague that night. I've never known anyone so excited as you were on that journey—as if you were drunk—until, suddenly, you were asleep in the car. And next day, after I'd left you with Lewis, you became all stiff, and reasonable, and determined. Both of you—like rocks—towards me and towards each other."

"It's better to pretend that than to pretend the other thing," she said in an airy tone.

"What other thing?"

"That we're madly in love for the first time. That everything's romance and plain sailing. That we see a honeymoon and no further."

"But you're happy?"

"Deep down." She threw up her head. "Ports are melancholy places. I shall be glad to be at sea." And she added: "Happy? . . . Not all dazzlingly happy. Perhaps I should be even that, if this were a spring day, not winter in Rotterdam. But that's feeling; and, if I'm happy now, I'm happy because I think; the feeling may come—I don't know. And whether I'm happy or not matters less than it did. If we are to live at all—with any real life, I mean, not a life of regrets and memories and shadows, then we must make our lives together, Lewis and I."

But Ramsdell who, though he knew the perils of her, saw in Julie the woman, and the only woman, for whom he would have abandoned reason, could not perceive, beyond what seemed but a friendly coolness between the two travellers, a possibility of love renewed. To him, as to all lovers, there was no love but his own; all else was friendship, no more; and between man and woman that had been lovers friendship was sparkless. He felt that these two were doomed, that they were attempting the impossible, and knew it; and, feeling this, he was suddenly possessed by admiration of their attempt. To this adventure they had been compelled; this was the fate, the irony, the unrelenting natural stroke that had hung always over the love that they had believed to be encircled. Now they must carry that love with them through the world, vindicating and fulfilling it. In the long run, he thought, consequence, which it seems possible to eliminate, always compels men to become either greater or less than they were—to become less in shrinking avoidances, or greater in acceptance; and he understood for the first time in what circumstance of love Lewis and Julie stood. They were not afraid of what might befall, but in awe of the prodigious and continuing power of what had befallen; and while it was still possible, from the very outskirts of the past, to look back with wonder upon the garden now closed, they were slow to advance into that external world towards which, out of their dream, fate and their own resolution were carrying them.

"I must go," he said. "There's no other train. And the captain is coming on to the bridge. Soon you will be away."

"Lewis, he's going," Julie called, and Lewis came up beside them. Little words were exchanged—messages to Enkendaal, promises of England whither Ramsdell would follow them in a week. Soon he was on the bridge-ladder and they were looking down on him.

"I'll go down to the gangway with him," Julie exclaimed, and Lewis also would have gone, but he understood suddenly that she wished to be parted from him for a little while, not to stand at his side and wait.

"I will come up again," she said. "Are we allowed on the bridge when the ship's under way?"

The captain had invited them, Lewis replied. He saw her run down the ladder like a seaman, facing outward, her palm under the rope; and turned away to look down again from the ship's side. If we sail now, he thought, we shall be beyond the harbour before dark, but there's little time left, and impatience drove him to look continually at the clock in the lighted chart-room where the captain was stooping over the table with a pair of dividers in his hand. At last the captain came out of the chart-room and went to the compass on the upper bridge. There was a grinding of capstans fore and aft, a creak of hawsers, a flop of hemp into the water of the basin. On the quay and in the ship itself the processes of going to sea went forward.

Long after the *Starling* was clear of the inner harbour, land remained in sight. The captain, coming down from the upper bridge, began to tell of the many voyages he had made across the North Sea, independently and under convoy, during the war. He was proud of them, and, though he said that he was glad that the risk of submarine attack was ended, there was a note of regret in his voice. Lewis was always eager for the talk of men that spoke of their own profession, and until the captain, wondering why his passenger stayed so long on deck when he might be snugly below, went up to the compass again, he was content. Alone, he became restless. He began to hear the lash and scud of the darkening sea, the low thud of the engines, the sharper beat of the auxiliaries, and to remember, with a shock of exile, the waterfall at Enkendaal. From that past he was now cut off, and he turned into the future with a determination to be bound by no regrets, to be freed from them by the final act which had brought him and Julie together into this ship. But it was a harsh determination, needing as yet all the support of his will. Chepping; Fells Square; Alison and Ford; he saw the old life returning. The same Julie who had been for so long separated from it in his mind—the idea of whom had, indeed, consisted in her detachment from this old, regulated life of his—would now share it; and he began to pity her, to blame himself for having so eagerly received her. There was, it seemed to him now, a great division between them—a division that must increase day by day and year by year if she was to maintain her own character in its integrity and he to fight again, in the world, his battle for spiritual independence. He could not cease to fight it; it was in his nature; vainly or not, he must fight it to the end.

The clamour of a rising wind was in his ears. Though the throb of the engines was under him, their sound was shut out. If Julie spoke, he did not hear her, and not until the pressure of her arm was within his own did he know that she was beside him.

"I have unpacked what we need," she said.

"But you didn't come up?"

"Not until we were clear of harbour. . . . Was that cowardly?"

The question touched him as none other could have done, revealing in her anew an aspect of herself which, in the despondency of waiting, had been withdrawn from his mind—a mingling of humility and adorable insolence against fortune which was hers, and hers only, like the flash and the surprising gentleness of her eyes. "Was that cowardly?"—knowing the answer, she could afford to ask that question; yet, though there was a challenge, a lilt of defiance in it, it contained also that baffling note of submission which, when she was a child, had made her, beneath all her challenges, so eager a pupil. The same challenge, the same gentleness, had entranced him when, on his first day at Enkendaal, he had found her with Ballater beside the lake; again when she had come up behind his chair in the Baron's room and had seemed to whisper to him; again as she took him for the first time through the darkness of her tower-staircase—always this mingling of contraries, of force and passivity, had shone in her and made her to him irresistible. It was her own light, by which she faced the world; her courage, her authentic spirit; was, indeed, herself—the origin and strength of his love for her. And it seemed to him now, as he looked at her, that he saw, not her only, but the spring of his own being, as though there were, and had always been, an identification between them more profound than their differences. It was as if, while watching a thing of beauty, he had begun to recognize and feel its beauty as a moving current within himself; and all his purposes were comprised in a single purpose—not to fail her. As she depended on him, so he on her; to fail her would be to fail in all things now. A fiery conviction in the same kind—quick in the heart, deeper and lovelier and stronger than the cold resolve that Ramsdell had observed—must have possessed her also in the same instant. She had felt a speaking tremor of his hand, had seen the movement of his head towards her, and they had told her what she wished to know—that, to whatever issue, he and she were staked finally on each other. She asked no more; nor he.

She watched a tug, frosted with salt, drop astern into the dusk. They spoke seldom, for the wind carried speech away, but they stayed a little while, hand in hand for their greater comfort, until the light was gone from the bronze clouds in the west, and the bow-wave, as it curled and spread under the bridge, began to shine in the increasing darkness.

1929–1931

AUTHOR'S NOTE

I AM reluctant to burden a story with a note of any kind, but it seems necessary to indicate what system I have followed in my use of Dutch and German names.

A novelist may suggest ancient nobility in England by an invented name, but the great aristocracy of Holland is so narrowly restricted and so well known that any fictitious title would give a false, and probably ridiculous, impression. I have, therefore, been bound to choose, in van Leyden, the name of a noble family extinct before my own sojourn in Holland. It has the right ring and may easily be pronounced by English readers; I have chosen it for these reasons only. The persons of my story are imaginary, and the family van Leyden has no connexion, even in my own mind, with any of my friends who received me and other English officers with generous hospitality during the late wars. I have borrowed in Enkendaal a setting and no more.

A watchful reader will observe what may seem to him inconsistency in my use or omission of the prefixes *van* in Dutch and *von* in German. The truth is that the use of them, particularly in Dutch, is extremely elastic and depends upon fine differences of meaning which even the kindness of the Dutch and German authorities whom I have consulted cannot reduce to a rule. For example, an intimate friend may speak of Leyden, not van Leyden; a snob who

433

wishes to affect intimacy may do likewise. In speaking of the Baroness van Leyden, I have used three forms: the Dutch, Mevrouw van Leyden; the French, Madame de Leyden, which is in Holland sometimes used when English is the language spoken, for "Mevrouw" does not come lightly from an English tongue; and "the Baroness," a form to which nothing in Dutch custom corresponds, but which was, within my own experience, more often used by Englishmen than any other, and was accepted. In each instance, I have relied upon my own ear, and, subsequently, upon the revision of my friends, who shall not, however, be held responsible for any errors I may have made by having their names coupled with my gratitude for their patience.

C. M.